MW00462736

Game, Set, Match

by

Nana Malone

Copyright 2010 Nana Malone

This is a work of fiction. Names, characters, places, and incidents either are the product of the author's imagination or are used fictitiously, and any resemblance to actual persons living or dead, business establishments, events, or locales, is entirely coincidental.

Game, Set, Match

COPYRIGHT © 2010 by Nana Malone

All rights reserved. No part of this book may be used or reproduced in any manner whatsoever without written permission of the author except in the case of brief quotations embodied in critical articles or reviews.

Cover Art by Kimberly Killion
Edited by Val Hatfield

Published in the United States of America

Dedication

To Erik, thank you for loving me, believing in me all these years, fostering my overactive imagination, not letting me get distracted, and most of all for making me laugh. That fraternity party was the best decision I ever made.

To my wonderful friend, crit partner, fellow Bravo TV junkie and sister, Misty Evans, I cannot thank you enough for taking me under your wings and helping my learn how to fly. I truly believe I wouldn't be writing this dedication if it weren't for you.

To Tendayi and Megan, thank you for keeping me writing, pestering me for more chapters and most of all, enduring my horrible spew drafts.

Every writer has friends and family who support them and keep them moving forward. To Naa Ardua, Cynthia, Fritz, Derrick, Marcie, Tricia, Nicholina and Reggie. I owe you more than you could ever know.

Mama, Daddy and Nortey. I love you. Thank you. I'm so proud of you all.

Chapter One

She's going to take Nick away.

Izzy Connors was going to lose her son. One midnight phone call, and Izzy's mind, body and soul ached from the sleepless night. Nick's birth mother, Sabrina Reems, had never been one for reasonable, rational discussion. Sabrina's words rattled in her head refusing to quiet. *I'm coming home in a month, and I want to see Nick.* She'd want to bully her way back into their lives and ignore the damning reasons for her continued absence.

How the hell was Izzy supposed to focus all day when she was in the fight of her life to keep Nick? Too bad her manager didn't care about her family dramatics.

Izzy squinted against the dazzling daylight warring for center stage with Simon's Ken-Doll good looks in her cramped and cluttered office. Using her hands, she blocked the glare of sunlight as he blathered on about her upcoming gallery opening, using words like, strategic and tactical and poised.

All very good words if he were giving a marketing presentation. But he wasn't. He was her perfect, MBA-strutting, stably employed, want-to-be boyfriend, Simon Jensen. The kind of man, who, if she married him, could help her accomplish the one thing she wanted the most. Adopt Nick. But she wouldn't, couldn't, use anyone to get what she wanted. No matter how badly she wanted to keep Nick.

She had a month until Sabrina's return, two weeks before her scheduled monthly meetings with the family court judge. She'd think of a solution before then.

Not like I have a choice.

Given Sabrina's history, Izzy had petitioned to adopt Nick more than once in the fourteen years she'd raised him. And more than once, the court had turned her down. Lack of stable income, the judge wanted to reunite mother and son, her race — the reasons didn't matter, the result was still the same. No adoption. She never should have agreed to the lopsided guardianship agreement with Sabrina.

"We have to think of your brand. Z Con will be a household name before we're done," Simon continued, unaware of her change in mood, his long fingers rubbing against the smooth line of his mahogany-colored skin.

She could always get a second job, not that her studio didn't make enough. It did. But the money went to Nick's school fees and college fund first, everything else second.

She glared at the wheatgrass shot on her desk, courtesy of Simon. She hated wheatgrass. Instead of a romantic breakfast date complete with mimosas and strawberries, he handed her a yogurt with granola, and a vile wheatgrass shot.

She stared at the murky green liquid and willed it to turn into champagne. It didn't. Like the rest of her life, wishing wouldn't make it so.

"Izzy, it's imperative …right people…the proper contacts… catapult…"

"Uh, hmm," she muttered, trying to focus on his words, but unable to force her mind to latch on. Echoes of Sabrina's voice the night before wafted into her consciousness. I'm coming back in a month. I want to see Nick.

Taking a deep breath, Izzy shoved the thought to a far corner in her brain and locked it in a trunk. She would think about it later. There was nothing she could do about Sabrina right now, and she had a life to tend to.

Izzy held her breath and took the shot, trying not to gag as the forest green liquid glooped down her throat.

Simon beamed at her. "See, that wasn't so bad, was it?"

She chose deft avoidance. "Simon, the gallery opening will be great, but I want to make sure we keep it small, intimate, you know, and —"

His booming laugh interrupted her, sucking all the air out until she felt as if she needed to ration her breathing. "Small? Honey, I don't think you get it. We're going to put you, Z Con-international photographer, on the map."

Her eyes searched his for some sign he was her Mr. Perfect. She wanted to feel something, anything. Anything beside the mild affection and sometimes annoyance over his continued assurance they were perfect for each other.

She waited for the breathless, giddy anticipation of longing to wash over her. Waited for the staccato rhythm of a heart in love to tick away in her chest. Waited for the heated blush to take a languid stroll over her skin leaving a wake of goose bumps.

The only thing she felt was queasy dread that she'd never experience those things. Or maybe it was the wheatgrass.

His chocolate skin and lean athletic build should make her heart prance whenever he turned his signature grin on her. His Blair Underwood meets Taye Digs good looks, should make her fuzzy and cozily dreaming of Sunday lie-ins complete with a steamy romp and Sunday paper. His pedigree, charm and zest for life, should have made him a dream candidate for the future Mr. Connors.

Should, should, should. Except, they didn't. Despite every reason to want him, not a single butterfly fluttered anywhere near her belly — or — lower. He was handsome, no doubt, but the last thing on earth she wanted to do was sleep with him. She'd done everything she could to discourage his feelings, but he insisted they were right for each other. Insisted she only needed time to get used to the idea.

She gave him another quick once over. Hot and heavy, he did not make her. More like lukewarm. But, according to her mother, what was marriage if not a strong steadfast friendship? Her mother loved Simon. Everybody loved Simon. Everybody except the two people closest to her, Nick and her assistant, Jessica. They both thought he was boring.

Casting Simon another glance, Izzy willed her lips into a smile and told herself love could grow on a person. Like a fungus.

He tried so hard to make her happy. He pushed her at break-neck speeds because he wanted her to succeed. He brought her breakfast every morning, just to make sure she remembered to eat. Too bad he includes the wheatgrass.

"Iz, I know your own gallery showing during Pasadena Art Night is scary, but I think you can do it. If anyone can, it's you."

If he'd stopped there, that would have been fine. Better than fine. Her brain could have accepted the statement as a cheerleader's pitch. Instead, he added, "I've already promised them forty pieces."

"Forty?" Shit. With the opening in three months, that didn't leave enough time to get them all canvassed, framed and ready to display.

Simon nodded. "Perfect number, right?"

She knew she needed to focus on the good news. The gallery opening was just the thing she needed to catapult her career. But the feeling of suffocation, instant and unavoidable, spread over her like a warm, wet blanket in the middle of August.

Tell him no. As quickly as the thought formed, she tangled it with thoughts of Sabrina. Simon had worked his tail off for two years to make her a name. He'd gotten her this far when, by rights, she should be living the life of a starving photographer in a one-bedroom hovel.

Any of her friends, if she'd had time for friends besides Jessica, would think she was insane for not getting with him. Too bad every time she thought of him naked, she felt the tickle of a giggle in her throat. And while it had been a long, long time since she'd done the do, Izzy knew giggling was not on the approved list of responses to nakedness.

"Izzy, are you listening to me?"

Busted.

She sighed and put down the balance sheets she'd been moving around her desk. She picked up a camera to clean as she always did when she needed to think. "Yes, Simon, I'm listening, but I'm not sure if I can be ready for a gallery opening in time. Things are kicking up again with Nick's school and tennis, not to mention Sabrina's coming back. This could finally be my chance to adopt Nick. I don't want anything to get in the way of that." Translation, you were insane to promise forty pieces.

"You can do it. It'll be great," he said in a rush. The way he always talked as if he were a chipmunk on caffeine.

She sucked in a deep breath. Replacing the lens, she told herself it was caution not fear that made her hesitate. "Keep in mind, something like that takes time to put together. I've never had my own gallery opening before."

Simon's lips rolled inward showing his poorly concealed annoyance at her hesitation.

"Izzy, I know how important Nick is to you. But your career is just as important. You can prove to the judge that your income is stable. Besides, a gallery opening of your own is a huge break. No more portraits of old ladies and babies and pets." He waved her appointment book in the air.

Simon finally noticed her lack of response. He placed the appointment book back on the desk and reached cross the desk for her hand.

Out of habit, she let him take it, even though her fingers twitched, desperate for release. He rubbed his thumb across her knuckle in an attempt to make her more comfortable.

"If push comes to shove with Sabrina, you know the court is more likely to let a celebrity black woman adopt a white kid, than a regular black woman with a job, a good job, but—you get my drift. You need to focus on what's important—providing for Nick. This opening will let you do that in ways you've never even conceived. When Nick was younger, you needed to be selective about jobs. He's fourteen now. It hurt your career not to be as available as other photographers, even if you were better. Your time is now."

He was right. She needed the gallery opening. It was the next logical step. "I know. I want to be able to do both." She leveled her eyes at him to make her point. "But, if it comes down to Nick or the gallery opening, you know what I'll choose, right?"

His smile displayed perfect Chiclets for teeth. "Damn, Izzy, you make me insane. But yeah, I hear you. You won't regret it."

She smiled, surprised she didn't need to force it. "Good. I'm glad we understand each other."

He held her gaze for a moment too long. When he looked away and stepped toward the window, she breathed her relief on a sigh. She didn't have the heart for the battle she knew was coming.

"One more thing, Izzy."

Oh boy. She prayed she could avoid the "Let's take this relationship to the next level," conversation for one more day. It wasn't the first time they'd had it, and she was too tired to have it again. Plus, Mrs. Wilks from Nick's school was due in at twelve o'clock for a portrait, and she still had to prep and set up.

He must have seen something in the rigid posture of her back because he didn't bring it up. "I made an appointment for you to do a celebrity spread. Sports Illustrated is thrilled at the idea of working with you again. They loved what you did with Lebron."

She felt the joy swell in her chest for the barest instant before she locked it away. "Okay, I assume you talked to Jessica, and she put it in my calendar?"

Shooting celebrities wasn't her favorite work, but Simon was right. It was good for her profile. Some celebrities were palatable, but the majority seemed to think she was the hired help, and she found it difficult to keep her tongue in check.

And it paid well. A job like that would complete Nick's college fund.

As she ushered Simon out of the gallery as quickly as she could, she wondered if it was a bad thing that his cologne made her think of balance sheets as opposed to satin sheets.
****

Hours after Mrs. Wilks had come and gone, Izzy dragged leaden feet to go and deal the deathblow to her son's happy normal life. With a sense of doom, she shoved away from her light table and proofs. Her stomach growled, which meant she'd forgotten to eat — again.

Casting a glance at the wall clock, she muttered a curse as she put away the proofs for her new Homelands book. Her publisher had called asking if she could get the photo book out earlier. As usual, she accommodated. Accommodating meant a happy publisher, which also meant a successful gallery opening, which meant she could take better care of Nick. For Nick, she could accommodate.

The clock chimed four-thirty, and she muttered another curse as she grabbed her bag. "Jessica, I'm heading to the house. If Simon calls, tell him he can reach me on my cell."

Jessica's head, topped with a fuchsia-colored bob, peeked out from around the receptionist's desk. "Sure thing, Izzy. Have a great night. And don't worry about the supplies that came in, I'll sort them and put them away before I leave tonight."

Izzy smiled a grateful thank you as she wondered if that was a new piercing she'd seen in Jessica's cheek. Ouch.

Jessica's non-conventional looks weren't for everyone, but the perpetual grad school student was organized, efficient, and a no-nonsense type. Not to mention, she was one of the few friends Izzy'd had over the years. One of the few Izzy allowed herself.

Not for the first time, Izzy was thrilled only a backyard separated her studio from her house. After long days like this one, the shortened commute helped improve her mood. She headed across the backyard, picking up two hackeysacks, a skateboard and a tennis ball, along the way. No matter how many times she'd told Nick to pick up after himself, he somehow managed to forget. A byproduct of being a teenage boy?

The moment she entered the backdoor, she knew Nick was home. Rap music blared through the stereo in the living room.

Izzy dropped her bags on the large kitchen island, and as her shoulders slumped, she groaned with relief. Recessed lights twinkled above and washed the kitchen a warm glow. Removing her shoes, she made her way toward the din.

"Nicholas Reems, you may not care about your ear drums, but I certainly care about mine. I need you to turn down the Snoop, okay?"

Was she really that old? "Well at least you know it's Snoop on the stereo," she mumbled. She dreaded the day when she would have no idea what her son listened to.

"Not your son yet, Izzy," she mumbled to herself. She couldn't get used to not thinking of him as hers. Every time Sabrina returned home, that one fact came back to haunt her.

Deep breath. You're going to do everything in your power to change that.

She swallowed and forced the bile back into the darkened depths of her belly where it belonged. She needed to tell Nick about his mother's call. Today. Before Sabrina called again and told him she was on her way home.

Izzy rounded the corner of the dining room into the living room and stopped as if rooted by super glue to the maroon runner between the two rooms.

Two blond heads jumped apart. One, the familiar sandy blond she'd been yelling at for days to get a haircut, the other, pale, almost platinum, matched to fair, near-white skin.

Nick reddened to the tips of his ears, and Izzy did her best to hide her smirk. Busted, punk.

Nick stammered. "M-Mom. I didn't hear you come in."

This time, she did smirk. "It's no wonder with the music as loud as it is." She inclined her head toward the waify blonde. "Who's your friend?"

A pixie-like girl around Nick's age, jumped off the couch to walk around. She also wore a pink shade of embarrassment like a well-fitted mask. Izzy took small solace that neither of the kids needed to rearrange their clothing.

"O. M. G. Izzy Connors, it's so awesome to meet you. Nick's told me a lot about you."

The use of her first name surprised her. She wished she could be one of those parents that thought it was cool for kids to refer to them by name, but she wasn't. Old school values instilled from her southern mother shined through.

Nick seemed to find his voice at last. "We've got a Trig test coming up. We were studying, Mom."

With their lips? Izzy tried to hide the knowing smirk that wanted to break free again. She turned her attention on the girl with a welcoming smile, or at least what she hoped was something near a welcoming smile and not the one her mother had used to chase boys from the house when she was Nick's age. "How about you call me Miss Connors. What's your name?"

The girl's wide blue eyes misted over with confusion, and Izzy wondered if she'd lost cool points.

"Samantha. Samantha Tisdale."

Izzy nodded. "Do your parents know you're here, Samantha?"

Samantha wrinkled her blond brow. "Uhm, no." Then she appeared to think better of her last statement. "No, ma'am."

She'd gone from Izzy to ma'am in three point four seconds. Izzy was only thirty-two, she wasn't a ma'am. She knew who Tupac was, after all, and Snoop. "Do me a favor and call your parents. Tell them you'll be on your way home in half an hour. Do you have a ride?"

Samantha shot a plea for help look in Nick's direction. Nick, true to form and his young age, provided no assistance and stayed silent.

"N-no, Iz…erm, Miss Connors. We took the bus."

Izzy nodded and turned her gaze on the lanky form to her right. "Nick, call Jessica. She's still at the office. See if she can take your friend home. I'm going to get dinner started so you guys have till about five-thirty to wrap up your studying."

Izzy ignored the look of horror on Nick's face when she mentioned dinner. "Samantha, why don't you come over for dinner one of these nights? Make sure it's fine with your folks first though, okay?"

Samantha's eyes widened. "Yes, ma'am. Thank you."

Nick looked stricken, but Izzy couldn't help feeling more buoyant.

In the kitchen, Izzy helped herself to a chocolate chip cookie. An honest-to-gosh real chocolate chip cookie. No soy, wheat germ or flax seed to be found. She needed it after that make-out scene. She tried not to think about the last time she'd made out with anyone. Too depressing.

Her baby was growing up into a man. Not your baby.

Because she needed the fortification, she shoved another cookie into her mouth and pulled out the casserole dish from the fridge. Thank God for their part time housekeeper. As much as she hated to admit Nick's fear of her kitchen skills had merit, she knew what her strengths were and what they were not. She'd never mastered the art of cooking. Nick's culinary skills were better than hers, any day.

Somewhere after five, Nick strolled into the kitchen. "Nothing happened, Mom, I swear."

Izzy shoved the casserole in the oven and prepared the potatoes for mashing.

"We were just studying." Then, in an attempt to change the topic, he added, "Grandma called."

Izzy turned to give him a look, "Studying? Is that what we're calling it now?" Then she smiled and added, "Nice try tossing your grandmother under the bus, but she can't save you."

Nick blushed again. With his height and burgeoning muscles, he looked older than most boys his age, easily passable for seventeen. But, at heart, he was still a kid.

"She's the hottest girl in school, Mom, and she asked me to study. What was I supposed to do?"

Izzy sighed and turned to face him, no idea how she was going to traverse this minefield. She didn't need another embarrassing round of the sex talk. "Look, Nick, I know you're interested in girls, but remember we had a deal. School first, always. Then the extracurricular activities you've committed to. Only after that come friends and girls. Remember the conversation we had about taking things slow and respecting women?"

Nick hung his head nodding. "I know, Mom, I just...I don't know."

She turned the oven on to preheat as the cooking label said. She wasn't concerned with the girl so much as she worried her baby was growing up faster than she could control. "Do you really like this girl?"

Nick shrugged. "I dunno, I guess." Then he wrinkled his forehead. "You're supposed to wait for it to preheat before you put the casserole in."

She turned to survey him. When had he grown up? How much time would she have with him? She pulled the casserole back out of the oven. "Fair enough, invite her to dinner here so I can get to know her, okay?"

He nodded and indicated the boiled potatoes. "I can do that." His gaze shifted, and he changed the subject. "Simon joining us tonight?"

His pretended nonchalance didn't fool her. Izzy looked up to find him grinning. No matter what she tried, the two of them had never bonded. "You're cheeky, you know that? What's wrong with Simon?"

"You mean besides being boring, thinking he always knows best, and his not noticing that we hate wheatgrass?"

Izzy tried to swat him with the towel, but he scuttled out of the way, laughing all the while. She sighed. Wished he didn't have a point. Now sober, she handed him the premade salad bowl from the fridge. "I have something to talk to you about, Nick."

There must have been something in her voice. He stopped smiling. Serious brown eyes stared at her. "What's wrong?"

Shit. She didn't mean to worry him. "No, Nick. Nothing's wrong." She moved to stand in front of him. Even at fourteen, he dwarfed her. "Your mom called. She's coming back."

He put down the salad bowl and crossed his arms in stubborn refusal. "When?" His voice was steady, yet — hardened. When had that happened?

She shrugged. "She said about a month. Not really sure with her."

She watched him work his jaw back and forth. The motion was familiar to her, especially as he got older.

"I don't want to see her."

She put her arms around him and waited till he relaxed and hugged her back. "Unfortunately, Nick, we don't have much of a choice."

Chapter Two

"Mr. Cartwright, do you care to comment on your relationship…."

Jason slammed the phone down mid-question. He took several deep breaths to release the tension in his body. When he couldn't control the muscles by will, he gave up the fight and let out a stream of curses. "Shit. Damn it. Shit. Shit."

Why is there such interest in my personal life? If the barracudas weren't camped out in the bushes to get a picture, they cyber stalked him and blogged about his latest party boy faux pas, or worse, somehow ferreted out his phone number no matter how many times he changed it. He tried not to imagine what they'd do if anyone found out why he and Arthur Michaels no longer trained together.

Jason bit back a wince as he maneuvered both crutches and lumbered onto the balcony. His knee sent simultaneous bursts of pain and itch up and down his leg. Once settled, he glowered malevolently at his crutches, not sure if they helped or hindered.

Damn, how the hell did I end up here? He was supposed to be Jason Cartwright, number one seed and a true force to reckon with, on and off the courts. In reality, he was Jason Cartwright, gimpy, almost-has-been hoping for a comeback. All thanks to Michaels. If his own trainer didn't believe in his comeback, who would?

Feeling the burn from gripping the handles of the crutches too tightly, he forced his fingers to release, finger by finger. He would take responsibility, needed to. No one else would. He was in this mess because he put his trust in Michaels. He was in this mess because he hadn't prepared himself for Michaels' betrayal. He should have protected himself. Now he had a torn ACL and a shattered career.

The hell with it. He was in this mess because Michaels was a disloyal prick. "Shit."

The doorbell chimed a series of cheery tones reminiscent of the Brady Bunch, and it did little to improve his mood. He ignored the now dull throb accompanied by the ferocious itch in his leg as he hobbled to the door, only pausing to ditch the crutches against the wood sideboard in the sun-drenched hallway. I could always use them to beat off the paparazzi.

With a shake of his head, he thought better of it and continued on to the door. He didn't need the paps to catch him giving one of their own a beat down from hell. Not that it mattered, they'd make up stories about him just the same. Only some of those stories would have the barest grain of truth. The paps latest obsession included actress Cienna Dunst and their supposed engagement.

He'd gone out with her a few times. Next thing he knew, Us Weekly splashed photos of them on the cover, with details of a Malibu wedding.

When he reached the door, he halted when he saw who awaited him on the other side — his manager, Aaron Banks, with his usual optimistic smile. Jason wasn't in the mood for optimism. But on the plus side, at least it wasn't a paparazzo with a flashbulb.

When Jason turned away without opening the door, Aaron let himself in.

"Hey, buddy."

Jason scowled. "I need to change those locks. What do you want?"

His long-suffering manager put on an affected look of pure dejection and pointed at Jason's face. "That look, there, on your face, it's not happiness to see me."

Already on his way to the kitchen, Jason didn't wait for another comment, the itch around his surgery scar too persistent to ignore. He needed a scratch stick. He sighed when he heard Aaron's heavy footfalls behind him. This wouldn't be a quick visit.

"Do I have a reason to be happy to see you?" He heard clattering in the hallway, and turned back to glare at Aaron.

"What happened to you last night at the club? All the girls asked where their favorite party boy went."

Was that the way people referred to him now? What happened to the day when the world knew him as a tennis player first? "I got antsy and had to get out of there."

"The VIP room was a rage. Samantha Ronson did her thing. Can't believe you ditched out. Everything cool?"

No, everything was not cool. Maybe he was sick of doing nothing but partying all the time. Maybe he was sick of the endless slew of hangers-on. Maybe he wanted to respect himself again. He bit his tongue. "Yeah, cool."

Aaron grabbed one of the crutches and hobbled behind him. When Jason reached the kitchen, he almost cried with relief at the sight of the one thing that could stop the constant itch. His housekeeper had left the wooden spoon on the counter next to the sink. He grabbed it and made quick work of wiggling the long end of the spoon into the brace, careful not to disturb the bandage around his surgery scar. Damn, that's good. He closed his eyes and let out a sigh of bliss.

"Damn man, with that look on your face, you'd think scratching was better than sex."

Jason cracked an eye open. "Right now, it is."

"Jase, if Cienna isn't up to the job, there are plenty more to take her place."

Jason opened his eyes. The last thing he needed was a woman. The damn paparazzi would have a field day. He gave Aaron a long look. "I doubt you braved the Malibu traffic to discuss my love life."

Tugging on his pristine tie, his manager smiled. "It's my job to worry about your love life."

"Oh, yeah? How is my love life part of your job?" Managers like him had a way of spinning anything to their advantage.

Aaron rolled his eyes, and spoke very slowly, as if dealing with a simpleton. "Your liaisons garner publicity. Clubs want you to host their New Year's Eve celebrations. Champagne companies want you as their endorsement angel. Fashion lines throw free swag at you like panties at a Bon Jovi concert. All of it means revenue, my friend." He leaned the crutch against the counter. "Besides, I maintain an active sex life from your castoffs alone, Bro."

Jason wasn't sure he wanted to be a commodity to buy and sell. But Aaron was right. It was all part of business. "You don't need my castoffs." If ever his friend had a downfall, it was women. He had a Patrick Dempsey look to him that got him all the women he ever wanted.

Pristine teeth flashed into a grin. "Yeah, you're right. I am a handsome devil. But, I didn't come here to talk to you about that." With a frown, he indicated Jason's leg. "Why aren't you on your crutches?"

Jason shrugged. "I'm faster without them."

Aaron's dark brows rose as he indicated the leg brace. "When do you lose that thing anyway?"

"Doc says another two days, but as you can see, I can move around okay. The therapy is doing its work." The lie rolled off his tongue with ease. He didn't need Aaron clucking over him.

"How is PT?"

He shrugged again. "It's a pain in the ass. I want to work faster."

Aaron gave him a rueful glance. "Haven't we been through this already? You come back too fast, and it's Wimbledon '05 all over again. Knocked out in the first round. You want that?"

Unfortunately, Aaron was right. If he wanted to come back strong for another go at a title before retirement, he couldn't rush it, so he'd have to take it easy. "No, I don't want a repeat of Wimbledon. I'm a little stir crazy is all."

All he wanted to do was a few hundred-miles-per-hour serves, but that wasn't in the cards for him yet. To make it worse, every time he went to physical therapy, the damned paps were there. The last thing he needed at a training session.

Aaron nodded. The two of them had been together since his first tour, both younger and inexperienced then. He saw Aaron's eyes narrow, gauging his mood. "You meet the new trainer yet?"

Jason shook his head and shrugged. "Next week, at PT." Some hotshot from USC. He had to be better than his last trainer.

A pregnant pause took the place of the questions Aaron didn't ask. Everyone else bombarded him with questions on his separation from Michaels. The press, his family, the occasional random stranger. None of them able to guess what could have caused the once unbeatable team of trainer and athlete to part ways so abruptly. Everyone asked about it. Everyone, except Aaron.

Why doesn't he want to know?

Aaron pointed to a photo on Jason's wall. The Masai tribesman's haunted gaze compelled attention with his bright red cloth billowing in the wind like a matador's cape. "You like Z Con's work?"

In a house full of expensive toys and gadgets, the photo was Jason's most prized possession. While the steel framed contemporary furniture often lacked life and depth, the photo warmed the whole room. From the moment he saw it, he always felt like the tribesman knew him, could see to his soul. From that acquisition, he'd been obsessed with the photographer's work. Jason had every Homelands book he ever made, Nigeria, Egypt, Ireland and New Zealand. Z Con's photos touched a part of Jason he'd buried years ago.

Jason gave him a quizzical look. "You know I do. You gave me that photo."

Aaron grinned that infectious smile. "I do have excellent taste, don't I?"

Rolling his eyes, Jason prodded. "So what gives? I saw you last night at the club. You didn't mention anything urgent then."

"I got you a photo shoot."

"You know I don't want to do any publicity right now, especially while I'm injured. Get me out of it." Aaron lived for the publicity, where Jason didn't. It was a long since sore spot between them.

"Sorry, Bro. Can't do that. It's for Sports Illustrated. Besides, we need to make your endorsers more comfortable with your position. If they think you're out for the count, the endorsements will dry up."

Money. It always came to that. "I'd rather focus on my recovery."

Brows drawn together in one of the few frowns Jason had ever seen from his friend, Aaron shook his head. "Sorry, Jase. It's my job to tell you like it is. You don't do voluntary publicity immediately, and you will be a washed up has-been. Your rep has taken a beating, especially since the press knows you better for your club preference than your court prowess. I need to keep you afloat till then."

Jason's jaw tightened. "Thanks for the vote of confidence."

"I tell it like it is. I had to talk SI into this interview and spread. You have more money than Croesus, but I know you. You need to play. We need to clean up your image, get people to focus on who you really are, a fucking tennis genius." His frown morphed into a determined smile. "Don't worry. We'll have you back in fighting shape in no time. Then everyone will see the truth. Jason Cartwright is a star. Always has been and always will be."

A sickening fog rolled over Jason. That's what he was afraid of. What if he couldn't do it? What if he was a washed out has-been at thirty-four? What if he should have listened to Michaels? He nodded noncommittally. He wondered when he'd become a liar.

A sly smile spread over his friend's face. The same smile he used whenever he went for a kill on a deal. "Would you cheer up if I told you the Sports Illustrated photo shoot is with Z Con?"

Jason put down the wooden spoon, unable to believe it. Giddy excitement tripped over synapses in his brain. He'd been trying to meet the elusive photographer for several years, ever since seeing a spread in National Geographic. "You're shitting me."

Aaron's grin widened. "No shit."

"Has he done SI before?"

Aaron nodded. "Did a spread on LeBron last year. I brought you a copy. It's in my car."

For the first time since his surgery and the scandal, Jason's spirits lifted. "I'm in."

Chapter Three

"So, you two finally steam up the sheets last night?"

"What?" Stifling a yawn, Izzy whipped her head up from her task to glare at Jessica. "Would you be quiet? Somebody might hear you." But even as she scanned the long hallway off the back kitchen for potential clients, she saw none.

Jessica giggled. "I'll take that as a no." She chugged the last of her latte and added, "You can relax, nobody's here yet. You know full well the looky-loos don't start till around six-thirty."

"Jess, not today. Please, I beg you. I can't talk about my love life when we're in the middle of a tart crisis." Today of all days, Izzy didn't need Jessica's needling. They had their monthly Arts and Tarts open house, and she was already a wreck. She and several other small gallery owners in the neighborhood hosted open houses every month starting in the late winter to draw in potential customers.

Arts and Tarts was initially supposed to be just her and the two gallery owners around the corner in the cheery Pasadena neighborhood, opening their galleries one night a month. But over the last two years, other shops had joined in. Before she knew it, once a month, most of the merchants in the neighborhood stayed open till nine, serving wine and desserts from the bakery on the corner.

Izzy had never meant for it to be a big thing, but now, local news wanted to come and film the first event of the year. And this month of all months, she had cash flow problems, so no tarts from the bakery. Thankfully, Jess and Nick baked, but she was nervous. Did they have enough? Would anybody notice her tarts weren't as tasty or fluffy as the tarts offered by her neighbors?

"Hey, I'm sorry. I know the stress you're under. I shouldn't tease you now. I'll resume tomorrow." Jessica tilted her head and gave Izzy her most encouraging smile. "It'll be great, okay? Don't worry about the press. Everyone will be focused on the great pieces and not your past."

"I hope you're right about that. I don't need that kind of attention. Though, do you think I'd get more sales?"

Jessica's pink bob shook from side to side as she chuckled. "You just worry about putting whipped cream on the tarts, and I'll go grab the extra trays from the bakery."

She shot Jessica a grateful, but rueful smile and resumed her work with the whipped cream, already mentally preparing for the Simon questions tomorrow. Pausing to rub tired eyes, she carefully spread dollops of whipped cream on the final tarts. It was the only job Nick or Jessica allowed her to do when it came to the baked goods.

She didn't enjoy the Arts and Tarts events, all those people poking around her work, never really buying anything. But until she opened at a gallery, it was a way to get a few pieces sold.

She checked the clock for the fifteenth time that afternoon. Damn. Late again. Since Sabrina's call, she'd been off. Her schedule, her internal clock, her relationship with Nick.

"Izzy, are you here?"

The click clack of Simon's footsteps echoed on the mahogany hardwood floor, reverberating down the hallway as he made his way to the studio's back rooms.

Crap. He was early, and she was far from ready. "I'm in the kitchen, Simon."

He joined her with the usual force of a tornado, a flurry of frenetic energy and exuberant enthusiasm. "Hello, sweetheart." He gave her a quick squeeze, and kissed her with a sound smack on her lips, stealing her breath. Though, more from surprise than breathless arousal.

The instant claustrophobia that clung to her like a sloppy drunk co-ed, forced her to step away from him and pick up the tart tray. Through measured breathing, she gave him a wan smile, the tray of tarts acting as a shield. Her stress wasn't his problem. Her mind latched on to the thought of forty pieces in the next three months.

She'd deal with that later. All she had to do at the moment was prep for Arts and Tarts, make herself look presentable and, fingers crossed, sell a couple of pieces. Any thoughts about her relationship with Simon could wait. Would wait until she could find time to breathe, analyze. She knew she'd eventually have to make a decision about their relationship, or rather their non-relationship. She knew she'd eventually have to decide to sleep with him or not, move their relationship forward or not. In some ways, it would be easier to avoid him. Like Dad. Like every other man in her life. Thankfully, she didn't have to decide today. Today, she could be grateful for the extra help.

"I'm glad you're here. I need help with the display for the Arts and Tarts and —"

Simon let out a puff of air and tapped impatient hands on the glass counter. His light gray suit was a perfect blend with the harsh stainless steel backsplash and appliances.

"Izzy, you can't be serious. Have you forgotten you have an appointment in ten minutes about the SI shoot?"

Damn it. Had she forgotten? She last glanced at her calendar around ten. There hadn't been anything about SI on it. Had there? Panicked, she looked at the wall clock again and wished for more time to prep for the open house. "Shit, I'm so sorry. I forgot, and Jessica is out and —"

He took hold of her wrists as though she were a chocolate-smeared three year old headed for a white couch. "Izzy. Focus. They'll be here any minute. You're not usually so out of it, what's with you lately?"

Jaw set, her temper threatened to boil over. She inhaled three deep breaths before she spoke. "I've got Sabrina, Nick, the studio, a judge who won't let me adopt my son, and a boyfriend-slash-manager who's promised forty pieces for my gallery opening without so much as a consult with me. You'll forgive me if I'm a tad forgetful."

He grimaced, contrite in an instant. "I'm sorry, sweetheart. I'm a prick. And a demanding one at that. I'm just working for your future."

For one scary second, her temper threatened to rebel against its leash, but she restrained it. She didn't want conflict. Simon was not the enemy. "I'll put these in the main studio and wash my hands." She caught a glimpse of her image in the wall mirror and made a mental note to do something about her hair as well. No one would take her seriously in pigtails.

Simon followed close behind, giving her the rundown of everything Sports Illustrated wanted for the shoot. "There'll be three separate shoots. One on Saturday…"

She tuned out Simon's voice as she turned into the studio's sale hall, where she hung all photos she'd sold that still awaited pickup. It was pitifully empty. Only three black and whites lined the hallway, all off to the same owner.

Voices trickled into her consciousness from the front hall. Her feet faltered. At first thought, her ears played tricks on her. A deep voice crackled like a glowing fire on a rainy night, reverberated off the walls. Heat flushed her body. Izzy tried to take a deep breath. Last time she'd heard that voice, he'd told her he'd be back in an hour. He'd left her aroused and alone. It can't be him. It can't be.

But she knew it was. The telltale Connecticut accent dripped from each word he spoke.

Her heart kicked up and added another thud to its usual routine. The last time she'd seen him, she'd been the picture of embarrassment after throwing herself at him. The pleasure-pain of nerves prickling with awareness assailed her.

Her hands gave an involuntary shake of the tart tray and she hurried to right it. Rounding the corner, half hoping it would be him, and half hoping-pleading-begging it wouldn't be, she let out a breath when she saw him — that same sandy blond hair and that same angled jaw.

Her fantasy, come to life, Jason Cartwright.

Oh shit. Oh shit. Oh shit.

She squeezed her eyes shut in the illogical hope that if she could no longer see him, he wouldn't see her. She whirled around, intent on escape, but slammed into Simon—tarts and all.

"Izzy!" Simon ground out, along with a few epithets.

"Crap, crap, crap. I'm sorry." She peeled one eye open to survey the damage. After an eyeful, she squeezed it closed again. If she didn't see it, it didn't exist. Though the image of white gloops on a grey Brooks Brothers suit left an imprint she couldn't ignore.

A surprised voice came from behind her. "Izzy? Izzy Connors? Is that you?"

Busted. Her option of retreat vanished into the ether.

Muttering under his breath, Simon excused himself and hurried to the restroom near the kitchen to clean up.

With no hope of escape, she took a deep breath, trying to force her heart to return to its normal rhythm. When that didn't work, she turned around anyway not sure what to say. Wow, that was a long ass hour, would come across as combative. And the last thing she wanted was a confrontation.

She settled on, "Hello, Jason."

His casual stance belied the speed and strength she knew he was capable of. Years of rigorous activity had hardened his tall, rangy body. Memories of kissing his square jaw and the light cleft in his chin assailed her.

Dark glasses masked his eyes, but Izzy knew behind them, she'd find intense heat able to strip her to the soul. His tousled blond hair was just as she remembered it, a little unkempt, as if he hadn't bothered with it. The sexy grin that had haunted her dreams for fifteen years showed off straight white teeth. He was every bit the Hollywood playboy portrayed in the press. And that devil-may-care sexiness would be the death of her.

Before she could say anything else, his strong arms and a warm musky scent enveloped her. Involuntarily, her body stilled like an ice sculpture as her breasts came into contact with the hard planes of his chest. Unable to process the situation, she heard a faint clatter as his sunglasses fell to the floor. She squeezed her eyes shut and tried not to think of the last time she'd seen him, the last time he'd abandoned her for Sabrina.

"Damn, Izzy, you look terrific." He set her down, but kept hold of one of her hands. Whiskey eyes poured warm amber over every inch of her body. "How've you been?"

The source of her greatest humiliation wanted to know how she'd been, as if they were old buddies. She reminded herself they, for all intents and purposes, were old buddies, until she'd made the mistake of pegging him as her first lover.

Behind Jason, his companion, with his rugged dark good looks and infectious smile, saved her from having to speak. Not that she could have. "You two know each other?"

Jason's smile flashed and made her want to do all manner of inappropriate things. Smash his head in with a pan? Strip him naked and see if he still looked as good as he promised? Launch a full TET offensive on him with her lips? Not necessarily in that order.

Jason ignored the question and asked his own. "You're Z Con?"

Simon returned from the bathroom, flustered, but just as jovial as ever. With one glance at her hand in Jason's, he placed a proprietary arm around her shoulder, and she felt the tingling heat of a flush envelop her body.

"Yep, this is none other than Z Con. It was great marketing, keeping the gender of the photographer a secret, shrouding my girl here in anonymity."

Izzy worked not to grind her teeth at the 'my girl' comment. Trapped, Izzy looked from Jason to Simon, back to Jason. Her voice made a reluctant appearance. "It helps with privacy."

Not sure whose touch to be most concerned about, she erred on the side of safety and removed her hand from Jason's. Then she shrugged out of Simon's grasp as well, glad to be free, glad to be able to breathe.

Jason's smile remained firm, and he picked her up again the moment she extricated herself from Simon. "Damn, I can't believe it's you."

Simon looked confused for a moment, then narrowed his eyes at Jason, he said, "I see you two are friendly."

Izzy tried to free herself from Jason's tight grasp, willing her arms to push against the sheet rock of his chest, not languidly roll around his shoulders like they wanted to. "Jason and I went to college together. Haven't seen each other since he left for the pro tennis circuit."

She heard the front door bell chime and was more relieved than she'd ever been to see Jessica, serving trays in hand.

"Erm, Simon, why don't you show these gentlemen into the studio. I need to sort Jessica out for a minute." And calm her speeding heart, but she couldn't tell him that.

While Simon directed them into the studio, she hung back to steady her nerves.

She watched Jason walk around the first set of displayed photos. She couldn't help the urge to know what he thought of them. A small part of her hoped he saw what she saw when he looked at them.

"So, are you going to tell me who those fine specimens of men are, or am I going to have to find out all on my own?" Jessica's voice broke Izzy out of her trance.

She pulled Jessica toward the reception desk where they could watch the men in relative secrecy. "Jess, I need you to pull the Mother-May-I escape plan in about five minutes, okay?"

Jessica looked back toward the studio. "Are you insane? You've got hot men in the studio, and you want me to come in and interrupt you?" Jessica took another look and whipped her head back at Izzy. "Cheese and Rice, Batman! Is that Jason Cartwright?"

Izzy's brow furrowed. "Cheese and rice?"

Jessica's bob flounced merrily. "Yeah. Lord's name in vain."

"Right, right, you're still into that Mormon rocker guy." Izzy nodded. "Yes, that's Jason Cartwright." She held up a hand. "Mother-May-I. Five minutes."

Jessica's smile morphed into a scowl. "You're crazy."

She didn't have time for resistance. "Please? I'll explain later, but right now, I can't really deal with more than one man at the moment."

Realization reappeared on Jessica's pretty face. "You know them?" Her voice trailed off, and as she took another peek, she added, "I call dibs on the McDreamy look alike."

"Jessica!"

"What? You got dibs already? Fine, I'll take JC. He'll do just fine."

"Be serious for a minute. I need you to do this. Okay?" Exasperated, she added, "You have a man."

Jessica must have seen the desperation on her face, because she acquiesced. "Yes, I do, but it's always good to have a spare." At Izzy's scowl, she sighed. "All right, all right. You okay, Izzy?"

She shook her head. "No. No, I'm not okay." Izzy tried to suck in a calm breath through gritted teeth. Now was not the time to lose control.
****

Jason tried to calm the adrenaline-heightened tremors in his hands. Izzy Connors. Judging by the way she'd stiffened in his arms, he shouldn't have touched her. The hug had been an impulse, and now his body paid for it.

He remembered every nuance about her. Her smell, her voice, her eyes, the way she'd felt in his arms. She looked just like he remembered her, from her thick, ink-black hair to her bee-stung lips. His mouth did its best impression of the Sahara when he remembered those lips brushing against his. He coughed to clear his throat and his mind. He'd thought about her for years. Tried to replace her. Now that she stood in front of him, his stomach felt as though he'd just sampled the finest scotch.

Watching her take long strides into the studio, he could tell this was her domain. She owned this space, standing tall and confident. Her face lit with pleasure when she walked by particular pieces.

He couldn't tell if she still played tennis, but she still had the body of an athlete. Moved like one. No wasted movements, every muscle doing its part in the balletic walk. Her simple silk blouse and leather belt accented her tiny waist and full breasts, her jeans showed off long, muscular legs.

She moved ahead of him to show Aaron a portrait at the far end of the studio, giving him a spectacular view of her peach of an ass. He smiled as he recalled how she'd always referred to it as her African trademark.

Fifteen years, and she hadn't changed. Not a bit. It took him several moments to realize she walked toward him again, lips moving. An unsteady smile passed her lips before she spoke again. "You see anything you like?"

Blood pumped in his ears as he thought his answer over. From the glower her manager shot in his direction, she wasn't on the available list, which nixed telling her exactly what he'd like. He indicated the portrait of the Masai woman on the wall. "I have a canvas of a Masai warrior. It's related to this one right?"

Her eyes danced. "Really? You have one of these canvases? We did a few of them in limited release mostly as marketing for the Kenya Homelands book. It's one of my favorites."

Then, as if she realized her proximity to him, she took a step back, and her smile faltered, replaced by a furrow on her brow.

Fifteen years, and she still could make him feel what he shouldn't feel. She isn't seventeen anymore. He shoved the thought aside. There was too much water under the bridge now. Far too late to think about what he should have done.

Aaron and Simon joined them at the photo of the Masai woman. Her lips quirked in response to Aaron's question about various locales for the photos, and deep dimples peeked out of both cheeks. Her wide, almond-shaped eyes, framed by thick lashes, lit up when Aaron relayed a story about his trip on Safari in South Africa.

In that moment, he could have killed Aaron. Jason stole a glance at Simon, adding him to the death toll. Simon's possessiveness was as defined as an Ansell Adams photo with all the back-off signals radiating off of him.

Jason had never been one to ignore a direct challenge for something he wanted. All he wanted was five minutes alone with her. Well, for what he wanted he'd need a lot longer than five minutes, but he'd start with that.

"Izzy, I'm so glad to have someone who knows me so well on these shoots."

She blinked at him and nodded, but it wasn't hard to notice the looks from Simon and Aaron. Aaron's more curious, but there was no mistaking the hostility in Simon's scowl.

Izzy's expression changed, her unsteady smile tensed. The four of them stood there in a bad parody of No Exit. They made several attempts at small talk, but none caught hold.

Finally, Aaron's eyes darted back and forth between him and Simon, and he directed Simon back to the far side of the studio to presumably discuss the shoots.

When they were out of ear shot, Jason leaned into her, caught a mild scent of jasmine and vanilla that made him ache. "Are you two serious?"

Her eyes widened. "What do you mean?"

Jason inclined his head toward Simon and Aaron. "You and Mr. Slick."

She wrinkled her nose and narrowed her eyes. "I don't see how that's any of your business."

He nodded, a little disappointed. "I'll take that as a yes. Does he make you happy?" He couldn't stop the question as it tripped off his tongue. Simon wasn't the kind of guy he saw her with. And you are?

"What part of 'It's none of your business' don't you understand?"

He gave her his best grin. "I have this condition where I filter out what I don't want to hear."

She might not have wanted to, but the corners of her lips turned up in an exasperated semblance of a smile. Dimples greeted him.

Taking his chance, he opted for innocuous and asked, "Why don't you come out to the house to play some tennis. I've got the courts available all day every day."

He watched her reaction with interest. Her eyes widened, and her lips parted as she shook her head. On a breathless whisper she said, "I don't play anymore." He wondered if she'd meant to inject a double entendre into her tone.

Curiosity piqued. Not ready to give up, he pressed, eager to elicit another breathless response. "You don't play anymore, or you don't play with me? I don't bite you know. You used to live for the game." He grinned, sure he'd probably pushed too far.

Her lips twitched as she attempted to contain her smile. He knew her well. Knew how she'd respond. Or, at least, hoped he knew. He changed the subject to a more comfortable topic. "You said you did the Masai prints in limited release? Do you think I can order a couple?"

"Yeah, of course. I have some contact sheets in storage I can show you if you like. Then I'll frame it up if you find a photo you want."

"Lead the way."

Her dark brows drew in. "What? Now?"

"Why put off until tomorrow..."

"Okay, this way." She led him through the studio to a work area, turning back to call out to Simon and Aaron as she unlocked the door. "I'm just going to pull some contact sheets to show to Jason."

The moment the door unlatched, Jason's eyes scanned the clutter of canvases leaned up against the wall and shelves stacked with supplies and boxes of contact sheets. Framing pieces littered the walls in no discernible order.

"Wow, this place is like a treasure trove."

She muttered something noncommittal as she scanned the names on some of the boxes, running her fingers against each one before moving on to the next. Her fingers traced the lettering on each box as if she read by brail. "I know they're around here somewhere…" Her voice trailed off as she scanned the top shelf. "There we go."

He stepped to assist her as she pulled the edge of a box out by her fingertips, careful to avoid tipping it over. "Are you sure you don't want any—"

Her gasp of shock and alarm propelled him into action. He rushed behind her and held the box still as it teetered between the brink of leveling back on the shelf or crashing on Izzy's head.

He adjusted the box, but it didn't stabilize, all he succeeded in doing was to shove Izzy further against the shelves. Not to mention, the semi erect length of him ground into the small of her back.

Izzy groaned out a curse.

Jason's body seconded her epithet. With every breath Izzy took, her body rubbed against his. Blood roared into his dick. "Are you okay?" he asked as he inhaled her scent. He felt her shove against the bookshelf, but he didn't budge.

"Let me go, Jason." Her voice came out squeaky and breathless. It only intensified the blood rush in his head.

"I'm working on it, but if you want me to stabilize this thing," he bit back a groan as she wiggled again. And if you want to keep your clothes on... "I suggest you don't move."

He shoved the box back on the shelf and gave her more breathing room, but not much. He moved back three inches and placed his hands on her waist to steady her. "Are you okay?"

Izzy dragged in gulps of air, one hand clasped her hand at her midriff. "Yeah. I think so. I didn't realize it was so heavy. Normally I — "

Her ramble cut off midstream. His guess, now that she was no longer in pain, she noticed the insistent penis pressed into the small of her back. He cleared his throat and tried for light and casual, but didn't release her. "If you wanted to get me alone, Izzy, there are less dangerous ways to do it."

She turned in his grasp to look at him and narrowed her eyes. "No one can be that egotistical." She shrugged. "Besides, you asked for a print. I'm not going to turn down a potential sale."

He bit back a hiss as she rubbed up against him—willed his hormones under control. Too bad they didn't listen to the command. Need crashed through him, and his erection twitched against her belly. He knew the moment she felt the movement, as her eyes flickered to where they touched, then back to his face.

In her gaze, he recognized the dilated pupils, awareness and apprehension. "I prefer the term confident to egotistical."

"Spoken like a jackass cursed with too much charm."

His hands tightened on her waist in reflex. He knew he should release her, but he couldn't do it. Not yet. He forced a smile on his lips, denying every instinct to rush. "Well, at least you think I have charm."

She blinked at him several times, shook her head. "Nothing fazes you, does it?"

His eyes fixated on her full lips, her pretty pink tongue peeking out to moisten her lower lip. On a groan, he lowered his head, watched for a reaction. Her full breasts rubbed against his suit as she dragged in ragged breaths. Commingling their breaths, he tipped her head up to look in her eyes. "Have you ever thought about me in all these years?"

She cleared her throat as her body leaned imperceptibly toward him. Before Izzy could answer, the woman with the bright pink hair poked her head into the storage room. "Iz, I've got the supplier for the frames on the phone. There's an emergency with your next shipment."

Jason watched as her gaze flicked to her assistant, then to him. "I—ah—need to take that." She extricated herself from his grip and rushed out.

She was lying. She'd always had that look of panic on her face when she lied. He knew a rescue when he saw one. He followed her out to join Simon and Aaron.

He didn't see her again before he left, but he'd managed to get her cell phone number from the wacky receptionist.

He told himself all he wanted was to apologize to her. To explain why he'd never gone back for her. But even as he completed the thought, he knew it was a lie. He wanted a whole lot more from Izzy Connors.

Chapter Four

An eerie luminescent moon hung low over the ocean as Jason slammed ball after ball over the net. He might not be able to run any balls down or serve yet, but at least he could hit some balls over the net. He needed this. Screw the fact he couldn't take a step without pain. He could hit.

It beat lying in bed and thinking about the state of his career. It beat thinking about how he could pull off a comeback. It beat lying in bed thinking about Izzy Connors. Of all the photographers in all the world.

One touch of her soft chocolate skin, and he couldn't get her out of his head. Her scent, her touch, her remembered taste. He needed his head in the game. Shit, it had been a long time since a sport magazine had wanted to do a feature on him, let alone Sports Illustrated. He couldn't have chosen better if he'd picked the photographer himself.

He just needed to get her out of his head. If only —

"Jason, baby, are you down there?" A woman's soft voice trailed down to him from the balcony.

Shit, Delilah. Awake and attention hungry. She wore one of his button down shirts as she padded down the stairs to the courts.

He'd never cursed their friends-with-benefits arrangement more than he did now. As a friend, he couldn't throw her out. But neither could he take the benefits she'd offered. "Hey Delilah, I see you're awake."

Her lips lifted in a sleepy smile. "I told you I never should have had so much wine. Especially red. Puts me out." She gestured to his shirt, the corner of her lip tugged up. "I hope you don't mind. I had to find something to wear out here since it's a little chilly."

He raised an eyebrow. "What happened to the clothes you wore over here?"

She angled her head to give him a smirk. Her hips sashayed from left to right as she sauntered toward him, careful to avoid the balls from the ball machine. "Well, I went upstairs to seduce you once I woke up, and you weren't there. I'd already taken all my clothes off."

In a blink, he perused her willowy, half naked form. Dark hair and pale skin gleamed in the moonlight. She'd left the shirt unbuttoned at the bust line, perhaps in the hopes of creating cleavage. It didn't work. But it's not like models were known for their bust lines unless they worked for Victoria's Secret. She was gorgeous and elegant and sexy.

Yet, he didn't want her. He'd made this date before he'd seen Izzy again, and now, all he wanted was her luminous dark skin under his hands, not Delilah's.

As she drew closer to him, his nostrils filled with the scent of expensive perfume. Her arms looped around his neck, and she whispered, "How come you're out here all by yourself? I could have come down with you." She indicated the leather upholstered benches. "We could have christened those."

He gulped past the lump in his throat even as he removed himself from her embrace. "We already did remember? Those used to be on the balcony."

Her brow furrowed as she stepped into his space, again she trailed fingertips down his torso. "That may be, but didn't anyone ever tell you, to christen things properly, you need to do it at least twice?"

Damn. He squeezed his eyes shut and willed the fevered attraction he'd felt for her when they met at Mr. Chow's six months ago to overtake him. Now, all he felt was mild affection. She wasn't Izzy.

If he felt like this already, and he'd only seen her once, he was in for a world of trouble.

"I think I might have heard that somewhere before." He stroked Delilah's cheek with his finger. "Tell you what, why don't you head upstairs to my bedroom. I'll use the outdoor shower to clean up, and I'll join you in bed."

A small pout marred her otherwise perfect face, but she didn't argue. "Okay, but don't make me wait too long."

He nodded his acquiescence even as he did a mental calculation as to which guest bedroom had an extra pair of clothes for him to wear in the morning, so he didn't have to wake her by going into his room when he woke up. She'd be disappointed, but better that, than he attempt to sleep with her while he imagined Izzy, beneath him, on top of him, in front of him. It was a recipe for torture. Not like he hadn't done it before, but he was too tired for charades.

He turned on the shower and hissed a curse as ice water sluiced his arm. As he sent a silent prayer that the water would warm, he unfastened his brace. Only one more day, and he could toss the albatross. Unaccustomed to the weight, his bad leg wobbled, but he remained upright as he scooted into the stall.

Stars illuminated the sky and winked at him as the water ran through his hair. He saw his bedroom light fade out just as he finished. His dick twitched in hopeless protest as the wish of accessible pussy winked out with the light.

As if on cue, his mind went to the one place he didn't want it to go. The vision of him and Izzy in her storage closet fanned his memory before he could prevent it. Every muscle he had tensed at the recall of her body molded to his, at the memory of her movements against him. The hitch he'd heard in her voice, the way her pupils dilated.

Shit. He'd never get any sleep this way. Wrapping his fist around his erection, he pumped the soap slickened flesh in a slow, deliberate motion. As blood surged to his groin, he pictured Izzy on her knees before him, all that glorious hair slicked back with water as she wrapped those luscious lips around him.

He could almost feel her tongue lap the length of him before circling the tip in a deliberate motion. He could feel her delicate hands, wrapped around his girth as she stroked in time to her suckling mouth.

Blood roared through his head. He slapped a hand against the shower stall to steady himself against his release. He bit off a stream of colorful curses as he dragged in gulps of air. He had to get Izzy Connors out of his head before she completely derailed his comeback.

Chapter Five

Izzy knew what obsession was. Knew the pain, joy, danger of it. But it didn't stop her rebellious brain from keeping up with the obsession. She couldn't take her mind off of him. The way he smelled, felt, sounded. And she, like a fool had wanted to fall for it. When did I become a masochist?

The way he'd held her as if they were the only two people in the world. That was classic Jason. She coaxed her previously focused, normal, non-obsessed brain into this parody of a working one. The way he'd brazenly asked her to play. Who said that? She could just imagine what game he wanted to play. He may have substituted the word tennis for sex, but she knew him better. She'd played before, and lost.

As hard as she tried to focus, she couldn't drag her mind back to work. Though, she supposed, if she had to choose between Jason's unceremonious reentry into her life or Sabrina's, Jason's was marginally more welcome.

Over the years, avoiding him wasn't an issue. They moved in vastly different circles. Los Angeles could be as immense and limitless as any galaxy. The only time she'd been unable to avoid him was televised tennis matches. She no longer played, but Nick did. And, as her bad luck would have it, he idolized Jason.

What she needed was a serious distraction. Maybe it was time to refocus her energies where they belonged, with Simon. With someone who was dependable and stable, and didn't say inappropriate things to her about coming to play —

Jessica interrupted her thoughts. "Your new Canon came in."

She looked up from the paperwork on her desk to see Jessica shifting from foot to foot in the doorway, excitement vibrating off her body.

"And are you going to tell me the deal with tall, blond and hot enough to melt in your mouth?"

Izzy worked to keep her grin under wraps. Jessica had shown remarkable, uncharacteristic restraint through a night of Arts and Tarts, the cleanup afterwards, not to mention taking pity on Izzy's world weary appearance last night. But now, it was morning. And she wanted answers.

Only, Izzy didn't want to talk about Jason. He already occupied far more of her brain power than she cared to admit. She considered exhaustion as an excuse but Jessica held the camera package in her arms, and Izzy had been waiting for that camera for weeks.

With a deep sigh of acquiescence, she mumbled, "There's nothing to tell."

Jessica placed the FedEx box on a shelf and plopped herself in the guest chair. Delicate, pierced eyebrow raised, she wouldn't let Izzy out of her trap. "Don't lie to me. You're terrible at it. I caught you two in the closet having a moment. A blind man could see the sizzle between you. Not to mention, I know you never miss one of his matches. Give me the deets."

Izzy cringed at her exposed secret and stood up to inspect the package on the shelf. She fiddled with the box, but resisted the urge to tear it open like a kid on Christmas. It's not like she had the time to play with it anyway.

"There was no sizzle, no tension. Nothing happened in the closet. He stopped a box from falling on my head. That's all." Hand on her hips, she huffed. "We're old friends. That's it. In fact, I wouldn't even call us friends. More like acquaintances." Her fingers played with the tape on the box as she angled her head to give Jessica a look. "And I don't watch all his matches. I do happen to love tennis, you know." She rolled her eyes for exaggerated effect, before she added, "Besides, isn't he getting married to that actress, the tiny, pert blond one?"

Jessica leaned forward. "The plot thickens. What's the matter, Iz, jealous? Are you two lost lovers?" Jessica rubbed her hands together with maniacal glee. "Even better than I imagined."

Izzy laughed and shook her head. "No plot. Just…" Izzy's voice trailed off as she searched for the right word. "Friends. Never lovers."

Not for lack of trying.

Jessica shook her head. "Even if I believed that, which I don't, but if I did, that doesn't change the fact you need to get some, and he's clearly interested. Even daft Simon couldn't have missed that. And I heard what he said about going to play at his house." She shivered. "So hot. I'd be more than happy to go and play with him."

"A, I do not need to get some. B, he is not interested. Trust me. And C, have you forgotten Simon and I might start something? And see earlier comment about Mr. Hot Enough to Melt in Your Mouth getting married." She sighed. "And don't call Simon daft."

Jessica snorted a dismissal. "When are you going to realize that you and Simon have no future? He's not what you need, no matter how much he insists he is. And that you can't believe everything you read in a trashy tabloid."

"This from the woman who lives and dies by Perez Hilton."

"Answer me this, Batman. Does Simon make you feel the way that Jason did yesterday?" Jessica continued to give her stern look, and Izzy grew warm under her discerning gaze. She didn't want to talk about Simon. Not with Jessica, certainly not with Jason.

She'd played Jason's conversation through her head since yesterday. How dare he question her relationship with Simon? Her relationships were her business. He'd opted out of her life years ago.

Izzy stiffened her spine. "What is your problem with Simon, anyway? You act like he's this major troll, but he's not. He's very attractive. For Pete's sake, he looks just like Blair Underwood."

"And he knows it."

Annoyed, Izzy said. "He's dependable."

Jessica sighed. "He's dull."

Izzy spread her arms. "He's committed to making something work with us."

Jessica shook her head. "When was the last time you were with your battery operated boyfriend and fantasized it was Simon? Oh yeah, scratch that, you can't picture kissing him, let alone doing The Do."

Izzy dropped her head into her hands and pushed her hair back off her forehead. "Is there any hope you'll let this conversation go?"

Pink wisps floated around Jessica's head as she shook it. "Nope. I care about you. You should be happy, and have real love. Not just date the guy who's convenient."

"He's not convenient. He's great. He—"

Jessica interrupted. "When's the last time your toes curled? When's the last time you had one of those passionate, mind-numbing kisses, so good you forgot your name? Can Simon give you that? I'm guessing Jason can."

Had she ever had that with anyone? The answer formed in her mind before she could stop it. Yes. With Jason. Izzy didn't like where this conversation was headed. It depressed her. "Look, not every relationship is supposed to be like that. We have respect for each other and enjoy each other's company. There's nothing wrong with that."

"Not if you're sixty. Even at that, I'm sure Grandma May wants to get some at some point. You can't have everything in your life so careful and controlled. It's not good for you."

"I'm fine. I like my life the way it is. I appreciate your concern, but it's not necessary. I know what I'm doing." She huffed. "Besides, I'm about to turn down the job."

Jessica stood, a frown pulling at her lips. "If you really think it's best to run away, I can't stop you. Like I said, I care about you. I watch the way you keep yourself so closed off from people, afraid to make a ripple. You can't live that way. No one can. Tell me you're in love with Simon all you want, but I saw that spark between you and the tennis hero. If Simon made you spark like that, I'd stay out of it and mind my own business. But he doesn't."

"Jessica, I'm tired. I don't want to talk about this anymore."

Jessica made her way to the door. "Yeah, I hear you. I have a date with Dingo anyway."

"As in the dingo ate my baby? What happened to the Mormon rocker?"

"I missed my favorite curse words too much. Anyway, back to you, just ask yourself this, how does Simon make you feel? How did tennis hero make you feel when you went toe-to-toe with him yesterday?"

Alive. Excited from the minute electrical charges she felt any time he touched her. Weak and jelly kneed as he licked those sexy lips of his and bent his head to kiss her.

But like hell, she'd tell Jessica that. Like hell, she'd let herself remember the feeling. Like hell, she'd let Jason Cartwright melt apart her carefully constructed defenses. She'd work with him because she had to, but she sure as shit wasn't going to play with him. He was dangerous to her, but she was ready for him.

****

Would anyone blame him for postponing facing his demons?

Jason had needed to kill a half hour before physical therapy, and he needed to take his mind off of it. Even if it put him in the direct path of his favorite paparazzi stalkers. The Grove wasn't normally a Pap hangout, at least not like the Ivy. He flicked through the GQ and paused over a Men's Health, but instantly put it down when he saw himself on the cover. He knew he couldn't avoid all media, it was everywhere. He only wished there wasn't so much of it everywhere. Finally, with another quick perusal, he found what he was looking for. A clue. And there it was.

The sub headline of Life and Style Magazine caught his attention. "Shocking scandal from the world of tennis."

How the hell had they found out? Had Michaels gone to the press? For weeks since he fired Michaels, Jason had anticipated him airing his grievances in the press. But he had nothing to gain by doing so, unless some rag wanted to pay for the sordid story.

Not that it mattered, because someone had leaked the story to the media. He scanned the cover for a clue. There wasn't one. Just allegations and innuendo. As he glanced around to make sure no one noticed him, he picked up the magazine and scanned the article.

"A high ranking men's tennis player has been named as a key witness in tennis's biggest drug case. An investigation by the…"

The article went on to talk about some vague items related to a DUI of the Australian number two seed, but not a word about him or Michaels. He thanked God for small favors and put the magazine back where he'd found it. Enough procrastination, he needed to face his demons.

An hour later, Jason stared at his opponent across the net, analyzed his stance, mentally calculated the serve, and anticipated his return move.

Jason told himself he wasn't nervous despite the tremor in his hand as he held his racket. His first day back at training. His first day back at seeing if he had a snowball's chance in the Sahara of a comeback.

His new trainer, Brian, raised his racket high and sent a spin serve over the net. Jason anticipated the serve, sliding with his good knee for a strong return. Brian ran for the ball, hitting a forehand return to Jason's right side.

Instinct urging his muscles into action, Jason started the full out run before his brain and his nerves could kick in. As his brain came online, he registered the slide and pivot he'd need to return. The instant he registered the pivot, his knee locked, and refused to cooperate. Slowing himself down, he trotted to a stop just before he could crash with the court wall. "Shit."

Brian ran to the net. "You okay, Jason?"

He gritted his teeth against the pain. "Yeah. I'm fine. Let's go again."

"Your knee's not up to it, we can take it easy."

Jason felt the scowl tighten his upper lip. He'd had enough of people telling him he couldn't do this. "What part about let's go again wasn't clear?"

Brian narrowed his eyes, but didn't argue. He took his position back at the base line.

Never mind a long day. Judging by his knee, it would be a long-assed cross-country journey to victory. Good thing he had a stubborn streak.

Chapter Six

The screech of tires filled the car as Izzy swerved to avoid the twelve-year-old Lindsay Lohan wannabe at the helm of the BMW. She squinted a mom look at the offender to deaf reception, the teen too busy yapping on her Bluetooth.

Taking a long breath to steady herself from the near miss, Izzy checked the clock on the dashboard as she pulled the dark green Corolla into a guest parking slot at Emerson Academy. As she hit the brakes, she strained to listen if the odd noise she heard was a bump or a thud. She knew she had to take the car in again, and mentally calculated her monthly budget.

Uniformed students milled around the entrance to the main hall and the parking lot. A few came off the tennis courts in their pristine white tennis uniforms. None of them Nick. She peeked through the windshield, trying to get a better view of the court, the slow setting sun a glare in her eyes.

The school fees were killer, but they had the best in-school coaching program in the country. Add to it twenty percent of the students went to ivy leagues, and she happily wrote that check at the beginning of every term. She could pay an arm and a leg to get Nick into one of those special training camps, but she couldn't afford that and a top notch school like Emerson. And as far as she was concerned, his education was more important than his tennis aspirations. That kind of thing had mattered to her father. Not that he'd ever met Nick, she thought with equal parts sadness and bitterness.

After a twenty minute mental check of the photos she wanted to use for the gallery, trying not to think about Sabrina, and trying even harder not to think about Jason, there was still no sign of Nick. Maybe I got the time wrong? It was his first day back to practice, and she'd wanted to be there to pick him up, and to talk to Coach Tisdale.

She considered getting out to find him, but took in her ripped jeans and unmade up face, and thought better of it. The last thing he needed was embarrassment when he wanted to fit in. She'd wait until practice was over and there were fewer students around before she got out to speak to Tisdale.

Star Wars music filled the car and had her digging around for her phone. Thanks Nick. Lately, she never recognized her own ringtone. Nick always changed it to something silly.

When she rescued the phone from the clutter of her bag, she checked the screen but didn't recognize the number.

"Hello?"

"You know, I recognize a rescue when I see one." The deep voice on the line sent shivers chased by a warm flush through her body.

Jason.

She didn't like the giddy sensation running through her. For Pete's sake, she wasn't a teenager anymore.

"How did you get my number?"

Her brusque tone didn't dissuade him. "Ouch, that doesn't sound like happiness to hear from me, Iz."

She sighed and reminded herself he was a client and, like it or not, she needed him. "No. It's not like that. Just wondering how you got my number."

"Your receptionist gave it to me." He paused. "So why were you in such a hurry to get away from me the other day?"

He sounded so endearing and wounded, she almost softened, until she reminded herself why she needed a rescue. She cleared her throat. "I didn't need an excuse, Jason. I—you didn't just call to harass me, so what do you need?"

He seemed unsure and faltered before he continued. "I meant what I said the other day about catching up, you know, getting reacquainted. It's been a long time."

The last thing she needed was to fall for that charming 'Don't mind me, I'm sweet and harmless' routine again. How many Hollywood starlets had fallen for that same shtick? Besides, how could he think they could just hang out and chat like old buds? He's Jason Cartwright, that's why. She scanned her brain for something diplomatic to say.

Cautious, she said, "Yeah, it has been a long time. But, I'm slammed with work. I'm actually waiting for an appointment now. We can catch-up at the shoot." Maybe that would be enough.

Or, maybe not. "Izzy, are you still upset with me about—"

She rushed to cut him off before he could thrust her into the throws of mortification. "Jason, I'm sorry, I have to run." Hanging up quickly, she stared at the phone. How the hell would she get through the photo shoots if she could barely talk to the guy?

Movement by the courts caught her attention, and she saw the familiar fair-haired lanky form exit with an older man in tow. She recognized the coach from the parent open house earlier that year. At fifty, Coach Tisdale could have passed for late thirties. Benefits of living in Los Angeles.

Nick indicated to the coach that she was there, and Coach Tisdale gave a perfunctory wave. Izzy waved back, but didn't bother with a real smile. They'd never hit it off, but he'd been a supportive of taking on a transfer student like Nick, so she cut him some slack.

Nick tossed his gym bag in the back before he slid into the front seat. "Hey, Mom, can I go over to Matt's for dinner? His sister can come get me and everything."

Izzy knew she was selfish for relishing every moment he called her Mom, but she couldn't help it. "Sure, as long as your homework is done."

He scrunched his face in the same way he always did when he was about to lie. "I don't have any homework." Taking note of her disbelieving expression, he amended his statement. "Well, not real homework anyway. I can get it done before school. It's only French."

Izzy raised her eyebrow. "Only French? Didn't you get a B minus on the last test?"

He shrugged. "Well yeah, but—"

Izzy didn't enjoy these types of struggles with Nick. She didn't want to be a soft parent, but the truth was she hated conflict and would do anything to avoid it. But she had to be firm. Just because discipline gave her nightmares of her strict father didn't mean it wasn't necessary.

"You know, there's been something I've been trying to remember." She gave him a look of mock forgetfulness. "Oh yes. There it is. I seem to recall a rule about homework. May I remind you, that you're the one that asked to go to France with the school this summer?" A trip she still wasn't sure she could afford.

Nick rolled his eyes. "Yeah, yeah. But it's just this one time. And I — "

Izzy shook her head in stubborn defiance and started the car. "Sorry, Nick. No dice. Besides, I thought we had plans tonight?"

His eyes widened, followed by a look of chagrin. "Ah, sorry, Mom, I forgot all about family night. With practice and all, I got caught up."

She gave him a soft smile. She didn't want him to feel bad. "It's okay." Then looking back at the coach, she unbuckled her seat belt. "Can you hang out for a minute while I talk to your coach?"

Nick wrinkled his brow. "About what?"

"Parent stuff." She climbed out of the car and walked over to Tisdale. As he finished talking to one of the parents, he looked up at her. She noted he didn't look too pleased to see her. Right back at you, Bub. She wasn't exactly eager to speak to him, but she was a parent first. If Nick wanted to hang out with Samantha Tisdale, then she wanted to make sure it was okay by her father.

Izzy clamped her teeth on one of her fingernails before she could catch herself and halted the action. She only reverted back to the old habit when she was nervous, like now.

There's no reason to be nervous. She was the parent. She had every right to act like one. Then why did she feel physically sick with every step? Because you're a chicken shit.

"Miss Connors, I don't have a lot of time today. Can this wait?"

Hello to you too. He needed a lesson in manners. She wouldn't slink away and hope she didn't have to deal with the situation

"This won't take long. I wanted to chat about the kid, well, kids really. I hoped to invite your daughter Samantha over to dinner sometime. I know, left up to Nick, it'll never happen."

His already thin lips set in a flat line. "Any particular reason you think my kid is interested in dinner at your house?"

She sighed. Neither his tone nor his stance leaned toward civil. "I just figured if she and Nick were going to spend so much time together, it would be nice if I got to know her better and you and your wife..." She looked back toward the car. "I like to know where Nick spends his time. Helps keep him focused."

Tisdale shortened the distance between them and crossed his arms. "Just what are you inferring? That my daughter is up to no good with Nick?"

Izzy backed up a step. "I think you mean implying." She stuttered as she added, "I-I didn't mean to imply anything like that. She was over at the house the other day and mentioned you didn't know where she was. I figured if we got on the same page about what the kids were up to, we could avoid future confusion."

The frown line in his forehead deepened. "Well you can rest assured, you have nothing to worry about. I keep an eye on my kid."

This hadn't gone the way she'd planned. She'd annoyed him. "I'm sure you do. I wanted you to be aware that she's welcome anytime and for us to keep the lines of communication open."

He huffed and worked his jaw. "Well, I'm aware. I'll handle my kid, you handle yours."

Hell. That was the last thing she wanted. She prayed he wouldn't take it out on Nick.

As she climbed into the driver's seat, Nick looked back at his coach for a moment but didn't ask about their conversation. He shook his head. "I was going to try out my Death by Burrito recipe tonight." Not usually one to sulk, he'd already let go of the fact he couldn't see his friend.

Izzy cringed at the Death by Burrito reference. "Food isn't meant to burn a hole in your mouth or your stomach."

"You'll like it, I promise. I think I used too many habaneras last time."

"If you say so." Izzy rubbed her stomach. She didn't think she'd recover from the last death by burrito she'd eaten, but she'd make an effort. He was a great cook. If only he hadn't had a penchant toward the deadlier spices.

They drove in companionable silence for several minutes. As they approached their exit to the artist nook of Pasadena, a more sober Nick asked, "When is she coming?"

It broke her heart. After the age of nine, he'd stopped asking about Sabrina. He usually enjoyed the times she was around, but never asked when she would blow in to their lives, or blow back out. "I wish I knew. I tried calling the number she left, but it was disconnected."

When he didn't respond, she peeked a glance at him. He looked so much like Sabrina with his dark eyes and olive tone to his skin, but he was nothing like her in temperament. He had an almost manic penchant for keeping commitments and promises. Izzy had a feeling she'd be paying a therapist to delve into that sometime in the future.

Her mother's voice rang in her head. Better out than in. "I know you said you didn't want her to visit, but I've been thinking, maybe it might be fun?"

He shrugged. "It'll be okay, I guess."

Not to be thwarted, she tried again. "Remember that trip to Mexico and the insane donkey ride? I swear, I'll never get on one again."

He cracked a smile, but still didn't say anything. Izzy wasn't sure if it was standard male silence or if he really didn't want to see Sabrina. "I know it's tough having her leave, but we can always enjoy when she's here right?"

When did you become such a good liar? Izzy hadn't enjoyed Sabrina's infrequent visits since Nick's trip to the hospital at age six for an appendectomy. Izzy had been frantic, but Sabrina never made it back home. When Izzy had brought it up on her next visit, Sabrina said what she always said, "You took care of it didn't you?"

That had been Izzy's last straw. She knew their arrangement was unique, with Izzy having legal custody of Nick, and Sabrina having an all access pass. Izzy was also careful never to say anything negative about Sabrina, but she had a feeling Nick knew how she really felt.

He stared out the window, watching the red lights of traffic.

"So, I'm going to petition the Judge again."

That got his attention. "Oh, yeah?"

"Yes. I told you I wouldn't give up."

"Yeah, I know. But what makes you think the judge will grant it this time? Which excuse of his no longer matters?"

She hated it that he was so astute. "Well, the gallery opening for one. I've got a Sports Illustrated shoot coming up too. That means a great income. Something more stable than a struggling studio. That'll make a difference."

He shrugged. "Not all the difference. Besides, you've done okay."

No, not all the difference. She still wasn't married, curse her luck for having a traditional Judge. And the primary reason, she was still black, and Nick was still white.

He glanced at her. "It's not your fault. You shouldn't have to marry some douche just to adopt me."

"Watch your language." She slid him a look. She knew what he wasn't saying. She shouldn't have to be white to adopt him. She sighed. "Maybe it won't matter this time around."

At the sullen look on Nick's face, Izzy opted for a change in topic. "So this thing with Samantha, you really like her?"

Nick's expression was still sullen, but he answered the question. "Yeah, she's okay."

"Okay? I caught you guys necking like…like…well, like teenagers, and you only think she's okay?"

Sullen expression gone, he now looked half mortified, half amused. "Geez, Mom, do you have to ask that? Who the heck says necking? What does that even mean?"

She laughed. "Well, yes, I do have to ask that. I'm your mom. And okay, you do have a point about the use of the word necking. C'mon. Inquiring minds want to know."

He shrugged. "Didn't we already cover this the other day?"

"Yeah, guess we did." She coughed behind her hand to mask the bark of laughter when the tips of his ears turned red.

"Well, she's the coolest girl in school. And she's fun. And she's Coach's daughter." He turned to stare out the window. "All the guys say I'm lucky she even talks to me."

Something about the way he said it pulled on Izzy's heart. She knew what it was like to be in the shadow of the girl everyone thought was perfect. She didn't want him hanging out with Samantha Tisdale for the wrong reasons. "Well, do you think you're lucky to be hanging out?"

Another shrug. "Yeah, she's cool."

Ah, to be the mother of a teenage boy.

Izzy mimicked his shrug. "Fair enough. Just keep it in mind. You don't want to be a follo—"

He rolled his eyes again and finished the statement for her. "Follower, I know. I want to be a leader."

Izzy feared she'd gone into Grandma territory. She was always trying to find that balance, but as he got older, she never seemed to find it.

He grinned at her, and Izzy squirmed behind the wheel, aware she was about to get a cross examination. "Can we stop talking about my personal life and talk about yours?"

Izzy laughed. "No! We cannot talk about my personal life."

"What about that pilot guy, Mick?"

"Mike, his name is Mike, and we were never dating."

Nick pretended he hadn't known. "Are you sure? Because he showed up at the Arts and Tarts the other night and spent a whole hour trying to butter me up. He could be the one, Mom."

Izzy laughed. "Doubtful." She eased off the freeway. "Besides, he's a potential client."

Nick sobered again, his face a mask Izzy hadn't seen on him too often. He looked too adult and world weary when he said, "You know, Mom, you don't have to avoid guys 'cause of me. I want you to go out and do stuff besides work."

A light prickling behind her eyelid signaled oncoming tears but she blinked them back. When had her baby become a man? She took his hand and squeezed. "Nick, me not dating seriously isn't because of you. It's because of me. I've chosen to focus on my career that's all."

He squeezed back. "If that's how you want to play it. But you should go out more, Mom." The devilish smile that would likely melt many a female heart as he got older was back. "With someone besides Simple Simon."

Izzy's laughter blurted out. Where did he and Jessica come up with this stuff? "Oh, you'd like that wouldn't you, Nick, my man."

Then she remembered she was supposed to be the parent. "And don't disrespect him. He's a very nice man."

Her impression of Simon's phrase whenever he saw Nick was spot on, and her son burst into a fit of giggles, once again looking like the child he was. "You make him sound like a librarian." He thought for a moment then added, "Maybe Jessica knows someone."

Izzy cringed then shook her head. The only men she ever saw Jessica with had more skin tattooed than not, and more piercings than she cared to think about. She shook her head. "I will not have my assistant or my son fix me up. I'm not that sad and pathetic yet."

"Well, you just let me know when you are. Half my friends have older brothers who think you're a total MILF." He shrugged. "I think it's gross, but one of them might—"

Izzy ignored the reference to older brothers and ran through the letters in her head, but couldn't figure out what MILF meant. "Dare I ask, what is a MILF?"

Nick shook his head. "Geez, Mom, don't you know anything? It stands for Mom I'd Like to—" A look of alarm crossed his features. He blushed, and continued, "Follow Around?"

She pulled into their driveway at the end of the cul-de-sac and shot him a glare. Somehow she didn't think that's what the F stood for. "Language."

"What? I didn't swear."

Izzy raised an eyebrow. "Sometimes it's the intent."

He muttered something that sounded like "Yeah, yeah," as he climbed out of the car.

As she followed him in, she wondered if she really had become so pathetic her son needed to fix her up. Catching a glimpse of her makeup-less face in the hallway mirror, she had a feeling the answer was yes. Before she could close the door behind her, her purse started to ring. The theme song from Buffy the Vampire Slayer filled the hallway. Izzy made a mental note to add Jessica to the list of people not allowed anywhere near her phone.

She juggled a camera bag as she dug into her purse. When she retrieved the phone, it took her a minute to realize it wasn't a call coming in but a text message. Once through the door, she used her foot to kick it closed and placed both bags on the floor. Her phone continued to incessantly sing Buffy at her until she tapped the message icon. She really had to figure out all the features on the blasted iPhone.

Izzy didn't recognize the number, but she instantly knew who sent the message. It's rude to hang up on someone, you know. Didn't your mother teach you better?

She absently wondered if she needed to change her number as she typed out a message. What are you going to do, spank me?

It wasn't until after she hit send and mumbled to herself, "That'll teach him," that she realized the suggestive nature of her message. Or rather, how he might interpret it.

As if on cue, the sounds of Buffy once again filled the hallway, and Izzy half expected vampires to waltz around the corner. She angrily pushed on the text icon. Is that an invitation?

The rush of liquid heat to her core as she stared at his message didn't bode well for her vow to ignore him. Playing games with Jason Cartwright would only get her hurt.

****

Izzy Connors was dangerous to Jason's focus and recovery. He had to stop thinking about her and stay on track. He'd already nearly severed a finger fiddling with one of the ball machines and almost dislocated his shoulder when lifting too much weight. He squeezed his eyes shut as he completed the last rep of leg lifts. Izzy's last message to him played over and over in his head. Had she been flirting? Did she have a secret spanking fetish? If it was anyone else, he'd know the answer, but she was different.

Not paying attention, he let the weights slam down too quickly. His knee shot bursts of pain up and down his leg at the shock. He let out a curse as he rubbed the throb until it abated. It hurt, but still felt better than the disaster match the day before. The aches in his muscles and the throbbing in his knee were his body's way of telling him he'd overdone it the past few days. But after seeing Izzy again, he'd needed to work off some of the tension. It wasn't everyday he ran into the one woman he'd let himself love.

The Izzy he remembered had been inquisitive and sweet. But the woman he'd seen the other day was neither of those. More like closed off and cautious. And dating that robot boyfriend of hers—Jason couldn't believe she was happy with him. Maybe she is. He quelled the burst of envy in his heart. He didn't have any right to it. She wasn't his.

He moved over to the treadmill and entered in the appropriate workout selection. All the while he tried to ignore the guilt he felt about the last time he'd seen Izzy. He should have called her. Had the opportunity to more than once. He should have gone back to see her. He should never have gone anywhere near Sabrina Reems. Should should should. He couldn't change any of that now.

He could have insisted on seeing her when he went back to campus, but he'd taken the easy route, Sabrina. He hadn't even thought about Sabrina in years, but seeing Izzy brought back those memories. Whatever had possessed him to choose Sabrina over Izzy all those years ago was long gone. He prayed he'd exorcised the desperate need for self-destruction.

For an hour, as he ran, the steady whir whir whir of the treadmill soothed his mind. One step in front of the other. He could do that.

"Anything you want to tell me?" His manager's steady voice came from behind him, startling him into tripping.

Not sure how to respond, he kept it simple. "Hi, Aaron." Does he know? Adrenaline poured through his body, urging him to run and release some of it. But he didn't. He kept his pace and schooled his expression. Aaron either wanted to discuss Michaels or Jason's poor showing in practice. Either way, he wasn't in the mood to rehash.

Too bad, because his manager wasn't in the mood to stay quiet. Aaron pulled out Jason's exercise report. "Is that all you have to say?"

Shit.

"I wish I knew what you wanted to hear, man." His heart rate monitor beeped at him, and he slowed his pace.

"How about the truth? How bad is your knee, Jason?"

"Not that bad. I'm recovering."

"Is that why Brian recommends a full physical analysis in two months before he clears you to play?"

Shit. Brian had no right. "What the hell does he know? The guy's a blowhard. I have no intention on waiting two months before I get the all clear."

"Damn it, Jase. Do I need to remind you that you selected this trainer? Plucked him out of obscurity from your alma mater? You're not going to find anyone this good in such a short timeframe." He slapped the folder on the neighboring treadmill. "This is the kind of shit you're supposed to tell me about. You can't keep looking me in the eye and telling me you're fine. If your knee's done, then I need to know that so I can restructure your career."

Jason continued to walk at a steady pace on the incline, ignoring the throb in his knee. Tread lightly. He surveyed Aaron's bloodshot eyes and disheveled suit before checking the wall clock. Eight in the morning. If he knew his friend, he was out past his bedtime so it might as well be dawn. "Look, don't listen to that idiot. Get rid of him. He doesn't know what he's talking about. How about you have a little faith and let me worry about my knee? You just worry about getting me in as a wildcard in a couple of matches in the next few months. I'll be ready." Jason flashed his all will be well smile at his manager.

"You can't fire him because he's telling you something you don't like. When are you going to learn that you can't charm and bullshit your way out of everything? Your career is serious. We need to figure something out if this trainer isn't working."

Jason wiped his arms off then ditched his heavy towel, using his forearm to swipe away sweat from his forehead. "I don't think you understand. I'm not trying to charm or BS my way out of anything. I'll be ready. On my own if I have to. Don't fire him, but you better tell him I'll be damned if I'll listen to some bullshit about not being able to do this. Even if you don't believe it, I do. Even if fucking Brian doesn't believe."

Aaron wiped a hand across his shadowy stubble. "Okay, look. I get it. You want your shot at a comeback. You're getting ready for a run on your old title." He placed both hands on the side rail of the treadmill. "You might not want to listen to Brian, but if you do some serious shit to yourself, and we're not prepared, you're fucked. No title, no more shots at a title. And, if we don't clean up your rep, no cushy broadcasting job, no training camp for the aspiring kiddies. None of it. Is that what you want?"

Jason leveled his gaze at Aaron. He clenched and unclenched his jaw, reminding himself that Aaron wasn't the enemy. "I hear you, but get Brian off my case. If I wanted doubters in my camp, I'd have kept Michaels around."

Chapter Seven

"I will see Izzy, if I have to physically remove you to do it."

Izzy's head snapped up from her light table at the commotion from the reception office.

"Over my dead body, Simple Simon. She's working her tail off to try and complete the impossible, thanks to your poor planning. You can't interrupt her."

A crash exploded down the hallway followed by colorful expletives from both Simon and Jessica.

"I'm her fucking manager. I know what's best for her career."

"Oh, remove that fucking stick up your ass, you pompous douche bag." Jessica's shrill voice echoed off of the reception walls.

"Tsk, tsk. How would your freak of a boyfriend feel about your language, Jessica?" Simon's voice chilled the air.

As Izzy rushed out of her office, her heart slammed against her ribs. Voices grew louder and harsher as she rounded the hallway.

"You're nothing but a small minded, little dicked, mother fucker, no wonder Izzy—"

"What the hell is going on here?" Izzy interrupted in a rush cutting off the rest of Jessica's tirade.

They stood facing off over the reception desk, tension and anger crackling between them. If Izzy didn't know better, she'd swear the tension was...sexual. Jessica's colorful red poodle skirt and matching sweater set a good barometer for her mood. Simon's ice blue tie shifted and gleamed, reflected the recessed lighting above as he loosened it. She looked like a sparkling firecracker and the look in his eyes bore frosty resentment.

Izzy tried to keep her voice calm. "Is there a legitimate reason you're shouting the studio down? Lucky for you there's no one in here right now. What the hell is wrong with you two?"

Both spoke at once.

"She wouldn't let me in to see you."

"He tried to bully his way past me."

She stared, incredulous. "You have got to be kidding me. What are you two? Children?" Before either could speak, she put up a hand. "Enough. Simon, I asked Jessica to keep everyone out, including you, so there's no need to verbally lambaste her." She turned to Jessica. "Thanks for doing your best, but next time, just come get me before it escalates. I can't have a shouting match in here. There could have been customers."

Both of them stared at her with a mixture of anger, antagonism and angst.

A red-faced Jessica muttered a brief apology, then bent to retrieve the discarded desk phone, paperweight and invoices from their scattered locations on the floor. Her contrite attitude toward Izzy didn't translate to Simon, however. He stared at her bent over form, eyes half lidded. He drew in several deep breaths, before turning to face Izzy again. There was something in his expression, Izzy had never seen before — uncontrolled, almost primal.

She dragged him back to her office determined to diffuse any potential flare-ups. Once ensconced in the relative privacy of the brightly lit room, she gave him her full attention. "You owe her an apology. I'd make sure you give it to her before you leave."

He stepped back as confusion lit his eyes. "Me? You're going to make me apologize? She's your assistant. She should know I have important matters to discuss with you, whether she likes it or not. And—"

Izzy narrowed her eyes to slits. "She's also my friend. She was doing her job so I could work. Apologize."

Izzy watched as the last of his annoyance seeped out of him, replaced with contrition.

"Okay, you're right. I was an ass. She just drives me crazy."

"Whatever it is, squelch it. I can't deal with your squabbles and still get work done."

"Actually, that's what I'm here about."

Izzy moved back to her light table. "What's the urgent matter that couldn't wait till this afternoon's meeting with the publisher?"

He quirked an eyebrow. "You mean besides you calling to back out of the photo shoot with Jason Cartwright?"

Blood suffused her cheeks under his intense scrutiny. "Oh, that."

"Yeah. That pesky little photo shoot with Sports Illustrated? Why would you jump to that solution without talking to me first?"

Yes, why had she tried to avoid talking to him? How was she supposed to explain working with Jason was a non-starter? Simon would read something into it. She opted for a safer excuse. "Look, I know you had to pull a lot of strings to get me the job, I just can't manage it and the gallery opening. It's too much."

"What is it you can't handle? It's a couple of shoots, Iz. This is Sports Illustrated. They'll do half the work for you. All you need to do is take glorious photos."

"I do more than that, Simon. I'm responsible for the art direction. I'm responsible for the mood, finding the stellar picture, looking into the soul of the subject." If he has a soul, she thought bitterly.

He didn't speak for several beats. Frowning, he asked, "Is it the subject you don't want to deal with? I caught some of the tension there. If it is the subject, I'll tell them it's a definite no and line something else up for you, but Sports Illustrated is a huge step in getting you where you're supposed to be. I don't want to tell them there are artistic differences if I can help it."

She bit back the bitter bile at his artistic differences retort. "I know how important SI can be. I'm not crazy about shooting the athletes and actors and stuff, but I can do it. I have done it."

"So it is the subject you object to."

Shit. If she said yes, he'd want an explanation, not only as her manager, but as her boyfriend. She wasn't ready to give explanations. If she said no, he'd think she was a difficult artist type, and she hated it when he made those kinds of references. She was a professional.

"No, it's not the subject."

"Good. Then there's no problem. You'll do the shoot." He took her hand and pulled her out from around the light table. He encircled her waist with his hands. "I'll make this as easy on you as possible. Anything you need, you just tell me, and I'll make it happen."

She leaned back from him. Knowing she couldn't ask him to make Jason Cartwright disappear without a trace, she opted for something in the realm of possibility. "How about less pieces in the gallery opening?"

"Well, how about we try something smaller. Besides, you know forty will give the critics a good range of your work and your talent. Anything else you want? How about I come to the set and make sure everything goes smoothly?"

Izzy hated having him on set. He always got in the way, tried to give direction. She'd have to babysit him to make sure he didn't waste SI's money. "Oh, no, you don't have to do that. I know how bored you get at shoots. It's a lot of sitting around. How about more time in my day?"

"Your wish is my command. I'll cancel the publisher this afternoon. Give you more time to work. But I think coming to the set will be fun. It's been a while since I've seen my lady work."

He seemed so pleased with himself, she didn't bother to tell him he'd make her job harder, not easier, and by going to the meeting in her place he'd only be giving her back the time he stole from his interruption. "That would be great, Simon. But honestly, don't feel obligated to come babysit me. Jessica will be on hand to make sure everything goes smoothly."

His jaw clenched at the mention of Jessica's name, then slowly unclenched before he spoke. "I'm not there to babysit you. I'm there to be your right hand. Jessica's capable enough I'm sure, but she's not me." He grinned and pulled her tighter. "Anything else milady wants?"

She screwed her face up, body tightening at the contact. "That you can provide me? Not that I can think of right now, but I'll take a rain check."

He smiled as he dipped his head. "Where's your sense of imagination," he mumbled against her mouth before nipping her lower lip.

In what could only be a practiced move, he shifted to pin her against her light table with his hips while both hands went to her face in what might have been an attempt at an achingly tender kiss. But it wasn't. Firm, coaxing lips slid over hers and demanded a response. He left her nowhere to run.

When in Rome. He wouldn't let her wheedle out, so she threw everything she could into the kiss and waited for the tingle of arousal to slide up her spine. Waited for the quickening and thrumming of heady heartbeat. Waited for the dizzying ladder of lust and longing. Hoped to replace the memories of Jason.

Traitorously, her heart and body sighed in resignation to a kiss from the wrong man. Not Jason.

The moment the image of Jason's handsome face peeked into her consciousness, she felt the sparks of telltale arousal. She remembered his clean, crisp scent and the way his arms slid around her in familiarity and sexually heated tension. Using her imagination, she molded herself against the lengthening heat of Simon's arousal. And wished for several moments that Jason's hands slid down her form in desperate need. That Jason's tongue slid in and out of her mouth, coaxing her tongue to dance with his. That Jason's erection pressed into her, insistent and aching for relief.

Jason, not Simon. Jason. Desperate to shake off the fog of her fantasy, she tore her lips from Simon's. The sounds of labored panting filled the air as they both tried to catch their breath. Though, her pants came with a healthy dose of self-loathing and remorse. Simon was finally treating her like a desirable woman, and the only way she could get turned on was to think about Jason? She needed therapy. And a drink. A drink and therapy. Maybe an exorcism too just for good measure. She'd try anything to wipe thoughts of Jason Cartwright from her head.

"Damn, Izzy, if I'd have known that was going to happen, I would have suggested we go up to the house." His lazy smile told her just what he wanted to do up at the house.

Feeling like a first class bitch, she disengaged from him. "I still have work to do."

He gave her a disappointed smile, but released her. "You're right. We can finish this later." He must have seen some of the panic flit across her face because he amended the statement immediately. "I'm not going to move too fast, Izzy. I want this to be perfect."

She listened to him walk out and murmur brief apologies to Jessica. Fantasies were normal she told herself. Healthy even. Many a woman had fantasized about George Clooney or Brad Pitt, or Jason Cartwright for that matter, while with their boyfriends.

Then why did she feel so guilty?

It took her almost an hour after Simon left to accept the realization that he had manipulated her into staying on the SI job. Not only that, but he'd also manipulated her into inviting him to the set. She was no better than she'd started off. She still had to deal with Jason, but now she'd have the added pleasure of Simon's company on the shoots.

Chapter Eight

Jason waited for Izzy, every nerve coiled in anticipation. The tension, his constant companion since the day in her studio, ebbed out of Jason's shoulders at the sight of her. Izzy. Not for the first time in fifteen years, she'd occupied more of his mind than he wanted to admit.

He shrugged into the suit jacket the stylist handed him and watched her set up. Her linen cargo pants fit her so well they showed her every curve and accentuated her long legs. Though, he had a feeling she wore them more for their utility than for fashion. The faded green t-shirt that clung to her breasts looked well-worn and lived in. An expensive-looking Canon camera hung from around her neck. He watched as she turned each knob, depressed each button. Her every gesture, efficient and erotic.

Stomach tight, he took a sip of coffee, grabbed one for Izzy, and headed across the tennis court toward her. He ignored the twinge of pain in his knee when he put weight on it.

Before he could reach her, a gangly blond teenager set down a tripod behind her and said something that put a genuine smile on Izzy's lips showcasing her dimples. Jason stopped mid-step, and stared as her eyes lit up and lips, full and wide, revealed that beautiful smile he remembered.

She used to smile at him like that. Damn, I've got it bad.

Behind the gangly kid, he caught sight of her manager and swallowed a curse. He hadn't anticipated trying to get close to her with the ever watchful eyes of her jailer on him. He considered his options and shrugged. Fuck it. What was the worst that could happen? He knew what he wanted, and the pencil pusher wasn't going to stop him.

He watched the boy saunter off before he approached. He offered the coffee and hoped he looked nonchalant. She took the cup with a grateful smile. But even though she smiled, he didn't miss the fact that she avoided looking him in the eyes.

"Good morning. Thanks." She took a sip of the dark liquid and moaned her pleasure as she gave him a quizzical look. "You remembered how I like it."

"Not hard. I've never met anyone who takes their coffee with equal parts sugar and coffee grounds."

Her lips parted as if she wanted to say something, but then they snapped shut. She indicated the Canon around her neck. "You ready to get started?"

Okay — all business and no chit chat. He'd expected that.

"Uh, yeah I'm ready when you are. You do these early morning shoots often?" He resisted the urge to hang his head in his hands, knowing he sounded like an idiot. His critics would guffaw if they heard his bombing pick-up lines.

She gave him a smile, a genuine one. Maybe all they needed was a little warming up period. Maybe he could remind her they'd been friends once. More than friends.

"Early mornings are a photographer's paradise." She noted his confused look and added, "It's the best light."

He nodded. "I know I said this already, but, it really is great to see you. I'm excited to work with you. You already know I'm a huge fan of your work."

She pulled a lens out of a camera bag and attached it to the camera. "You're right. You did say that already."

Fair enough, she wouldn't give him any wiggle room. With every one of her efficient movements, he caught a whiff of jasmine and vanilla. "It's true." When she merely fiddled with the camera, he added softly, "I've missed you. I don't think I realized how much until I saw you again."

She gave him a long measured look, eyes boring into his soul. He returned her stare and stubbornly refused to break the connection. Midnight eyes drew him in, and he took an involuntary step into her space.

Her eyes widened and pupils dilated. When her lips parted slightly to reveal the tip of a pink tongue, he couldn't drown out the blood rushing in his head.

"That charm of yours get you far?"

Before he could respond, a voice behind him broke the connection. "Mom, I put the film cameras in the red bag, and the lenses for them are in the blue one. The rest of the digital lenses are—" The gangly teenager Jason had seen carrying her equipment stopped and stared at him.

Mom? His mind struggled to process the single word. His body still staggered from his response to her as he wondered if he had heard right. The boy was blond and far from biracial. Adopted? But she'd always said she didn't want kids.

The boy continued to stare at him agog until Izzy poked him in the ribs, and he finally spoke, blurting out, "Holy shit, you're Jason Cartwright." Eyes wide, he turned to Izzy and added, "Mom, you didn't tell me you were shooting Jason Cartwright."

With a bemused look, Izzy made introductions, but not before she corrected him. "Watch your language. Nick, meet Jason. Jason, this is my son Nick."

There was that word again, Mom along with son. Unable to immediately find his tongue, Jason smiled and held out his hand clasping the teenager's hand, scrutinizing, looking for any signs of Izzy. After a moment, he gave Nick a smile he usually reserved for the red carpets. "Nice to meet you, Nick. You're a tennis fan?"

There was something familiar about the boy around the eyes, but he couldn't place what it was. He couldn't picture Izzy as a mother. Granted, he didn't put much stock on motherhood or parenting for that matter, his own parents screwed up bad enough to make him never want children. Parenthood was an important job. One most people weren't suited to. Absently, he wondered what kind of mother Izzy was.

Nick sputtered and rambled a stream of consciousness. "Am I a fan? Gosh, yeah. I watch every match you play. It totally sucked about your knee. Coach says I play my forehand just like you do. None of the guys are gonna believe this. God, if you could—"

"Nick," Izzy interrupted him, a bemused smile played across her lips. "Slow down. Jason and I have to get to work." She cast a glance in Jason's direction. "But maybe if Jason has some time, he could talk to you between shots and after."

He wanted to laugh at the exchange, especially when the kid realized he'd sworn within earshot of Izzy. "Yeah sure, we can chat all you like."

When Nick beamed at him, Jason realized how misleading his height was. He stood about five feet eleven inches, but Nick couldn't have been older than thirteen, maybe fourteen. If he was Izzy's, that meant she gave birth when she was sixteen or so. Jason had known her when she was sixteen. She must have adopted the kid.

Izzy pulled a racket out of one of the tennis equipment bags and indicated the other court. "I figured you could take some swings while we got to work."

Nick looked uneasy, shifting glances toward Jason, like he didn't want to leave. "Are you sure?"

Izzy brushed hair out of her face. "Well, it's either that or you can hang out with Simon."

They both looked toward her manager, out of place in his Brooks Brothers three-piece suit and tie, yapping away on his phone. Photo shoots as a rule were informal places due to long hours. He wore a suit, but he was talent. What was Simon's excuse? The stylist had paired the suit with stark white tennis shoes and a skinny tie, making him just this side of dressy casual and uber-fashionable. Nick made a face. "I thought maybe I could help. Carry your bags, set up the lighting and stuff."

Amused, Izzy said, "But you hate to play assistant. Is this how you want to spend your midterm day off? You never—" She stopped talking at Nick's desperate look.

"I can do it. I'll stay out of your way. I swear."

Izzy blinked at him and shrugged. "Jessica should be in the back with the assistant art director. Go tell her you want to be a gofer for the shoot. She'll get you working."

"Really, Mom?" Pure joy lit up Nick's face with a thousand watt smile.

She nodded and grinned. "Yeah, really. I would have asked, but you usually don't want to do this kind of stuff."

Nick blushed. "Course I want to help. I also don't want to get stuck with Simp — erm, Simon." With a grin, he headed off across the green, but not before stopping to say, "I'll see you later, Mr. Cartwright."

Mr. Cartwright? He wasn't that old was he? "You can call me Jason."

Nick shook his head and cast Izzy a look. "If it's all the same, I'll keep calling you Mr. Cartwright."

Jason glanced between Izzy and Nick. "Okay. Whatever works. I'm flexible."

"This is so dope."

Izzy shook her head as she watched Nick run off. "When did kids start using dope again? I'm cutting off that kid's BET." Giving Nick another dubious look, she added, "His MTV too, for good measure."

Jason barked out a laugh as they watched Nick bounce away.

"Thanks for being so nice to him. He sometimes has a confidence problem. Could you tell?"

Jason scanned the courts. Several assistants carted camera bags to the shooting area on the court.

He laughed and added. "I noticed he lacks for things to say, too." Suddenly sober, he added, "He seems like a great kid." He meant it. The gangly teen had Izzy stamped all over him—in spirit if not genetically.

Izzy nodded. "Thanks. You're pretty much his idol."

Instead of asking if she watched matches along with him, he said, "I wish I'd known. I'd have gotten you tickets to an open or something."

She halted and took a light reading of his face. "Oh, we've been. We were at the US Open last year."

His stomach flipped. She'd seen him win, then she'd seen him lose that crushing defeat to Nadal. "Why didn't you come through to see me after the matches? We could have had dinner. I could have shown off for the kid. We could have— reconnected." I could have told you the truth.

****

What lie would he accept? Izzy squirmed under the scrutiny of his gaze. Not knowing where to look, she looked where was most comfortable, at her camera. She fiddled with the knobs to appear busy.

"I figured you probably didn't remember me or were too busy with reporters." She prayed that didn't sound desperate or worse, pathetic. In truth, it had been more along the lines of she couldn't face him, couldn't relive the memory of the last time she'd seen him.

He stared at her, whiskey eyes probed hers. "We both know that's a lie."

Unable to take the truth in his eyes, she looked away and set up the first round of shots. Why was he looking at her like that? It made her uncomfortable and heated enough to sweat.

Izzy positioned him and snapped away, while she attempted to lose herself in the cool methodical process of the photos. He wasn't a difficult subject to shoot, with the angles of his jaw, aquiline nose and full lips. The camera loved him, especially in shadows.

Most photographers cherished the creation of a photo, the art and the passion. Not her. What she prized the most was the truth in it. The camera held the inherent truth about life. Photoshop might spin a brilliant tale, but raw film was pure and honest. It was impossible to hide in black and white.

Izzy snapped another few images before stopping to switch lenses. As she moved, she could feel his eyes on her. She didn't dare meet the stare, because every time she did, she saw interest. Keen interest. But she knew better. He'd built a social career on being the good looking, womanizing, paparazzi darling.

As they moved to the next set of shots, Izzy tried to ignore Jason's intent looks as best she could. But he made it increasingly more difficult with each shot. The intensity was perfect for black and white, but not perfect for her. *Why does he always do this to me?*

He'd turned her down, hadn't he? The way she figured it, she'd gotten off lucky when he walked away from her. Or not gotten off at all to be honest. Jason wouldn't turn her world inside out again. She stole another glance at him and sighed. She had her pride.

As if trying to fill the silence, he tried small talk. Asking about other photo shoots, her clients, how her parents were. When she mentioned her father had passed away, he looked genuinely sad. For the most part, he kept things light and impersonal, which suited her fine.

It was only after they moved to the next series of shots that he was close enough to speak to her and break the no personal questions barrier. His gaze locked on hers. "So, the dweeb over there." He nodded his head, indicating Simon who flashed a feral grin in their direction. "Is he your..."

He let his voice trail off forcing her to complete the sentence for him. She knew the verbal tactic, but chose to answer anyway. Maybe if she said boyfriend, he'd leave her alone. "Simon? Yeah, he's my..." She could play the game. Let him believe what he wanted about Simon. She didn't owe Jason explanations.

He nodded, and his brows drew in. "As long as he makes you happy."

She snapped a photo, noted the change in shadow over his masculine features and switched angles. He'd gone from dark and handsome to brooding, dangerous. Clearing her throat, she put a safe distance between them before she responded. "Very."

Seemingly unperturbed, he nodded. "That's good." He then smiled at her with a devilish gleam in his eyes. She almost dropped her camera.

The powers that be really should outlaw that smile. Or at least make him carry a permit to wield it. It went beyond dangerous. Women everywhere would drop their panties. But, his outlaw smile notwithstanding, she knew better than to turn away from the full onslaught of those sensuous lips. His smile had earned him heartthrob status first on the court, then around the world. The magazine would want to see it captured in its full brilliance. She almost lost her balance when she leaned in to get a closer photo. Strong and steady, he reached a hand out to help balance her.

The moment their hands came into contact, she held her breath, trying to ignore the zing she felt from the warm heat of his hand. God help her. She pulled her hand free from his, telling herself he didn't affect her. "What about you? I read you and Cienna Whatshername are tying the knot."

A guarded look instantly replaced the polished smile. "You should know better than to believe what you read in the rags."

"So, she doesn't make you happy?"

"There's nothing there. It's the media's imagination. Besides, we were talking about your love life, not mine."

"No, we are not talking about my love life. It's not an available topic of discussion."

He smirked. "Why not? You're afraid it'll be apparent you don't love that pencil pushing douche bag?"

She whirled on him. "Who the hell are you to presume to tell me how I feel? He's wonderful. Patient and dependable." Why did it sound like she was describing a car?

"Dependable, huh? Tell me something, Izzy. When did you become so uptight?" He looked around and lowered his voice. "I can tell just by watching you two together. You can't stand his touch. When did you decide to settle?"

She took her cue from him and also lowered her voice. No need to have the whole set gossiping about her personal life. "Not everyone can live their lives carefree with no consequences, switching out partners like they were underwear." Her breath came in sharp and ragged. Why did she let him get to her?

He gave her a wry laugh. "Is that what you think?" The look he gave her was predatory. "There was a time when you would have gladly jumped on me. Or have you forgotten?"

She spun away from him briskly, praying that he couldn't read the mortification in her eyes. She sucked in one long, deep breath and steadied herself. Turning back to him, she smiled without humor. "That was a long time ago. I've developed some taste since then."

He stood, and she realized, not for the first time, how tall he was. Arms crossed over his chest, he asked, "What's your real problem with me, Izzy?"

Besides you tormenting my dreams? She ignored the rapid pace of her heart or the red haze that crept into her vision and took a step forward. "I know who you are, Jason. Or at least your type. You dissect my life and show disdain for the choices I've made. All the while, you've gotten away with murder most of yours. Taking the easy route. You use your charm like a shield, protecting you from having to get too close. I see you in the magazines. For someone with your talent, you could be a role model, make a difference in someone's life, but it's far easier to be seen at all the clubs running around with the latest starlets. At best, you're all charm with no substance. What happened to the kid who wanted to be the best in the world and that's all that really mattered?"

An emotion passed over his face she could read. It could well have been pain. Before he could retort, she sighed and put up a hand. "Enough. We have a long shoot. It'll get longer if we snipe at each other."

He seemed to let it go and went back to his supine position for several minutes while she set up the next shot. Attempting to fill the tense silence with what he probably thought a safer topic, he asked, "So, Nick calls you Mom, did you adopt him?"

She frowned. Something inside her shriveled. Another reminder of how the world viewed her. She didn't want to discuss Nick with him. Jason was batting a thousand. "I wondered when you would ask."

His brows drew together. "I'm curious. You're too young for him to be yours."

"Not to mention he's too many shades of white to be mine?"

He looked sheepish and a little wary. His mind no doubt wondered if he'd stepped into another mine field. "Well, uhm, yes."

She backed up, snapped several shots with her wide angle lens in place. She then moved in close enough to catch his scent, clean and earthy. "Jason, can you look down at me for a minute?"

He complied, and she depressed the shutter release. "Nick is my son in every way that matters."

He gave a long sigh looking defeated. "I'm only curious, Izzy." His eyes roved over her face. "I never pictured you as the soccer mom type."

Izzy straightened her spine. "What's that supposed to mean?"

"Last time I saw you, you were about to take over the world. No prisoners. I remember you saying you didn't want a family."

Had she said that? "That was before I took one look at Nick. Plans change. Other things become a priority in your life. For me, it was love at first sight with him." She turned her attention from her camera to him. "But a superstar playboy wouldn't know anything about the pull of family."

The moment the words were out of her mouth, she wished she could bite them back. His wince said it all. Her verbal jab hit its mark and wormed its way to his soul.

Considering his history with his parents, she knew better. She should have anticipated his questions about why she was a mother. Their damaged parents were a few of the things they'd bonded over in school. They'd spent endless hours talking about how they wouldn't want to screw up kids that way. She sighed and lowered the lens for a moment. "I'm sorry." Hands spread in silent apology, she added, "I had no right. The Nick situation is a little sensitive."

His eyes softened and bared a new vulnerability for the camera. He was silent for several moments as if weighing her apology. "I guess you get a lot of questions." He smiled and added, "It seems like you've done a great job with him."

Izzy wrapped up the shot for a break, and Nick materialized with two bottles of water, as if his ears burned. From the corner of her eye, Izzy saw Simon coming their way across the green, and she bit back a groan. She didn't have the patience to deal with him right now. She cast a pleading look in Jessica's direction. At the very least, she could distract Simon.

"Hey, Mom, since you and Mr. Cartwright are friends and all, I thought we could invite him for dinner next Sunday night."

Izzy felt the wire mesh of a cage close in around her and prayed Jessica would hurry over as Simon's steps drew closer. Jason stared at her, and her darling son helped to ensnare the trap. Her heart picked up its pace as she darted a look at Jason. "Oh, Nick, I'm sure Jason has plans already, we can't really expect him to—"

Jason didn't let her wiggle out of it. "I'd love to come to dinner. Thanks for the invitation, Nick."

Simon and Jessica both drew up just in time to hear Jason's acceptance of the dinner invitation.

In typical Simon fashion, his appearance seemed to suck all the air out of the room. "Did I hear someone say dinner? I can make us some reservations at Il Sole."

Jessica snorted a response. "You don't have to steal the kid's thunder, Simon. It's his invitation."

Accustomed to playing pseudo peace keeper, Nick groaned. "No, nothing like that. I just invited Mr. Cartwright to dinner at our house since him and Mom are friends."

Izzy carefully kept her gaze from Jason's. What should have been a simple declined dinner invitation had quickly bloomed into a Shakespearean drama, with Jessica poised for battle, Simon intent on exerting his will, Nick pleadingly hopeful and Jason—amused. Damn him.

Simon plastered on a charming smile. "That sounds even better. Less formal, with old friends. We could make a whole night of it. I have a couple of ideas I'd like to run by you—"

Not liking the icy way Simon uttered the word friends, Izzy opened her mouth to interrupt, but Jessica beat her to it. "No, Simon. Nick's too polite to tell you, but you're not invited. He wants a night with his idol, not a business dinner." Simon sputtered as Jessica rolled her eyes at him before turning a dazzling smile in Jason's direction. "I'm sure Jason and Izzy want to catch up too."

Wait, what? That wasn't how this was supposed to go. "Unfortunately, tomorrow night won't be possible. I'm swamp—"

Jessica, Simon and Nick spoke at once, for the first time, all three on the same side, though, for different reasons.

"What woman wouldn't want to spend the evening with someone as charming as Mr. Cartwright here." Jessica gave her a smile that was all innocence before turning a more conniving version toward Simon. Damn it. Whose side was she on anyway?

"Mom, c'mon. You don't have to work every night," Nick wheedled.

"We'd all love to have dinner with you. I'd love to hear all about you and Izzy at school. It'll be a good catch up time." Simon beamed at Jason, as he ignored Jessica's attempts to unsettle and uninvite him.

Trapped, she looked around at all four of them. Nick's hopeful face, Simon's plastered expression, Jessica's ill-concealed jubilation and Jason's smug grin. Fuck. "I'm sure Jason's far too busy to join us on such short notice."

"Like I already said to your future tennis prodigy here, I'm wide open and looking forward to it." Nick looked happy, but she felt far less than happy as Jason added salt to the wound. "You gonna cook me something special, Izzy?"

Nick and Simon pulled faces, but Nick spoke the shared sentiment. "I don't think you want her to do that, Mr. Cartwright. Maybe Maria could make—"

Was her cooking that bad? She smiled at the three men malevolently. "Nonsense, Nick. I'd be happy to make something nice for dinner."

Before running off again, Nick gave Jason the no go signal.

Jason didn't seem to heed Nick's warning and gave her a look that told her he meant business, despite Simon's presence. "I look forward to dinner, Izzy."

As soon as Nick was out of earshot, she turned to Jason. "You don't have to come."

"Are you kidding? It'll give us a chance to catch up." He turned his superstar grin on Simon. "Like Simon said, old friends, together for a whole night. And I can learn about your life. Besides the fact you're a photographer, and you have a son, I know nothing about you."

Simon interjected, "Don't forget the best girlfriend a guy could ask for."

"How could I forget something like that?"

Izzy chewed her bottom lip even as she shot a look of reproof to Simon. "This isn't something you can just say you'll do and be flighty about, Jason. I won't have Nick disappointed."

Jason's eyes darkened, and he worked his jaw. "I'll be there."

Chapter Nine

Several hours after Izzy shooed an overexcited Nick off to bed, the sound of music reverberated from Izzy's purse. She didn't want to talk to anyone. But it could be Sabrina. Her mother. Simon, with a job.

Annoyed, she tossed off the jasmine scented quilt and padded over the cold hardwood floor to the dresser. The moment she opened her bag to rifle through it, sounds of 2 Live Crew's, Me So Horny filled the air. Stunned, she didn't know whether to laugh or throw her phone under the bed. She'd have to buckle down in the morning and read the damned manual to change it.

If she hadn't been so annoyed, she'd see the humor in song choice given the indication on the LCD. Jason. Damn him. Couldn't he just leave her in peace? She selected the message icon and held her breath in preparation for the message.

Did I mention you looked beautiful today?

Fairies beat wings of need deep in her belly. He had a way of reducing her to an awkward seventeen-year-old without much effort. Forget leagues, Jason Cartwright played games out of her conference.

Using both hands she tapped out a response. What's the matter, Cienna not up for a cuddle?

His response was instant. I'd rather spend the night with Izzy Connors.

Wisely, she chose not to answer. She stumbled back to bed and sank into the comfort of her mattress. Flopping on her belly, she willed sleep to come. To her frustration, memories of Jason danced through her consciousness.

He was the last person on earth she'd ever thought she'd see again. But now he was back. And she couldn't stop the flood of emotion that came with his reappearance. The swell of anger that tightened her chest when she thought of how he left. Her heart beat a snare drum of excitement when she saw him now or heard his name on the news. The raw lust that coursed through her veins and threatened to liquefy each cell when she caught his gaze on her. She hadn't been prepared for any of it.

For fifteen years, she'd tried to not think of him. As if it was that simple. She'd done what she could to tune out any gossip or rumors about him. Of course, that had been increasingly difficult since any number of magazines splashed him on their covers every other week.

She didn't need the flirtation. She didn't need to be the focus of anyone's attention. She was perfectly happy, she lied to herself as heavy lids drooped shut.

Izzy trembled as Jason's hands gripped at her waist. She wanted him. Only him. "Jason…"

A low moan sounded in his throat, and he wrenched his lips away from hers. "Izzy, wait, we…"

"I don't want to wait."

He groaned when she pulled his head back to hers. Firm lips molded to hers. When she parted her lips to allow him deeper entry, he took full advantage. His tongue thrust and teased as it mated against hers.

Izzy couldn't believe this was about to happen She'd dreamed about this since she'd first laid eyes on him. She ran her hands over his broad shoulders. Heat radiated off of his body and scorched her fingertips as they roamed. Emboldened, she let her hands roam lower.

"Izzy, oh m…" He didn't finish the thought when she unsnapped the button of his jeans.

She'd never been so bold in her life. But tonight, she could do anything, say anything. Including caress the hard length of him. She drew in a sharp breath, and her gaze flew to his. There was no way they would fit together.

He must have seen the alarm on her face because he bit off a colorful curse and stepped away from her. "Izzy, we can't do this. I—I can't do this."

"Why not?" She told herself she wouldn't cry. That didn't stop the pinpricks of tears from stinging her lids.

He leveled his eyes with hers. "This isn't right. It shouldn't be like this."

He didn't want her? This time, she couldn't keep the tremble from her lips. She'd gotten it wrong. He trapped her face in his strong hands, despite her attempts to wrench away. Wasn't she humiliated enough?

"Izzy, sweetheart. I want you more than I've ever wanted anyone in my life." He looked down and smiled ruefully. "You feel how much I want you."

She blinked tears out of her eyes. "Then why are you stopping me?"

He took her hand and sat her down on the bed. "For once in my life, I'm trying to be the good guy. You deserve the good guy."

"But you are—"

"Izzy, if I were the good guy, I never would have kissed you. You're sweet and perfect, and I want you so bad I can't think straight most of the time, but this isn't right."

She tilted her chin up and crossed her arms. Every bit the petulant seventeen year old. "Jason, I know what I want."

He shook his head and indicated the bottle of wine on the peeling Formica counter of the shabby kitchenette. "Really? Then why did you need the influx of liquid courage?" He sighed before adding, "You're seventeen."

She glared at him. "I'll be eighteen in a couple of months. If you don't want me, all you have to do is say so." She sobbed as she continued. "I can't believe I listened to Sabrina."

He kneeled in front of her. "I don't know what Sabrina has to do with this, but she doesn't matter. I care about you enough to want to wait till you're fully sober and fully aware of what you're doing. I can barely breathe, I want you so bad. But for you, I can be a good guy."

She hated to admit it, but her head was swimming. She'd had way too much wine. But it was the only way she'd have ever had the courage to go after what she wanted.

Bleary eyed, she asked. "Can you hold me for a minute? You don't have to stay long, just for a little while."

He smiled at her. "That I can do."

He pulled her into his arms on the bed and held her tight, kissing her temple as he caressed her back. After several moments, his phone rang. They ignored the insistent ringing at first, but the caller wouldn't give up.

The moment he picked up the phone, his body language changed. Shoulders tensed and voice tight, he turned to her. "I have to go take care of something. I'll be back in an hour, I promise."

Izzy sat bolt upright from her dream, sheets tangled around her ankles. Damn it. It wasn't enough that he haunted her waking hours, but memories of him had to take over her sleeping hours too? Her entire body felt flushed from the memory of Jason's kiss. The flesh between her thighs tingled and throbbed begging for release from a man's touch. From Jason's touch. No! Not Jason. Simon.

Izzy flopped on her side, trying to will the feelings of need back into their lockbox. Sleep wouldn't come quickly today. What's the point? She rifled through her happy drawer and pulled out her battery operated boyfriend. "How nice it is to see you again, B.O.B."

Shifting position, she turned B.O.B onto mild vibrate and closed her eyes in anticipation of the predictable bliss. At first, she kept the vibrations low to reflect how she liked to be teased.

Teasing her slickened folds to coax them into response, she pinched her distended nipple, hoping to speed the process along. But nothing happened. She needed incentive. Maybe picturing Simon was what she needed. If she could imagine herself with him, maybe she could feel something.

Frustrated, she increased the speed of vibration, closing her eyes and tried to picture Simon — the way he'd kissed her the other day. Simon's tongue traversing her dew slickened folds. Simon's strong hands massaging her breasts, plumping them into response.

Simon inserting first one finger, then two into her, groaning as her juices dampened his hand. Simon's dampened fingers circling around her nipple. His gaze locked on the puckering bud. His head lowering to the nipple, tongue peeking out to tease before tasting.

In her mind's eye, she pictured his head lowering with aching slowness. Blond locks tousled and tangled from her attempts to draw him closer. Blond? That wasn't right. Black men didn't have blond hair. Her eyes flew open, and she sat up as she moaned with the need to climax. Why couldn't Jason leave her in peace even now?

Flopping back on the bed, she groaned. Might as well go with it. After all, it was only a fantasy. Not like it was real. She closed her eyes again, shifting to make room for B.O.B.

Jason's roguish smile flashed in her brain, and she whimpered as the need crashed into her blood. She pictured his head lowering to her nipple covered in her essence. Tongue traversing around the nipple, he mumbled. "Mmmm, delicious." As his teeth grazed and his lips suckled at her nipples, his fingers acquainted themselves with her folds. He mumbled love words as he paid homage at her breasts. "So wet…hot…beautiful…"

Izzy moaned his name as her fantasy took on a mind of its own.

Jason finally released her nipple with a pop and lowered himself between her legs. "I've had a teaser, now I want the whole thing."

His first lick forced a full body shudder form her. His second ripped a moan from her throat. On his third, he circled her clit slow and easy, refusing to give her the harder stimulation she needed. He circled the distended nub with his lips and hummed.

Izzy's hips bucked off the bed. Calloused hands gripped her hips to keep her in place. "Oh no you don't. I want my feast." With his thumbs, he parted her plump folds and took in the view. "Gorgeous."

She whimpered his name and a plea. He rewarded her by licking a path of heated need all the way from her clit to her perineum and back again. He repeated the process, though this time, he stopped at her clit, placing a soft kiss directly above it.

"Jason…more…"

When he didn't give her what she wanted, Izzy peeled open her eyes to look at him. The purple latex of B.O.B. looked back. Damn.

She needed to get over her Jason fantasy before it ruined her life. Why couldn't she get over her mental blocks? She and Simon cared about each other. They were friends. Maybe they could be more than friends. Besides, she needed to focus on the reality of her life, not the fantasy she wished her life could be.

How long had it been since she'd had sex? It couldn't be that long ago. She counted back the months but had to stop after she ran out of fingers. Damn, over a year. And if she remembered right, it hadn't even been that good.

Well, I have no one to blame if I sit around and don't do anything about it. She brushed her covers aside and hopped from the bed to find the perfect seduction outfit. She could just call Simon to come over. He'd moan about the late hour, but this way, he wouldn't be able to refuse her.

Finding the wispy bits of red lace in her drawer, she changed in a rush, arranging herself on the bed in what she prayed was an alluring manner. Extending her arms trying to take a picture, she realized that wouldn't work. Spying the dresser she smiled. Perfect. She set the timer, quickly hopping back on the bed before she could chicken out.

The camera clicked, and she giggled. Jessica would never believe this. She'd never done anything so daring. She picked up the phone and hastily typed out a message with the attached photo. "I'm so lonely. Want to come over and keep me company?"

She selected speed dial number one and hit send. When the little message envelope said sending, she lay back with giddy anticipation. Any moment now, Simon would call and tell her he was on his way from Century City. That he'd dropped everything and couldn't wait to be with her.

Any moment now. Except, as she waited for the message to send, she noticed the area code as 323, not Simon's 310. Panic shot through her, cold and fast, knotting icicles of tension in each muscle. Oh shit. "Oh no. No, no, no, no, no. Oh Shit. God, if you're up there, please tell me I can recall that message." She shook the phone and tried to stop the send process. When that didn't work, she sped through the message options looking for some sort of recall button.

Oh God, oh God, oh God. This could not happen. It was a dream, a terrible, horrible nightmare. All she had to do was wake up. She pinched herself, then muttered curses at the frisson of pain that shot up her arm. "Ow. Damn it."

Defeated, she sunk onto the bed, shoulders slumped. She was grounding Nick tomorrow for changing her speed dial numbers. If it was Jessica, she was so fired. After several deep breaths, she fought back the tears in her eyes. She had no one to blame but herself. Nick didn't tell her to be irresponsible. Jessica didn't stuff her in the see-through lace and tell her to try her hand at seduction. All of it was her stupid idea.

Fuck.

The sounds of Star Wars filled the room, and she stared in horror at her phone LCD. Jason. Equal parts shame, misery and fury washed over her and rendered her unable to move. Maybe he'll hang up and leave me alone? The phone stopped ringing, and she would have cheered if she'd been able to move. Though, her cheer didn't last, as the phone rang again. Jason—again.

I can't be a sissy all my life, can I? Forcing the motion of her fingers, she answered, stumbling over her words. "Look, I'm mortified enough. Nick changed my speed dial settings, and you were first, but it was supposed to go to Simon, and now you have it, and I—"

"What's your game, Izzy?" His tone, husky and lazy, washed over her like much needed sunlight.

"I—I—It's not a game, Jason. It was a mistake, a complete horrible, nausea inducing have-to-pack-it-in-and-move-to-Timbuktu sort of gaffe. I'm embarrassed, and I never should have, but Nick messed with the phone and I was lonely and Simon…" She trailed off when she noticed the sounds of a highway in the background. "Are you driving?"

Voice still husky, he let out a brief, pained chuckle. "This is one of the times I regret living in Malibu. Babe, it'll be a while to get to you, but maybe we can start with phone sex. I already know what you're wearing, so how about I start with are you wet?"

Izzy couldn't process his last question, because she was too focused on the first thing he'd said. On the road. From Malibu. Shit. And because the fates loved to see her squirm, she realized with painful horror that she was wet. Oh God. Heat suffused her skin all over, and she prayed for a hole to open and swallow her. I am not having phone sex with Jason Cartwright. "Jason, don't come over. I beg you." She didn't recognize the silken husky voice as her own.

A horn blared in the background. "You're insane if you think after what I've seen, I could pretend I haven't."

"Please don't. This was a horrible mistake. I swear I will never do anything so reckless again in my life. Please don't come over."

"Too late. I need to see if you taste as good as you look." He mumbled a curse. "I don't care if I have to wake every neighbor you have. I'm seeing you tonight."

Damn, she didn't stand a chance if he kept at her like this. Any woman in the world would be beside herself to have Jason Cartwright breaking traffic laws to get to them. Any woman. Every woman. How many women had he seduced with the smiles and the sexy voice and the urgent pleading in his voice? That thought had her rationale returning to her.

"Jason, you show up here and wake up the neighbors, the press swarm this place in a heartbeat."

That brought him to his senses. "Shit. You don't play fair Izzy Connors."

Neither do you. "I — uhm. I really am sorry again. How about we both just forget this ever happened? We still have another shoot to do. This will be something we can laugh at and humiliate me with twenty years in the future or something. I am so sorry, Jason. Never again."

Jason was so silent for several moments she thought he'd hung up. "You never did answer my question, Izzy."

Confused, she stuttered, "Wh — what question?"

"Are you wet?

Chapter Ten

Five days, and Jason could only think of Izzy. Five days since they'd talked. Five days since he'd seen her in her lingerie.

He needed to have his head examined. What kind of fool chased a woman who said she wasn't interested, dared the laws of physics and the Malibu Police department by driving a hundred-twenty miles an hour in a rush to get to said uninterested woman. Though, in the fool's defense, she'd sent him a photo hot enough to rob him of all common sense for weeks to come. He'd see her tonight. Tonight, boyfriend or not, he'd see her in her lingerie again. Tonight, he'd get an answer to his question.

"You want to tell me about the fight?"

Jason's head snapped up from the contract he signed, automatically filtering out the restaurant's din. Château Marmont was not his ideal place for a meeting, but Aaron loved it, the chaos, the energy. "What do you mean? What fight?"

Aaron shrugged. "I heard you and your lady photographer went all De la Hoya vs. Mayweather."

"De la Hoya vs. Mayweather? Where do you get this stuff?" He shook his head and chuckled. "It was nothing. We just had a little difference of opinion."

His manager leaned forward, eyes searching his face. "What aren't you telling me, Jase?"

"Nothing."

"You think I didn't notice the tension in the studio with you two?"

"You're a pain in my ass."

Aaron swigged down the last of his Scotch. "Yeah, I might be a pain in your ass, but if there's a problem with your photographer, I need to know. This Sports Illustrated cover and spread is important, especially with you injured. Your endorsements depend on good press. If it's not working out with this photographer, I can have her replaced."

The skin on his arms prickled at the thought of having Izzy replaced. That was the last thing he wanted. What he wanted was more time with her, alone time, not less. He didn't want her replaced. "We work together fine. There are some minor complications we have to deal with."

Aaron raised his empty tumbler in the direction of their harried waiter. Ice cubes clinked in the empty glass, reflecting shards of rainbow light from the setting sunset off the French doors. He looked every bit the expensive sports agent. He and Simon would make fast friends, Jason mused.

"What is the history with you guys anyway? You into her?"

"When did you start prying? Besides, it's not like that." Liar. "She's an old friend. And, she's got a kid. Kids equal drama."

"Ouch. No one wants to deal with Baby Daddy bullshit." Aaron ignored the warning look and continued. "If you're just old friends, why do you have that look?"

"What look?"

"You know, the look. The one you get when you can't get someone out of your head. Remember that thing with the heiress? You obsessed about her for months."

Jason groaned at the reminder of the oil heiress. "Dude, I was twenty-two and dumb. You can't hold it against me."

Aaron shifted his focus for a moment to check out the long limbs of the red-headed It-Girl on her way to a table. A vibrant jade green gaze flitted over their table before narrowing in on Jason with the focused precision of a laser.

"Damn, what I wouldn't give for a piece of that," Aaron muttered.

Jason's eyes skimmed over the red head's body. Memories of a drunken coat closet incident surfaced in his mind. Maybe Izzy was right, and he had pissed his life away with a series of meaningless encounters. "Not worth it."

Aaron's eyes widened. "Oh man, her too. You're a dog. Give the rest of us a chance."

"Oh, c'mon. It was three years ago. I've changed my stripes."

"Yeah right." Aaron stretched over the table to take his pen back from Jason. "Look, you've got two more shoots scheduled with the Connors chick, are you two kids going to play nice?"

He had every intention on playing nice with her tonight. "It's under control. There won't be a problem." He didn't want to share with Aaron that he was on his way to Izzy's after their meeting. None of his business.

"If you say so. Besides, if you have chocolate fever these days, we can get you a date with that actress Grace Umber or somebody like that. Or, even better, one of the Jenkins sisters, the ones coming up the tennis ranks. Now how's that for publicity? Tennis legends in love — endorsers love shit like that. Sasha..." Aaron used his hands to imitate her breasts. "She's a real powerhouse."

Chocolate fever? More like Izzy fever. He liked women, all kinds of women. Tall, short, black, white, they all helped drown out that empty feeling. At least they had, before Izzy. "Jesus, do you have to be so lewd? I don't need a fix-up."

"I'm just saying. If you're into black girls now, let's at least hook you up with one that can get you some press. The Connors woman is a hell of a photographer, great body if you like ass, and not a bad rack at all, but I mean it wouldn't kill her to wear a little makeup, right?"

Was Aaron really that much of an asshole? Better yet, was he blind? She might not lacquer herself in the makeup and trappings of all the extra stuff, but she didn't need it. "You know, sometimes I wonder why we're friends."

Aaron grinned. "Because I'll tell you how it is. You need that kind of honesty."

Jason rolled his eyes. "Whatever, man. I gotta blaze. I have plans."

"Jase, before you go, do you want to talk about our situation?"

"Our situation? Does that mean our money is up for grabs? I thought we already agreed there was no need to talk about it. I've got it covered."

"Not so fast. Your Kellogg's contract is up for renegotiation."

"Yeah, I know. I thought we agreed to sign with the same term as before and renegotiate a higher fee after I win another Open or Grand Slam."

"Yeah well, the Kellogg's guys are dragging their feet. I sent them the contract last week, but they haven't even come back to me for changes."

The hairs on his neck pricked up, and he scooted to the edge of his seat. "What are you saying?"

"I'm saying, it might be time to prepare yourself to not have Kellogg's on your roster of endorsers."

He slumped in his chair. "Shit."

Aaron rolled his lips inward. "I'm sorry, Jase."

Jason's heart hammered a tattoo into his chest cavity. Aaron was kind enough not to point out what would happen to his other endorsements once they found out about Kellogg's. "Is there anything I can do to stop it? Anything? Come let them watch a practice? Something to prove I'm not worm food yet?"

"Let's not go that far, but just so you know, I'm working on it. Besides, we don't want to reek of desperation. Like you said, you worry about you, and I'll worry about the rest."

And what if Kellogg's had it right? Jason refused to dwell on the negative thoughts dragging dark clouds over his mood. He would be back. He had no other options. He navigated through the throng of tables in Château Marmont's dining room as he strode into the lobby in a hurry to get to Izzy. The swarm of photographers trapped his feet in virtual cement. Were they there for him or someone else? He considered going out the back door, but with a single flashbulb, was too late. He'd been spotted. Damn.

"Jason…"

"Over here, Jason…"

"Can you tell us about the allegations you and Michaels didn't part on good terms?" Damn, was that going to stick?

"Jason, can you tell us when you and Cienna are getting married?"

They weren't ever going to let go of that one were they?

"What about the rumors that you're gay?"

That was a new one.

He was stuck. It was too late to go out the back, so he had no choice but to go out the front door, which meant, best case, he would be late to Izzy's. Worst case, he wouldn't make it. As the swarm of flashbulb bees grew, he gritted his teeth — worst case.

****

Izzy's mind was on murder. All she had to do was find the inventor of the skinny jean and shoot him, maybe tar and feather him first. Even better, squeeze his ass into a pair of skinny jeans, tar and feather him, then shoot him. It had to be a him, no woman would put another woman through the torture.

"Aaarrrggghhh!" She jumped and wiggled. When all else failed, she lay on the bed, but after all her efforts, she was only able to pull the jeans halfway up her thighs. "What the hell possessed me to think I could pull off skinny jeans?"

Nick knocked at her door. "Mom, you okay in there?"

What a question to ask. She felt the blush tinge her cheeks. It was also one there was no neat answer to. She mumbled, "Yes, I'm fine."

She heard him shuffle off, and she stared down at her legs. Once well-muscled and toned legs had long since lost that sleekness of youth. Though still toned, they weren't as muscled. Oh, if only to have the ass of a seventeen year old again. You're not seventeen anymore. You'd better remember it. Not like Jason hadn't already seen everything she had to offer. Heat flooded her face. He'd promised never to remind her of last Sunday night. Could he be trusted?

She discarded the skinny jeans onto the towering pile of clothes on her bed, which now resembled a brightly colored pig sty. With a sigh, she grabbed a pair of high-waisted jeans, now all the rage when she let Jessica drag her shopping. Was it her imagination or did the dark denim make her ass look twice as big? What happened to slimming dark colors?

What if he doesn't come? If she bothered with the makeup and the clothes and the hair, and he didn't show, she'd kill him. As she stared at the clumpy black spiders on her lashes, she wondered how old her mascara was. She hoped Jessica would know how to fix it.

Primping. She was primping for some idiot man, something she promised she'd never do. He was a hot idiot man, but that didn't make it better. So much for the promises made to herself. Note to self: Only make promises you can keep.

She hated herself for that, but something stopped her from calling him to cancel. She'd dreamt, fantasized, about him for years. The seventeen-year-old girl in her wanted to believe in fairy tales. The woman in her wanted to exorcise the memory of him once and for all. And tonight with Nick, Jessica and Simon as her witnesses, there would be an exorcism.

There was another soft knock at her bedroom door before a bleached blonde wigged head popped in. "Hey lady. I'm here to lend reinforceme—" Jessica stopped and stared at her.

Izzy looked down at her outfit, jeans and a button down silk blouse. "What's wrong with my outfit? Was I not supposed to tuck in the blouse?"

Jessica's gaze moved from her outfit to her face, and she wrinkled her brow. "Uhm nothing's wrong, besides the mom jeans, nineties worthy top and the tarantulas on your eyelids."

Izzy looked down again. This time noticing how the high-waisted fit of the jean made her look extra curvy and how much the canary poet's shirt reminded her of one she'd had in eighth grade. Not to mention she could feel her eyelashes every time she blinked.

She inhaled trying to take a deep breath around the blooming anxiety, but her lungs refused and constricted. "I'm doomed."

Jessica rolled her eyes. "No, you're not doomed. It's fixable. How much time do we have?"

Taking a glance at the clock, Izzy let out a moan of dread. "We have thirty minutes." Then staring at the mom jeans again, she felt the panicky increase of her heart rate. "I'm useless. Maybe I can still cancel."

That statement earned her a derisive look from Jessica. "Are you insane, Boss Lady? There is a hotter than hot, sexy man on his way here to spend time with you. This is the first real date you've had in months."

Izzy was quick to correct her. "No. This is not a date. If it is, this is the first date I've ever had with three chaperones. Nick invited him over. This is not a date. Period. End of story." She wrinkled her brows. "Besides, I go on dates with Simon."

Jessica rummaged through the closet and tossed a pair of jeans at her. "Right, right, Simon. Please see earlier comment about real date." Next came a white puff-sleeved top and chunky gold lamé belt. As a finale, gold ballet flats followed. "The shirt is fine if you have a sleek pencil skirt. But not today. Those jeans are the curse of curvy women everywhere, only made for runway models that double as coat hangers."

She changed into Jessica's ensemble suddenly feeling more comfortable, more like herself. "I don't know what possessed me to even buy those pants."

Jessica sat her down and pulled out the makeup remover. "You didn't buy them remember? The photo spread for that designer? Those were a gift."

"Later, remind me to kick that gift horse in the kisser."

"What in the world did you do to your eyes? I can barely get this stuff off."

"Never been an expert with makeup. Sorry. At seventeen, my focus was always tennis, then books. Never my looks."

"C'mon, I've met your mother. Cici is a cosmetic line's dream. She didn't get you into it?"

Izzy shrugged. She wished. But she'd been under her father's tutelage, not her mother's. "Dad always said it was better to be strong and smart than pretty. Makeup and sexy girly clothes weren't allowed in the Major's house."

Jessica snorted. "Sounds like a swell guy. He and I would have gotten along like gang busters. I'm sure your mom made sure there were at least some boys. Nice, nerdy, pencil pusher types." She waggled her eyebrows.

Izzy laughed. "Not that I could have held their interest. Dark skinned, jock, book worms were hardly the rage back in North Carolina. I chose University of Southern California over the University of North Carolina just to escape the dictatorship."

Jessica wielded the blusher brush and dusted her cheeks. "Sixteen is awful early to go to college across the country all by your lonesome. I'm surprised you didn't become a wild child. Lord knows I would have." She paused and considered. "Never mind, I was born a wild child."

Izzy laughed. "You'd think, but the Major and Mom moved to San Diego to be closer to me, so no freedom for the inner wild child. And then after I stopped playing tennis, there was Nick. Save the occasional big night out, and even then I stuck to lip-gloss."

"Well, if there was ever an occasion. You can say this isn't a date all you want, but I know chemistry when I see it. The way he looked at you at the shoot, I sense unfinished business."

Izzy shook her head after several strokes with the hair brush. Jessica snatched the brush from her hand. "If you're about to put that gorgeous hair into a ponytail or pig tails, you might as well let me do that after I'm done with your face. She dabbed lip-gloss onto Izzy's lips, then smiled. "Perfect."

Izzy stared in the mirror. She looked — great. Pretty even. Trendy, but not like she'd tried too hard. She didn't even know what to say about the makeup. She looked like herself, only — more. "Jessica, I don't know what to say. I look, I look… Damn, I look fantastic." Pinpricks behind her eyelids warned her of the impending tears.

"We're not done yet. We still have to take care of your hair. While I fix it, tell me about Mr. Hottie McCartwright."

Jessica brushed, then teased and added the odd bobby pin or two. Izzy sat in front of the vanity and let Jessica work her magic. "There's nothing to tell really. We went to college together. He used to date Sabrina."

Jessica halted the brush, mid-stroke. "You lie." Shaking her head, she added, "Let him go, Girl. This one is tainted."

Izzy chewed her lip. "Yeah, tell me about it." She took a deep breath before adding, "I was the youngest on the team when I arrived all fresh-faced and not yet legal. Coach assigned Sabrina as a big sister to make sure I adjusted well." Fat lot of good that did me.

"College early, and you made the team? You must have been really good to play for USC."

Izzy laughed without mirth. Her tennis life was a long and distant memory. "Well, it's been a long time since I played. Besides, the Major wouldn't have it any other way. Anyway, Jason used to pay me a lot of attention, trying to be nice to the new kid, I guess. I, like the idiot I was, had a huge crush and mistook the attention he paid me as — more." Izzy let her voice trail off before she continued. "We were all close until he started to date Sabrina. She didn't like him spending so much time with me, so he stayed clear."

Jessica applied bobby pins to Izzy's hair. "The curse of Sabrina."

Izzy sighed. "Yeah, the curse all right. Sabrina was volatile, free spirited, temperamental. They were off and on a ton. Finally, when she broke up with him, she encouraged me to go out with him—as if I'd want her cast offs. She was obsessed with the fact that I'd never had a boyfriend."

"What? No!"

Izzy nodded. "Yes. She knew about my crush. I think she thought it would be funny."

Jessica scowled, suddenly rougher with her brush strokes. "Oh, hell no."

Izzy winced but kept her mouth shut. She knew better than to complain. "One night, after their break up, Jason came to see me to talk." Izzy ignored the flutter of her stomach. "We kissed."

Jessica whooped her delight. "Tell me, tell me, is he as good as he looks?"

Izzy cleared her throat, more aware of the heated thrum of her heartbeat. "Yes, he's good. But we didn't get very far. He stopped us."

"What? Oh, no." Disappointment written all over her face, she asked, "Why?"

She shrugged. "I don't know. I think he was freaked out because I was so young and naïve. I'd also had a little to drink… make that a lot."

Jessica looked contemplative. "Ah, liquid courage. If you held your liquor then, half as well as you hold it now, it was really noble of him."

Noble, yes, but it didn't lessen her humiliation. "He held me for a bit, told me not to worry about it. But Sabrina called him with some emergency or another and he ran off."

Jessica's brow furrowed and she dropped the brush. "Wait, he left you to go after her?"

Izzy nodded. "Like a moron, I waited for him for five hours. As far as I know, he left for his first national tour the next day. I've only seen him on TV since."

"Hmmm. So this whole situation is either kismet or a tornado in a crowded city."

"You got it. We just need to stay civil long enough—"

Star Wars music interrupted her, and her stomach took a long slow roll through a bed of thorns. He's calling to cancel.

Jessica handed her the phone frowning at the display. She grabbed the phone willing it not to be Jason. Please don't be him, please, please, please.

"Hello?"

"Izzy? It's Jason."

The warm timber of his voice washed over her and raised the hair on her arms. There was still the possibility, still hope.

"Listen, I am so sorry, and I hate to do this, but the paparazzi have swamped my car. The cops are here trying to break up the mess. It's impossible to get out of here. I'd still come, but I would bet money they'll follow me, and you don't want to deal with that kind of mess. Can I get a rain check?"

The paparazzi? Was he serious? His voice, his tone, transported her fifteen years. But this time, it wasn't just her Jason let down. Helpless to stop it, she felt the quickening of her heart rate, the tight quick swallowing of her breaths, the tension roll onto her shoulders. She didn't mean to shout, she told herself. Didn't mean to spit venom with every word. Didn't mean to lose her temper. Bad things happened when she lost her temper.

"You selfish, selfish, selfish son of a bastard's left nut. I told you. I told you not to do this. You never should have accepted the fucking invitation. He's a kid that worships you. Jason, you can't spend your whole life as the devil may care Golden Boy and not give a shit about who you hurt. Your word has to mean something, you fucking prick."

"I'm sorry. I tried. Don't overreact. I promise I'll make it up to him, you, both of you. I'll smooth it over. I just — "

He hadn't changed in all these years. Still focused on himself alone. As hot rage transformed into icy ire, she said, "Don't overreact? That's my kid. You know what? Don't. I'll deal with the aftermath. I always do. You just continue on being you. Go deal with the paparazzi. I'll handle Nick." She didn't give him an opportunity to respond before she hung up. Nothing had changed. He was still the same old Jason.

Her hands trembled she stared down at the phone. Jessica whistled, then rescued the phone from her clutches. "You know, in the four years I've known you, I've never seen you lose your temper."

Fifteen years was a long time. Fifteen years hadn't changed her. Fifteen years hadn't brought forgiveness. Emotion rolled through her body, the thick, wet disappointment and fury.

Chapter Eleven

"You're only his foster mother, you have no rights."

Izzy bit her lip as she tried to blink away the tear on her lower right lid. "How can you say that to me? I've been his foster mother for over ten years, surely that must give me some rights."

The frown lines on Judge Robertson's brow deepened. "Miss Connors, by law you don't have any. If Miss Reems comes home, can prove she's clean, and remains so, it's best for the child that we place him with her. The idea is to keep families together as often as possible. You know this."

Izzy clenched and unclenched her fists. "I'm his family. I'm the only consistent family he has. His own grandparents didn't want him. His mother threw away her chance. Staying with me is what's best for him."

"I understand you're upset, but do I need to remind you about the guardianship agreement you signed? Until you can get the mother to sign away parental rights, you cannot adopt the boy." He sat back in his chair, voice softening. "Look, Izzy, if the mother continues to show she's unfit, he'll stay with you. Moreover, she's proved unfit on more than one occasion. You might not have to worry."

"But there's no hope for adoption."

"You know the terms of adopting him. I'm sorry, but you and Ms. Reems are going to need to come to some sort of agreement."

****

Where the hell was he supposed to hide his sick fascination? Clutching his magazines, Jason moved with swift efficiency and tried to find the best hidey-hole for his stack of tabloids. The design team from Sports Illustrated rearranged his place for the shoot and removed every trace of the unsightly — all except for his dirty stash.

His heart rate kicked into a higher gear when he spied the production van in the drive. Izzy was here. He threw the magazines into the closet before he opened the door for the diminutive Production Assistant. He told himself he wasn't nervous about Izzy being in his home. She was like every other press person that had ever been allowed inside his sanctuary. Except she's not another press person. She's Izzy.

His ears wouldn't soon forget her choice words to him. At the time, he'd felt like shit, but what was he supposed to do? The Paps had been all over him, and he hadn't been able to leave. When he had finally been able to break free, they'd followed him for miles. It was the reality of his life, and he didn't want to bring that on her. He'd done it for her. You did it for yourself. He needed to do everything he could today to make amends.

He should have gone, paparazzi or not. But no, he'd taken the easier route out, and now she'd make him pay for it. Was she right about him? Had he spent most of his life taking the easy way out, assuming he could get away with anything just because he was Jason Fucking Cartwright?

The more he thought about disappointing Nick, the worse he felt. Nothing like having it pointed out he'd disappointed a child to make him feel like the world's biggest dirt bag. And not just any kid, her kid, his biggest fan. How could he honestly think it wouldn't be a big deal?

He glanced around at the crowd of people in his living room and kitchen. No Izzy. Like a fool, he searched for her in the clown car of a van in his driveway. Pathetic. "You're an idiot." He muttered to himself and shoved away from the front windows to get dressed.

He dressed in the stylist-provided outfit and went into the dining room where the hair and makeup people convened. The dining room was on the opposite end of the house so he didn't hear her come in, but he felt her. His nerves were on edge, and the short hairs on his neck stood at attention. The air changed the moment she walked into the room.

She took one look at him and nodded a hello, but didn't say anything. Addressing the makeup artist, she asked, "How long before he's ready?"

The woman with the makeup sponge in her hand waved. "About ten minutes. He's got a natural tan, so there's not much to do."

Izzy nodded and made her way out the back door toward the tennis court. He watched her as she went and tried to read her. She didn't give any indication of anger. She was a professional, so he hadn't anticipated her to lay into him. But, he had expected her to say something. Anything.

He looked around for Nick with the hope to apologize, but there was no sign of him anywhere. He recognized the disappointment for what it was and bit back a curse. His plan was to apologize to Nick and maybe get back in his good graces. The other night was supposed to be the most normal night he'd spent in months, and it had been ruined by the arrival of the paparazzi. How had the paparazzi known he'd be there?

Jason gritted his teeth, and Madeline, the makeup artist, paused her ministrations. "Something wrong?"

He forced himself to relax. "Just anxious to get on with it."

She gave him a brilliant smile that told him if he'd be up for it, so would she. "We're almost done here."

She was sweet and had a body molded with curves designed to get men into trouble. Two weeks ago, he'd have taken her up on the silent offer and not thought twice. But not today. Even before Izzy, he'd started on the road to being a decent person, and he didn't intend to go back.

Once he was ready, he went out to the courts. A PA ran over to hand him one of his rackets. Wrapping his hand around the familiar grip, he felt on even ground. He was made to play.

Izzy strode over to him. For a moment he remembered her as she once was, in her tennis whites, long, chocolate colored legs devouring pavement as she ran down every ball. He smiled at her, and she faltered for the briefest instant before continuing toward him.

All business, the first words she spoke to him were related to the shot. "Okay, this will be a little different from last time. The light will change on us, I think there might be some rain this afternoon, so we'll try and get all our shots this morning."

He glanced up at the sky. "Yeah, I think you're probably right."

She ignored him. "We'll get some photos of you in your house later today with a minimized crew. Sound good?"

It wasn't really a question, more a quiet directive. "Yeah, sounds fine," he muttered under his breath. There was something in the way she didn't look at him.

She settled herself behind her tripod and metered the light. She adjusted her lens, then cast him a glance that gave him an inside-out chill. When she approached him again, camera in hand, her death glare filled him with dread. With her every step, he wasn't sure what to do, where to look.

Her lips turned up, revealing straight even teeth as she reached him. He attempted to swallow around the lump in his throat. Just because she showed her teeth didn't mean it was a smile.

"You don't look relaxed. I'll need you to loosen up a bit."

He nodded and took a deep breath as he waited for his annihilation.

She leaned into him, dropping her voice low enough so only he could hear. "Jason?"

Unable to think for the fog in his brain, he leaned into her and muttered, "Mmm?"

Her non-smile deepened, displaying sweet dimples he longed to kiss. "The last guy who messed with my kid's feelings ended up with no left nut. Care to take your chances?"

His ears buzzed, brain unwilling to process her statement. "Uh, n—no."

She grinned at him, and her eyes twinkled. "I'm glad to hear it." She turned to walk back to her tripod, but paused. "Oh, and by the way, I expect you to apologize."

Not entirely sure if he should worry for his left nut, Jason took his position at the net and followed direction as best he could for the next two hours. Most photo shoots took a lot of energy and effort, but Izzy was easy to work with. She kept to the range of things that were comfortable for him, attuned to him and his not-quite-healed injury. He even started to have fun when he started lobbing shots over the net and managed to make her smile a few times.

The earlier tension seemed, for the moment, abated, replaced by something that felt familiar. Not to mention she was good at what she did. He knew that from the earlier shoot, but he didn't take her efforts to make him comfortable in front of the camera for granted. Several times, she called him over show him a photo and ask him to tweak an expression.

When they moved locations into the house, most of the crew packed the van and prepared to move out, leaving only Izzy, Madeline, and a production assistant.

He changed into the black shirt and pants the stylist had laid out for him. When the PA positioned him on the couch, shirt parted to reveal some skin, he felt — exposed. The blinds had been closed and let in only a sliver of light. Not that there was much light as the clouds rolled in. Several candles were lit, and artificial lights set up.

The whole set up made his expansive and impersonal living room warm and intimate. Izzy shooed Madeline and the PA into the kitchen telling them she'd call if she needed them for anything.

She rearranged his position and stood back to examine him. Frown lines marred her otherwise smooth skin. She reached for him, unbuttoned another button on his shirt. He felt the heat from her fingertips as they grazed his skin. A familiar twitch in his pants throbbed, acting as a reminder of how easily she could affect him. He shifted so she wouldn't notice and cleared his throat in the wild hopes of clearing his head.

But by the look on her face, she wouldn't have noticed a tidal wave. Her eyes were clear, but oddly unfocused as if she saw something else. She stepped back again—analyzed. Frown lines deepened, and she widened the opening on his shirt. This time, when the tips of her fingers grazed his pectoral muscle, an electric charge sent shivers up his arms. His hand snapped out to grab her wrist before she could inflict any more damage.

All moisture left his mouth as he fought the want, the need, to pull her the five inches he needed to taste her. He watched as her pupils dilated and lips parted in invitation. All he needed was five inches. The tip of her tongue peeked out and moistened her bottom lip. In reflex, his hand flexed on her wrist, and he heard her sharp intake of breath. He could take what he wanted, what she wanted. He could pull her in and make the decision for her. But he wouldn't. If he kissed her now, while she was still pissed, he'd ruin any real chance he had.

Needing to diffuse the tense electricity, he breathed, "I didn't realize you wanted beefcake." He cleared his voice again, not recognizing the husky timber as his own.

Startled, her eyes focused on his. "What?"

"Beefcake."

She stepped back, forcing him to release her hand. "Oh, sorry. Uhm, not beefcake. More strength, elegance and sex."

Jason swore he could see a faint blush tinge her cheeks. He needed her to stop doing that. He wanted to retain his sanity. "A lot of women read Sports Illustrated?"

Her lips tipped up in a small smile, revealing the briefest hint of dimple as she took position behind the camera again. "You'd be surprised."

Maybe he would. He'd be more surprised if the next hours in the house went by as quickly as the hours outside. Now, with no massive crew milling about, no caterers, and no makeup people, it was just him and Izzy and damned uncomfortable. Willing his brain to think about anything other than sex, he brought up the only thing he could think of to relax her. "Can I ask you a question about Nick?"

****

Izzy glanced up from her camera, sneer forming on her lips before she remembered her new mantra. No use being angry with fools. Schooling her expression, she focused on the shot, wanting the safe ground. She needed the shoot over as quickly as possible. Everything he did made her tingle. Made her aware. His movements weren't deliberate, but her system felt the havoc. He was too close, and she was too pissed at him.

She was pissed at the world, her mother, and her knack for driving Izzy insane, Simon, Sabrina. The only two she wasn't angry with, were Jessica and Nick. Now, she had to deal with Jason. How hard could that be? He was only hotter than sin and had broken her heart more times than she cared to count. She could do this. Feign complete indifference. She'd managed it for fifteen years.

Breathing deep, Izzy forced herself to relax. If she was tense, it came out in her photos.

"Ask away. He's my pride and joy." She switched to the wide angle lens she preferred for portraits, all the while watching him, wary.

Jason smiled and shifted his position. "You know, your eyes light up when you talk about him. You don't even light up like that when you talk about your photos."

She shrugged and snapped. "It's a different kind of pride, I guess. From the moment he came into the world, it's been love at first sight." Something wasn't right about the angle. "Can you move back into the shadow?"

He adjusted until half his face was in the shadow. "Did you know his birth mother?"

Izzy's mouth lost all moisture. Of course he would ask the one question not up for discussion. She knew it had to come out, but Sabrina's name was the last she wanted to utter. I have nothing to hide. I can just tell him. That didn't stop the waves of nausea.

She moved to reposition him further into the shadows, careful not to look into his eyes. If he looked at her eyes, he'd be able to read the hurt. She steeled herself for his response.

The whisper slid off her tongue. "He's Sabrina's son."

Jason's head reared back, and his nostrils flared as if the name alone was a slap. "Sabrina's?"

Because of his extreme reaction, the tension dissipated in her belly. *He thinks Nick is his.* Izzy let out a bark of laughter almost dropping her camera in the process.

"Oh God, Jason, you should see the look on your face." Racks of laughter dissipated her control. One hand holding her side, she shifted and placed the camera on an end table. She shook her head at him, she said, "He's not yours. I did the math." As she sobered, sadness infiltrated her heart. "It was one of the first things I did."

His horrified shock half morphed into something more stoic. "I didn't think he was mine."

She raised an eyebrow at him, smirk in place. "Sure you didn't. Your subconscious probably put two and two together when you saw him. It's hard not to. He looks a lot like her."

Jason's breath blew out, steady but harsh. "I didn't realize it at first, but now that you've said it, he does look like her, especially around the eyes." As if suddenly all the unanswered questions started to rattle in his brain, he asked, "But why does he call you Mom?"

With practiced ease, Izzy mentally placed solid stones in the wall around her heart. "Well, you know Sabrina. Motherhood was tough for her to get used to. She needed some help, and I was there. I've raised him, sort of a foster mother."

"So where is Sabrina now?"

His frown formed lines in his brow, and she clicked. She turned away and replaced one lens for another. And now for la piece de resistance. "Funny you should ask. She'll be back in a few days." Her every nerve ending tensed in anticipation of his response.

He didn't react to her statement. Still not satisfied with her answers, he asked, "So how is it you came to raise Sabrina's son exactly?"

She cleared her throat and moved back to the safety of the camera, her sanctuary. "When Sabrina found out she was pregnant, we were in an apartment near school. She'd just gotten an internship at Blue House Records."

Jason shook his head. "I can't even picture Sabrina pregnant. She never seemed the type."

Izzy smiled wryly. "Yeah, I know. She freaked out about it." Izzy shrugged. "She'd been dating a couple of guys…"

Izzy watched Jason's brow wrinkle. "So she didn't know who the father was?"

"No. Or, if she did, she didn't tell me. Either way, despite her fear, she was determined to keep him."

"I had no idea she had that part of her."

Izzy shrugged. She was so accustomed to never saying anything negative about Sabrina for Nick's sake. She didn't have to hold back to Jason, but she didn't know where to start. It wasn't for any love lost with Sabrina. Izzy's problem was she didn't know how to be honest about her true feelings for Sabrina.

"Sabrina's Sabrina." She shrugged again. "I think she wanted the baby to prove to herself that she was nothing like her mother."

"God, that lady screwed her up."

Izzy was tired of making excuses for Sabrina's behavior. "The sins of our fathers. But at some point Sabrina became an adult. Her choices were her own." She snapped several photos in succession, enjoying the play of emotions on Jason's features.

Jason nodded at that statement. "When did she get bored with the mommy and me stage?"

"It wasn't so much she was bored, more didn't know what to do as a mother. I was still in school, and I'd come back from class to Nick's crying. Sabrina changed him and fed him, but he was a baby, they cry. She didn't know how to take it, so she'd leave. The first time, she was gone for two days."

Jason stared at her shocked. "You mean she just left him there?"

Izzy glanced in the direction of the kitchen. She didn't need the rest of the crew to know her business. "Keep your voice down." She then added, "I had quit the team by then, so I was home, thank God. But it was scary. I didn't know if she'd ever come back."

She asked Jason to stand and move toward the fireplace and mantle. "Why didn't you call Social Services?"

Izzy thought back to the number of times she'd almost made that call, and a fist of ice formed in her belly. "I loved him too much. I didn't want to put him in the system."

"What the hell did she say to you when she got back?"

"You know Sabrina. She pretended all was well. Came back with toys for Nick and a new outfit for me."

Incredulous, Jason asked, "You didn't read her the riot act?"

Izzy repositioned the lights around him. "I've never been good at confrontation. And after Dad and everything with the team, I was broken in some way. I couldn't confront her and she knew it."

"Bullshit. You used to read me the riot act all the time. Your temper was never too far behind your smile. Why did you quit the team?"

Oh boy. Izzy could only deal with one thing at a time so she deftly avoided the topics. "I guess after Dad died, I had no one to play for anymore. I lost track of who I played for most of the time. It's a long story. Anyway, Sabrina developed a pattern of running off, usually for days at a time, sometimes a week here or there."

"You took care of him didn't you?"

"Yeah. It became a real problem once when Nick was sick. Pneumonia. I took him to the hospital, but they wouldn't let me make decisions for him. It took me a day to track her down."

Jason stared at her and worked his jaw. "Jesus, Izzy."

"Don't I know it? She cared about Nick enough to not want anything to happen to him. At first she only gave me custodial rights. Eventually, she signed over guardianship to me."

"I can't even fathom that. You were only a kid."

Izzy hadn't been able to either. "My mom was around then. Helped me out." She shrugged. "When he was four, Sabrina vanished for six months. He's called me Mom ever since. Just never in front of Sabrina. She'd never have been able to take that."

Jason looked contemplative. "So she just shows up when she likes."

When he put it like that, it didn't seem like such a good idea. "I try and do what's best for Nick. It's not easy but I have to do it. She's his mother." Izzy moved in for close-ups of his face.

His lips formed a thin harsh line. "You're his mother."

Adjusting her lens, she said, "Loosen up your face. The shadows make you look angry and predatory." When he did so, she said, "She's his mother. I'm just the one who gives him love like one."

Jason looked out the window that faced the courts. "You gave him plenty. He turned out okay so far."

Izzy didn't know what to do with the compliment. It was all she'd ever wanted to hear from anyone. "Thanks." Then, because they were in a rapidly darkening living room and he was too close for comfort, she coughed and changed the subject. "So, why don't you tell me about your friends, the paparazzi." She could have bitten her tongue. Stupid, stupid, stupid. She didn't want to talk about the other night. "Never mind, forget I said that. As long as you apologize to Nick, we're good.

"Izzy, I —"

She held up a hand. "Maybe we should start with something else, less…" Her voice trailed off. She didn't know what to say. What did anyone ask a superstar? "What about the messy thing I saw in the paper that one time?" Lame, but it was the best she could do. The close quarters were messing with her synapses.

She couldn't read the entire look on his face, but there was something hard about his expression. "Which mess? Because if you believe the tabloids, I'm in a few messes."

She told herself she wouldn't ask about his love life. Not that she cared either way. She told herself who he dated was none of her business. She wasn't interested. Liar. "Let's start with your love life. To hear it told, you're the Lothario of Malibu."

He barked out a laugh with a mischievous gleam in his eyes. "Why so interested? You jealous?"

Izzy scoffed and rolled her eyes. Then wondered if the effect was too much. "What do I care about your love life? Though you took a ridiculous interest in mine."

Jason only shrugged. "I need a break from dating and the whole scene."

A break? Izzy could only imagine what it must be like to have a social calendar so full she needed a break. "What? You need a break from the throng of beautiful women?"

As if recalling his question about Simon, he quirked his lips into a wry smile. "The only people's happiness most of those women care about is their own. Take Cienna for example. I'm pretty sure her publicist leaked rumors of the impending nuptials. It ups her status with the tabloids."

For a moment, with the shadow on his face, there was a vulnerability she couldn't place. She hoped she'd never know what it felt like to have herself used as a means to get ahead. "I'm sorry, I'd hate to be used like that."

He shrugged as if unfazed. "It's a game we all play. The press can act as life-giving nectar, or they can rip your foundation out with a jackhammer. It's just how it is."

She nodded as if she understood, though Izzy was so far removed from the world of the rich and famous it was laughable. "Is that what happened with you and your trainer? Did he jackhammer at your foundation?"

He looked shocked, and she rushed to add, "I have a tendency for prying. So tell me to shut up if you don't want to talk about it."

"No. It's okay. Michaels was a good trainer for a while. But then he got greedy like a lot of people do. Before I knew it, he'd do anything to win. Couldn't stick by a losing horse."

"I'm sorry he lost confidence in you. But he'll be sorry in the end."

"Don't be so quick to pick sides. How do you know I'm not a losing horse?"

She shrugged. "I just know."

Something flashed in his eyes, and she adjusted the angle of her camera and took the shot. Instinctively, she knew that was the one photo she'd request for the cover. The combination of regret, gratitude and determination was powerful.

He cleared his throat. "One minute I'm on my way back to the top. The next, I'm parting ways with my longtime trainer. Everyone thinks I'm nuts, but I couldn't work with the guy anymore. Not after what he did. It's all about to blow up in my face probably. Then it's bye-bye to my career."

He looked haunted. Izzy resisted the urge to touch and comfort him. "I doubt it. You always manage to come out on top. When you want to, you work harder than anybody I've ever seen. Everybody will see that come Wimbledon."

His expression was self-deprecating. "I don't know about that. They would prefer the bad boy stay the bad boy. I'd mess with their world view if I stopped acting like—what did you call me? Oh yeah, an overindulged child. Now they'll see me as the guy that ruined several careers."

The vulnerability in his eyes had her snapping away.

"Everyone knows what kind of talent you have, your strength, agility. That's what will matter in the end. No matter what anyone says or what they write about you. What you do on the court is what matters. If you can leave the other stuff behind and focus."

His smile was sad. She wanted to say more, but she heard the faint sound of a ringing phone. The PA called from the kitchen. "Miss Connors? Your manager is on the phone.

She did her best not to roll her eyes, but she was only half successful. "I'll call him back."

Jason inclined his head in question, but she ignored it. The inquisitive look was immediately replaced with a rakish smile. All traces of earlier vulnerability gone. "Let's talk more about my strength and agility."

That was the Jason she remembered, the one always trying to tease a smile out of her.

Once she had all the shots she needed, he helped her pack up her lenses and equipment. The PA and makeup artist left the house first and drove off in the second van.

Jason walked her to the car carrying all her equipment, refusing to let her carry anything. "Jason, don't be ridiculous, I can carry my own equipment."

"I know. I'm working at my chivalry. Let me see how it feels, okay?"

"Fine, do as you like." She said fine, but what she wanted was to get out of Dodge as quickly as possible. The moment they were alone, she felt the tension spark between them. She didn't need him to be nice to her. When he was nice, she remembered they'd been friends. And forgot that he'd broken her heart.

She climbed into the beat up Corolla. "Let me know if you have any questions about the photos."

He cleared his throat and hesitated before he closed the driver's door for her. "Izzy, I'm really sorry about the other night. Please let me make it up."

Shit. Why did he have to look so sexy in that black shirt? "I—you know what, Jason, no harm no foul. It's already forgotten." Maybe he'd let it go.

"Then let me take you out for dinner?"

She didn't need this. She didn't need the sweet Jason she remembered. She didn't need him to be vulnerable and nice and sexy. "I don't think so. It's probably best if we keep the past in the past, you know?"

He looked like he wanted to say something else, but refrained. He stepped back from the car and returned to his front steps.

Ready to be back in the safety of her sanity, Izzy turned the key. The ignition clicked but didn't catch. "Oh please, oh please, oh please," she muttered under her breath and sent up a fast prayer, frantically wondering where she was going to find a mechanic in the middle of Malibu.

She turned the key again with another prayer. Click.

Concerned, Jason came down from his perch on the front steps. "You're going to need a ride, huh?"

"I'll just call a tow truck and a mechanic. I don't think the last van is too far away, they can come back and pick me up."

His gaze was concerned. "You don't like to rely on anyone do you, Izzy?"

"I — uhm…" She couldn't tell him it was the safest way to avoid disappointment. She needed a good reason to decline his offer, other than the fact she didn't want to be in a confined space with him. Other than the fact she didn't trust her emotions when she was near him. Other than the fact his scent made her want to do things she'd only read about in romance novels. Other than those reasons, she couldn't offer up one.

His voice was even. "I'll move your stuff to my car. Let me get my keys, and I'll take you home."

Even though another prayer was probably a hopeless cause, she sent one up anyway. Dear God. Please don't let me act like a fool with this man.

Chapter Twelve

Tension, thick and sexual, filled the space between them. Jason considered rolling down a window to let some air in, but the night was too chilly. The drive from Malibu to Pasadena took longer than normal, thanks to traffic. And he felt every moment of it. For the first time, Jason noticed the claustrophobic effects of the car, as the endless seconds ticked by.

He slid Izzy a glance. Her rigid posture said she wasn't thrilled about the close quarters either. The Porsche wasn't big enough for all of her equipment, so he'd promised to chauffeur over the rest tomorrow.

She seemed content not to talk much, but the way he figured it, they couldn't sit in the car in silence for the next few hours. The trip up the coast, under normal circumstances, only took an hour. But given the congested brake lights, it would take at least two to get her home.

He was normally comfortable with no chatter, but the heavy silence made him feel as though they were sluicing in a sea of tension.

He needed to say something. Anything. He forced his body to obey the command. But in that moment where his lips followed the order his soul betrayed him and spilled out the last words he wanted her to hear. "I'm sorry I didn't come back to you." Damn. Where had that come from?

Out of the corner of eyes, he saw Izzy shift her body, angling her knees away from him toward the passenger door. Desperation etched her profile. "We don't need to talk about this."

His brain worked for a way to retract his statement, anything to keep from going into it, but he figured the damning words were already out. No use keeping the rest of it in. "I know you think I left and never looked back." He paused and drew in a breath, letting it ebb out of him slow and steady as he silently counted. One, two, three. One, two, three. "And in some ways it's true. But I thought about you—a lot. At the time, I thought I had a good reason."

She turned her head and gave him a view of her elegant curved neck as she looked out the window. "Right."

"Look, I know I was an ass. Immature for leaving like that. Everything you could call me, I've already called myself. It was a stupid decision, and I would reverse it if I could."

She whipped her head around to face him, dashboard lights reflecting in her eyes. "What? What could have been so important?" Then she shook her head and turned back to the window. "Forget it. It's not important. It was so long ago."

"I owe you an explanation. I always felt bad about how I walked out on you."

"What? Why? Between Sabrina and the girls on the tour? I'm sure you never gave another thought to the pathetic girl that had a crush on you."

He muttered a curse. "I never thought you were pathetic."

Her derisive scoff boomed in the tight space. "Really? Because Sabrina told me all about how you laughed at me."

"That's a lie," he spat. "I never laughed at you."

"Why would she lie?"

The vise around his heart tightened around its captive. "Because that's what Sabrina does. Because she's a master manipulator. Because she thought I was in love with you."

****

Bursts of frenetic pulses started in Izzy's belly, then spread all over her body, all encompassing. She placed a hand above her diaphragm with a hope to quiet the spasms there. She tried to block out his words. But her brain refused her attempts at banishment. It insisted on echoing his words again and again against the cavernous walls of her consciousness. I was in love with you. I was in love with you.

"Wh — wh — why would she think that?" She didn't recognize the squeaky voice for her own.

"Because it was the truth."

Her left hand shook, and she placed it over her right, still pressing against her diaphragm. "But, but, you laughed at me. She told me how you'd laughed at my attempts to throw myself at you."

He shook his head. "Where would you get that from? It never happened. It's not the first time she's lied." Exasperated, he punched an open hand against the rim of the steering wheel. "More than once, I let her almost leave my life in ruin. The year I was with her I spent in this intense fog, completely impenetrable."

As her brain plucked at his words, Izzy tried to make sense of them. "What do you mean it's not the first thing she's lied about? She didn't start spiraling out of control until after Nick was born."

Izzy watched his jaw clench and unclench, watched as he pulled in breath after breath.

His voice came out, ragged and harsh. "That night I left you, she told me she was pregnant."

Her lips formed a silent O. The final remnants of the Hershey's Kiss she'd eaten that afternoon swirled in her belly and threatened a reappearance. "What?"

His hands tightened around the steering wheel. His voice chilled as he spoke, and a slithering shiver spread over her body. "When she called that night, she told me I'd better get over to her place, or she'd make sure I didn't get to leave on the pro tour."

Izzy chose not to focus on the one word that could shatter her world. Pregnant. Instead, her brain tried to make some sense of what he told her. "How could she stop you from leaving? Everyone expected it."

He tensed his jaw once, then again before he spoke. "Something I'd rather forget." He cleared his throat before he continued. "When I went over to her place, she was high and pissed off, the way only Sabrina could get."

He deftly dodged a piece of debris in the road, careful of the rain-slicked path. "She went on and on about how I'd ruined her life and knocked her up and she'd never forgive me."

Reason finally broke through the confines of her shock and confusion, and Izzy found her voice beside him. "But she wasn't pregnant. She didn't get pregnant with Nick until several months later."

His heavy breath filled the tension-thickened silence in the air. "Yeah I know. We'd always used condoms. I knew her history of manipulation. I needed her to prove it to me. I wasn't going to blow my future on one of her manipulations. If she'd been pregnant, I would have done what I needed to do, stayed and supported her and the kid. But like hell I was going to chain myself to her if she wasn't pregnant."

Confusion and bewilderment swirled in her mind. All along, there had been a reason why he left her. Years of self-doubt, rage and disappointment threatened to spill out. "You would have done the right thing."

He turned toward her, pinning her with a harsh glare. "Don't make me a hero, Izzy. I ran out and bought one of those home tests. I brought it back, ready to call her bluff."

Unable to hold the anger in any longer, Izzy blurted out, "But who does that? Who lies about something like that?"

Jason kept his eyes on the road ahead. "When I got back from the store that night, she cried and put on the Sabrina show. Told me she'd made it up." He tightened his grip, swerving to avoid clipping a car. "I wanted to get as far away from her as humanly possible."

She didn't know what to do. What platitudes would be enough to soothe? She wanted to face him, she wanted to offer an apology of sorts, but didn't know what she could say. She hadn't told the lie, but she felt for him just the same. She raised a hand to his face, then drew it back into her lap. "Jason, I'm so sorry. She had no right."

He shook his head. "I would've killed her if she hadn't been so pathetic."

"I don't know how you didn't. I might have. Why would she lie?"

He shook his head, quirking the right side of his lips up in a wry smile. "You don't get it do you?"

When she blinked at him several times, he gave a humorless chuckle before he spoke. "Simple jealousy."

Izzy could see him steal a glance at her face. "You know I never even thought about it. I was just..." Her voice trailed.

He loosened his grip on the wheel as he exited the freeway. His voice softer, he said, "Izzy, I'm sorry I didn't show. I was too angry and immature to handle any of it the right way. So I took off."

Not knowing how to take the apology, she stared at him. For years, she'd imagined what she'd say to him if given the opportunity. Imagined what she might feel. However, after what he'd told her, all she felt was the blinding numbness. "I don't know what to say. Not sure how to feel."

"I wanted to call you a million times, but I just thought it would be better if I left you alone. You were still so young. You didn't know what you wanted. So I went on a bender for two weeks."

"It was so long ago, Jason. It doesn't matter now." Even with her words, her brain was unwilling to let it go. "You weren't scheduled to leave for weeks. What did you do once you could see straight again?"

"I went to training camp early and focused on being who I was supposed to be. I told myself you'd be happy, and I could live with that."

She watched him navigate the exit toward Pasadena, glad to be out of the traffic. They sat in companionable silence for the remainder of the trip, neither sure of what to say, now with the air cleared up. When he pulled into her driveway, he smiled at her. "Door-to-door service, milady."

She gave him a genuine smile. "Thank you. You didn't have to drive me all the way out here."

"It was the least I could do. Your photos will save my public image. Giving you a ride is part of the bargain."

Before she alighted, he reached out and placed a hand on her arm to halt her. She stared at his hand and relished, for a moment, the tingling sensation. He angled his body toward hers, and she reminded herself to breathe. In and out. In and out.

His gaze searched hers as if seeking permission. He leaned in as he brought their heads into closer proximity. No matter how many times she told herself to calm down and tried to practice her diaphragm breathing, she couldn't stop the erratic thud, pound, thud, pound of her heart.

When he spoke, the low timber of his voice spread though her like chocolate fudge. "Would you mind if I came in real quick to apologize to Nick?"

She told herself the hollow feeling that followed his words wasn't disappointment he hadn't kissed her. She'd told him to apologize. He was making good. She couldn't fault him for that. "I think he'd like that."

Three weeks, ago, if anyone had told her Jason Cartwright would stand on the threshold of her house about to walk in, she would have had a good laugh. Yet, here he was, and here she was, in an awkward first date parody.

Because her hands were full, Izzy rang the doorbell. Moments later, thunderous footsteps rushed toward them, and the door yanked open. A panting Nick stood before them, ear to the phone. "Holy shit. Sam, let me call you back." He hung up with a snap of his cell.

Izzy watched his transformation with amusement as Nick's demeanor shifted from confident and nonchalant to awkward and nervous. In a well-established homecoming ritual, she went in with her bags, and Nick grabbed the other camera bags from Jason, moving toward the kitchen.

Behind her, Jason closed the door and followed them into the kitchen with halting steps. Clearing his throat, he said, "How's it going, Nick?"

A powerful blush stained Nick's cheeks, and he stammered a response. "Mom said you didn't think you'd be able to come around for awhile."

Izzy cringed. Nick's voice held no reproach, but the combination of tough question plus expression of childish innocence would make anyone's insides squirm, curl and wriggle like octopus tentacles.

Jason flushed and had the good sense to appear contrite. "I'm sorry about that. I couldn't get away on Sunday. But my schedule has opened up, and I'd like to make up for the other night. How about a tennis lesson?"

She watched as her son's eyes widened to reveal grapefruit sized eyeballs. "Are you serious? You would do that?"

Jason smiled one of those movie star smiles. "Yeah, we'll set something up. Maybe have you come out to the house if your mom says it's okay."

Izzy flashed Jason a look that said she'd make sure he followed through. "I'm sure we can work something out." Heading into the kitchen, Izzy pulled out a casserole for dinner and turned the oven on.

Nick followed and attempted to wrestle the dish from her hands. "Mom, I'll heat it up. You don't want to take a chance you'll mess it up, especially if we have company."

Jason leaned against the doorjamb and grinned. "I think I'd be willing to take my chances."

Nick grimaced at him. "No. You wouldn't. Why don't you ask her how she scorched the pot the other night with a simple task like boil water?" Nick glanced at his mother. "I love you, Mom, but you just can't cook."

Izzy glared at Nick. "You act as if I haven't kept you fed for years."

Nick ignored her glare and responded with a sunny smile. "Thanks to a housekeeper and my own expert culinary skills."

Izzy rolled her eyes. "Look, I can put in the casserole and set the timer. You go wash up." She turned her attention to Jason before she added, "Will you stay for dinner? It's the least I can do since you drove me home."

One of his lazy, slow burn smiles guaranteed to singe her nerves, inched across his face. "Yeah, I'll stay."

Nick's grin flashed as he ran off to wash up. "So cool. The guys are never gonna believe I had dinner with Jason Cartwright."

Jason smiled at Izzy. "Thanks for the second chance."

She shrugged. "I've been with you half the day. You haven't eaten in at least as many hours as I haven't eaten. The Hershey's Kisses in the car don't count. I might as well feed you."

Nick came back freshly washed and chattering a mile a minute. But it wasn't long before they all smelled something burning. What temperature was I supposed to cook the casserole?

Nick ran over to the oven, yanking it open allowing a tower of billowing smoke into the kitchen.

Nick shook his head. "I swear, Mom, it's like you were born without the culinary gene."

"I can cook," Izzy blustered as she waved a napkin around to clear the air. She couldn't help sneaking a look over at Jason who still stood in the doorway. When she saw the smile, she considered an attempt at a vanishing act.

Nick's blond hair flopped in his eyes as he cleaned up the counter tops. "Heating up Maria's dinners doesn't really count, Mom. And you're supposed to remove the cooking label Maria puts on the dishes before you put them in."

Izzy watched, fascinated as laughter spilled out of Jason. His laugh did more than transform his face. It lit her up from the inside.

"Oh, Izzy. It can't be that bad, can it?"

She grinned at him and went to the fridge. "I'm afraid so. Have a seat, can I get you something to drink? A beer?"

"Water's good enough."

She handed him a bottle and plopped herself on a stool at the island. "So our dinner options are pizza, Chinese and Thai. All deliver."

He took a swig of the cold liquid and smiled at her. "Thai'll do. And if anyone asks, I'll tell them you made a delicious curry."

Watching Nick at the garbage, disposing of the charred aluminum casserole lid, Jason stood and rolled up his sleeves to lend a hand. For the next hour, Izzy felt like Jason was part of the family.

She actually enjoyed herself, without thought to all the work she had to do, upcoming shoots, Nick's school, Sabrina. She enjoyed having him in her space, didn't feel crowded at all. She'd always told herself she didn't need anyone else except Nick. Convinced herself companionship was all she needed, not warmth and family and love. She hadn't felt this giddy in years.

Maybe I was wrong.

Nick told Jason about his coach, school, Samantha, and filled him in on Izzy's misadventures. She tried to play down any exploits and asked Jason about his life outside of tennis. The shrill ring of the phone broke the happy family spell, and Nick ran to answer it, giving Jason and Izzy their first extended moment alone since he'd arrived. An irrational part of her wished for the shield that Nick provided.

"So, what's the story behind Z Con? Your photos—I don't remember you traipsing around much with a camera in school. Is it something you started after graduation?"

At his unexpected question, she brought her gaze up to meet his and blinked several times, trying to determine the best way to answer. "Uh, no story really. I started taking pictures when Nick was a baby. I got lucky. I had a job on campus, and when my boss saw some photos of Nick, she asked me to shoot her wedding." She shrugged. "After her wedding, she gave my name to the Times. I worked freelance for them until graduation. Got a couple of breaks, blah blah blah. Eventually, I had to get an agent. I've been unbelievably fortunate."

"Not many photographers I know can afford their own studio. Let alone a studio in Pasadena."

She laughed. "Oh that. You forget my major was Economics. You live in tight quarters, save every spare dime that doesn't go to food and rent and diapers. Invest it. Work like a dog. Oh yes, and toss in a mother who's able to babysit for free. You too can live in Pasadena." Shrugging, she said, "I bought this place with the studio in the back. Now I have the classic struggles of a small business owner—keeping the studio in the black, school fees, college funds. I'm very grown up these days."

"You make it work though. You've built an unbelievable life."

She hated the pity she saw in his eyes. "I was lucky. Had a lot of help along the way, and I had family."

"Don't forget talent."

His charm would be her undoing. She laughed. "Yes, let's not forget my talent." The start of her photo career was not something she normally discussed. She loved her work and the peace it brought her, her camera was the best therapy she could ask for after the Major died. She hated to think about the first few years on the hustle. The way she'd needed help, the sleepless nights worrying about bills, taking every job that came her way. It depressed her. So, she did what she did best. Deflection.

"I, uh, developed some of the photos from your first shoot. Do you want to see them?"

His eyes squinted slightly, as if recognizing her avoidance technique for what it was. If he did, though, he didn't call her on it. "An advanced look?" He put his hands in his pockets and smiled that sexy smile of his. "I'd love nothing better."

She glanced up at him, the dark pools of his eyes looking clear to her soul. "Follow me."

Chapter Thirteen

Like all mice and children before him, Jason followed the piper. The rain had finally stopped, leaving soft sodden grass behind. A light wind wafted a flower fragrance toward him. Her perfume? Unable to keep his eyes off of Izzy, he watched her lithe movements. At five foot seven she wasn't small, but her frame was petite, except for her ass — of which he had a spectacular view. The khaki skirt she wore molded over her butt and gave his imagination some ideas. Some things never changed.

As she walked him through her office into the main studio, he noted the changes to the studio. There were two photos of him against the far wall. He'd only recognized them because of the shoot location, otherwise, he'd have thought they were someone else. In one, shadows over his face revealed a vulnerability in his eyes he didn't know existed, or rather, tried his whole life to extinguish.

For several beats, an internal silence drowned out the soft pitch of her voice. He stared at the photo and willed the openness to disappear. Waited for it. But it didn't disappear. There it was for the entire world to see.

A lightheaded feeling reminded him to breathe. He filled his lungs with oxygen before he turned his attention back to Izzy. She stared at him, head cocked.

"What's wrong?"

Her photo captured his bare soul, and she wondered what was wrong? Feeling unsettled, he shook his head. "Nothing — I guess I'm not used to anyone seeing me." He looked back at the photo. "Really seeing me, anyway. It's disconcerting."

A smile lit her face as she walked over to the photo and crouched next to it. "I loved this photo the moment I took it. I hope you don't mind that I created a canvas for it. The way the shadows play over your face, there's such sadness there — as if you'd spent your whole life hiding from something." She looked back up at him. "What were you thinking about?"

Even if he felt inclined to remember, he wouldn't tell her. She already saw too much. He shook his head and walked over to the other portraits in the studio. "Don't remember."

She angled her head up at him and keen eyes surveyed his every move. "It's okay. Everything I need to know is in that photo."

He ran a hand through his hair in an effort to shake the discomfort. "In case you didn't know this before — you're good. I didn't even know I had that side of me."

The corner of her mouth quirked up revealing a dimple in her right cheek. She strode toward the photo next to him. "You know." With a half shrug, she added, "You just choose to hide that part. It's easier to be what people expect you to be."

Because she was too close to the truth, he changed the subject by turning his attention to the photo next to him where clouds billowed off a mountain rolling toward earth. "Where'd you take this photo?"

Allowing the diversion, Izzy stepped closer to him, and a hint of jasmine and vanilla enveloped him. In that moment, he knew this impromptu photo tour was a bad idea. He wanted her, but when he had her, it wouldn't be a quickie in her studio. He'd waited too many years for her.

She must have noticed the tension in the air because her voice took on a breathy husky quality. "South Africa. I had a hell of a time pulling the car over on the wrong side of the road to catch the storm rolling off of Table Mountain." Her dimples deepened with her smile. "Nick thought the clouds were going to swallow us up."

The dark thunderous storm clouds at odds with the russet color of the mountain and the sun-kissed rainbow pulled at something in him. As if the photograph understood how what he wanted to do and what he should do warred with him.

"Izzy, I—"

She turned to face him, eyes wide as if she knew what he wanted to do and wasn't sure if she would let him.

Jason looked at her lips as she nibbled the corner, like she used to when she was nervous. Full and ripe, they invited him to taste them. Rolling his shoulders to loosen the tension, he closed the gap between them. He could ask for forgiveness later, but now, all he wanted to do was taste her perfect lips.

Before he dipped his head, he flexed and unflexed the hand at her waist giving her a moment to walk away. But she didn't. Her lips parted and the tip of her delicate pink tongue peeked out moistening her bottom lip. Body tense, he reached for her, massaging the back of her neck and her waist. "Izzy." They stood like that for several moments as he worked the tension out of the back of her neck. He reveled in the feel of her delicate skin beneath his hands. She raised her head to look at him, and his body screamed for closeness.

In the instant before their lips met, their breath commingled, and he felt the energy ebbing from her. What was meant to be a soft testing kiss, immediately changed to a more urgent one the moment her tongue met with his — teasing and tasting.

Unable to stop the roaring, insistent, beat of his blood, and unable to calm the need, desperate for satiation, he deepened the kiss. Encouraged by her arms wrapping around his neck and her pliant body pressing into him, Jason shifted his hand from her waist to the small of her back and pressed her closer.

Her arms tightened around him, and he couldn't think for the howl of blood that rushed through his head. He was mindful they were in her studio and Nick could come down at any moment, but he couldn't pull his lips from hers.

Soft and moist and hungry. Wow. He brought his hands up from her waist to cup her face. "Izzy."

She mumbled something unintelligible into his mouth. He didn't want to stop. Couldn't think of enough reason to stop. He nipped her ripe lower lip.

She rewarded him with a moan and wiggle, effectively rubbing her feminine core against the length of him. His erection surged and struggled for freedom from the confines of his jeans. Reflexively, his hand clenched in her hair. Instinct and need clouded every rational thought to take it slow.

She responded by raking a hand up from the base of his neck up through his hair. The action sent sharp tingles to each of his nerves. Straining for control, he ripped his lips from hers, using the hand tangled in her hair to hold her motionless.

"Damn — Izzy." He rasped out her name as he drew in several generous breaths. Jason felt her hesitant attempt to disengage her hips from his, and he tightened his grip in her hair as his dick threatened to explode. "Do. Not. Move."

Her own harsh breaths mingled with her husky words as heavy lust lidded eyes fluttered open. "I'm s — sorry, I — "

"Shh. Trying — get — control." His inability to form cohesive sentences surprised him. He'd been with plenty of women, but none of them ever made him feel like he had an electric current connected to his dick. He dragged in another breath.

"Why?"

****

Was this what heaven felt like? If so, Izzy didn't ever want to leave. She couldn't believe she was in her studio making out with Jason Cartwright. Couldn't believe Jason needed to get himself under control.

None of this was her life. It had to be a dream fantasy she'd wake up from any moment now. Had to be.

But she didn't wake up. Jason's body pressed insistently against her, and all she wanted was for him to bury himself inside her until the fiery ache in her core extinguished. For the first time in a long time, she felt bold and out of control and to her surprise, she liked it. More than liked it. It made her feel alive and beautiful and sexy.

"Why do you want to be in control, Jason?" She rotated her hips against his, and he ground his teeth. His hand tugged on her hair almost to the point of pain. Almost.

"Damn it, Izzy—"

She silenced him by licking his bottom lip before she suckled it. His reaction was instant. In a swift movement, both hands gathered up her skirt going straight to her ass, cupping it, using it as leverage to pick her up. On instinct, she wrapped her legs around him.

He braced her against a wall and adjusted her position so that his key directly positioned against her lock. The zinging pleasure drowned out any rational thought she possessed. All she wanted to was to feel like this forever. Liquid heat continued to pool at her core, and she moaned his name.

His right hand spanned her waist, reaching up to cup her breast. She rolled her head back in pleasure, inviting him to feast on her neck. A rakish grin spanned his face as he bent his head. His lips made contact with the soft fabric covering her right breast.

Through the fabric, she could feel his hot breath as he rubbed his lips over the bud again and again. She hissed out a curse when he repeated the motion with his teeth.

She could hear the humor in his voice as he switched attention to her neck. "You like that do you?"

She moaned a reply.

He growled a response. "Good." His thumb danced a pattern over her nipple as he laved the spot he'd bitten. "This too?"

Unable to form a coherent thought, she tightened her grip with her legs.

In some dark corner of the dust covered part of her mind, she knew she should stop. Knew she would not have sex with Jason in her studio with her son less than a few hundred yards away. Knew she was just a diversion for Jason for now, and come tomorrow, he would forget and discard her.

She was going to hell. Might as well decorate her hand basket. Because if she was headed for hell, she damned well wanted to go for a good reason. Even the thought of going to hell couldn't stop her hips from choreographing an ancient dance in time with his. Didn't stop her body for preparing for his to claim hers. Didn't stop the need that zinged from the edges of her toenails to the ends of her hair.

She told herself she'd be able to stop in just a minute. That she needed to feel alive for just a few more minutes before she could go back to her normal staid, respectable self. Every woman deserved to make out like a teenager at least once, didn't they?

Jason's lips found hers again and commanded them to respond. His tongue cajoled hers to come out and play. "So sexy."

His eyes met hers, and Izzy read every bit of need he felt in their depths. Breath hot and fevered against her neck, he whispered, "I haven't been able to get you out of my head since that photo."

"Mmm hmm." Completely incapable of speech, all she could do was move her hips in an effort to bring him closer.

"Are you wearing anything like that under these clothes?"

"Jason—" Her breath caught as he switched their position to a work table, working his hands between them.

They slid under her t-shirt, exploring the skin beneath. All the while, his eyes never left hers. When his hands closed over her breasts, he bit off a curse. "Damn, you're perfect."

Fingers shaking, she wrestled with his buttons, drawing his shirt open. Taking in the muscled planes, she muttered, "Likewise."

Impatient, he worked up the layers of her skirt.

Panic threatened to break through her hazy sex fog. "Jason, I—uhm—"

"Shh, relax. I just want to check something,"

The blood roaring in her head forced out any capacity for coherent thought. "But, I—"

His fingers slid over the satin band of her underwear, thumb nestled against her clit. "Baby, you never did answer my question."

For every two strokes, he coaxed a moan out of her. "Wh—what question?"

He grinned and stroked again. Once. Twice. "In the photo—were you wet?"

Tension coiled in her sex. All she wanted to do was continue her hurtling speeds toward climax. "Jason, please."

He paused his stroking to slip his finger along the edge of her panties. His finger lifted the edge, and slid past springy curls to reach her core. "Shit—Izzy. You're so soft, ready." He groaned into her neck.

"I want—" Before she could finish the thought, the crackle of the intercom interrupted her.

"Mom, food's here. Where's your wallet?"

Jason ripped his lips from her neck, spouting a litany of four letter words. Spell broken, Izzy dragged in a breath and struggled to unlock her legs from his back. Disengaging from him on shaky legs, she strode to the other side of the studio to reply. "Uhm, check the big black camera bag. I didn't take my purse to the shoot." She prayed the waver in her voice wouldn't betray what she'd been up to.

With trembling fingers, she rearranged her button down and khaki skirt and patted down her hair in an attempt to pull herself together before she faced Jason. Once she'd readjusted her bra and shirt, she turned, only to find him directly behind her. Alarmed, she attempted to take a step back. Damn he has the feet of a ninja.

"Hey, relax," he soothed.

Easy for him to say. If the tabloids held any truth, he did this sort of thing all the time. She, on the other hand, did not. "I am relaxed." Then because she couldn't think of anything else to say, she added, "Dinner's here."

He nodded, his eyes narrowed. "Please don't do that whole closed up thing on me." He took her hand inclining his head toward the work table. "I didn't mean to get carried away. I'm sorry if it was too much."

Damn. Did he have to be sweet too? At the risk of sounding like the rank amateur she was, Izzy shook her head. "I'm just not used to—that. Rather, I'm not usually so impulsive."Gah, I'm a moron. "I mean, I don't run around doing…" Gah, shut up! Shut up now! Her lips slammed shut.

He still held her hand. As he caressed her knuckles, he asked, "Even with Simon?"

Instantly annoyed, she tried to disengage her hand. But he didn't release her. The last thing she needed was a reminder that she'd just been crawling all over him.

Shame and spite made her lash out. "Are you jealous?"

The smile he gave her teetered on a ledge between predatory and sheepish. "Maybe I am."

She scoffed. "Yeah, right."

He still didn't let go of her hand as he tugged her toward the door to the backyard. "Is that so farfetched?"

She smirked even as she fell into step with him. "Honestly? A little. Yes. You're out every night with models and actresses and professional athletes. Not to mention royalty if the tabloids are believable. I doubt I compare."

He halted as they reached the backdoor to the house. She noticed the harsh set of his mouth and his tightened grasp of her hand, and she wondered what she'd said wrong.

"All of them, Izzy — they never compared to you."

Izzy stared into liquid pools of amber and knew she was in trouble. She couldn't flirt with danger and make it out unscathed. He was a professional playboy, and she was nothing but a rank amateur.

His musky scent enveloped her. The tingling in her lower back was strong enough to make her jump. This is no good.

She didn't need hot and heavy. She didn't want hot and heavy. She was a relationship girl. What if he just wanted sex? Her eyes lowered from his fierce gaze to his lips. It would be so easy to tip her head up and —

No, she resolutely told herself. She would not go down this road. Not with Jason. He was a complication she didn't need. Especially not with Sabrina on her way back. Not to mention he had his own complications. She cleared her throat and deftly moved around him.

"I find that hard to believe."

She twisted the knob but stopped once she heard the chattering voice. Her heart hammered against the walls of her chest and threatened to push through the confines of her chest cavity. She recognized the bubbly voice. Jason must have as well, because he stopped behind her and gripped her hand almost to the point of pain.

Her stomach threatened to spill out bile and partially digested Hershey's Kisses. She was glad Jason was there, because she never would have been able to open the door.

When they entered, a nauseous-looking Nick stood near the island, lean, tanned fingers held by a smiling brunette. Without releasing Nick, the pretty brunette with cat-like eyes, turned and smiled at them. "Well, well, the gang's all here."

Chapter Fourteen

Sabrina? Seeing her again, feelings of insecurity overwhelmed Izzy. Would Jason respond to Sabrina's beauty as he always had? Would Nick beg to live with his mother? Stop it. She chastised herself. It did her no good to worry about the future.

She plastered what she hoped was a cool and collected smiled on her face. "You should have called, Sabrina. We could have picked you up from the airport." And had some freaking warning, she added silently.

Sabrina's cat-like eyes tipped up as she gave them all a beatific smile. "What and ruin the surprise? You know how I love surprises."

Noting Nick's hand clutched in Sabrina's, Izzy swallowed the acrid taste of jealous bile. She forced herself to remember Sabrina was his mother. She had a right to touch him. Izzy shouldn't be jealous. Oh what the hell. If she wanted to picture herself using a camera strap to strangle her beautiful, perfect, ex-best friend, then she'd go right ahead and do so. Though, she felt a moment's satisfaction as she noticed Nick try to disengage his hand from his mother's.

Sabrina looked from Jason to Izzy and back again. No doubt she wondered how Jason fit into the equation. Given what Jason had told her in the car, Sabrina had deliberately kept them apart.

Izzy gulped in a breath and held onto it until it burned. Sneaking a sidelong glance at Jason, Izzy braced herself for the inevitable lust she'd see there. Once, she'd watched those eyes fill with lust and craving for Sabrina. Now, his eyes gave Sabrina a cursory once over, a cool appraisal. She saw disgust, mistrust, and worse, apathy. Maybe he was over her after all.

Sabrina let out a breath, but she did not release Nick, even though he struggled against her grasp. "Izzy, you look great."

Izzy wondered if she had that thoroughly kissed look about her. Or worse, a look of guilt. She couldn't help it. Jason had always been forbidden to her for some reason or another. He'd always been Sabrina's. Old feelings were hard to bury.

"Jason, I'm surprised to see you here."

Jason's eyes narrowed, and he showed even white teeth, which the uninitiated could mistakenly perceive for a smile. He shoved his hands in his pockets, inclined his head and gave her a smile that was mostly malice. "Sabrina."

Sabrina arched a delicate eyebrow at the both of them and stilted her head. "You two seem cozy."

Izzy felt an emotion close enough to guilt flit across her face. But as quickly as it appeared, she hid it. No use letting the devil know he owned her soul.

Beside Sabrina, Nick finally managed to free his hand. Her smile, a usual radiant glow, went brittle and sharp, and Izzy couldn't help the jolt of elation.

"My baby and I were just getting reacquainted."

Izzy's eyes widened, but she remained silent. The four of them stood around like rookie bomb techs afraid to make the first move toward a bucket full of napalm. Nick scowled, and Jason shifted his weight. None of them spoke.

After several tense moments, Nick broke formation without a word. His gangly form disappeared into the living room. The slamming of the front door a clear signal of his thoughts about her visit.

Sabrina drew her brows together, whirling to glare at Izzy. "You know, I'm getting the impression none of you are happy to see me."

Jason's lips tightened. "What do you expect, Sabrina?" He turned his attention to Izzy and asked softly, "Where does he go when he's upset?"

Her stomach curled in on itself, desperate to go after Nick, but knowing she had to stay and deal with Sabrina. "If he's not in the studio, there's a basketball court about three blocks over. You might find him there."

Jason nodded and headed out after Nick. But not before giving her a meaningful look. "You okay here?"

She squared her shoulders and nodded giving Sabrina a level look. "Yeah, I've got this. Just see if he's okay." It wasn't like Sabrina hadn't been here many times before. But this time Izzy wasn't the same old Izzy. Jessica's Krav Maga classes notwithstanding, Izzy was stronger than before. She could handle Sabrina.

When they were alone, she didn't speak as the two of them stood in the kitchen squared off, tension sparking, ready for battle.

At last Sabrina broke the silence, indicating her bags. "Is the room on the right still mine to use?"

Izzy's eyes tightened, and she shook her head. "No."

Confusion made Sabrina wrinkle her nose and put on her persuasive voice. "Oh c'mon Izzy. I need a place to crash. You wouldn't toss me out on the street, would you?"

When she took too long to ponder that question, Sabrina grabbed her small bag and headed toward the bedrooms.

She startled when Izzy spoke. "Sabrina, you know I won't put you out because I think it's important that Nick see you. I know you're manipulating the situation. For now, I'll let it go. But I'll be damned if I give up my bedroom. You can use the spare bedroom at the end of the hall."

Sabrina straightened her back and turned to give Izzy a long look. "You can't mean to put me in the small bedroom? That bedroom is no bigger than a closet. I need space, not to mention my own bathroom. I can't share a bathroom with Nick. Teenage boys are filthy."

Izzy smirked. "It's too bad you feel that way. I'm sure you'll be more comfortable at a hotel, because that's what I have to offer." The muscles in her jaw clenched and unclenched several times as she bit back words with physical force. "That's the way it goes, Sabrina. I won't have you disrupt our lives. You'll be sharing the bathroom with Nick."

"Why can't I have Nick's room?"

Izzy stared, mouth agog. "It's Nick's room. You came uninvited after not telling us when you'd arrive. You'll take what I offer, not dictate the rules."

Sabrina nodded slowly. "Yeah, okay, fine."

Sabrina started dragging the suitcase when Izzy stopped her again. "And Sabrina, I want you gone in a week."

****

On shaky legs, Jason marched out into the darkness like the hounds of hell wanted a piece of his ass. Sabrina, shit. She was the last person he'd thought he'd see again. When Izzy said she was coming back, his brain didn't compute the fact he might see her.

Unfortunately, that fact was now as painfully clear as a sledgehammer to the head. The last thing he'd wanted to do was leave Izzy with her, but he needed to find Nick. So instead of ushering Sabrina out on the same broom she'd flown in on, he chased after a boy he wouldn't know how to comfort.

Jason felt the barbed wire tighten around his gut as he hung a right at the end of the driveway. He realized he neared a jog, so he slowed his pace. He didn't need to rush. He knew exactly where to find Nick. When he'd come in with Izzy, there'd been a basketball by the door. He hadn't seen it on the way out, so it was a safe bet Nick had opted for physical exertion to forget his woes. A method Jason understood.

His slowed pace also had to do with the problem of not knowing what to say to the kid. Somehow, "I'm sorry your mom is a drug addicted lunatic," didn't seem appropriate. How the hell was he supposed to know what to say? Kids had never been his strong suit. Mostly because they scared the shit out of him. He knew how easy it was for an adult to mess with a child's psyche and do permanent damage.

Nick was lucky. At least he had Izzy. Jason didn't have an Izzy when he was a kid. He'd had absent parents and a string of nannies he couldn't remember now. The few times his parents had paid him attention, he'd immediately wished they hadn't.

The hollow thud thud thud sound of a basketball against pavement met Jason long before the sight of Nick attempting three pointers did. Not sure of what to say, Jason took a seat at one of the courtside benches and watched.

Nick handled the ball with the practiced ease of a natural born athlete, and Jason had a feeling Nick could play any sport he wanted to. But he'd chosen tennis just like his mother. Both of his mothers.

After five minutes, Nick called out, "I'm not going home, you know."

Jason wondered at what age running away lost its shine and gloss. "I don't blame you."

Warily, Nick cast him another glance. "You're not here to make me go back and play nice?"

Jason quirked a brow. "Is there any chance you feel like going back and playing nice?"

Every bit of Nick's expression read, Get real.

"Fair enough, I'm not here to make you go back then."

As if not sure whether to believe him, Nick continued to play, but kept looking over in Jason's direction.

After another ten minutes, Nick bounced the ball toward Jason. Understanding the male version of "I'm ready to talk now," Jason shrugged off his blazer and picked up the basketball. Basketball wasn't his main sport, but he'd played a couple of years in high school. When he sank a shot from the paint, Nick looked at him wide eyed.

"You can ball?"

Jason wasn't sure whether to laugh at Nick's astonishment or take umbrage. "Yeah, I got a few ups. Haven't played in a while though."

Nick surveyed him with renewed interest as he took his place fetching rebounds. "You ever think about playing basketball instead of tennis?"

"If you'd have asked me when I was young, I might have said yes. But everyone expected me to play tennis, so I did."

Nick hustled after a wild ball. "You didn't want to play tennis?"

Jason considered. Tennis was such a part of his life early on, there was no real consideration he wouldn't play. Basketball and other sports were a way to keep in shape for tennis. His parents choreographed everything about his tennis for his future development and potential. Somewhere along the line it had become his salvation. "I did want to play. It just so happens, everyone else wanted me to play too."

Jason's next shot missed the mark, and he traded places with Nick. He watched as Nick took his first shot. The ball arced high and slid into the basket like a woman putting on a silk dress. "Your parents play too?"

The last time Jason talked to anyone about his parents, a different man had sat in the Oval Office. "Both of them played, though I doubt they did it for pleasure."

Nick nodded solemnly. "Mom doesn't play anymore. Though sometimes she looks like she wants to."

Jason's nerve endings did the locomotion at the mention of Izzy. "Did she used to play with you?"

Swoosh. Another ball slid though the basket with ease. Jason had a feeling he'd be the permanent rebound guy the rest of the night. "Nah. I guess she stopped playing when Grandpa died. Before I was born. She used to be my coach."

Jason nodded and wondered where the conversation would turn given the weight of the avoided topic. "I can imagine. She was an amazing player."

Nick stopped in mid-shot. "You actually played together?"

Jason thought it better not to ask what Nick meant by played together. "Yeah. She was powerful. Never afraid of the net. Used to get after it."

"That's how she is sometimes when she's taking photos. She's got this total focus." Nick grinned. "Like this one time, she bungee jumped off this bridge in Zambia because she wanted to get this perfect shot of a rainbow on Victoria Falls."

Jason's mind tried to reconcile his memories of a young and spirited Izzy with the more sedate older version. "Sounds like fun. A little dangerous, but fun."

Nick smiled a smile that said he'd never admit it, but his mom was the coolest. "Yep, every summer we go somewhere different. Mom takes pictures, and I learn about culture and stuff. Usually just the two of us."

The next question was out before Jason could put the brakes on it. "Is Simon going with you guys this summer?"

Nick missed his shot. As he and Jason traded places again, he said, "God I hope not, I can't stand that dweeb." Then as he realized he probably shouldn't have said that, he gave Jason a sheepish smile. "Sometimes Jessica comes, which is cool. When I was little, she used to come too."

Jason didn't have to ask who she was. Nick's shuttered gaze told him enough. Jason knew he was the last person on earth to talk anyone through complex family dynamics, but he wanted to help. "I guess seeing her just now was kind of a shock. When was the last time you saw her?"

Nick shrugged. "A few months ago, I guess." He shot a string of two pointers to make Kobe Bryant proud before he added, "Mom lets her stay with us so I can spend some time with her."

"How do you feel about that?"

The steady rhythm of swoosh, thud thud filled the air for several minutes before Nick answered. "Mom, Izzy, says it's good for us to keep a relationship. But I don't want to."

"Have you told her that?"

Nick fired another shot which hit the rim, threatened a mutiny, but went in all the same. "She doesn't understand. She tries to make it better 'cause she feels bad she can't adopt me."

Jason felt an unfamiliar tightening in his chest and prickling behind his eyes. Shit, he was going soft. Had he been this astute at thirteen? "She's in a tough spot, I guess." Grabbing a rebound ball, he asked, "What's stopping the adoption? Sabrina?"

Nick shook his head and shrugged simultaneously. "The judge says it's because there isn't consent from both birth parents. Which is lame. I really think it's 'cause Mom's black."

Jason held onto the rebound ball, shocked. "I'm sure that's not the reason. Maybe they want to see if Sabrina can get herself together."

Nick gave him a look and raised an eyebrow. "Whatever. Mom says we're a family no matter what."

It never occurred to Jason the hurdles Izzy had to face to raise Nick. She'd given him a clue during the photo shoot, but at the time he assumed she was sensitive about the subject. Now he knew she had cause. He cleared his throat before he said, "She's right you know, about you being family." And because Nick had been honest with him, he added, "She's a better mom than I had."

Nick studied him, eventually nodding as if he understood the truth Jason shared with him. "Yeah. She's cool."

"You think maybe she's worried about you? The way you took off and all?"

Nick slumped in his hoodie. "Yeah. Probably." Picking his head up to look at Jason, he said, "I don't want Sabrina to ruin everything."

Jason couldn't agree more. "I know the feeling."

☐

Chapter Fifteen

Razor edges of a chainsaw slashed through each of Izzy's nerves. Thanks to Sabrina's late arrival, numerous clattering trips to the bathroom and five am roaming and puttering about, Izzy hadn't slept all night. After waiting two hours for Nick and Jason to return, all she'd needed was a good night's sleep. Too bad she didn't get it. Sabrina didn't know the meaning of good houseguest.

Izzy recognized and understood the game in startling clarity. They'd played it several times. Sabrina was pouting because she hadn't gotten her way. Every other time she'd come home, Izzy gave up the master bedroom, ran out and shopped especially for her visit, bent to Sabrina's will. But not this time. She couldn't be bothered. She'd had enough of accommodating everyone in her life.

Slamming her bedroom door, she cringed. Thank God, Nick was already on his way to school. He'd never let her forget it. Curls of dread clawed at her stomach as she approached the spare bedroom on tip-toe. Midway through she stopped and strode with her normal gait. Why bother? She wouldn't tiptoe in her own house.

Though, as Izzy passed the spare bedroom, Sabrina's voice filtered through the door. On the phone. Talking in hushed murmurs. Unable or unwilling to stop herself, Izzy leaned in and darted a furtive glance down the hallway. No way in hell she wanted Nick or Jessica to catch her eavesdropping.

The sounds were muffled, as if Sabrina deliberately lowered her voice, but Izzy could catch the thread of conversation.

"I know you have no reason to believe me given my history, my father's, my brother's. But I'm clean this time."

Izzy could hear a soft rapid thump thump thump on the hard wood and could just picture Sabrina's leg moving in rapid succession up and down as she sat on the bed.

"I need access to my trust fund now. How the hell am I supposed to live without any money for two years?"

Her ears strained and her heart raced as she heard footsteps approach the door. She whipped away from the doorway, flattening her back against the hallway like a cockroach in daylight. As the footsteps faded, she let out a breath. Decency and politeness should have her off to work, but ever since Jessica had told her to find her inner bad girl, she couldn't seem to find a decent bone in her body. She leaned closer to the door, careful not to jangle her keys.

"Look, I'm supposed to have that money within six months of leaving rehab, as long as I'm clean. I've been out for four already." She paused. "I don't give a shit what my mother wants. She has no right. There has to be something you can do."

The tone and volume of the last comment made Izzy jump. But she didn't move out of earshot.

Sabrina's voice took on a hint of desperation. "Okay, look. Maybe I can borrow against it. I have some personal debts to pay off, and they won't be willing to wait two years for payment." There was a beat of silence, then she added. "Look, these are not the kind of guys that will accept a bank transfer. I need to deliver the money in cash."

Izzy knew when she'd heard enough. As she shuffled down the hallway toward the kitchen, she wondered why she always got her hopes up that Sabrina was clean and out of her old life. Some things never changed.

Finally in the sanctuary of her studio, she turned on some Nina Simone to match her morose mood and settled in for a long morning of reviewing proofs of Jason. If anything could temporarily take Sabrina off her mind, it had to be Jason.

She always preferred to compile an absolute yes list of images she couldn't live without, before she compiled a list of maybes. Her only problem was, with this subject, she had a mountainous list of absolute yeses and hardly any maybes or nos.

Even the flat two-dimensional photos of Jason caused her blood to stir. She picked up the negative sheet containing the vulnerable photo he'd admired the night before. Immediately, images flashed though her mind of Jason picking her up, anchoring her against the wall.

No matter how many cold showers she took, or how many cups of coffee she drank to clear her head, she could not erase the branding scorches of his hands from her body. Heat flooded her core in preparation. Izzy groaned as she tried to refocus her attention on the comp sheets. What a hell of a time to get a libido.

She needed a chocolate chip cookie. She cast a glance at the window to the backyard as she wondered if she could make it into the house unseen and unheard to grab a cookie. I'm an idiot for avoiding my own house. As she whittled down her selection of keepers, Izzy realized she needn't avoid the house. Trouble would always come to her.

Down the hall, she heard the sounds of Jessica singing along to Nina's bluesy tones. But the singing abruptly stopped, followed by a battle of wills. Jessica's snotty voice was Izzy's thirty second warning. "Do you have an appointment? She's very busy." While Jessica was occasionally snotty to Simon, she'd never been outright rude, and her tone at the moment bordered on bitchy.

Of course, Sabrina being Sabrina, she didn't heed Jessica's testaments and barged right in. Jessica, hot on Sabrina's Prada-covered heels, followed, protesting every step of the way. "Izzy, I'm sorry, if you want me to call the police, I can."

The corners of Izzy's lips threatened to curl, but she kept them under control. She wasn't kidding about the cops. They'd been called in before when a patron had refused to pay for her portrait session. Jessica didn't play. And she had always loathed Sabrina.

"It's all right, Jess. I can handle it."

Jessica looked mutinous and glared at Sabrina, but she turned to leave. "Yeah, all right. But just holler if you want me to call them."

Izzy made a mental note to give Jessica a raise if she sold a few photos at the gallery opening. She didn't bother to halt her selection process of photos she worked on. "What do you want, Sabrina?"

"Gosh what a frosty welcome." She cast a narrow-eyed glance in Jessica's direction. "When are you going to get a presentable secretary, Iz?"

Izzy glanced up and wondered what kind of gilded, delusional world Sabrina lived in. "She's a friend. She's also good at her job."

Sabrina rolled her eyes. "Oh right, but come on, the way she looks? Please, I'm surprised she doesn't scare off your clientele."

Izzy felt the familiar throbbing in her clenched fists and forced her fingers to release and relax. "She's an asset. Any client who disapproves, I can go without their money."

Sabrina glanced toward the door again. "Would she really call the police?"

"Yup. She would." Izzy wanted Sabrina out. If she looked at her too long, she was likely to say some things Nick might regret.

Sabrina shifted her weight. "Look, I know I'm a disruption to your life and everything."

"Do you really? Did you give any thought about what your visit would do to Nick?"

All traces of the initial bravado swinging Sabrina vanished, and she sat down nervously on the stool across from Izzy. "I'm here because of Nick."

Izzy couldn't hide the shaking contact sheet in her right hand. It took her several moments to realize her hands were behind the shaking.

"What about Nick, Sabrina?"

With a deep breath, Sabrina swiveled around in the stool. "I know the past several years have been rough. And it's been my fault."

Yeah right. As Sabrina rattled off what sounded shockingly like an apology, Izzy wondered how much of this conversation tied into the earlier one she'd overheard? Last time she'd been clean for four months before her inevitable descent. Izzy'd heard it all before. This was the amends part of Sabrina's recovery. Damn, do I look like a father confessor?

"Izzy, I've done unspeakable things to you, to Nick. Over the last several months, I've been taking stock of the right thing to do."

Izzy stood, attempting to stretch out the crick in her neck. Too tired to reign in her temper, she said, "I'm sorry, Sabrina. But what's different this time? I've heard all of this before." Not to mention she knew what Sabrina was really doing home.

"Izzy, I know I shouldn't ask you for anything."

"You're right. I've given you enough. You're a taker. And if it suits you, you ask for forgiveness later."

Sabrina's face fell. Softly, she said, "I'm not all bad."

Izzy said nothing, waited for the impending demand.

"Okay, I admit, I do need your help."

Of course you do. Whenever Sabrina needed something, it was something she couldn't get for herself. Given how resourceful Sabrina was, the favor must be a doozy. Izzy did her best to stop the tingling sense of dread climbing her spine. "What's so bad you'd come back after last time?"

Sabrina cringed. "Look. I know after what I did, I had no right to say those — unspeakable things to you."

Izzy set her hands on her hips. "You mean the statement you made about a second rate mammie not being able to raise your son, as the cops carted you away? Save your apologies for someone who gives a shit."

A deep blush climbed up Sabina's neck and cheeks as she stood to clasp her hands around Izzy's. "I was high, Iz. I didn't mean it. You've been the closest friend I've had in years."

Staring down at the pale manicured hands that gripped her chocolate ones, anger and resentment washed over her as it threatened to snap her thinning hold on her temper. "If that's how you treat your friends, God help your enemies."

Sabrina sighed as she released Izzy. "Look, I'm serious about my recovery this time. I'm lucky I didn't end up in prison. I'm lucky Nick isn't in some shithole foster home."

"Serious this time, are you? You plan on saying sorry to your piece of shit dealer after you stole from him? I doubt he'll accept the apology if you can't pay him."

Sabrina had the wherewithal to appear ashamed. "I'll make good on my debts and keep you out of it."

Izzy couldn't help the sneer. "I thought one of the conditions of you going to the treatment center instead of jail was no contact with your former life?"

"It is. And I intend to keep my end of the bargain. I'm clean now. I swear to you, I'll do whatever I can to stay that way." Sabrina took a breath. "I just need you to do one thing for me."

What did she need, a kidney from Nick or something? Izzy didn't have any money. "Jesus, what is it?"

"Would you consider sharing some of the responsibility of raising Nick. Like maybe joint-custody or something?" Sabrina looked around as if expecting to see someone around the corner.

A sudden pain behind Izzy's eyes threatened to blind her. This was not how the conversation was supposed to go. Sabrina was supposed to ask for money, and Izzy was supposed to refuse it. This wasn't in the script. "Over your dead body."

Sabrina took an uncertain step back but leveled her jade green eyes. "He's my son."

"Why would you want partial custody now? You've never shown any interest in raising him before." Izzy forced out the words as she fought for breath. Her brain worked overtime to try and figure out Sabrina's angle.

"I need him. He'll remind me of why I need to stay clean. He needs me too. He needs his mother."

"You say this to the woman who raised him when you were too high to do so?"

Sabrina slammed a hand over her eyes. "Shit, I'm sorry. I didn't mean it like that. I meant we need to get to know each other."

Izzy didn't possess mass quantities of the idiot gene, no matter what Sabrina thought. "You want me to give an addict custody of my son? I must really look stupid to you. The ans—"

The desperation in Sabrina's eyes stopped her mid-tirade and made her switch angles. "Look, we both know you don't want custody. So why don't you tell me why you're really here. This has nothing to do with you wanting some involvement in Nick's life. Do you need money or something?" When she saw Sabrina's fleeting look of guilt, Izzy slammed her hands down on the work table. "You're unbelievable. Get the fuck out. Nick doesn't even have any money."

Except in his trust fund. Nick's grandfather had begrudgingly set up a meager trust fund for him when he'd been born. They hadn't approved of their daughter or their grandson. They'd never wanted custody of him or even offered to see him.

Given the Reems family had a history of addiction, Nick couldn't access the trust till he turned twenty-five. Izzy didn't even know how much was in it. Only family could act as executors of the will—only family with custody. Truth dawned on Izzy with the force of a semi truck. If Sabrina couldn't get access to her own trust fund, she could access Nick's if she had custody. Who the hell stole money from a child?

Sabrina's mouth fell open, and her eyes welled with tears. "You think I could be so evil and unscrupulous. I'm not malicious, Izzy. I really do want to get to know Nick. I'm only trying to help out."

"You're a piece of work. Get. The. Hell. Out."

She hadn't meant to yell, but her raised voice brought Jessica running, blue hair flying. Izzy waved Sabrina out. "Get out."

For the first time, Sabrina's eyes held a note of defeat. "Izzy, don't do this. I want to help. You've got a great career lined up. I have nothing. I need him."

"My well rounded ass you want to help. You want access to his trust. I'm not the same little girl you can manipulate. I fight back."

Sabrina worked her bottom lip, brows drawn together. "Izzy —"

So angry, she couldn't control it, Izzy blurted, "Don't you dare, you stupid cow. Get the hell out of my studio!"

She knew she had to get fresh air before she lost it. She ran out of the studio, past Jessica and into the backyard. Oh God, not again. She couldn't let the panic take over. She would not lose control.
****

Jason dove for the ringing phone. His knee felt better, and he couldn't resist the urge to test it at any given opportunity. It hadn't even been sore after his one on one session with Nick.

"Yeah, hello."

"Mr. Cartwright, do you care to comment on Art Michaels' accusations that your career is over and you're running a smoke and mirrors game on the public?"

How the hell had they gotten this number? He hung up without a word. Once he heard the dial tone, he hit speed dial number two. Not bothering with a greeting to Aaron, Jason said without preamble, "I'm going to need a new number."

"Hello to you too. The hounds of hell get a hold of your number again?"

Contrite, he said, "Hello, Aaron. Yes, the hounds got a hold of the new number. I swear we've got a leak."

"Unfortunately, we can't really do anything about it. All we can do is limit the number of people with your personal information. Just be grateful it's not your cell phone. I'll have the number changed today."

"Thanks."

Aaron paused for several beats. "How you holding up?"

Jason shrugged, forgetting Aaron couldn't see him. "Okay, I guess. The calls are a pain in the ass, but the worst is the paparazzi camped out in front of my house."

"Have their asses arrested."

"I wish. They're camped in a row across the street. And I don't technically live in the gated section of Malibu. They still have a clear shot to my front door. They can see me coming and going. It's not ideal."

"Well as long as you stay put, they won't catch you doing anything."

Annoyed, Jason rubbed his shoulder. "Well, I don't really have much choice but to stay put if I don't want unnecessary attention. Since Michaels' statement, all the speculators are running around like teenaged boys with their dicks cut off."

"Like yesterday's news, no one will think about it tomorrow. He can't say anything negative about you. He values his ass too much. He may be pissed he's not your trainer anymore, but he won't perjure himself. So all he can do is insinuate. We could go after him if you want."

Jason sighed and willed away the tension in his shoulders. He wouldn't expose Michaels yet. "It's not worth it. Good thing I don't give a shit about my rep, otherwise this would kill my chances with the ladies."

Aaron laughed a mirthless laugh. "If only women were your problem. Give me a client with woman troubles any day."

Jason heard the knock at his door and contemplated not answering. But he expected the door to door mechanic about Izzy's car, so he went to answer. The slender brunette with the wide aviator glasses was the last person he'd anticipated or wanted to see.

"Aaron, let me call you back."

"Hi, Jason." She removed her sunglasses and adjusted her purse in movements no doubt meant to entice.

"Fancy seeing you here, Sabrina. You've given up tormenting Izzy and the kid?"

Delicate almond eyes blinked up at him. She smiled a brilliant smile meant to put him at ease. "It's nice to see you again, Jason."

When he didn't respond or let her by, she reached up and wrapped cloying arms around his neck in a hug. He wanted to leave Sabrina where she stood on the porch, but knew it wasn't prudent, considering the paparazzi. He stood aside.

She coolly walked by him as if she belonged there, making sure to brush up against him on her way in. She sauntered through the foyer in a white linen dress like she owned the place. As always, she looked like sin with mischief in her eyes and a promise on her lips. "You know, Jason. I get the impression you don't want me around?"

He gave her a mock innocent look. "I don't know where you got that from."

"Are you going to offer me a drink?"

"What would be the point? You're not staying." With tilted head and narrowed eyes, he added, "Besides, I thought you were clean and sober now?"

"I am clean and sober, thank you. Doesn't mean a girl can't do with a glass of water." She made her way to the window. "God, you've got a fantastic view of the beach."

"We both know you're not here for the small talk or a glass of water, so what are you doing here? You didn't come all the way from Pasadena to shoot the shit."

She gave him her best 'Oh just amuse me' look. "I swear, you act as if I can't drop in on a friend. Maybe I just wanted to see your pad."

"Just like you dropped in to see your kid?"

For a split second, he swore he saw genuine pain in her eyes. "What the hell do you know about my kid?"

"Not much. Except he's a great kid, and he turned out that way through no effort of yours."

"Maybe that's what he needed."

Not sure what she meant, Jason dropped the subject. "What do you want?"

She pursed her lips. "I'm sorry I interrupted you and Izzy last night." A cat-like malice in her eyes belied her next statement. "I think you two would make such a great couple."

"That would be a first. Didn't you do everything you could to make sure we didn't go anywhere near each other?"

"See it how you like."

Jason laughed. "You're a piece of work, lady."

"So are you. Let's not forget that."

"Yeah well, we all have to grow up sometime."

She sidled up to him. "Is that what you've done? Grown up?"

He removed her arms from around his waist. She'd always been able to elicit an instant sexual response from him. Not anymore. "That won't work anymore, Sabrina. I'm tired. You can either tell me what you're doing here, or you can get out. Your choice."

She mastered an insulted pout. "Okay, fine. I came to you because I need help."

He rolled his eyes. "Yeah, no surprise there."

"I need to borrow some money."

"That's a joke, right? First, you said borrow, implying your intent to pay it back." He continued, "Next, you forget you're an addict. Never give an addict money."

"It's not for drugs. And I would pay you back. I swear. I'm in a tight jam."

"So you thought of me?"

"Exactly. I've got some characters determined to get their money, and I've got nowhere else to go."

Some things never changed. "Izzy said no, huh?"

She blinked several times. "What does she have to do with me coming to you?"

"Just proud of her for telling you no."

Sabrina rolled her eyes. "Let's leave Izzy out of this, shall we?"

He stared at her. Sabrina had always been self-centered but he'd never thought her to be cruel and uncaring. Izzy raised her son as her own and all Sabrina could think about was herself.

"So, Izzy said no, and now here you are."

She shrugged.

"You need to be careful where you lay your head, Sabrina. Sleeping with dogs and all that. I'm not going to help you."

She surged to her feet. "What, why? You know I wouldn't come to you unless it was important."

"You know why."

"Like hell I do. You owe me at least this."

"I don't owe you a thing."

A malicious smile spread across Sabrina's beautiful dark features. "I wonder how Izzy would feel if I told her about our last night together."

Jason felt the blood trickle and drain out of his face. "Too bad you can only play that card if she means something to me."

A smile, calculated and chilly, spread on over her lips. "Don't be a fool, Jason. Izzy's always been your Achilles heel." She sidled up to him like a leach on the hunt for blood. "And from your guilty expressions last night, she still means something to you. It's a no-brainer. I need a hundred grand. You give it to me, and I won't ruin your chances of true bliss or whatever."

A bead of cold sweat burrowed between his shoulder blades. "A, I won't give you a dime. B, you tell her about us, and I'll make your life a living hell."

☐

Chapter Sixteen

"What the hell do you mean there's nothing I can do? There has to be something." Izzy stared at her lawyer, Bryce Jacobs, over the expansive oak desk, hoping if she stared long enough, different words would come out of his mouth.

"I wish I could tell you different, Iz. But the ball is in her court. If she tries for custody, she'll have to stay clean for more than six months, prove she's capable of taking care of not only herself, but Nick. When was the last time Sabrina held down a job?" Disappointment etched on his face, he added, "I wish there was more I could do, but for now, we wait."

Izzy stood, her hands planted on Bryce's desk for leverage. "So I'm just supposed to let her continue to disrupt our lives? I can't live like this. We've got to have some kind of closure." Biting on her thumb nail, she added, "Nick deserves it."

Bryce shook his head which dislodged a shock of prematurely gray hair into the center of his brow. "Just because you agreed to allow her to see Nick doesn't mean she has to be in your house, you know."

Izzy knew. But knowing didn't stop the guilt from washing over her every time she thought about kicking Sabrina out. She would never be able to explain to Nick. "I have to do the right thing for Nick." Biting her lip to help force incumbent tears back, she added, "Am I a horrible person because I want her to fail? I want her to fall off the damned wagon. I want my son to myself."

Bryce sat on the corner of the table. He put a hand on her shoulder to comfort her. "No, you're human. Look, no judge would give her custody right now given her extensive past. And while she still has a right to see him, we can fight to have that visitation monitored."

"This is my fault. All of it. Maybe I should have called child protective services all those years ago. Saved myself the pain."

He shook his head. "You never would have forgiven yourself. This is Sabrina. You'll have to be patient. Soon enough she'll fashion a noose out of the rope."

"In the meantime, I need to be on the lookout for anyone who looks shifty. If she invites that slime into our home—"

He followed her lead toward the office door. "First things first. Anything out of the ordinary happens, you call the police immediately. You can't do what you did the last time and square off with a drug dealer. Sometimes, I think you have a death wish." He took her hand. "If you even suspect she's using, get the police involved. It'll go on the record."

His smooth manicured hand generated enough heat to chase off the chill in her bones. She nodded as she forced a brittle smile. "You're right." It was time to take control of her life.

She let herself out into the hallway. One of her Ghana Homelands photos, "Village on Stilts," greeted her. She knew the photo was there, but it didn't stop the rush of surprise and pride every time she saw it.

Izzy quirked an apologetic smile at Bryce's assistant Lydia. Lydia had a penchant for trashy gossip mags. Izzy felt bad she hadn't thought to stop by the newspaper stand downstairs before coming in. "Sorry, Lydia. No Us Weekly for you today. I forgot to stop."

Lydia's thin lips curled into a tilted uplift of a smile. "Not a problem. I have the TMZ RSS feed."

Desperate for something to lift her mood, Izzy sidled up to the desk and selected two Hershey's Kisses from the candy bowl. She was very proud of herself that she knew both what TMZ and an RSS feed were. "C'mon, let's have it, what gorgeous Hollywood hunk is coming out as gay? Inquiring minds and all that."

Lydia tapped to the next page. "Nothing that good this week. Although—" Wide blue eyes twinkled with excitement. "That gorgeous tennis guy, Jason Whathisname? He's already dropped Cienna for a new chick. Some brunette." She sighed wistfully and added, "I so totally would."

Izzy stopped mid-chew. The melted chocolate acted more as a throat irritant, than nectar of the Gods. For the briefest of instants, Izzy wondered if someone had taken a photo of them together leaving his house. You're black, princess, not brunette. She reminded herself. For an instant, her heart did a panicked flutter in her chest as she considered someone might have a photo from their hot and heavy session in the studio.

Izzy hoped she didn't sound too curious with her next question. "Another star I suppose?"

Lydia shook her head. "You can't see her face in this picture. Only the back of her dress. But they're kissing for sure." She turned the monitor so Izzy could look for herself.

The brunette's head slightly obscured Jason's face in the photo, but the height was right and the house was unmistakable. Unfortunately, so was her white linen dress.

Sabrina.

****

Jason couldn't remember the last time nerves had tickled his spine. "You have no reason to be nervous you idiot," he mumbled to himself as he walked through the Z Con studio reception area.

Jessica, now blue-haired, flashed him a broad smile. The serene lilt of her lips reminded him of a Cheshire cat.

"Hi, Jessica. She in?"

"Izzy?" she asked, as she played with her pen and batted her lashes. He nodded, and she winked at him. "She's in the studio to your right."

Not sure what he was supposed to do about the wink, he gave her a wan smile. "Er, thanks." As he walked down the hall to the studio, he was sure he could feel her gaze on his butt. But he'd be damned if he'd turn around to look.

The jazzy sounds of Nina Simone met him before he stepped into the studio. Izzy bent over a table afforded him a spectacular view of lush curves wrapped in snug fitted jeans. If he kept looking, he'd be tempted to touch. No doubt, Izzy wouldn't want to give Jessica that kind of show.

He cleared his throat, but she didn't turn around. "Izzy?"

He moved behind her, but she still didn't turn until he brushed her exposed neck with his fingertips. In a swift move, she grabbed his wrist and whirled on him, fist at the ready.

Ducking out of the way and securing her fist behind her back, he blew out several harsh breaths. "Shit, Izzy."

Eyes wide with alarm and surprise, she stammered an apology. "Oh, God, sorry. I didn't expect, I mean, God, I'm sorry." In another swift movement, she released herself and took a step back.

He opened his hands palm out to give her some space. "Remind me never to piss you off."

"Crap, I said sorry." She pulled up a stool for him. "I didn't expect you to—well anyone, actually, to come up and touch my neck. It was reflex."

With her hair down and the sun streaming in to kiss the light brown highlights, a soft halo formed around her hair. A memory flashed—Izzy's lips, her firm body pliant against his. Those sexy mewling sounds she made when aroused.

Mouth dry, he cleared his throat in an attempt to get some moisture. "Some reflex."

Her smile went thin as she used a remote control to turn down the music. "Well, you shouldn't sneak up on people."

He laughed. "What? I called your name several times. You had your focus on your own world."

She shrugged. "Yeah, well, when I'm working, I get a little absorbed. The loud music helps me concentrate."

"I notice you still listen to Nina Simone when you want some focus."

"You remembered that? It was so long ago."

Of course he remembered. Izzy in focus mode was just about the sexiest sight he'd ever seen. She could literally block out the world and devote undivided attention to the task at hand. It was surreal. "Of course I remember. I got you her greatest hits when you won the conference title that year."

"Oh yeah. I remember now. Not much really changes, I guess."

There was a hint of sadness in her voice he couldn't place. He hadn't prepared for awkward. On his way over, he prepped his heart and body to deal with any of her reactions to Saturday night. Unfortunately, awkwardness didn't make the list. They hadn't had much chance to talk after he'd taken Nick home. Maybe he should have called before coming over, but he'd wanted to surprise her.

Walking over to the table, he noticed the photo she laid the matte for. An African man, years of wisdom in his crinkled eyes, stared back at him. It was the same photo he'd bid on at an auction, but lost.

The photo that spoke to him. Even though the man in the photo was near the end of his life, his eyes still held secrets. As if there was part of him he kept hidden.

"You know I bid on this photo in an auction about a year ago, I didn't get it. When can I get a crack at those Masai prints?"

She looked up, brows furrowed and eyes wide. "Shit, I forgot. I'll sort that out sometime this week."

"At the time, I didn't know it was your work. But it spoke to me. I tried everything I could, but I still lost the damned auction."

A nervous tongue peaked out of her lips. Mesmerized, he watched as it tracked moisture over her lips. She parted her lips as if to speak, but then she pressed them back together.

Unable to resist, he brushed a lock of hair off her shoulder and rubbed it between his fingers. Feeling like a teenager asking for his first date, he smiled nervously. "So, we didn't have a chance to get dinner on Saturday. I thought I'd make that up to you tonight if you're free."

She took a step back, literally, if not figuratively, putting some distance between them. "I don't think so Jason."

Had he done something wrong? He stepped back and put his hands in his pockets. "Is there a reason why not?" This wasn't the way it had gone in his head.

She shifted from one foot to the other and moved to the small desk in the corner. "I just don't think it's a good idea. What we had—" She waved her hands. "Or didn't have for that matter, was a long time ago. There's no need to go there again."

He clamped his jaw shut against his annoyance.

"Okay, I, uh, I guess I'll get out of your hair then." Confused, and not sure where he'd gone wrong, he headed toward the door.

Her soft voice stopped him before he could reach the studio door. "Were you going to tell me that you saw her?"

Shit. A tingling of awareness pricked his skin. Sabrina. He lowered his voice a pitch. "She came by, Izzy. All on her own."

She lifted her head to glare at him as she swiped a lock of her thick full hair out of her face. "It's none of my business what you do with your personal life, Jason. But I'm not stupid. I'm not a seventeen-year-old kid throwing myself at you anymore."

He furrowed his brow. When the hell had he fallen through the rabbit hole? With every racing beat of his pulse, he told himself to relax. "What are you talking about?"

At the table, she tapped a few keys of a keyboard. As if by magic, an image of his front door appeared on the screen. She turned back to her matting table without a word.

He looked at the screen and cringed. He didn't need to get any closer to know what the photo looked like. There, in all their splashy glory, were he and Sabrina in what looked like an embrace. Damn it. To make matters worse, the headline read Bad Boy Dishes It Up With Sexy Brunette.

"Izzy," he implored. "I know how this looks, but it's not like that."

She sighed and looked up from her board. "You're right."

He filled his lungs with the sweet air of relief. She wasn't going to overreact. She understood how the paparazzi could manipulate photos. Though, as he further searched her face, he held onto the deep breath as if it would be his last.

"I know how it sounds. But it honestly doesn't concern me. It's none of my business."

He took two halting steps over to her matting board. "Do you think I'd be with Sabrina? And to add insult to injury, come here, ask you out? That doesn't make any sense, Izzy."

She hesitated, and then straightened her back. "It didn't make any sense then either. Did it? I'm not interested in playing games, Jason."

He stood directly in front of her until she had no choice but to look him in the eye. "I'm not playing games with you. I came here today because I wanted to see you. End of story. I felt something."

She scoffed. "Of course you felt something the other night, you wanted to get laid."

The surge of anger crashed through his veins, but he reigned in his temper as best he could. She'd always been able to rile him. "Oh, it would have been nice to get laid, but I'm way beyond the age of trying to play games to get some." Because she forced his emotions to churn, he added, "And sweetheart, let's not get it twisted, you were the one all over me all those years ago."

She reeled back as if he'd slapped her, and he wished he could take back the harsh words. But they were already out. Fuck. How the hell had they gotten into a fight? "Look, she came over to ask for money. She's in some kind of trouble."

Eyes wide, she blinked at him. "Did you give it to her?"

"Are you kidding? Whatever trouble she's in, Sabrina will have to get out of it on her own."

Izzy sat down looking at her hands. "Did she look like she was using again?"

"I don't think so, but I don't know. She said she needed it to make amends or whatever." He shook his head. "She's a piece of work."

Izzy's shoulders slouched. "I don't know why I thought this time would be any different."

"I didn't give her anything. She knew the cameras were there. She played you all over again."

She squared her shoulders. "And you're not?"

Chapter Seventeen

Izzy slammed her phone down at Simon's tenth text of the day. She would have to deal with him, tell him once and for all they weren't going to be together.

After a few kisses from Jason, she knew to her core, she couldn't fake it. Since the night in her studio with Jason, she planned to get it over with, but with Sabrina and Jason, and lawyers and the gallery opening, she couldn't focus.

As the sounds of Sean Paul blared from the radio, as she danced around her room sorting laundry and let the sounds of dancehall soothe her soul.

She couldn't postpone the inevitable.

Jessica sat cross-legged on the bed going over final details of the gallery night. "The timeline is almost set. Press is scheduled to arrive at seven, but I promise they'll be a little late."

While Sean Paul prompted her to "Shake that ting ting" Izzy tossed the pile of darks into the hamper and searched under the bed for her dark jeans. "Okay, so I'll want to arrive about a half hour later. Do the interviews I need to, then make myself scarce."

Jessica's expression softened. "You don't need to do that anymore, Iz. No one cares about the past."

"Maybe you're right, maybe you're wrong, but all it takes is one reporter to dig around about my past. Maybe they don't care anymore, but I don't want to take that chance."

Jessica chewed her bottom lip. "Look, I know you don't like to talk about it, but I came on long after it all went down. I don't even think I have the whole story."

Izzy turned down the radio and eased herself onto the bed. "I guess it doesn't make a difference now. My sophomore year, I was in the semi's for the NCAA Singles Championship. Between finals and classes and applications for every internship under the sun, I was under a ton of pressure. Got run down and contracted Mono."

"Damn."

"Well, anyway, I considered dropping out to let the wildcard take my spot. I was in no condition to play. My dad was there, like he was for every other match I've ever played, and came back to the holding pen to give me the failure isn't an option speech." Izzy puffed in a breath. "We got into a huge fight with him insisting no daughter of his was going to quit."

"Shit, how's that for supportive?"

"Tell me about it. Anyway, I went out on the court and played the worst set I've ever played. Part of me knows I was sick, but the other part of me knows I did it out of childish spite. Anyway, Dad screamed at me from the stands. Every time I missed a serve or faulted."

"Sounds like a winner."

"I finally got fed up, flipped him off, and screamed at him to fuck off." Izzy wiped a hand down her face, trying to erase the memory. "I walked off the court to get my gear. When I looked up at him, people crowded around his slumped form."

"What happened to him?"

Izzy leveled her gaze and Jessica. "He had a heart attack. By the time I made it up there, someone was doing CPR, but he didn't regain consciousness. When I realized what had happened, I lost it."

"Oh, honey. I'm so sorry."

"I don't remember much about that time, but I'll always have the news clips to remind me. Apparently, I threw myself on him screaming about how it was all my fault and I couldn't believe I'd done this to him. Mom says I didn't eat or sleep for a week. I totally lost it. There was a lot of press at the tournament. Must have been a slow news week, because every night in the sports section, they'd cover my breakdown in the news. People speculated on my mental state."

"That's horrible."

"Yeah, tell me about it. I haven't played since, and I hate press. When I hired Simon, he suggested the name change to protect my anonymity. Though, every now and again, during the Tennis NCAAs, someone busts out some of that archive footage."

"Shit. I don't know what to say."

Izzy shook her head. "Don't say anything. I don't want to talk about it." To solidify the change in subject, she scanned the piles of laundry, adding, "Have you seen my dark jeans anywhere? The ones I wanted to wear on my non-date?"

Jessica rolled her eyes. "I wish you wouldn't call it a non-date. He wanted to show up." Jessica hung herself over the edge of the bed to search for the jeans. Unable to find them she shrugged. "Maybe the gnomes took them."

"By gnomes, you mean Sabrina, who's made herself at home by borrowing my clothes?"

Jessica nodded. "The very ones. Look at the bright side though." She indicated Izzy's tank top emblazoned with the text I'm a MILF. "At least your missing clothing has forced you to wear my present. It suits you." She cackled.

Izzy gave her a wry smile as she thought of Sabrina. Unclenching her jaw, she reminded herself to take Bryce's advice—be patient. Wait her out. Not easy, in theory or in practice.

Izzy peeked out the window, listening to Nick jabbering into his cell. "When you were a kid, were you on the phone half as much as Nick is?"

Jessica's green-tipped, blue head bobbed up and down. "Oh, hell, yes. Girls are worse. Be glad they're not on their way to Vegas for a drunken wedding."

Izzy dropped the t-shirt she held and whirled to face Jessica. "Don't play with me. I still haven't had a chance to suss out the new girlfriend over dinner."

Jessica shook her head in awe. "Yep, I can feel the awkwardness now. You, her, and a whole interrogation scenario. Nothing says nice to meet you like a serious mom grilling." Her smile softened. "I think you're a great mom for going into interrogation mode. A ton of parents don't even bother these days. They don't want to be too intrusive."

"Did your parents do that?"

Jessica grinned. "Nope. Too intrusive. Besides, my friends would have scared the shit out of my mother."

Izzy wasn't sure if she should be grateful Nick didn't stage a mutiny. Maybe her traditional values made her overprotective. Izzy wished she could hold onto Nick's youth for a little while longer. "I don't doubt it." She couldn't resist another glance at her son, the gangly boy-man.

Her line of vision didn't escape Jessica's keen gaze. "Relax. You were in love once."

Izzy had some vague memories of being a teenager and in love.

With Jason.

Shoving the thought back under the bed, she tried not to think about Jason and Sabrina in living color on the TMZ.

She shook her head to clear the imagery. "Yeah, well, we didn't have all the methods of communication then. I mean for heaven's sake, AOL had rudimentary chat. Now, Nick's got a cell phone, email, IM, text messaging, a Facebook account and a webcam I cringe to think about what he does with when I'm not home."

Jessica perked up at the mention of text messages. "Speaking of text messaging, any more texts from the delicious Mr. Cartwright?"

"No. Not from him. A whole bunch from Simon, though. I think it's time to have a come to Jesus with him. It just won't work." As she uttered the phrase out loud for the first time, she watched her friend's face with anticipation.

Jessica sprang up and upended a pile of clothes. "Woohoo! Now we can get your groove back, girl." She twirled in excited glee. "No more pompous jackass thinking he owns the joint. Bust out the single lady anthems."

Tentative, Izzy sat down on the bed. "So, you're happy about this?"

"Are you kidding? Nick and I have waited for this moment for months. I can't believe you'll finally yank the shit out of that trigger."

"Well, given the other night, it's pretty obvious he's not the one I want."

Jessica put her hands on her hips. "What other night? I sense withholding."

"The night of the last shoot, my car died at Jason's place. He brought me home and stayed for dinner. I showed him some early proofs, then one thing led to hot make out session."

"What? Isabella Connors, you dirty slut. I love it. Tell me everything. Are those lips as soft as they look? His hands as big as they seem?" Her eyes widened in gleeful excitement. "Did you get to sample the goods?"

Izzy couldn't help but laugh. "Yes, lips, very soft, but knowledgeable. Yes, on the big hands, the better to cup my sizable ass with. As to any sampled goods, no." Not for lack of want.

Jessica collapsed back on the bed, a dreamy expression on her face. "You lucky bitch. Please, please, please tell me you had on cute undies. A nice lacy pair or something?"

"Sorry to disappoint. Basic Victoria's Secret sateen." At Jessica's incredulous expression, she added, "Well I didn't get dressed in the morning thinking, 'Today Jason Cartwright will see my undies.' Besides, it's not like he hasn't seen the goods anyway."

"Oh yes, the sexting incident."

Izzy cringed with the embarrassment and guilt. "Never again."

Jessica wiped away streaks of tears as she howled with laughter. "Dude, that shit would happen to you."

Izzy picked up the hamper and made her way down the hall to the laundry room when the doorbell rang. "Nick, can you get the door?"

Nick didn't respond, and the bell rang with a persistent chimes. She dropped the basket and trotted to the door. For several moments she stood staring at Jason as if she'd never seen him before. They had one more photo shoot, but she'd planned to be emotionally ready to deal with him. Surprise visits were unfair.

Because he didn't say anything and stared at her, grinning like an idiot, she spoke first. "What are you doing here?"

Hands raised in a peaceful gesture, he said, "I'm here for Nick. He asked me to come around and go through some match film with him."

Perfect. Even her own son conspired to torture her. "He's in the back. You can go through to the kitchen."

When he didn't budge, she glared at him. "What?"

He shook his head and stepped into the foyer. "Nothing. I'll head back."

As he sauntered to the back yard, Izzy caught herself taking in the view. She knew staring at his ass constituted a desperate and depraved act, but she couldn't help herself. "God I've got to get out more," she muttered under her breath.

Before he disappeared around the corner to the kitchen, he leaned back and said, "I've got to say, I'd agree."

Not until later, as she loaded the washer, did she realize she still wore her MILF top.

****

Jason let himself into the backyard still grinning about Izzy's tank-top. Wearing short shorts with her hair in a ponytail, looking barely legal, she didn't seem like any MILF he'd ever seen.

He couldn't help thinking about the way the tank had showed off an expanse of belly. The Izzy he knew had always been conservative in her dress. Maybe she'd changed.

Nick cut his conversation off. From his tone, Jason made the assumption he'd been talking to a girl. "You ready to check out some footage?"

Nick ambled over and gave him a now-typical, one-armed, man-hug. Jason knew the familiarity of the one-armed man-hug, but the foray into the world of "down" handshakes following the hug baffled him.

"Yeah. Thanks for coming by. Mom let you in?"

Pretty sure Nick meant Izzy, Jason nodded. "Yeah, she did. She seemed pretty surprised to see me though."

Nick cringed. "Sorry. I mentioned I wanted to review some tapes with a friend. I think she assumed I meant someone from the team." He shrugged. "Since you're not her favorite person right now, I figured I'd let her think what she wanted."

Jason tried to stop the quirking up of his lips. "Okay, but next time, check with her. I don't want her to come down hard on you."

Nick nodded in agreement. "Okay, can do. Though, Mom's never come down hard on me, unless I screw up pretty bad."

Jason followed as Nick led him into the house. "That's good. I doubt you'd ever screw up that bad. My mother loved to get on my case."

"You were a screw up?"

Jason thought back to his childhood and grinned. Then, remembering his teenaged audience, he curbed the grin. "I got into a little trouble."

When they settled in the family room, Jason was surprised at how comfortable he felt with Nick.

Jason paused one of the tapes to point out Nick's opponent. "You see what happened right here? He's getting ready to come into the net."

Nick leaned in. "Yeah, it's where he always gets me. I always misjudge and end up putting a ball into his racket I can't chase down."

Jason nodded. "Yeah. You want to be careful. Lucky for you he has a tell." Jason went to the screen to identify the opponent's footwork. "Notice the weight change?" Waiting for Nick to nod, he went on. "He does it every time he comes into the net. Like a bad habit."

Comprehension lit Nick's features. "No shit. Oh yeah." Then looking at Jason he grimaced. "Sorry."

Jason almost laughed out loud. Figuring humor wouldn't go over well, he said, "You should hear my language on the practice court."

At Nick's smile, Jason went on. "I suggest, against this guy, to go in with that strong forehand of yours. When he comes in, put the ball in the corner. He won't catch on."

Nick's eyes widened. "I'll be able to get him every time. Beating him has been real hard before. Now I have a chance."

Jason smiled. Pride welling in his heart. "You always had a chance. You didn't understand till now." He shrugged and added, "Might only work for a little while though. His coach will coach him out of the habit eventually. For now, it'll take care of your problem of giving up those crucial first games to him."

Nick nodded. "I can do that. The coach for Emmetsville doesn't seem to care about anything as long as they win. He's tough to beat."

"I'm sure you can. You'll need to stay focused."

Nick popped in another tape and brought sodas for the both of them. When he settled back down, he pierced Jason with a worried stare. "Can I ask you something?"

Jason's nerves skipped and jumped to life. He didn't like the seriousness in Nick's voice. "Sure." His mind raced for a kid appropriate answer to a slew of possible questions.

"You used to date my mother."

It was a statement, and not a question, so Jason waited for the rest.

"Was she always like this?"

Jason let out a breath. Again, he couldn't decipher if Nick meant Izzy, or Sabrina. "Was she always like what?"

Nick shrugged. "All about herself, I guess." Shrugging again, he shook his head. "I dunno. Not interested in anyone else."

Sabrina. Jason breathed a sigh of relief, but he struggled with what to say. He opened his mouth, but Nick interrupted.

"You don't have to be super nice about her like Mom is. I know she tries for my sake." He quirked his head in a nonchalant teenager's way. "She doesn't want to ever say anything bad about her, 'cause she wants me to have a relationship with her, or something."

Jason wondered if Nick was really thirteen. He already possessed more wisdom than he should at his age. "Izzy's number one concern is you. She wants you to be happy."

"Yeah I know."

Understanding he should address the question about Sabrina, Jason took a deep breath. "Your mother —" Changing his mind, he started again. "Sabrina is lost. Always has been. She's always been searching for love and acceptance in all the wrong places."

Nick didn't face Jason but gave Jason a sidelong glance as he swiped his hair out of his face.

Jason continued, "Because she's always been hurting inside, she can't relate and identify well."

Jason frowned. How could he dissect someone he hadn't seen in years? "She wants someone to love her in the exact way she needs, and when things don't happen how she wants, she searches for love somewhere else. When she does find love, she doesn't know what to do, so she runs."

Nick pondered for a minute. "Why does she treat my mom the way she does?"

A prickle of sweat rolled down Jason's back. He hadn't realized reviewing some tapes would turn into an inquisition. "Uh, well—"

Nick gave him a look that said he knew Jason was trying to find a graceful lie. "You don't have to make up an answer."

Damn. He didn't want to lie to the kid. "Because your mom lets her." Truth was the truth. Izzy had always let Sabrina steamroll her.

"Oh. Okay. Do you have a thing with my mom?"

Jason choked on his coke, the sweet liquid running down his chin. He swiped at it and laughed. "God, you're gonna make a great lawyer one day. What's with the twenty questions?"

Nick smiled. "It'd be okay." He indicated his head in the direction of the bedrooms. "I wouldn't mind if you wanted to take her out or something."

Wow. Jason hadn't been so nervous since asking out Mary Lou Sims in the sixth grade. A small part of him was touched at the gesture of Nick's blessing, but he didn't want the kid's hopes up. "Your mom is great, but it's, uhm…"

"Complicated?" Nick offered.

Jason nodded. "Yeah complicated." Good save.

Nick shook his head. "That's what adults always say. Then they tell kids to be honest about what we're feeling and stuff."

Nothing slipped past this kid.

Jason needed to get back on solid ground, so he changed the subject back to tennis. "What's your plan? Are you going out on the Juniors round this year?"

The noncommittal teen shrug made another appearance. "I dunno."

Relishing the idea of not having the spotlight on him, Jason prodded, "What's not to know?"

"Mom says I don't have to go if I don't want to." He took a deep breath. "Coach seems to think everything's all final and set. Keeps talking to me as if we're heading out on the road together."

Jason nodded encouragement to keep going. "You don't think you're ready?"

Nick took a sip of soda. "I guess I'm ready, but I guess I feel like I have to. What would you do?"

He thought about it as he took another sip. "What is it about Juniors you're not into?"

Nick glanced toward the bedrooms again. "I'm not sure I want to play tennis forever. I think I need to think through some stuff. Get a chance to do the school thing and friends thing."

He had a point. So many of the kids who went to the Juniors circuit ended up chasing the dream, unsure of what to do when they discovered not everyone could be the next Sampras. "Sounds like you've given it a lot of thought."

Nick furrowed his brow. "I also don't want to end up like Mom."

Jason stopped mid-sip of his soda, put his drink down, and leaned in further toward Nick. "What do you mean?"

"She used to love the game. She lived for tennis. At least that's what grandma says. I guess she lost it after her dad died, and she hasn't played again." He looked confused. "She'll hardly pick up a racket to play with me."

What had happened to her? "Maybe she's just more focused on other stuff now and has lost the urge to play?"

"I dunno. Sometimes she acts like she wants to, but then she doesn't." He shrugged. "Like she's scared."

They reviewed another tape before Jason had to leave. He hadn't enjoyed that kind of companionship in ages. Somehow, he'd found a friend in a thirteen-year-old.

Before he left, he gave Nick some advice. "It's important you commit yourself to the things you do. It's even more important you speak up about the things you don't want to do. Be honest, and let whatever happens happen. At least you'll be honest with yourself."

Nick nodded in understanding. "Thanks, Jason." Then catching himself, he amended. "I mean, Mr. Cartwright."

"How about you call me Jason when your mom isn't around."

Nick nodded and gave him a sheepish smile in return. He lifted his baseball hat to shift hair out of his eyes. The sunlight hit his face, and Jason could see all of Sabrina in the set of his eyes and the outline of his nose. He could also see something else. A faint purplish bruise under one of his eyes. His gaze honed in on it, sharpening.

Nick flushed. "It's no big deal."

Cold ice settled in Jason's stomach, wrapped around the organ and squeezed. He kept his voice even. "What the hell happened?"

Nick squirmed. "Nuthin."

Jason rocked back on his heels. "Sure doesn't look like nothing. Someone do that to you?"

Panic flashed in Nick's eyes. "No."

"Did some asshole at school do that?" If some idiot hit the kid, he'd make a special trip out there to let them take a crack at someone their own size. Though given Nick's height, it didn't seem likely that some teenaged boy would have the stones to step to him. "C'mon, Nick. I could do this all day. You need to tell me."

In that moment, Nick looked every bit the kid he was. Big brown eyes pleaded with him. "Please let it go. It's no big deal, won't happen again."

Realization clawed at his gut. Sabrina. "Fuck. When did this happen?"

"Please don't tell Mom. You can't."

Jason tried to step back in the house, but Nick blocked him. "Nick, I need to tell your mother. Sabrina hitting you is way out of line and unacceptable."

"Please don't. Mom already laid into me when I told her I got hit by a loose ball. She thinks I got into a fight, but she can't prove anything. Things are already tense enough around here. Sabrina will be gone soon. And it wasn't her fault anyway. I think she was high. And I talked back. Called her a bitch. I shouldn't have, but I was so angry and…" He sucked in a jagged breath cutting off the verbal diarrhea for a moment. "Please. I trust you. Please don't make everything worse."

Shit. The pleading in the kid's voice broke his heart. Nick couldn't face his mother now, but Jason wouldn't let this go. Sabrina had more than overstepped the line, and he was going to make sure it didn't happen again.

Chapter Eighteen

"Hello gorgeous." Izzy whirled her head around at the sound of Simon's voice. Careful of her position on the ladder, she gave him a quick smile and turned back to focus on her wall hanging. Also to get a handle on her nerves.

"Two secs—I want to see if this hanging goes here." Inching down the ladder, Izzy took several steps back to survey her work. She was playing with frame types for the opening.

"Izzy, everything looks great, but the studio can do this for you, if you just let me—"

She cast him an irritated glance. "It's important to me I be able to make the decisions and choices."

He gave her his patented, "Whatever makes you happy" look.

She wanted to smack him, but turned back to stare at the canvas of the young Masai girl. Tension and nerves rode her most of the morning. She shouldn't take it out on Simon.

"I think I don't want to split up the pieces by region. I should combine the ones that speak to each other."

"Well, it's your gallery opening. Has Rachel from the Hudson Gallery called yet? She can review the layout and…"

Izzy tuned him out. She focused on the sorrow and loneliness in the Masai girl's eyes. A thought flashed, and she hunted through the framed photos lying against the wall. When she came across the one of the children in the Chinese village of Wampei, she smiled. Most of them had run toward her grinning, but one small boy hung back, scared and alone. She'd chosen to focus on him. His bright red cap would offset the red robes of the Masai girl.

"Earth to Izzy. Are you listening to me?"

Brought back to earth, she sighed and pulled out the framed photo, dragging the bulk toward the wall. "Yes, I'm listening. Sorry, I'm trying to map out how this is going to go in my head."

He moved toward her. "I know. I just want to review some logistics with you." Taking her hand, he pulled her into the office. "I have a surprise for you. A couple of surprises actually."

She didn't care for interruptions while she worked. "What is it Simon? Can it wait? I'm in the zone."

Once in her office, he went around to her chair and laid out several pamphlets with pictures of beautiful women in black tie attire and beautiful jewels. The exuberance ebbed from him in waves, so infectious she almost laughed. One of the reasons she'd selected him as her manager was his faith and excitement about her work. If he hadn't been excited, she wouldn't have hired him.

He grinned at her, unable to keep his excitement in. "Do you remember Jennifer Dubois?"

Izzy searched her memory. "The diamond lady?" The Dubois were well known for their diamonds and even more famous for their association with celebrities who wore their sparkly designs. "Yeah, I remember her."

"Well she loved the Arctic landscape photo you sent her so much, she wants you to wear their designs at the opening."

Diamonds? Save some solitaire earrings from her mother, she'd never really worn diamonds. Not the real deal anyway. "This is a joke, right? Why?"

"No joke. She wants her designs taking center stage with the press corps."

Izzy couldn't quite process the information. "Center stage?"

"Well, maybe stage left as your photos should be the focus. You get the idea."

Her head swam. She'd thought the gallery opening was like every other small showing she'd done. She selected the photos, the gallery got them framed and hung, she made a guest appearance toward the end of the night and she could run away. They'd never been a big deal. "Did you say press? I don't do press. You know how nervous I get. We had a deal—I'd do the pre-press, and then I'd escape."

His grin fell a fraction. "C'mon, Izzy, this is great news. We need the press. The time has come to unveil Z Con."

Izzy tried to quell the rolling motions of her stomach contents. "What if she doesn't want to be unveiled. We had a deal."

"We discussed no press in the past, but USC was a long time ago. No one remembers what happened but you. The press is eating this up. Not to mention, with them in attendance, you'll get more exposure."

Izzy shook her head vehemently. "What if I don't want more exposure? You put too much on my plate as it is."

He came around the desk and took her hands. "Busy work is what's on your plate. You're a famous photographer. I want to take you to the next level. You're ready. You shouldn't be doing portraits and engagement photos."

What if she liked them? "I am at the next level. I like doing—"

He shook his head. "No, Izzy. You do those things, because you're afraid you won't survive if you don't. Newsflash, Izzy. With openings like this, you'll get to a point where you don't even think of money."

"I need to think about money. It's not just me on my own." Her stomach twisted. This was the last conversation she wanted to have. The argument was stale. She often turned down work because of time she'd already committed to small projects.

Frustrated, he ran his hands through his hair. "Izzy, you've filled Nick's college fund to the brim. You —"

Men. He'd never understand. "Not just the college fund. His current school fees. They're astronomical. Making sure he has the best I can provide him. This house, his future. I don't expect you to understand."

He took hold of her shoulders. "I do understand. He's a great kid with a terrific mom. I'm trying to give his mom the best of what I can offer, as her manager and —"

Izzy interrupted before he could go on. She would garner more sales if there were press at the event and not just before. She didn't want to fight with Simon. Especially not now. "Okay, fine. I'll do one press interview. You decide who with. I don't want my life or Nick's to become fodder for tabloids or anything."

He grinned and dropped his hands. "You got it. So does this mean you're not going to wear the diamonds?" He waved the pamphlet of show diamonds in her face.

She grabbed at it. "Let's not be hasty."

He laughed and pulled her in for a hug. She didn't resist at first, happy to be in a familiar camaraderie. They were friends, after all. Expect they weren't, exactly. He worked for her. Or the other way around, depending on perspective. Note to self: Get more friends I don't pay for.

When he held on for several beats too long, she struggled to move out of the embrace.

"Izzy, I—"

Shaking her head, she said. "Simon, don't." She wiggled out of his grip and took a step back. "I can't. I don't want…" Her voice trailed. How could she do this without hurting him?

The expression on his face was equal parts disappointment and determination. "We've been dancing around the subject of us for months, Izzy. Maybe even years. We would be good together."

They'd been dancing? Izzy wished somebody had told her as much. She hated dancing to a song she didn't pick herself. "Simon, we've got a great working relationship and friendship, I don't want anything to get in the way—"

A determined set to his jaw, he asked, "Would it help if I quit my job?"

Panic stared creeping up her spine. Why wouldn't he let it go? "No, Simon, it wouldn't." Then, with more conviction, she added, "I don't feel the spark with you. You're terrific, and maybe we confused our friendship for more, but the chemistry isn't there." There. It was out. Her hands clamped on the desk, and she waited for the inevitable to happen. Acrimony, arguing, anger, disaster.

Nothing happened, save his annoyed expression. Izzy felt the tension flow out of her shoulders. She'd confronted him and everything had turned out fine. At least everything seemed fine. He didn't hate her... maybe.

Simon didn't seem heart broken or disappointed, rather more determined than anything. "I can't say I'm not surprised you feel this way right now, but give it time. When things die down, we'll g—"

Hadn't he heard her? "Simon? I'm so sorry, but more time isn't going to do anything. It's not going to work."

"Well, I refuse to accept that."

Her eyes widened as she stared at him. "Are you refusing our pseudo breakup?"

He put his hands on his hips. "Yes. I guess I am."

Exasperated, she stared at him. How was she supposed to break up with him when he wouldn't let her? Hell they weren't even dating. "Simon, look, I don't want to hurt you, but I want to spend some time on my own exploring myself, and er, things." She shifted from foot to foot. She was usually the one on the receiving end of breakups.

A dark scowl marred his normally handsome face. "Other men?"

Shit. Why had she left it open ended? Now she felt like a total bitch. No, no no. You can't do things in life because other people want you to. In some ways, her life would be so much easier if she wanted to see him naked. However, she couldn't muster the urge.

"I'm sorry if I hurt you, Simon. I didn't intend to."

He nodded as he shoved his hands into his pockets. "Tell me one thing, Izzy. Does this have anything to do with the tennis player?"

She hadn't anticipated the question, and it sent tension slamming back onto her shoulders. She swallowed around the lump in her throat. "Jason? No, this has nothing to do with him."

Simon stood up straight and stiffened his spine. "Are you sure? I deserve the truth."

Izzy shoved aside the feelings of guilt and disappointment when she thought of Jason. "No, Simon. I told you. He's an old friend." If she used the word friend loosely.

Simon shrugged. "Yeah, sure, fine. It's none of my business. Though, if you're going to choose the hot-shot white boy, be aware of what you're getting into."

The tension she felt turned to anger in a flash. "You can't make this about him, Simon."

"Like I said, none of my business. I'm only trying to protect my investment in your career. The guy is no good. He uses women like tissues. He parties all the time. No telling what kind of shit he does at those clubs. You want someone like him influencing your teenaged son? You'll be splashed in the tabloids like some socialite party whore. We've worked too hard to let him happen to your career."

She narrowed her eyes. "So much for being civil adults."

"I'm not trying to pick a fight with you. Since you're choosing the tennis pro to help your position with Nick's custody, make sure he comes up lily white."

A breeze blew through the open window, hitting Izzy's skin and cooling the sweat forming. The nausea was back. This wasn't how the conversation was supposed to go. "I told you, Simon. Jason has nothing to do with this. This is my decision. Even if he did, how dare you insinuate I'd use him to help me sway the court. You know me better than that."

"Maybe I don't."

He didn't say anything as he left the office. Needing the additional support, Izzy lowered herself onto the edge of her desk. "That went well."

Chapter Nineteen

The juices of competition flowed over Jason like a comfortable hot spring. He stared at his opponent across the net, analyzed his stance, anticipated his move. With two bounces of the tennis ball, Jason served and quickly followed with a run up to the net anticipating his opponent's return.

But his opponent didn't do what he expected. He lobbed the ball to Jason's right, forcing Jason to make a run for it. In a classic Jason Cartwright move, Jason sprinted as he anticipated easing into a slide move, but at the last moment, all the muscles around his knee tensed at the thought of the slide forcing Jason to run past his target. Shit.

"Are you getting slow in your old age, Jase?" Aaron taunted him from across the net.

Jason gritted his teeth as he took his position, anticipating Aaron's serve. He had to get his head in the game. If Aaron beat him, he was in worse shape than he thought. "Shut up, Aaron."

"All right, all right, no need to get testy." As he palmed the ball before bouncing it again, he added, "I mean, if you're not up to it, all you have to do is say so."

Gripping his racket tighter, Jason tried to calm himself. I can do this. This is nothing. It's not like the guy is Nadal. "Shut up and play, Aaron."

"Whatever you say, buddy. Though, next game I want to put a little wager down."

Aaron threw the ball high and slammed with all his might in an effort to get an Ace. Jason's return was swift and efficient. Slicing over the net, it left little room for a return volley.

At least some things didn't change. Aaron ran for it, but couldn't get a swing in before its second bounce. Jason bit back his grin. "My serve."

As he positioned himself at the baseline again, he allowed himself to gloat a little before focusing his concentration again. "What was that about a wager, Aaron?"

He chuckled when Aaron flipped him the bird. As he analyzed the wind, his angle, and Aaron's position, he bounced the ball. Once, then again. Tossing it high, he slammed the racket with enough force to add a spin. Aaron huffed as he chased the ball, grunting as his racket made contact. His return went wild, sailing over the fence and into the yard.

Jason went to retrieve another ball, but Aaron signaled a time out as he leaned over to suck in gulps of air. He lifted his head to peer at Jason. "I see part of you is still working right."

Jason unlocked his jaw, wondering if he could make it through Wimbledon with only part of him working right. "I guess you don't want that wager anymore?"

Aaron sneered, but gestured to Jason's knee. "Your knee holding up?"

"It's holding." He almost choked on the lie. He'd need to do something if he wanted to be up to playing snuff anytime soon.

"That's great news." Aaron scrutinized his face. "Why don't you look happy, man?"

Jason plastered a fake smile on his face. "Oh, I'm happy."

Harsh laughter filled the air. "C'mon, Jase. We got a lot going on right now, but you have an, I need to go on a serious bender look about you. What's wrong? The press?"

Jason grabbed his towel and tennis bag as he followed Aaron up the stairs to the house. "What could be wrong with my life? The press follow me around like I leave them breadcrumbs. I'm busting my balls for some impossible goals. And I have an ex-trainer trying to smear me in the press. Everything is nifty."

"Well impossible goals are what we need. Let's not forget what a beating you took after last year's US Open. Then the whole Michaels scandal. Let's not forget the clause on your endorsements about placing in one Grand Slam tournament a year."

Jason grimaced. He didn't need reminders about the state of his future. "You're right. I need the press. I need a good profile. I'm new and improved."

Aaron preceded Jason into the brightly lit living room. "You look like you need an afternoon off. What do you say we hit the showers and head out to the Playboy mansion? Word is the playmate of the year's going to be at the pool party. We can catch some sun, and you can practice being very well behaved in the presence of gorgeous women."

Once inside the house, Jason dropped his bag. There was a time when a trip to the Playboy mansion would be just what the doctor ordered. He had other things on his mind today. "I have to pass. But you go on and have fun."

Aaron whirled. "You're kidding me, right? Please. Tell me you're kidding. I need you there. How am I supposed to get your leftovers if you're not there?"

Jason chuckled. "Somehow, I think you'll do just fine without my leftovers." He shrugged. "I have something to take care of this afternoon."

Aaron spread his legs and put his hands on his hips in challenge. "What is so important you'd miss the playmate of the year?"

Jason shook his head. "You remember the kid I told you about, Nick? I need to—"

Aaron's jaw went slack as he stared at him. "You mean you're giving me the I need Prozac face over a kid?" He shook his head in disbelief. Aaron plopped down on Jason's sofa. "When did you grow a heart?"

Jason rolled his eyes as he took a seat. "Clearly, you haven't been inflicted with the same malady."

"Heck no." Aaron placed a hand over his heart. "In here lies a lump of coal and a vodka on the rocks."

"You're an ass. Besides, I thought you said I needed to raise my profile. Do some good for the community."

"If all goes well this afternoon, I'll be a well-sated ass." Then, as if realization just settled on him, he added, "Wait, are you talking about the photographer's kid?"

"Do I hang out with a lot of kids?"

Aaron sat forward in his seat. "What is all this baby's mama stuff you got yourself into?"

"I'm not embroiled in any drama. Not like the kid's mine or anything. Believe it or not, I like him. He's a good kid. Will be a great player."

Aaron's eyebrows lifted. "And as a byproduct of coaching, you get yourself some of that ass? There are easier ways."

"Dude, do you ever think about what comes out of your mouth before you say it?"

Aaron flashed a grin. "I'm one of those lucky souls born without a brain-to-mouth filter."

"Some people call it rudeness."

Aaron shrugged. "Look, if you want to get some of her fine specimen of ass, then drive your butt out to Compton or wherever and get it."

"Pasadena," Jason corrected.

"Huh?"

"She lives in Pasadena."

Aaron threw his hands up in surrender. "More the better. You can take the Porsche without worry of carjacking. Regardless, my point is, go out there, get some and get your fill. But don't get tangled in all the other stuff going on with her kid. It'll get messy. Let her sort it out."

Jason scowled. "I'm starting to not like you."

"Aw, that hurt my feelings. At least I'm honest." He softened his tone as he added, "Look, I get it. The darker the berry, the sweeter the juice. She's got a hot little body. But she's not the only hot little body in the world."

Jason clenched his fists, took a breath, and counted to three. When measured breaths didn't work, he counted to ten. They'd been friends for too long for him to kill Aaron. Besides, he thought to himself, the blood would be a bitch to get out of the rug.

"I'm not interested in taking out any random girl. Anyway, I think this conversation is over."

Aaron's eyes narrowed. "You upset, Jase?" As if sensing he should back off, he put up his hands and sat back, signaling he was no threat. "I didn't mean to ruffle your sensitive feathers."

"I don't want to hear anymore."

Aaron blinked at him. "Geez, are you really into her? I didn't realize."

Jason released his breath in an attempt to expel some of the bubbling anger inside him. At first, he'd pursued Izzy because of their physical connection, but seeing her work, seeing her with Nick, even seeing her temper spark, reminded him of the girl he used to love. He liked her. "Yes, I'm into her, so maybe you can stop talking about her like a piece of meat."

"All I'm saying is, in this town, status matters. You honestly want me to believe you'd take your little photographer friend to meet your parents? All that ass, as bodacious as it is, is not made for your kind of life."

Unable to form a coherent thought with the blood pressurizing in his brain. Jason stood and walked to the door. He opened the stainless steel panel and glared at Aaron. "Get out."

Shoulders slumped, eyes bulging, Aaron stared. "Are you serious, man? C'mon, we can't hold a philosophical discussion?"

"Not about this. I'm not doing this with you right now." Holding the door wider, Jason lowered his voice. "Out."

Aaron grabbed his tennis bag and his keys. Stopping at the door, he looked at Jason. "Look. You'll cool off in a couple of days. Just keep in mind what I said about the kid, even if you don't want to listen to the other stuff. She'll be pissed if she thinks you're using the kid to get close to her."

Jason watched Aaron walk down the front stairs to his car. Angry energy pulsed through him as he picked up the phone.

The voice on the other line didn't sound like the pink-haired punk rocker he'd met. "Z Con Design Studio, this is Jessica. How may I help you?"

"This is Jason Cartwright. Is Izzy in all day?"

Her voice softened. "Yeah, she's with a client now, but she's free the rest of the afternoon."

"Great. Do me a favor and don't tell her I'm on my way. I don't want her to become mysteriously unavailable."

He could almost hear the smile on the other line. "I think that can be arranged."

He hung up with Jessica and grabbed his keys, then, taking in his sweaty appearance in one of the windows, he opted for a shower first.

Twenty minutes later, he was on the road to Pasadena. Izzy might not want to see him, but for Nick, she'd hear him out.

When the ringing sounded in his ear from his Bluetooth, he answered automatically. "This is Jason."

"You're out of time, Jason. I'm going to need your yes answer now."

Jason navigated the freeway to Pasadena as he adjusted his Bluetooth. "There you go again, Sabrina. Assuming you still have some kind of hold over me. You know what they say about assuming."

She let out a stream of curses worthy of a trucker. "You're the one who'll be making an ass of himself. You need to go ahead and play ball now, before things get dangerous."

"You wouldn't be threatening me, would you? 'Cause I can't tell you how bad an idea that would be. I wonder how the police would feel about your little extortion scheme here. I think it's a felony."

"Damn it, Jason. This kind of money is a drop in the bucket for you. Just pay me, and I'll be out of your hair."

"Skunk."

"What the hell are you talking about?"

"You're like a skunk, Sabrina. No matter how many times you wash the smell out, it sticks around. Even if I wanted to pay you, you'd only be back for more."

"Jason. You need to listen to me. Our bullshit aside, I owe money. If I don't pay it, some goons are going to make Izzy's and Nick's lives hell. You might think I'm a selfish bitch, but I don't want to see them hurt."

Would she really turn her drug friends on her own kid? A cold chill crept into the base of his spine, climbing it like ivy in the springtime. She wouldn't. Even Sabrina wasn't that cold. Though it wouldn't be the first time she'd resorted to violence with him. "Wow, you've gotten better and more elaborate at your lies." He took the exit for Izzy's. "Try them out on someone who's not a chump."

Chapter Twenty

Izzy heard the ruckus in the front lobby and cringed. Her head ached from another long night of worrying about the gallery opening, Simon's cold shoulder treatment and Sabrina.

The dull pain throbbed steadily between her eyes. Her whole body felt like lead, otherwise, she would have peeked to see what the fuss was about. But, exhaustion and the need to complete the final descriptions for the gallery photos, drove her to stay in her seat.

The ruckus and din, accompanied by heavy footsteps, drew closer to her office door. Izzy looked up from the paperwork to find Coach Tisdale barging through the opening with Jessica at his back.

A cold chill skipped up her spine. Nick. "What's wrong with my son?"

Jessica crashed into Coach in her rush to get to the office before he did. "Izzy, I'm so sorry. I know you didn't want to be disturbed, but he just came in past reception and refused to come back at another time and—"

She interrupted Jessica. "It's okay." Directing her attention back to Coach Tisdale, she asked, "Is Nick okay?"

Jessica excused herself, but not before shooting the older man a death ray glance.

Coach Tisdale stared after Jessica as blue hair flounced out of the office. He shook his head. "What kind of home are you providing for that kid?"

"I beg your pardon?" Pissed, she shoved her hair into a ponytail. "You still haven't told me if that kid is all right or not." Izzy, exhausted, had to sit back down.

"He's not all right. I don't know that the hell you're doing to him, but he's messed up."

Fear thundered through every nerve ending. "Where is he? What's happ—"

Tisdale looked confused. "He's at school."

Relieved, Izzy sat back down. "Then, Coach, please tell me what you're talking about. I'm too exhausted to try and figure it out on my own."

He leaned forward planting his hands on her desk. "Don't act like you don't know you're throwing away his future. This is all your fault. A talent like his—"

The herd of elephants wearing tap shoes in her head refused to stay still. She snapped and shouted, "What the hell are you talking about? You barge into my place of business, scare me half to death, insult my home and then my parenting. Before we go on, I'd like to know what the hell you're talking about."

"What, are you deaf too? Nick told me this morning he won't be going to Juniors this year. Some nonsense about wanting to be a normal teenager for a little bit. You've pushed him into making the wrong choice. You've ruined his future."

Izzy allowed herself several deep breaths. Nick wasn't in any imminent danger. He'd just made a decision. "I don't understand what the problem is, Coach? Nick thought long and hard about his decision. He didn't decide overnight."

He rolled his eyes. "I can't believe the courts put someone like you in charge of the kid, especially his future. What the hell would you know about his future prospects?"

Anger infused and fueled the demon elephants in her head. She barely heard the remainder of Coach Tisdale's mutterings over the stampede. She stood and crossed her arms. "Because Nick believes in you as a coach, I'm going to make the assumption that when you say someone like me you mean someone who doesn't play tennis anymore."

She huffed in a breath and gave him a look that said she knew all about his insinuations. "I'm going to make the assumption you have my son's—because that's what he is—best interests at heart, and that's why you're so passionate about this."

He stammered. "I don't know what you think I'm insinuating but—"

She put a hand up to stop him. "I'm not finished yet." She gave him a smile devoid of mirth. "I'm going to assume your only concern is Nick, and not your hopes of having the exposure that being the Juniors' champ coach would garner. Because, if you don't have his best interest at heart, if and when Nick is ready to play Juniors, there are a million tennis coaches that would love the opportunity to coach him."

He straightened and gave her a long look. Without saying a word, he stalked out. Izzy took a deep breath and sank into her seat. This was the last thing she needed. She tried to forget the words now etched in her mind. Someone like you. She told herself he was angry, and he hadn't meant to come off like a bigoted jackass, but she couldn't muster that lie.

The truth was, ever since she'd taken over guardianship, there had been a handful of people, black and white alike, lining up to tell her why a black woman shouldn't have custody of a white kid. Normally she would have done what she always told Nick to do in those situations—keep focus on what mattered and not worry about the rest.

However, she didn't feel like listening to her own sage advice. She slumped down in her chair. She didn't realize she was crying until the salty acrid taste of a tear hit her top lip.

The door opened again, and she swiped at the tear. The last thing on earth she'd let that ass of a man see was her tears. "Came back for more, did you?"

Where she expected Coach Tisdale's leathery features, she found Jason's blond head. He stepped in to the office looking confused. "I get the impression you were expecting someone else?"

Seeing Jason in her doorway, she couldn't help the overflow of emotions. First one tear escaped her lids, then another, then several more.

He came over to squat by her chair. "Hey, hey, what's wrong?"

Annoyed at herself for the tears, she swiped at them with a tissue and stuck her chin up. "I'm fine."

He nodded. "Yes, you look fine. What, with the tears and all."

She couldn't help the cross between a cry and a laugh that escaped her lips. "I'm okay, just pissed off."

"Liar. This have anything to do with the guy storming out of here a minute ago?"

"The asshole?" She nodded. "Yeah, but he's Nick's asshole of a coach."

"I don't remember you being a crier, so he must have said something to rattle you. Is Nick okay?"

"Nick's fine." She sniffed. "I'm the one lacking. Supposedly, I talked Nick out of going to Juniors. Seems I'm unfit."

Jason gripped her knee. "What did he say, Izzy?"

She knew that look. She'd seen that kind of singular rage from him in college when one of the players on a team with no minority members made a few comments. Jason disqualified himself from the meet and knocked the guy out. They were too old for high school antics. "Nothing, Jason. I handled him."

She could see him work his jaw, but he didn't press her. However, if she understood the core of him, he wouldn't let it go. "I hate to do this to you, but I'm here to talk to you about Nick too."

This couldn't be good. Not her day at all. "You think I'm a bad parent too?"

He didn't crack a smile. "Not funny, Izzy." He took a breath. "You're not the one who needs parenting lessons."

She was scared now. "Spill, Jason. I can't handle the games today. You came all the way over here."

He looked uncomfortable, as if sitting across from her was the last thing he wanted to do. "Nick asked me not to say anything, so I didn't the other day, but you need to know."

Nick didn't normally keep things from her. "My kid doesn't keep secrets." Although, he hadn't told her about his Juniors decision or the truth about the bruise on his face.

He looked even more uncomfortable. "The bruise on his face — I suspect he was trying to protect you."

She nodded. "Yeah, he said he used his face to catch a loose ball. I suspect he got in a fight, but he didn't say."

"Sabrina hit him, Izzy."

For several long moments, she sat shock still. At first, she couldn't process Jason's string of words. Then, she tried to process Nick's secret-keeping. When she finally got around to processing what Sabrina had done, she was on autopilot, the calm center before she exploded. She marched to the back door. Before she could open the stainless steel framing, Jason spun her around and held onto her. "No you don't. You don't get to go and murder her. Death's too good for her. Take five and breathe."

She tried to wiggle and free herself, but he held her too tight. He kept murmuring that they were in it together, that he'd help her. She wasn't interested in any of it. She wanted to go give the bitch what she deserved. Why wouldn't he let her? "Let me go, Jason. What you assume I'm going to go angry black woman on her? Geez, you're as bad as Tisdale." She struggled some more to no avail. "I can control myself, you know."

Refusing to let go, he brushed soft kisses against her temple. "I'm not letting you go until you stop shaking." He squeezed her tighter.

She hadn't realized she'd been shaking. She lifted her hand to have a look, and sure enough, she noticed a telltale tremor. Shit. Full of anger and pain, she collapsed against him and let him hold her.

"That's it. Relax." He rubbed slow circles into her back. "When you feel strong enough and ready, we'll go over there together."

Several minutes ticked by with them standing there like that. Finally, he loosened his grip. Strangely, she didn't want to leave the safety of his shield. She looked up at him. His jaw was set as he stared toward the house.

"Thanks. I can go up on my own. I don't even know if she's home. She dragged herself in at four in the morning, or so. She may have left again for all I know."

Jason's jaw clenched. "Two things, Izzy,"

She paused, hand on the door.

"One, I'm going in with you, not because I'm worried about what you might do to her, but because I want her to know she won't get away with anything like that again." He trained his gaze on her. "Two, don't ever compare me to Tisdale. It pisses me off." He stepped into the yard ahead of her without a backwards glance.

****

Jason led the way through the backyard, spurred by a combination of guilt and anger. With every step, he couldn't help but think he should have pressed Nick to tell Izzy what had happened. Alternatively, that he should have called Izzy the night before.

He opened the kitchen door and for several seconds, didn't trust his eyes. The kitchen looked like someone had ripped it apart. Broken dishes and glass lay strewn around the floor.

He shoved Izzy back several steps. "Stay here."

She looked like she might argue, so he turned her around to give her a little push and locked the kitchen door behind him. When he stepped through the disarray of the kitchen into the dining room, he knew the mess wasn't Sabrina's attempt at a temper tantrum. Someone had broken in.

He heard the footsteps behind him and whirled around. Izzy stepped through the back door, shock and disbelief on her face. "What the hell happened?"

Walking toward her with quick strides, he took her hand and tugged her with him. "We need to go." He glanced at her when they were back outside. "How the hell did you get in?"

"I live here remember? I have a key."

He didn't stop once they were outside, instead led her back to the studio's office.

"What the hell is going on around here?"

He wondered the same thing. But he had an idea about the answer "Not sure. But I'd bet Sabrina's involved."

Once in the studio, he called Jessica into the office. He sat Izzy down and grabbed the phone.

As soon as he spotted Jessica, he asked her to get Izzy some tea or something that would help calm her down. Jessica took one look at Izzy's drawn, pinched face and hustled to the kitchen.

Jason rattled off the address to the police. When Jessica came back in, she bore a mug of steaming liquid and the mail. She handed the mug to Izzy and dropped the mail on the table.

She gave Jason a questioning look before heading back out.

"Jessica, have you noticed anyone strange hanging around?"

She wrinkled her forehead. "Anyone strange like how?"

"Like someone you've never seen before. Anyone who didn't belong in the neighborhood. Strange like that."

She shook her head. "Besides me, no. Everything's been normal." She glanced at Izzy. "Except for Miss Bitchy and Coach McNasty, I haven't noticed anyone."

Izzy stared off into space not joining the conversation. Jessica's lips formed the exaggerated question, "Is she okay?"

Jason nodded and hoped it was true.

He glanced at Izzy before continuing. "There was a break-in at the house. The police will be here in a minute. Could you show them back here, please?"

Eyes wide, Jessica stared at Izzy. If Izzy saw her, she gave no indication. "Uh, yeah. I can do that." She turned her attention back to Jason and asked, "Do you want me to pick Nick up from school after practice?"

Surveying Izzy's condition, he checked the time and nodded. "Let him go to practice, but I want you to stick around until he's done and bring him to the studio. We'll figure out where they'll spend the night later."

"Okay I got it. Izzy, no rush at all, but I think the bill for the frames is in the mail on your desk. You'll want to try and pay attention to it tomorrow because they won't deliver the rest until you do."

After Jessica left, Jason knelt in front of Izzy. "You doing okay?"

She didn't answer.

He tipped her chin up. Her skin was soft and cool to the touch. She appeared not to see him at first, but eventually her eyes focused, and she looked at him. "Jason, what the hell is going on?"

He wished he could be more helpful, but he didn't know what else to say or do. All he could think of was to rub her knee and tell her it would be okay, but he didn't know that for sure. "We'll figure it out. I promise."

He moved the mail to perch on the corner of her desk, sending letters scattering to the floor. As he bent to pick them up, one in particular caught his attention. There was no address on the outside.

He turned it over to check the other side. Spidey sense drilling at his brain, he tore it open.

Expressionless, Izzy stared at him. "What is it? Why are you opening my mail?"

He clamped down his jaw. Shit. Out of the envelope spilled several black and white photos with one common theme, Nick. Some of the photos included Izzy, but Nick was in all of them. A type written letter fell out. Before he could stop her, Izzy picked it up.

"Pay up, Sabrina. I don't want to turn Martinez loose on such a pretty family." She choked on the last word, barely able to get it out. Shaking, she handed the letter to Jason. "I know who Martinez is. An enforcer for Tony Rodolfo's merry gang of dealers. Martinez is a sadistic bitch who's roughed Sabrina up more than once before."

He took the photo from her and shoved it back into the envelope along with the photos. He'd give it to the police when they arrived.

He didn't bother calling Jessica back in. The police would question her. Likely, someone added the photos to the mailbox after the mailman had already filled it. Jason didn't hold much stock in tracing it, but that was up to the cops.

He kept his voice low. "Izzy, look at me."

She looked at him with weary, vacant eyes, and his heart lurched. She looked about ready to crack. At the very least, she needed sleep.

"Izzy. You and Nick can stay with me tonight."

When she didn't respond, he added, "I'll call a crew to come and clean after the police get done."

She still didn't respond. He had no idea what to do. He'd only ever had to worry about himself. He couldn't imagine the torture she was going through worrying about Nick. He sighed. "I'd say Jessica should pick Nick up early from school, but he can't really come home so…" His voice trailed off. He needed her to say something. Anything.

She finally spoke, and relief washed over him. At least she wasn't catatonic.

"We'll stay at Jessica's. It's near Nick's school."

"You'll stay with me. I have the room, and I can take Nick to practice in the morning."

Panic danced in her eyes. "I don't want, I wish, I…" Her voice broke, and he pulled her up to gather her in his arms. Shit. This was a real crisis, and all he had to offer her were a couple of hugs and platitudes.

"I have good security, the room, and I'm stubborn. Once we're done here, we'll pick up a few of Nick's things and go to my place, okay?"

A sob racked her body, but she nodded. "Okay."

Jason heard Jessica talking to the police and pulled back to look at Izzy. "Go ahead and wash your face. I'll take them up to the house. You can come up when you're ready."

She nodded and headed into the bathroom adjacent to the office. Before she closed the door, she looked at him. "Jason, thank you."

He didn't know why, but the simple words made him feel like a fraud, as if he didn't deserve the thanks. Because as much as having her in Malibu was for Nick's protection, he wanted her close. He wouldn't give up the opportunity.

Is this what Sabrina had meant? She might be completely self absorbed, but she wouldn't turn on her own son. No one could be that cruel or evil.

Sabrina could.

Entangling himself with Sabrina was worth it to keep Izzy and Nick safe, but he also knew Sabrina, she'd hold that over their heads for as long as she lived. She'd never let them be. She would punish Nick for Jason's feelings.

Izzy's frail haunted look flashed in his mind. He knew her well. She was already in shut down mode. What good would telling her do? If he paid Sabrina, he'd do so to keep Nick safe. No strings attached. He'd suffer the consequences gladly.

Knowing what he needed to do, he pulled out his cell and made the call. A crisp and efficient female voice answered the phone. "Cartwright Trust Bank. This is Melanie speaking, how many I direct your call?"

"Hello, Melanie, this is Jason. I'd like to make a wire transfer."

"Certainly, Mr. Cartwright. Lovely to hear from you again. If you will just hold, I'll put you through to Francis."

He waited patiently as Francis picked up the line. With a deep breath, he authorized the transfer of one hundred thousand dollars to Sabrina's account.

It took him less than three minutes to secure the final nail in his coffin. He told himself he'd done the right thing to keep Nick and Izzy safe. Too bad it was the one thing Izzy wouldn't forgive.

Chapter Twenty-One

Izzy noticed three things as she snuggled deeper under the covers. It was too bright in her room—had she forgotten to pull the shades? Her sheets felt softer than she remembered. An unfamiliar musky scent enveloped her.

It took her brain several moments to register the scent of male didn't belong in her bed. What a wonder she remembered the smell, considering her sex drought.

She pealed her right eye open and peeked around for the source of the fragrance. Expecting the usual sunset color of her room, she blinked as stark white walls met her gaze. Slowly, memories of the day before seeped into her consciousness. Coach Tisdale, Jason. The photos of Nick. Her brain snapped into focus. Nick.

She sprung from the bed, hurriedly searching through her overnight bag for bottoms to cover her legs. She called out for him, but no one answered. Bleary-eyed, she checked the clock. Six-thirty. Shit. She'd overslept. She'd never be able to get Nick to the courts to practice in time.

Unlike most kids his age, he didn't sleep in, never had. His one fatal flaw. Kids should sleep in, especially on weekends. Automatically, she grabbed her camera, but since she couldn't find her shoes, she had no choice but to go down the stone staircase barefoot. She glanced at one of the steps dubiously. Once her feet hit the ice cold surface, she realized going down slowly wasn't an option.

Downstairs, sunlight washed through the windows and kissed all the furniture with morning light. Izzy searched, but still no Nick or Jason, but she did locate the tennis shoes she'd worn the night before and slipped them on. The French doors to the porch and outer grounds were open. Sounds of the waves crashing against the rocks over the cliff carried over the grounds. She could also hear the thwack of racket hitting ball.

At least she didn't have to drive all the way back to Pasadena so Nick could get some practice in. Padding out to the deck, she watched Nick toss his ball strong and high for a serve and hit it with enough force to elicit a grunt.

Jason gave Nick some instruction. "Good serve. You're strong. One thing, I want you to work on some forehand volleys at the net. They'll come in handy against Michon in the exhibition tomorrow."

Nick's response didn't carry, so she started down the stairs to meet them on the court. A few stairs down, she turned back around to grab her camera.

Once at the sidelines, she had a clear shot of Jason and Nick working at the net. Nick said something to make Jason laugh, and Izzy's libido interrupted the steady thud thud of her heart.

God, the word handsome didn't suffice. All muscle and sinew. She snapped several photos. Checking the digital display, she would swear that these photos were better than any she took for SI.

They still hadn't seen her yet, so the both of them were natural in the photos. No matter that he'd been the subject of thousands of photos, Nick always seemed to pose when he knew she had a camera on him.

Nick slammed a forehand volley over the net, and Jason grinned again. "That's exactly what I'm talking about. You want to leave your opponent no options."

Something about Jason's smile made her stomach clench. This was the man she'd known. A memory of the day before, when Jason held her, flitted into consciousness.

He'd been gentle and caring, had taken care of most everything with the police. He'd held her as if, by sheer will, he could stop her from breaking apart. His presence so strong that the foremost memory of one of the worst days of her life was not of Coach Tisdale, or the break-in, but of Jason holding her as she cried. Jason taking care of everything, protecting her.

And later that evening, he'd explained to Nick about spending the next few days, through the weekend, at his house. He'd gotten Nick settled then bundled her up in his bed. And he'd held her until she'd fallen asleep.

Jackass bad boys didn't behave like this. They partied, they drank, they had sex with lots of women. It didn't match. Who was the real Jason?

Nick waved, and Jason turned. They both smiled and made their way across the court toward her. Jason stood taller, though not by much. Nick was already taller than three quarters of the boys in his class.

Something in their strides made Izzy do a double take. What she usually called lazy plodding by Nick, was a sexy predatory gait in Jason. Their walk, in some measures, the same, only one more matured, neither one of them in a hurry to get anywhere.

Shit. She blinked, tying to expel the similarities she saw. I'm overreacting. Plenty of men walked that way, part of the male genetic makeup. Especially athletic men, graceful, fluid, lithe.

As they approached, they smiled similar smiles. It's impossible. God couldn't be that cruel. Shit. She couldn't believe she'd never put the two together before. Though, she'd never really seen them side by side like this.

The tilt of their heads, and the slow lazy smiles to match their slow lazy walks, were identical. Her heart hammered double time in her chest. She told herself not to freak out. Maybe she needed more sleep. All the stress and strain had taken a toll.

Nick, taking no notice of her mood, started in on her with his usual string of verbal diarrhea. As usual, she caught only mere snippets of the teenager code. "Mom…Jason said…then we did…and did you catch the volley…can't believe this house. It's…freaking dope."

Izzy could only do what she always did — listen closely and wonder where all her youth had gone. There was a time when she'd had the ridiculous teen speak to a science.

Jason smiled at her. "I thought you were going to sleep in. We didn't want to wake you."

She looked between the two of them, now noticing the similarities. Nick's hair, shaggy and unkempt, differed in color from Jason's. Nick's hair had the sandy color of youth, from the sun. Jason's was a darker shade of blond.

Izzy could recognize Sabrina in Nick's nose and the set of his eyes. There were distinct similarities between the shape of Jason's and Nick's jaws and the way they smiled. But she stared into the face she'd seen every day for the past ten years like she saw him for the first time.

Unable to continue staring at the two of them, she sputtered out a response. "I thought I needed to get you to the school for practice."

"No need with a court here."

Jason indicated the house. "We should probably get breakfast."

Feeling bad he'd opened up his home to them and she'd kicked him out of his own room, Izzy thought she should repay him. "You don't have to go to any trouble, we can help get breakfast together.

Nick interjected. "Uhm, Mom, I think maybe you should let me—"

She interrupted him before he could finish. "I'm perfectly capable of whipping up some eggs."

Nick looked at Jason and made no attempt to hide the warning shake of his head.

He had a point about her cooking being more of a death sentence than a repayment of kindness. She sighed. "You know, when I said I could whip up eggs, by I, I meant Nick."

The rumble of Jason's laughter as they climbed the stairs into the house, reverberated around them, reminding her of Nick's laugh.

Sabrina owed her some answers. When Izzy found her, she'd shake the truth out of her.

Chapter Twenty-Two

Izzy leaned over her portable light table as she analyzed the photos from the morning. She searched for something, anything, to disprove her gut. Jason is not Nick's father. Sabrina might be many things, but a magician she wasn't. The math was all wrong.

The longer she stared at the photos, the more she wondered if the impossible was, in fact, possible. What if…

"You're cute when you concentrate."

As the warm timber of Jason's voice washed over her, her internal temperature rose. Women all over LA dropped their panties at the sound of his voice. She didn't want to be one of them. Maybe not exactly the truth, but she'd stick to her delusions for now.

She glanced at the clock, and her jaw dropped. Past ten. "Did Nick get to school okay?" In a haste, she attempted to shove the morning's photos into her project folder.

Jason was too fast for her. "Yeah, he got off fine. Are those from this morning? How did you get prints of these so quick?"

Izzy pointed at her portable printer. "I know they're digital, but I still love my trusty light table. I don't have negatives, but I like to get some light behind them."

"Were you able to get a hold of Sabrina?"

"I tried. All I got was her voicemail. I left her a message about the house. Told her we needed to talk."

He rocked back on his heels. "Izzy, I'm sorry I didn't tell you about Nick's bruise right away. I should have insisted—"

She put up a hand. "No, you did the best you could. Kids are tough. The right balance between earning their trust and doing what's best for them isn't easy."

Without saying a word, he moved over to her side of the light table and extended his hand. "C'mon, I have a surprise for you."

Dubious, she inspected his hand for the trap. He waggled his fingers and teased her into acceptance. "I don't do so well with surprises."

Jason cocked his head, his smile, equal parts scrutiny and charm. "You used to love surprises. Whatever happened to that Izzy. I liked her. Let's bring her back."

Stifling the girlish urge to giggle, she allowed him to tug her to the back deck. "Nah, she's gone. I shot her in Reno just to watch her die."

"Smartass."

Izzy screwed up her face. "What, you don't like Johnny Cash?"

He rolled his eyes as he positioned her on the deck. "Close your eyes."

"Why?"

"Just close them, woman. Damn, you could drive a man to drink."

She closed her eyes, making sure to use as much exaggerated reluctance as she could muster. No reason for him to know how thrilled she felt. "What's your drink? I figure if I'm going to drive you to the act, I might as well provide the alcohol."

The low rumble of his laughter made her knees wobble. As she stood there, eyes closed, late morning sun on her face, she wondered if he gave any thought to their kiss the other day. She may have said she didn't want anything to do with him, but her body certainly didn't agree.

She felt him shift behind her, fully moving into her space. Warmth and a musky, woodsy scent followed him, making her almost beg for him to hold her. Taking hold of her shoulders, he turned her body to an angle.

"Okay, you can open your eyes now."

She peeled her eyelids open. Her eyes took several seconds to adjust to the onslaught of light. On the chair in front of her lay a racket. The handle wrapped in pink tape.

Izzy swung around to survey him. "I don't understand."

"What's not to get? The racket's for you."

She folded her arms across her chest and tried to sidestep him, but he wouldn't let her pass. "I don't want a racket. I'm grateful, but I don't play anymore, Jason."

"Why?"

"Because..." Izzy shut her eyes in an attempt to escape from his probing gaze. "I don't. Not anymore."

"But why, Iz? You were a star. You loved to play."

"Jason, you haven't known me in years. A lot has changed. Tennis isn't my life anymore." Frustrated, she ran her hands through her hair. "Not everyone wants to be in the spotlight like you."

To keep her in position, Jason put his hands on her shoulders. "Izzy, no one's asking you to suit up to play center court at Wimbledon. I'm just asking you to pick up the racket and have some fun. I saw you as you watched us. You looked like you miss it."

She removed his hands from her shoulders. "Look, you've been great, letting us come to stay here. I appreciate your help and hospitality more than I can say. But I won't have you pushing me into this. Why do you care if I play or not?"

Jason shoved his hands in his pockets. "Izzy, I'd give anything to see your face light up again. Yeah sure, I see some of the joyful Izzy when you look at Nick, but when's the last time you experienced pure bliss and enjoyment for yourself, your pleasure. I only wanted —"

"Enough. God, why does everyone think they know what's best for me. My mother, Jessica, Simon, shit, even Nick's in on the game. And now you. I'm perfectly capable of taking care of myself. I know what I need. What I want."

Jason tucked his head and peered at her from under thick, dark blond lashes. "Yeah okay, I understand. You're pissed. I was presumptive. Thought I knew what would make you happy." He turned to the sliding glass door. "I'm headed to physical therapy. I'll leave a set of keys to the Mercedes in the garage in case you want to go anywhere. Since I'll already be in town, I'll pick Nick up from school."

"Jason, I —" Thinking better of it, she softened her tone. "Thanks. I'll be able to get some work done."

"I want you to think about it, Izzy. What would make you happy?"

****

Jason pushed himself far beyond blood-engorged veins and sweat-soaked T-shirt. He focused his mind on the punishing workout. Pushed his body until every muscle screamed for release, then pushed them further.

He'd thought about calling Aaron before therapy, but given their last conversation, he wasn't in the mood. Why talk it out when he could sweat it out? He'd only meant to lighten Izzy's mood. Instead, she'd compared him to her slimy, too-close-for-comfort manager, and her mother at the same time. Not fair.

She acted like he'd dropped her off at center court for the US open, handed her a racket and told her good luck. He'd hoped to, at the very least, get her to hold the racket again. Maybe hit a couple of balls around, remember how she used to feel before she held the weight of a two ton semi, or at least the weight of a boy, on her shoulders.

He hadn't thought she'd fight him so hard. It was only tennis. A game. The one thing they'd shared in common. The one thing able to put their tenuous relationship on some kind of even keel.

Maybe he shouldn't have pushed. But ever since Nick had told him she hadn't played since her father's death, he couldn't help himself, charging in on his white horse, or racket, practically brow beating her into playing. He couldn't force her to play or heal.

I'm an idiot. Just because they'd gone after each other like kids on a honeymoon didn't mean she'd given him permission to take over her life. They were different, and at different points in their lives, but every nerve in his body screamed they still mattered to each other. Or at least, she still mattered to him.

One scorching kiss in her studio did not a relationship make. No matter what feelings she'd stirred in him. She'd already been real clear she didn't trust him. Have you given her any reason to?

She was right. Enough people in her life tried to influence her one way or another. Took advantage. Sabrina. Her father. Jason had only met him twice, but from what he remembered, the Major didn't suffer fools and made it clear everyone was to follow his edicts or else.

The old man had been hard on her, pushed her to be perfect and over-achieve at everything. She went to college early, played tennis on a professional level, got terrific grades. The perfect athlete. The perfect friend. The suffocated daughter.

Now, like the moron he was, he'd pushed too hard. Izzy had never said no to anyone or anything. Except him. Maybe that should tell him something.

Jason pushed through the throbbing pain in his knee to complete the last set of leg lifts. Sweat dripped from his hair in hot, messy streaks down his face. He should have asked her if she'd consider playing again, instead of getting ahead of himself and assuming. She had every right to be wary of him. Hell, if he were her, with their history, he'd run far and fast.

Damn. He hadn't even had the sense to ask her out on a proper date. Sure, he'd gone by her studio to do that, hoped to pick up where they'd left off, but strolling in with a hope and a prayer would hardly sweep anyone up in a wave of emotion.

Every other woman he knew clamored to spend time with him. Wanted to hang around at the parties. If he bought them a gift, they fawned over him. But not Izzy. Ornery, obstinate, unimpressed Izzy pushed him away and insisted on something real. He couldn't ever take the easy route with her. She made him work.

At one point he'd loved her for it. Love. If he didn't watch himself, he'd end up just as in love with her now as he had been then. Would that be so bad? It had been so long since he let himself care about anyone, he took a moment to re-familiarize himself. She might not believe he had feelings for her now, but no matter what it took, he'd prove it.

Chapter Twenty-Three

Izzy's singular sense of confusion warred with her annoyance and her guilt for top billing in her mind. As she ambled around the living area, unable to process her argument with Jason, the vast, empty expanse of the house added to her feeling of desolation. As usual, when faced with a challenge like Jason, she opted for self preservation. Without much effort, he managed to push the limits of her safely-constructed world and challenged her carefully-constructed walls. With a simple gesture, he exposed her fear.

It's just a stupid racket. Then why did the sight of the pink, taped handle fill her with icy terror? I've handled dozens of Nick's rackets. However, never, not once, had she considered playing.

She hated to admit it, but Jason had a point. For the first time in years, as she watched the sun spread rays over the court, watched the joy in Nick's face, she thought seriously about playing again.

Why punish Jason because he'd noticed the need, the desire, and aimed to please? Because you don't trust him. He was slick. He'd had enough practice with his assortment of ex-girlfriends and lovers.

He said he wanted her to be happy. After all these years, he still cared about her. Never mind his past with Sabrina. Never mind their history. Never mind her pride. Maybe she needed to give him a chance. A real chance. Not the half-assed one she'd attempted before.

Unable to stand the silence in the house any longer, she pulled out her cell. Jessica answered before the end of the first ring.

"Hiya, home slice."

Izzy shook her head. "Have you been watching BET even after I cut you off?"

"Nope. Urban dictionary. It's the dog's bollocks." Izzy heard papers shuffling. "You should check it out, you know, so you can keep up with me and Nick."

The dog's bollocks? She rolled her eyes. "Any messages?"

"Just Simon wanting to know your whereabouts. Not to worry though, I told him you'd run off with an exceptionally handsome rich guy. He didn't sound pleased. Your mother called too. You made the news in San Diego."

Great, just what I need. "Anyone else? Sabrina call? Come by the house?"

"Sorry. No sign of her supreme bitchiness. The cops are done though. Jason called, said his cleaning crew would be by tomorrow. You guys playing nice over there?"

"Yep, sure. Define playing nice."

"Damn, Izzy, what did you do?"

"Why do you assume I did anything? He's the over-charming, slick one who thinks he can get away with murder because he's Jason Cartwright."

Jessica's three-second silence seemed to stretch longer than a college overnight. "Okay, look, I didn't butt into your life when you let the harpy come and stay with you. I don't say anything, or rather not much, when you date guys who don't make you happy. Nevertheless, I've had enough."

Izzy tried to interrupt. "But, Jess—"

Jessica continued as if she hadn't heard. "You need to stop living in the past with Jason. He obviously cares about your wellbeing. You people need to have it out and stop dancing around your issues. Maybe he's not Mr. Relationship, but when was the last time you let yourself have some fun with someone. Carpe diem. Stop focusing on the past."

Izzy hated it when Jessica had a point. But then, she'd already come to the same conclusion herself. She looked over toward the light streaming in from the deck and sighed. "Jess, thanks for sticking around over there, and for kicking my ass. I appreciate everything more than you know."

Jessica giggled. "No prob, Bob. It's time you let someone take care of things for you for a change."

"I'm working on it. Listen, if Sabrina calls… "

"Understood. Tell her to call you." The second line shrilled in the background. "Iz, hottie, lawyer-guy is on the line. You want me to take a message?"

Bryce. "No, I'll call him right now."

After hanging up with Jessica, she immediately called Bryce. "I understand you're looking for me."

"Iz, where you been? I've been calling you at home since last night. Tried your cell, went straight to voicemail. Are you having some torrid love affair you're afraid to tell me about?"

Why was the idea of her having a torrid love affair so amusing to everyone? "No. We had a break-in at the house yesterday afternoon—"

"Geez, Izzy. Are you guys okay? Do you need anything? Where are you now?"

"We're fine. Nick was at school, and Jess and I were in the studio. I've taken Nick to stay with a friend in Malibu."

"Where's Sabrina?"

"The katrillion dollar question. I don't think she came home the previous night. Haven't seen her. The police were at the house getting some evidence earlier, but she didn't make an appearance."

"I'm calling with some more bad news, Iz."

Her heart hammered two quick beats against her chest, before locking in place waiting for the news.

"Sabrina filed for sole custody of Nick yesterday."

Even though she'd expected the news, even though she'd known it was coming, it didn't stop the crushing weights of dread and defeat from settling on her shoulders. "That's just perfect."

"Do you think she had anything to do with the break-in? It'll help your case if she did."

After she briefed him on the details of the photos of Nick, he let out a low whistle.

"Man, that friend of yours comes with her own cargo carrier of trouble. But, this can be good news for you."

Izzy almost dropped the phone as she considered what would happen to Sabrina if she was involved with her old dealer again. "Bryce, I'm worried about her. She's been so adamant about being clean. I'm sure she's using again."

"Good, ol' Izzy. The woman makes your life hell for several weeks, threatens to take away your pride and joy, and you're worried about her wellbeing. That's why I love you."

Frustrated, Izzy reminded herself, not to grind her teeth. She didn't need an achy jaw on top of it all. "I am who I am, Bryce."

"Fair enough. Regardless of what else is going on, Sabrina being MIA is still a good thing. I've got a date scheduled with the judge next week to review the current custody arrangement. In light of the latest developments…"

"Yeah, I know." Despite everything, Izzy couldn't shake the worry that something wasn't right.

By the time she hung up with Bryce, called her mother, convinced her mother she needn't drive up from San Diego, Izzy had had enough.

She didn't need her mother and Bryce probing about where she and Nick were staying. She didn't need Bryce reminding her about her Sabrina problems. She didn't need Jessica reminding her she had poor coping mechanisms.

Without thinking about it, Izzy tossed her cell phone on the couch and padded out to the deck. Without allowing herself to fear it, she picked up the racket. Without allowing herself to feel any negativity about it, she tromped down the long stairway to the tennis ball machine and flipped the switch.

Taking position across the net, without any thought to Nick, Simon, Sabrina, or Jason, Izzy flexed her hand around the pink handle and swung.

☐

Chapter Twenty-Four

Am I crazy to sneak into my own house? Jason tiptoed into the foyer, unsure if he should expect a torrent of curses. After physical therapy, he'd deliberately avoided going home, figuring they both needed ample time to decompress. Now, as he shut the door behind him, he couldn't dissipate the tension knot in his stomach. Lucky for him, Nick provided ample distraction with his fluid stream of consciousness.

"I still can't believe you came to pick me up in the Porsche. Did you see Steve's face? His dad may have a Porsche, but Jason Cartwright didn't pick him up from practice. So awesome."

Jason couldn't hide the smile that tugged at his lips. "Glad I could help. Any time you want to have some friends out here to practice or something, let me know."

"For realz? That'd be dope."

"Yeah, for realz."

Nick beamed a megawatt smile, and Jason felt an unfamiliar tug on his heart. "So you wanna play a little Madden?"

Knowing there was a right answer and a wrong answer, Jason glanced around for Izzy. Not seeing her, he figured, when in doubt, do the right thing. "Somehow, I have a feeling your mom would want homework first."

Nick's eyes bugged out of his head. "C'mon. Today's Friday."

Damn. When did he cross over into the uncool zone? "Shower, homework, dinner, and then Madden."

Nick gave an exaggerated eye roll. "You sound like Mom. Where is she anyway?"

"She trained me well." Looking back around, he added, "Wherever she is, hopefully, she's not doing any damage in the kitchen."

While Nick headed for the shower, Jason went on the search for Izzy. Six or seven people could get lost in the house and not find each other for at least half an hour.

After searching all the likely locations, he headed out to the balcony. Over the rail, he had an unobstructed view of the tennis court. In the same tank top and linen pants she'd been wearing when he left the house, hair in a ponytail and sweat drenched, Izzy slammed ball after ball over the net.

He trotted down the stairs and grabbed a spare racket as he joined her across the net. He used the racket like a broom to clear the spare balls off the court and turned off the ball machine.

Izzy scowled at him. "I wasn't finished yet."

"I figured you'd get more satisfaction out of putting a face to the ball."

Arms akimbo, her scowl didn't dissipate. "I don't want to talk."

"Who said anything about talking?" He moved back to the baseline. "Shut up and play."

That was the only warning he gave her before he sent a topspin serve her way. As he knew she would, she chased it down and returned serve with a grunt-filled backhand. As he anticipated the trajectory, he took three trotting paces and sliced an overhead drop shot behind her head.

She made an attempt to chase it, but slowed as the ball bounced for the second time. "Aren't you supposed to be injured?"

He shrugged. "Aren't you supposed to be good?" He bit back a grin as she displayed an elegant middle finger.

"Shut up and serve."

"Fifteen — Love." His next serve wasn't as fast, but Izzy's return was quicker and more controlled. She still had it. As he ran after her forehand, he calculated the next set of logical moves.

But Izzy didn't play by the rules. As soon as she returned his forehand, she ran up to the net. His next shot made it five inches beyond the net before she returned it clean and fast to his right side. Shit. He'd never be able to return it. He watched it fly by, knowing the pain that awaited him if he put too much pressure on his knee.

"What's the matter, Jase? Your knee acting up?" Her eyes gleamed with the thrill of competition.

Fuck, I'm screwed.

They went on like that for the rest of the game. Izzy hit shots to his right as often as she could. Some he returned, most he didn't.

As she wiped her face with a towel during one of their breaks, she sliced him a look. "Cut it out, Jason. I can beat you on my own. I don't need you giving me points."

He took a swing of water. "I wouldn't dream of it." Trotting into position, he prayed she stopped hitting to his right. He didn't know how much more of it his knee could take.

Lining up her serve, she sliced it over the net. His return was clear and sure. Hers was more wobbly, but it still hit its mark. He drew on the weaknesses he remembered from her playing days and took into account she might not be in as good a shape as she was, he ran her around the court. When she hit her final shot to his right, he gritted his teeth as he watched it go by. Damn it.

She ran up to the net and motioned him over. Wiping at the sweat on his brow with his forearm, he had no choice but to obey.

"What's going on?"

His narrowed eyes tried to focus on her face and not the way sweat molded her t-shirt to her breasts. "What do you mean?"

Her elegantly arched eyebrow traveled a path up her brow. "I can see what you're doing. If you want to keep playing, cut that shit out."

"I assure you, I'm not doing anything on purpose."

"Bullshit."

"Watch your language, sweetheart." He grinned.

"You expect me to believe we're tied? I'm not that dumb. Stop giving me all the shots in your right pocket. I'm sick of it. I'm not going to drop my undies for you just because you let me win."

He ground his teeth against the vivid image in his mind. "If you think I'd give you a win to see you naked, then you underestimate me."

"Then learn to chase down a ball or two because I'm not going to sleep with you if you let me win."

Her voice joined the likes of his own, Aaron's, Brian's and Michaels. The roar of doubt and insecurity drowned all other sound from his brain. All he could hear was Michael's voice telling him he'd never make another major tournament without the assistance of some serious drugs and a miracle.

"Fuck, Izzy. Don't you think if I could return on that side I would?" He tossed his racket and ran his hands through his hair. "I would love to chase down your returns and see what you're really made of. But I can't. I'm done, Izzy. Shit, at this rate, I'll be lucky to get a job as a tennis pro." When she still stared at him in confusion, he repeated himself. "I'm done. I'll give it another month, but in all likelihood, I can't play tennis anymore."

Izzy considered Jason for several moments before speaking. "Can we get back to the game now that you're done feeling sorry for yourself?"

His brow furrowed as he blinked several times. "Didn't you hear me?"

"Oh, I heard you." She shrugged and added, "I just don't believe in wallowing."

"Wha—"

She splayed her hands to stop him. "Before we get into another full blown fight, let me ask you this. Since you've been back at physical therapy, what have you focused your brain power on?"

"Getting better so I can get back to what I do. My livelihood. My life."

"Since when did you make tennis your whole life? My father was like that, and it nearly killed me. The need to be perfect. What everyone will think. It doesn't matter."

"This from the woman who spent the last thirteen years hiding from a racket."

She cringed as the jibe hit. "You have a point." She looked around at the scattered balls. "But at least I can face the demons, thanks to you. You plan on hiding behind your injury for much longer?"

"This should be good." He crossed his arms. "I guess you have a theory."

She shifted her weight from one foot to another. "Just this. You're an amazing player. Outside of all this fame bullshit, you're terrific. They used to call you the Tiger of tennis. When did you give up being that? If you're still in recovery, then fair enough. But what I'm seeing in your eyes, every time I hit to your right, isn't pain, at least not all pain. It's fear. What do you plan to do about it?"

He stared at her and wondered why she saw to his soul when everyone else skimmed the surface. Why, she, of all people, could see him so clearly. The answer wasn't one he was ready to swallow. At least not yet. He picked up his racket, moving back to the baseline. Tossing her a ball, he called out, "Forty — thirty. Advantage, Connors."

****

"Are you sore?"

Izzy's eyes snapped from the page of her book to peer at Jason in the balcony doorway. "A little. I'm sure it'll be worse tomorrow."

"I can guarantee it. You want a massage?"

She barked out a laugh. "Is that a tried and true Jason Cartwright seduction tactic?"

He grimaced. "Would you hold it against me if I said yes?"

"Well, at least you're honest. I'm choosing to look at it as flattery."

"I owe you a thank you."

"Yeah well, I owe you an apology. I've been a royal bitch."

"I've seen worse.

She put her book on her lap and eyed him up and down. "How's the knee?" She watched as he rotated his leg.

"Truth? I'm a little sore, but I feel great. First time anybody's forced me to use my knee in weeks."

"Everyone let you get away with feeling sorry for yourself, huh?"

He rubbed his jaw. "Everyone except you."

She grinned. "Glad to be of service." She sobered and added, "You're better than that, Jason. You never used to let anyone dictate to you what you could and couldn't do. You shouldn't start now."

"I think I've had enough self-reflection for one night." He eased himself onto a stool. "What prompted you to play today?"

Her heart beat a rapid beat in her chest as she considered her answer. "I just needed to hit a few." At his raised eyebrow she sighed. "I've been like a pressure cooker for years. Today, my little whistle sang."

"When I gave you the racket earlier, you looked scared. What changed?"

She figured she might as well tell him the truth. She'd forced honesty out of him. He deserved a little reciprocation. "I realized today I've been hiding most of my life. Make that all of my life. I'm carrying around a lot of resentment about it."

"This have to do with your dad?"

"The day he died, I had a fight with him. I was pitching a fit because I was hurt and didn't want to play. I've never lost my temper like that before. I ended up playing. But as I did, Dad had a heart attack in the stands."

"Shit, I'm sorry, Izzy."

"He died that night. I've carried that blame around for years. Until today."

"His death wasn't your fault."

She shrugged. "Yeah, I know. I've always known. Didn't stop the guilt. Afterward, I lost it. I couldn't function for weeks. The press was there, the whole team saw it, saw my meltdown."

"That's why the press makes you so crazy now?"

She nodded. "Once I sold some photos, I spent years praying no one would put the pieces together and ask questions."

"Now I get the name Z Con."

"It's silly, I know. But once I hired Simon, he thought it would be a great way to build in anonymity and buzz all at once. Great marketing he called it."

Arms crossed over his chest, he leaned back on the stool. "While we're on the subject, what in the world were you thinking going out with that douche bag?"

She dropped her head in her hands to stifle the giggle and scrubbed her hands over her face. "I know. We only went out a few times. Going out with him just seemed like a good idea at the time. You know I broke up with him, and he refused?"

"Smart guy. I wouldn't let you go either."

Not sure how to take the blatant flirting, Izzy changed the subject. "You got a phone call earlier, is everything okay?"

Faint color tinged his cheeks. "Why would you think anything's wrong?"

"Your energy. You're still tense around the mouth. If it's none of my business, just tell m—"

Mischief hugged his words. "You spend a lot of time staring at my lips?"

Shit. "Yes. I mean no. I mean, with the photo shoots, I—uh, in the past few weeks, I've spent a lot of time looking at you, capturing your moods etc." She was glad she'd put on long sleeves before coming out onto the deck. Despite the warmth of his embrace, cool air danced across her skin, and her hairs rose in response. What were gentle summer breezes in Pasadena were magnified tenfold at the beach. She moved from the settee to the railing and stared up at the stars.

"No need to worry about me. It was just something I had to take care of."

"Sorry for prying. My first thought when someone has a problem is how I can fix it. What's the solution?" She shrugged and turned back to look at the surf. "I know that's a typical male response. Most women want to talk it out. Not me. I prefer action, something solid."

"You like to take care of things. Nothing wrong with that. But who takes care of St. Izzy?" As he asked the soft question, he moved behind her to envelop her in his masculine warmth.

Warm liquid pleasure flowed through her muscles and eased her tired joints into a languorous state. You can take care of St. Izzy anytime. Pulling the air brake on her runaway train of thought, Izzy cleared her throat and tried to think clearly.

She tried for cheery. Cheery meant she could pretend he didn't have an effect on her. "Whatever's got you bummed, maybe I have a solution. And if not a solution, I have a shovel or two."

"You would really help me move a body?" His sexy smile was evident in his voice.

"Izzy Connors, problem solver at your service." With every loosened muscle, she tried not to moan with the pleasure zinging over her synapses. "Picture the marketing logo, me with a shovel and a grin."

His thumb traced circular patterns along the column of her neck and paused at the nape of her hair. If she'd been in the mood to lie to herself, she would pretend the shiver was a result of the chill, not the pleasure patterns Jason's hands wove on her neck and shoulders.

"I can see the campaign now. I'll keep you in my rolodex for the paparazzi."

"I never really thought about how all the trappings of fame must affect you. They're a major pain in the ass huh? I can't even imagine it."

"Trust me, you don't want to imagine it."

She turned to face him. "It doesn't ever get easier, does it? The people hiding in the bushes, coming up to you during dinner. I mean a normal life is hard enough without cameras following you everywhere."

Even though she'd turned to face him, he didn't release her. He drew nearer, warming and mingling the air they breathed. "The whole world watches and waits for you to screw up. It's a lot of pressure."

Gravel weighed his voice down. "You want to save me from the evil paparazzi, St. Izzy?"

Her skin prickled at his suggestive smile, she muttered, "Something tells me you don't need saving."

His hands slid from their position on her shoulders, smoothing out the curves of her back and coming to rest in the dimples of her lower back, just before no man's land. By reflex or by design, his hands pulled her in and steadied her more firmly against his wall of a chest.

Hard solid planes of muscle surrounded her, enveloped her. He drowned all reason, and every excuse she had for not taking what she wanted melted away.

She told herself she should make some glib comment to dissipate the tension. She should remove herself from the embrace before she made an idiot of herself. She should ask him to let her go and she'd be safe, happy, sheltered.

She tipped her head up and brushed his lips with hers. For the second time in her life, Izzy was lost.

At first, he seemed content to let her take the lead. He made no move to take the kiss deeper, allowed her to explore at her own pace. Nevertheless, when she leaned in, wrapped her arms around his neck and brushed her breasts against him, his calloused hands tightened at her waist as he pulled her core against his heat. Angling his head, his tongue probed her parted lips, demanding something deeper, more primal.

Izzy didn't recognize the mewling sound coming from her own throat, but she recognized the growl in Jason's throat for what it was. Desire. Possession.

Need swirled. Unable to sate the clawing heat burning at her core, she tried to get closer.

He was the one to break the kiss. Harsh rapid breaths poured out of him. "Damn, Izzy. You're killing me."

Izzy licked a patch of skin on his neck and savored the salty taste of him. "Mmm—hmm…"

For every kiss she planted along his neck and collar bone, he responded by squeezing his large hands around her ample bottom. "Sweetheart, the last thing I want to do is stop you, but maybe we should go—"

She ignored his words and rubbed herself against the thick pulsing heat in his jeans. Feeling bold, she removed one arm from around his neck, bringing her hand around between them, encircling his erection with her fingers.

A stream of creative four letter words streamed out of Jason's mouth as his right hand abandoned its post on her ass to move to her breast, thumb deftly stroking her nipple though her blouse.

"Baby, we should really go inside, we don't even have to go upstairs, I have a spare bedroom—ah, honey, you keep that up, and I'm not going to last very—ah shit…"

Unable to shake the need for him, and missing the delicious tingling sensation from his hand on her breast, she resisted his attempts to tug her inside.

He placed both hands on either side of her face, he held her gaze for several seconds. "You're sure?"

At her nod, he bent his head, his lips ravaged hers in what she could only call a kiss of promise. His tongue tasted and teased, explored just past her lips and withdrew until she knew he meant to drive her mad.

Hands still on her face, he urged her backwards until her back hit the back of the railing.

Lifting his lips off hers, he smiled. "Hold tight, sweetheart."

Following directions, she wound her arms around him. His large hands took hold of her bottom, and he picked her up, urging her legs around his waist. He placed her on the railing, and his hands went to her breasts, never breaking the connection of their lips.

Deft fingers made quick work of the front clasp on her bra. He unhooked it, but didn't bother to take it off. Izzy grasped his thick hair in attempt to get him to deepen the kiss, but he wouldn't let her take control. He took his time and tasted.

Fire roared deep inside her, and she wondered how she could have gone almost her whole adult life and never felt like this before. Both his hands took a slow path from her flat belly and inched up to breasts that ripened for him, full and heavy. His thumbs traced the undersides of her breasts wrenching a gasp from her throat.

He clasped his large hand over her breast and gently kneaded. Delicious sensations zinged through every cell and traveled at rapid speed to the core of her femininity. "Oh God, Jason."

He nipped her bottom lip to silence her. "Easy baby, we don't want to wake Nick." Removing his hands, he once again lifted her in his arms. When he put her down again, they were secluded further back on the balcony. From there, no curious onlookers on the trails could see them. If Nick came downstairs for anything, he couldn't see them from the sliding door. They were alone, secluded in the shadows.

After settling her back down, his hands flew to the buttons of her top. Undone, he opened the front panels exposing her breasts to moonlight and air.

"Good God, you're beautiful."

Urged on by his mumbled love words and the rhythmic pulsing of her inner core, Izzy tugged at the hem of his polo shirt, pulling it past his already tousled blond locks. Bronzed muscles gleamed under the moonlight.

For a moment, she could only stare at the broad shoulders before her, not believing she was actually there, in Jason's arms about to live out every fantasy she'd ever had.

He dipped his head, and laved the tip of her right breast. When she gasped his name, he moved to the other one, paying them equal homage.

Scoring her hands on his back, Izzy rode the climbing peak of pleasure, praying, begging it wouldn't stop.

Jason traced kisses from her breast, up the column of her throat before reclaiming her lips for his own, his strong hands gripped the hem of her skirt, shifting the folds of fabric until they hit mid-thigh. While the fabric stopped its ascent, his hands didn't slow theirs. Calloused fingers traced a pattern over her inner thighs until they reached the satin of her panties.

He lifted his head from hers, his eyes darkened to almost black. "Do you want me to stop?"

Surprised, Izzy blinked several times. "No. God—don't—stop… "

A slow smile spread across his face as he continued to hold her gaze. His thumbs traced a pattern at the edge of her panties. Unhurried and languorous. As if he had all the time in the world. He held her gaze as his thumbs hooked under the elastic and came into contact with her slick folds.

Izzy's eyes slammed shut upon his first stroke, before opening wide again. "Mmm, Jason, please—I…"

"So—wet…"

"Jason—I—need—"

"More…"

Chapter Twenty-Five

Jason hooked a thumb under the band of her silken panties and slid them down to gain better access to Izzy's silken folds. God, she was pretty, every inch of her.

He gritted his teeth and fought for control. Every instinct begged him to unbutton his jeans and bury himself to the hilt. With every murmur and mew from her, his blood surged and throbbed through lust-thickened veins.

"Jason..."

He nipped at her full bottom lip and relished in the sweet taste of her. "Mmmm?"

"I want—"

Smiling, he slid a finger into her tight channel. "I think I know what you want..."

A long moan escaped from her throat, and her tight core continued to slicken around his finger. Shit. Any more of this, and he'd lose control and slide himself inside of her before she was fully ready for him. He'd waited fifteen years to have her. He could wait another few minutes. Or, at least until she crashed over the peak she flirted with for the past several minutes.

"Baby, you feel so good." With every lick and love bite, her body responded as if she'd been made for him. He traced a path from her neck to a peaking chocolate-covered nipple. He rubbed a thumb across the peak and watched, fascinated, as the tiny nub hardened with arousal.

"Mmm." He leaned over her and moistened the smooth tip with his tongue. Sweet and rich, he couldn't get enough. He nuzzled, tasted, and suckled. Moving over to the other peak, he laved and paid worship at the ripe mounds. He'd fantasized about the taste of her for so long. Unable to wait any longer, he paused at her breast, unable to move away.

He struggled for control against the painful surge of blood in his erection, he ignored the screaming voice in his head. Rush, Hurry, Inside. Inside her now!

He anchored her thighs to the rail and kneeled before his promised land. Her soft petals beckoned him. As he darted his tongue to trace over her pleasure center, her hips rose and bucked under him.

He gripped her tighter, kissing the inside of her thigh. The low growl in his throat restricted his breathing. "Gorgeous, you taste incredible." He wasted no time acquainting himself with every hidden nook and fold. His tongue traced a path to her clit and only paused to pay homage with light circular motions. He stopped just short of direct simulation.

"Jason, don't tease me!"

He chuckled when she tugged his hair and pulled him closer to her, urging him on. On his upstroke, his tongue traveled the length of her silken folds, flattening against her clit, only pausing to tease the bundle of nerves.

On the down stroke, he explored the cave of her femininity as far as he could go, savoring the flavor of her, which beckoned him to taste, to explore, to brand. He repeated the routine, and only stopped to alter it when he slid a finger into her slick channel, mimicking the ancient rhythm his dick screamed to partake in.

Finally, his hands felt the telltale quiver in her inner thighs. Felt her whole body tense. Heard the harsh ragged breaths tear from her. He slipped another finger inside her, but didn't let up on the steady rhythm, in, out, in, out.

He didn't want her moans to carry upstairs and wake Nick, so he swiftly changed positions, and moved up her body to clamp his mouth over hers and absorb her cries. Feeling the gentle, pulsing spasms around his fingers, he used his thumb to stroke the concentrated bud of nerves. Once, twice, again a third time. All the while massaging the soft weight of her breast.

To tease her, he slowed his fingers, wanting to draw out her response. His thumb stopped, and she rewarded him with a raw moan that told him everything he needed to know. She was hotter than any woman he'd ever met. "You like that, princess?" he mumbled against her lips.

She answered with a moan.

He smiled. "Oh, no, you'll have to tell me."

She gave a choked cry on a breathy moan. "Yes. Yes, I like it. Just please—"

He nipped her lower lip, then used the tip of his tongue to salve the tiny wound. "What the lady wants, the lady gets.

He returned to her clit and circled the tiny bud, gently applying pressure. He murmured coaxing words in her ear as he urged her to relax. "Easy does it, baby. Just relax and let me love you." Gently retracting and inserting his fingers, he kept a steady pace, until the slick muscles of her core began to milk his fingers, pulsing, seeking. His body quivered in answering time, begging for release. Screamed for it.

He felt the trembling in her legs and coaxed her onward, determined to bring her to a shattering peak before he took. Before he buried himself so far into her tight sheath, he'd never be able to separate from her again.

Izzy's head snapped back, and her legs locked around him. "Jason—Oh my—" On a gasp, she came apart again, pouring liquid heat over his fingers.

Spent, she sagged against him. He held her shaking form, anchored her to him and placed kisses on her head.

After several moments, she lifted her head to stare at him. "What have you done to me?"

The corner of his mouth tipped up. "Nothing you didn't like." His voice softened, and his fingers moved within her flesh. "You feel okay baby?"

She didn't say anything, but raised her hips in time to his movements. God save him. He could spend the next several years exploring every inch of her and never get bored.

"You're not too tired to—" He didn't get a chance to finish his thought, before a beaming smile spread across her face.

"I've been waiting for this since the moment I met you."

Her hands shook as she went for his belt. He attempted to help her with his free hand, but she brushed him away. The determined look on her face told him he was in for trouble. When she unbuckled his pants, she didn't bother to free him from the confines of his jeans, but instead shoved her hand inside and encircled his rigid length.

He hissed a breath and counted to five. When the counting did nothing to quell his body's careen toward complete release, he tried to going for ten. He almost made it too, until her silken finger discovered the wet drop at the tip begging for attention.

He muttered a curse as his hips bucked in response to her searing touch. A knowing smile hinted at the corner of her lips.

Eyes heavy lidded, she used her finger to spread the dew across his straining head.

"Izzy, God—"

"Jason..." She pumped the length of him before shifting her hand further down to massage his balls.

Eyes crossed, he hissed out a halt. "Izzy, wait. If you—" He squeezed his eyes shut and allowed her one more pump before he halted her hand with his. Peeling open his eyes, he anchored one arm around her wrist and drew nearer to her.

The sight of her ripped a groan from his chest. She was so responsive, so wet. She looked so hot, wanton. He dipped his head to trace the tip of his tongue along her lower lip. "Delicious."

A sensual knowledgeable smile spread over her mouth as she took her delicate hands to his hips in an attempt to get his jeans off.

"Here, let me..." He pulled out a condom and placed it on the railing. His hands went to help her with his jeans. "That last button can be tri—" Movement over her shoulder caught his eye.

"Jason, hurry—"

His arms tightened around her. "Shh. Sit still for a second."

His eyes scanned the surf, wanting to convince himself he saw a bird of some sort or a dog. The flickering shine of the moonlight on glass told him his gut instincts were correct.

He gritted his teeth against the mixture of anger and lust. "Baby, listen very carefully. I need you to stand up and keep your face buried in my chest. I'm going to walk us back inside."

Izzy wrinkled her brow and stared at him. "Your chest is not my first choice for where I need to bury my face, but whatever turns you on, I—"

Jason groaned out a laugh. Some idiot with a camera was capturing their every move, but she still managed to make him laugh. For a single second, he considered her offer, but he couldn't compromise her if his gut was right. "I'd prefer you buried your face somewhere other than my chest as well, but I think we have company out on the surf."

"Shit." Izzy tried to whirl in his arms to see what he saw, but Jason kept a tight grip on her shoulders.

"No. You don't want to do that. Let's get inside, and I'll call security."

He knew the moment the enormity of the situation snapped her addled brain back to reality. The sex fueled haze cleared from her gaze, and she went rigid in his arms. "Shit, are you serious? Someone's really out there?"

And then like slugs after the rain, realization crawled on the pavement sucking up the torrents of truth—whoever was out there could have seen everything...Could have photographed...everything.

"As serious as my blue balls right now. Someone's watching us."

Izzy scrambled and squirmed in an attempt to get to the balcony door, but Jason held her tight. Cradling the back of her head in his palm, he began the delicate backwards dance around the deck furniture to the door.

Holding her so close, he could smell the lingering scent of her arousal mixed with the sea air and the sweet jasmine vanilla of her shampoo. Trying to ignore the urging twitch of his erection, he maneuvered them to the glass door.

Once he placed her in the doorway, he settled her away from him. "Go have a hot bath. And, do me a favor, stay away from the windows. The last thing we need is to have some pap hotshot get a grainy photo of you."

Izzy wrapped her arms around her body, unable to ward off a shiver. "What are you going to do?"

"Give whoever's down there a one way ticket to dropping the soap."

Chapter Twenty-Six

Sexual frustration didn't suit him. Every nerve ending Jason had was raw and ragged with lust, longing and something...deeper. He'd spent the rest of the night trying to find the paparazzi slime on the shores then filing a police report. By the time he made it home and back to Izzy, it was four in the morning and far too late to continue where they'd left off.

Saturday, the magic spell that had cocooned the two of them had evaporated into the night like their stalker. They'd spent the whole day, and most of the night, with Nick, shuttling to and from practice and spending time as a pseudo family.

For the first time in his adult life, he'd felt like an awkward teenager trying to talk to her in the bright light of the morning. Every time they'd caught each other's eye, they were swift to avert their gazes, lest the awkwardness envelop them.

He cared about Izzy more than he ever let himself care about anyone or anything. Jason slid her a glance across the expanse of his car as they drove to Nick's exhibition match. He was a fool if he tried to pretend he wasn't falling for her—again.

He could get used to the early Sunday morning drives to matches. Could get used to the family getting ready to cheer Nick on, or maybe himself. He'd never been too close to anyone. And judging by the sleepless nights, sweaty palms and ticking bomb in his chest, the whole falling in love thing might kill him.

The police and cleaners had finished up with her house, so after the match, they'd be going home. No more Nick. No more Izzy. As if they'd never been his.

He didn't like the hollow feeling in his stomach. They'd only been around for two days, but he would miss them. He'd never known staying home and playing board games could be more fun than going out on the scene, but it had been.

Izzy caught his gaze and smiled tentatively. Something wicked in her gaze had him convinced she and Nick had conspired against him to win at monopoly and cards last night. He'd have to play them again to be sure.

Though, cheating antics or no, nothing surprised him more than how easily Nick and Izzy's tight circle of closeness expanded to include him. He hadn't felt the sense of family in so long, he'd almost forgotten his need to belong.

Izzy smiled at something Nick said and turned around to talk to him. Jason knew she hadn't forgotten about Thursday or Friday, but at least she didn't have the weary look around her eyes any more. If he'd been able to give her some peace for a couple of days, it was enough.

When they arrived at the country club, Nick unloaded all of his equipment and headed to the locker room to join his team. He got about five feet before he came back and gave Jason a long look. "Uhm, thanks and stuff."

"For the practice? Any time. I should thank you. I needed the court time."

Nick shook his head and tossed a furtive glance toward Izzy who spoke to Jessica on the phone. "No. I meant for Mom. You kept her from losing her shit." He sucked in a deep breath, then he looked away. "It was cool of you."

Jason watched Nick walk away and didn't know what to do with the flood of emotion. One second, he'd felt good and even-keeled and in control. The next, he felt touched and emotional.

Once Izzy hung up with Jessica, he escorted her to the stands. They found three seats for themselves and Jessica when she arrived.

"So are you going to tell me what he said or not?" Izzy asked.

"He just wanted to thank me for the help with his forehand volley."

She looked at him as if unsure whether to believe him, eventually nodding. "I'm glad he said thank you. Him being a teenager, you never know these days."

Jason laughed. "I'm sure he has his teenage moments, but he's a great kid. I don't know how you survived all by yourself." He still couldn't picture a barely legal Izzy trying to care for a baby, with Sabrina no kind of help at all. Plenty of women coped all the time. But for Nick and Izzy to turn out so well proved her resilience.

"I had help." She shrugged and opened up her program. "You would have done the same."

Nick's match didn't start till the third round, so Jason sat back to watch the matches, the adrenaline, the improvisation reminded him of his youth. A few of the players were really good. He could see their future potential in each of their strokes. One or two were completely outmatched, but these were high school players, after all.

Midway through the second match, a commotion at the bottom of the stairs took their attention from the matches. He peeked over the edge of the stands and saw the brunette curls whisk by security. Sabrina.

She also saw him and called out, "How's my money maker?"

Shit. On his right, Izzy exhaled a sharp breath. "What the hell is she doing here?"

He needed to get rid of her before she ratted him out to Izzy. "Did you tell her we'd be here?"

Izzy groaned. "My bad. I put his schedule on the fridge. I didn't think she'd actually show up to one. She never has before."

He patted her hand. "Relax. I'll deal with her before Nick even makes it out."

"Are you sure? She's not really your problem."

Oh, he was sure. "I'll be back in no time." He maneuvered through the stands and was on Sabrina before she had a chance to protest. Wrapping a hand around her wrist, he tugged her down the stairs away from nosy eyes and ears.

As he pulled her through the country club's gates away from the courts, he picked up the faint hint of alcohol. It was too early in the morning for drinking. But not like he hadn't showed up to many a meet, pores oozing alcohol.

Once he had her in the lot, he pulled her to a stop. "What the hell is wrong with you? You can't let the kid have one good thing?"

She stared up at him and tried to brush past him to go back inside. "What the hell? You think because you're playing happy family with Izzy and my son, you're now an expert on parenting? He's my kid, I'm going in."

He blocked her path. "No you're not, Sabrina. You've never cared before, why would you start now?"

She raised a hand as if to slap him, and he caught her wrist before she could make impact. His lips formed a smile, but he kept his voice flat and cool. "You think you can try the shit you pulled on Nick with me?" He released her. "You won't like the results, Sabrina. Walk away."

Stricken, she stared at him. "What do you mean what I pulled on Nick?"

Did she really think she could lie and get away with it? "I know you hit him."

Her eyes darted up to the stands. Typical Sabrina, worried about how to cover her own ass. "Yeah, Izzy knows too. Honestly, I'm amazed you're still breathing. If I were her, your body would be in the middle of the desert by now."

She sputtered. "He pretty much called me a tramp. My own son. What the hell else should I have done? You act like Izzy never spanked him for anything. Kids like him need discipline."

"I think you know there's a difference. You hit him out of anger. He's too old to be spanked." Confused, he asked, "You didn't get Izzy's messages?"

She chewed her bottom lip. "I didn't listen to them. I went home and saw the cops so I split. I figured she wanted to let me know not to go home."

Jason shook his head and made to go back to the stands. "Not your home. Leave the kid alone, Sabrina. If you don't, you'll deal with me."

Hands fisted at her sides, she yelled after him. "You know, Jase, you act awfully high and mighty considering." She teetered and waved her arms to steady herself. "What do you think your precious Izzy would say if I told her you paid me to shut up?"

Hot fury turned the icicles in his blood to steam. "You and I both know I only paid you because Nick is in danger. Danger you put him in. You think Izzy isn't going to turn loose every lawyer she has available when she finds out the break-in was your doing?" He shoved his hands in his pockets. "Do us both a favor. Take the money you have and walk away."

Her hands trembled as they grabbed at the front of his sweater. "You don't understand. Tony, my dealer, he's charging me interest. I need to get out from under his thumb. He'll kill me if I don't give him the rest of the interest."

"How is it you never think to walk away? You could have couriered the money to him. You chose to stick around." He shook his head. "I'm not giving you another penny."

Sabrina's pretty features contorted into something hollow and ugly. "I'll tell her. I will. You have to give me that money."

"You tell her I gave you the cash, and I tell her you were behind the break-in." He shrugged. "Looks like we've reached an impasse."

"I thought you'd do anything to protect your son."

He stopped, but didn't turn around. She's lying. "We always used a condom. I wasn't dumb enough to touch you unprotected Sabrina."

She laughed. "As if they always work. Not to mention, you were too drunk and out of it to put one on."

"Izzy said the math was wrong."

"Yeah, but she doesn't know about you coming back does she?"

He half turned and gave her a benign smile. "Too bad you've already cried wolf before. I know better than to believe your lies." He left her standing there and made it back to the stands in time for the third match. He swallowed the guilt he felt when he saw Izzy's sunny smile. He couldn't tell her now. Soon. I'll tell her soon.

As the match started, he and Izzy both inched forward in their seats. He willed Nick to remember everything they'd talked about and stay relaxed.

Nick's first serve was firm and strong, but Michon was also quick and athletic. He chased everything Nick put over the net. Izzy watched silently, but Jason guessed by her clenched hands and the grim set of her mouth, she might be more nervous than Nick.

Jesus. Is this how being a parent felt? Aching pit of the stomach, jumping nerves, worry over their happiness. He didn't think he could take the stress. He never got nerves before his own matches, but now his stomach was a butterfly exhibit.

Nick went to the net for his forehand volley, but his feet were off, so Michon was able to return the ball and win the game. The opponent was good, but Jason knew Nick was better. Nick just needed to know he was better.

****

Something wasn't right. Izzy could feel it. When Jason came up the stairs without Sabrina, she'd been so relieved, she hadn't focused on it. But, now that the boys were taking a break, she could see the tight lines of tension around his mouth.

"I see you came back."

"Of course I came back. Did you think I'd up and leave in the middle of the match?" He shook his head before she could answer. "Never mind. I think I know the answer."

She sighed as guilt and uncertainty washed over her. "It has nothing to do with you. Every time I see her it just does that to me. I'm sorry."

He might have said, "It's okay," but the lines of tension deepened around his mouth. She wanted to pry, but had a feeling it wouldn't do her any good. She didn't want to get into another fight about Sabrina during Nick's match.

Nick and Michon came back onto the courts and Izzy resumed her usual pose on the edge of her seat. She was so tense, she almost jumped out of her seat when she felt Jason's hand on her back rubbing slow circles between her shoulders.

She managed to relax back in her seat at Nick's first serve. Without warning, once the serve was over the net, Nick charged forward and returned a forehand volley into the left corner. The referee announced the point to Nick. Wearing a grin, Nick glanced into the stands.

Izzy beamed and clapped. He was so beautiful, her boy. For all the trouble Sabrina had brought into their life, at least she'd brought Nick into the world. He was Izzy's universe, and she loved to see him happy.

She looked at Jason as he returned her grin, but there was something else in his eyes she couldn't read. Tenderness there and…something else. "You taught him that. He's usually afraid to go to the net."

"I taught him, but he's the one who tried it." The pride in his voice, unmistakable.

For the first time in his playing career, Nick won a match against Adam Michon. Izzy swore Jason cheered louder than anyone else, including herself and Jessica combined.

When he could, Nick ran up into the stands to join them. He even let Izzy hug him, something he usually tried to dodge in front of his friends. Ah, the world of teenage angst. After all, what kid wanted his mom to hug him in public?

What surprised her was the hug Nick gave Jason. When she saw them embrace, she knew she deluded herself by trying to pretend there wasn't the possibility Jason was Nick's father. Side by side, the resemblance was uncanny. She'd have to find Sabrina and pin her down.

On the way out of the stands, Jason turned to her. "This was fun today."

For the first time in weeks, she'd been able to relax and enjoy herself for a couple of hours. "Yeah it was. Thanks for hanging out with us, and for everything else."

He nodded, and an odd smile quirked his lips. "So I know your gallery opening is next week."

She groaned. "Don't remind me. I still have so much to do. I'm a bit behind since I haven't been at the house or studio the past few days."

He stopped her for a moment to let Nick and Jessica walk ahead to the parking lot. "I was hoping you'd let me come to the opening."

Let him? "Uhm, well yeah you can come. Why would I stop you?"

A long steady breath escaped his lips, and he gave her a bemused look. "I know we haven't had a chance to really talk about Friday, or about that damned picture of Sabrina and I…"

She cringed and shifted uncomfortably. "Yeah, about that. I overreacted about the photo. It just brought back a million memories I didn't want to deal with. You've been great to us for the past few days, and you didn't have to be."

"No, I deserved the response. I'm working at being more honest more often, so I should have told you she came to see me." Jason took another quick breath. "But I don't want to talk about that."

She raised her eyebrows.

"Uh, damn, this is harder than I thought it would be. But, I, uh, I don't want to just go to the opening. I'd like to take you to the opening. As your date."

Her eyes widened, heart skipping like river rocks across water. "My date?"

"Yes. Your date. You do know what a date is right?"

She didn't bother to tell him it had been so long since she'd been on a real date she'd forgotten the rules of conduct. "Yes, I know what a date is." Barely. "I think I can manage that."

The sexy smile he often displayed was back and turned into a full scale grin that deepened the creases around his eyes. "Good." He started walking toward the parking lot to meet Nick and Jessica. "And Izzy?"

"Yeah?"

"I promise I'll show this time."

Chapter Twenty-Seven

Izzy hiked up her dress to step into the black strappy heels. Her nerves were having a dance party with butterflies in her stomach. She fastened the teardrop chain, courtesy of the Dubois family. The diamond hit her at the lowest point of the V-neck dress, which unfortunately was very near to her navel. I never should have let Jessica talk me into buying this thing.

She fastened the dangling diamond earnings to her ears and examined her image. She fixed a stray hair and went in the family room to wait for Jason. She told herself she wasn't watching and waiting for the pot to boil. "Relax, Izzy. He'll show today." She told herself.

Before an event, she was always too high strung to deal with people, so Nick and Jessica left early. That was their routine. And because she would have to stay late, Nick usually stayed at a friend's or at Jessica's. Simon would meet her at the event. He claimed he had no acrimony after their breakup, but their relationship still wasn't back to normal.

Thankfully, Sabrina hadn't made another appearance since Nick's match. Although, part of Izzy wished she had shown. They had some ground to cover about Nick and Jason. Uncertainty accompanied the now familiar tingling in her spine when she thought about Jason and Nick.

When she realized she had nothing to do except wait for Jason, she sat on the couch and fiddled with her clutch. Glancing at the clock, she tried to quell the anxiety the last two weeks produced.

She reminded herself that the police were driving by the house every night. Jason had helped install a new security system as well as provided very discreet security for Nick at school. He'd done so much for the two of them in the last two weeks. Made sure they were safe. The Jason she'd come to know in the past few weeks was very different than the one she'd seen in the media over the years.

Maybe the bad boy was the persona and this was the real Jason. This was certainly the Jason she'd loved years ago. She was so busy in her own musings, she barely heard the insistent knock at the front door. Only after a more pronounced knock did she recognize the sound. She took a deep breath and checked her image in the hall mirror one more time before she answered.

Jason, in his Armani suit splendor, stood in the doorway giving her his best prom date grin. Dark eyes tracked over her body, and she felt his raw hunger for a split second before his mask of refined class slipped back into place. Throat dry, she tried to smile and felt her lips quiver. "You look amazing."

The grin on his face stayed intact, but there was a predatory gleam in his eyes that made her legs wobbly. He took her hand and pulled her toward him. "That's my line. Except, I would have delivered the line with more conviction." His right hand came up to caress her face, and he tilted her chin up. "I would have added ravishing." He kissed her left cheek just near her lips. "I would have added gorgeous." He mimicked the petal soft kiss on her other cheek.

He tilted his head, and as if drawn by a magnet, she did the same in the opposite direction, expecting the kiss, wanting the kiss, needing the kiss. To her frustration, his lips hovered over hers for several beats, and his lips curved into that lazy smile of his. "Or maybe, I would have just said, Wow."

When he backed away, Izzy stifled a groan of frustration. The tingling in her belly tracked its way somewhere distinctively lower, and she felt the need to sit down before her knees gave out.

She searched her mind for something sophisticated to say, but couldn't think of one thing. Speechlessness was not a usual affliction for her. He was good, and she was out of her league. For once, she gave herself permission to just enjoy it. Who knew how long she'd be able to feel like the most desirable woman on earth? "Wow sounds good. I might use that sometime."

He stood close enough for her to feel the chuckle rumbling in his chest. "I'll give you licensing to use it, but you will have to pay."

She smiled up at him. "I'm a shrewd business woman, you know. I don't want to over pay for licensing."

He kissed her cheek again. "I think we can work out a fair price." Taking her hand, he tugged her to the driveway. "Come on. We can't have the lady of honor arrive late to her own party."

"You're right, Paris Hilton I'm not."

Instead of the two-seater Porsche she'd figured he'd drive, or the Mercedes he'd driven the previous week, a limo sat in the driveway. "Jason, what is this?"

"I figured you should probably act like the star you are, so I wanted you to arrive in style. Too much?" His brow wrinkled in worry.

His concern touched her and made her want to bubble up with laughter at the same time. "A little. This event is just an intimate gallery opening. I'm not a star."

"That's where you're wrong. You're a star to me." He escorted her into the back of the limo and slid in behind her.

Izzy had been in a limo before with wedding parties and events like that, but she'd never splurged for anything as nice as this limo with its flat screen televisions and a bar stocked with Cristal.

If this is how the other half lived, she could get used to it.

****

Jason didn't know how he would keep his hands off of Izzy. Holding his champagne glass, he watched her smile and chat with members of the press and the guests that had poured in to see the show. To the casual observer she would appear poised and elegant seamlessly floating from guest to guest, easily engaging in conversation. But he knew differently. He saw the deep intake of breath, the way she steadied her center before she faced each new person.

With every move of her body, her dress flowed around her. The way her dress sat on her slim shoulders gave the illusion it could fall off at any moment if not for the lush curves of her breasts and her ass. When she'd opened the door at the house, the vision of her in brilliant white had nearly blinded him.

As far as he could tell, she wasn't wearing a bra, and he'd been almost unable to stop the itching need to palm her breasts and test their lush weight. The diamond chain she wore around her neck only accentuated their full rise.

For once, she'd worn her hair down. The waves gently framed her face and shoulders, flowing down her back. The combination of her thick black hair, her stark white dress and dark luminous skin forced all the air from his lungs. And he wasn't the only one staring.

Every time a male member of the press clamored to get close to her, Jason had to quell the jealous urge to shove the guy through a wall. And that was the least of what he wanted to do to that slick manager of hers.

For several hours, he'd watched Simon slip his hands to Izzy's waist and urge her one direction or another. When Simon leaned in to brush Izzy's hair off her shoulder and whisper at her ear. Jason drained his glass and tried to find something to take his mind off the sight of the interloper.

He'd been trying to give her space to do what she needed to do. After all, she was technically working. Every half hour or so, he made his way over to her to make sure she didn't need anything. Or sometimes just to tell her she was beautiful. But for the most part, he stayed out of her way. This was her show, not his.

Because the press was there, he wanted to make sure this night was about her. Not about his tabloid exploits. Not about his attempt at a comeback. Not about anything that didn't have to do with her. Their arrival together hadn't gone unnoticed by the press, but when they'd attempted to talk to him, he'd always directed the conversation toward Izzy.

For the most part, it seemed to work. He'd deal with any fall out tomorrow when it came. He noticed Nick and Jessica hiding out in a corner, and he went over to join them. After all, the three of them were the misfits of the guests. Neither of them belonging there. Nick looked young Hollywood hip but mildly uncomfortable in his suit. Jessica had her green and blue mane in a bun and wore a simple black dress without a tattoo in sight, looking serene and pretty in her simplicity.

And of course there was him. He was really the one that didn't belong here. He'd been part of this world for most of his life, but he'd never been accepted. Never wanted to be accepted. He always did the opposite of what was expected of him.

Nick brightened up when he saw him. "Dude, my mom's photos are making a killing. Jess just took stock. We've sold all but six so far."

Jessica nodded. "Not that you don't already know we've made a ton of sales, seeing as you've bought four so far."

Damn right he'd bought four. He'd have bought another one as well if the mayor hadn't beaten him to the punch. "Guilty as charged. There are a couple of these I've been trying to get my hands on for years."

Nick looked at Jessica. "You think if she sells all of them, she'll be in a good enough mood to buy me that Vespa I asked for?"

Jessica laughed. "Don't push your luck. Not to mention you're still a couple of years shy of being able to drive."

Nick shrugged, but didn't look defeated. "You just wait. I'll wear her down."

Distracted by the sight of Izzy in his peripheral, Jason half smiled at Nick. Something in the determined set of Nick's clenched jaw made his stomach flip. Could Sabrina have been telling the truth?

But he had used a condom. He always had with Sabrina, never trusted her to be faithful. He knew the truth, but it didn't stop him from wondering, almost wishing. The train of his own thoughts surprised him enough that he looked for a way to excuse himself.

As luck would have it, he didn't need one. Simon sauntered toward their general direction. He nodded to Jason. "Cartwright. Nice of you to support your photographer." He gave Jessica the type of empty vacant look reserved for elevator rides. But to Nick he turned a beaming smile, "What's happening, Nicky boy?"

Nick scowled at him. "I hate it when you call me Nicky boy."

Jason was relieved he wasn't the only one not feeling the love for Simon.

Simon blinked several times as if unsure of how to respond. Jessica, sensing his weakness, sprung her attack.

"Don't bother, Nick. This schmuck doesn't understand the finer points of how to talk to people."

Simon turned cool eyes in her direction. "I see you attempted to put yourself together for the event. How does it feel to be without your piercings and combat boots?"

"Probably the same way it feels to walk around without a soul, the way you do."

Jason looked between the two of them. "Look, maybe you guys want to keep your voices down. Today is Izzy's day."

Both turned to him in unison. Jessica's face flushed, and her eyes went wide. Simon's eyes dilated and his breathing turned rapid. Jessica muttered an apology, but Simon didn't bother. He turned his attention to an approaching Izzy, who sent a beaming smile in their direction as she walked by.

Jason would have sworn he caught the moron staring at Izzy's ass. Not that he could fault him. The way the material skimmed over pert roundness—Jason had caught himself staring more than once.

Unfortunately, Nick also noticed Simon's attention to Izzy. Scowling even harder into his glass of soda, he asked, "Do you have to look at her like that?"

In total agreement, Jason picked up another glass of champagne off a passing tray and said, "Tell me about it."

Jessica looked back and forth between the two of them. "I think things are a bit testosterony for my taste. If you'll excuse me…" She abandoned them to follow a tray of canapés. Simon stared after her for a long moment before heading in the opposite direction.

Nick looked up at Jason. "So you gonna ask her out, or what?"

Having just taken a sip of champagne, bubbles tickled his nose, and Jason choked. "What?"

"My mom. Are you going to ask her out? I've seen you guys sniffing round each other."

Somehow this kid always had him off center. "Well, Nick, we are sort of on a date now."

Nick pondered that for a moment then nodded. "Okay, good. She hasn't ripped your head off yet, so that's a good sign, right?"

This kid was too astute for his own good. "Yeah, in my experience it's generally a good sign."

Nick looked over at Izzy. "And she looks happy."

Jason wondered what kinds of things kept Izzy from being happy so he could get rid of all of them. "I want her to be happy."

Nick shifted his eyes from his mother to Jason. "I wouldn't be cool with it if you did something to make her unhappy."

Jason recognized the territorial pissing and half respected it, half wanted to laugh since it was coming from her son, and not her father. "Understood."

Jason spent much of the rest of the opening hanging out with Nick. He talked to the occasional politician and Hollywood type, but funnily enough, he felt most comfortable with the kid. The same kid who pretty much told him if he messed up with Izzy, he was a dead man.

As the last guests made their way out of the gallery, Izzy discussed instructions for shipping with the gallery owner. When she finished, she walked over to him and gave him a brilliant smile. "Thank you so much for hanging out through the whole thing. I know these things can be a bit dull."

He took her hand and pierced her with a look. "First, customary practice is to take your date home at the end of the night and not leave her to hitch her way home. That won't usually get you a second date."

Her laugh was clear and loud and made him want to hug her to him and capture that laugh as his alone. "I suppose that is the custom for dates."

Relief washed over him that she hadn't tried to suggest this wasn't a date. "Yes, it is. Secondly, I love to see you do your thing. Your photos are beautiful. Everyone should appreciate them."

She smiled shyly. "Thank you. Except for everyone to appreciate them, you should have to give up a couple of the ones you bought. Jessica said you bought six."

He shrugged. "Let everyone else get their own. I'm keeping my six."

She laughed and shook her head. He loved her laugh, the way she threw her whole self into it. "Fine, you can keep the ones you bought, but I really must insist you release the ones you've got on order." She spread her arms. "Where are you going to put all of them?"

He knew exactly where they were all going to go. "You let me worry about that."

"Have you seen Jessica? I need her to sign off on some order and delivery forms with the gallery owners before she leaves."

Following her toward the offices and coat check, he asked, "Are you sure she didn't take Nick home?"

She shook her head. "No. Well, yes, she did that earlier. He's got a sleepover with a friend tonight. I saw her come back though."

"I last saw her in the midst of giving Simon a proper what-for about something."

She flashed him a grimace as she searched the main office. "I hope they didn't kill each other. I suppose I should be grateful they didn't get into a bitch fight in the middle of the opening."

He wondered if he should tell her about their earlier sparring match, then thought better of it. Let her believe everything went smoothly. No reason to ruin her image of a perfect evening. "Yep, we'll thank God for small favors."

"I don't know what it is with the two of them. They were never the best of friends, but it's gotten worse of late." She chuckled. "Part of me wants to tell them to either go ahead and shoot each other, or go ahead and sleep together. At least that way, we'll all get some peace."

The clashing images of uptight Simon and punk rock Jessica in flagrante forced a snort of laughter out of his lungs. "Somehow I doubt we—"

A thud from the coat check interrupted him. The two of them exchanged a curious look before simultaneously heading in the direction of the noise. As they approached, the thud turned into a series of thuds and increased in frequency.

Izzy put her hand on the doorknob, and he flashed his out to meet hers. "Iz, wait. We might interrupt someone." He raised his eyebrows to add emphasis to his meaning.

"Oh c'mon, who has sex in the coat check? It's so cliché. I mean—" Her voice cut off abruptly as she swung the door open.

The sight of the broad back of a charcoal gray suit jacket and bare brown male ass wrapped by pale feminine legs greeted them. Eyes squeezed tight, Jessica's head rolled back as she moaned. "Yes, Simon. Harder. Yes—"

Izzy closed the door on a rush of air and avoided his gaze. Shit, was she still hung up on the guy?

Jason cleared his throat and rocked back on his heels. "I'm sorry you had to see that."

Eyes wide, she leveled a gaze up at him. "Are you kidding? This is fantastic." As she pulled him away from the door, she giggled and chattered at high speeds. "They'll finally stop sniping at each other, and he'll finally stop giving me attitude about breaking up with him."

His eyebrows drew in. "So you're not upset?"

"Why would I be?"

Unsure, he rubbed the end of his nose. "I don't know, your best friend and your ex going at it in the coat closet."

"In case you haven't noticed, I'm not with him for good reason—absolutely no chemistry. If they make each other happy, all power to them." She smiled and sidled up to him at the end of the darkened gallery hall. "And, in case you haven't noticed, I came to this event with the world's sexiest man."

"Well I won't argue with a beautiful woman. You and People can't be wrong." He took both her hands and drew her closer. "So, am I to take you home, or am I to take you to Malibu?"

The look she gave him made the blood rush out of his head and zoom about two feet south. "Is that what we're calling it now? Going to Malibu?"

He couldn't help the laugh that burst forth. He shook his head and said, "I guess that is what we're calling it now." Leave it to Izzy to diffuse some of the thick tension that surrounded them.

Turning serious, she gave him a long look and nodded. "Let's go to Malibu."

Chapter Twenty-Eight

"Hey, why so far away?"

Jason bit back a groan as she patted the seat next to her. Everything about her sent a siren call to him. Her perfume, her satiny skin, the rise of cleavage that peeked out above her dress. His fingers and tongue itched to taste and tease and explore. Not to mention plunder and ravage and live out every dirty fantasy he'd ever had about her. If he touched her now, they'd never make it into the house.

He shook his head to clear the lust thickened cobwebs and croaked out, "Not yet, I want to look at you."

She dipped and angled her head, her lips parted in a feminine smile. All the while, she patted the seat again more insistently. "You've been looking at me all night. I want you to touch me."

Damn, he wanted to touch her. His hands ached as they remembered the feel of her full breasts. He wanted to feel her hair through his fingers and kiss the nape of her neck and a slew of other things he wouldn't be able to stop once he started. "And I want to touch you." He shifted to give himself more room in his pants. "I want to take you home and treat you like the princess you are. Not go at it like two teenagers in the back of a Buick."

She considered him, then narrowed her gaze. Delicate French tipped fingers adjusted the material of her dress, bringing the sleeves into perilous danger of slipping off her slender shoulders.

He coughed, desperate to clear an airway to his lungs, as his eyes snapped to the line of material just above her breasts. He prayed and willed it to slip off. His fingers gripped the edge of the leather seat, but he didn't join her. Stubbornly, he set his jaw, and gave her a smile somewhere between wolfish and pained.

Her resulting grin made his dick swell and leap against his trousers. She studied him for a several moments before she shifted to showcase the slit in her dress. Crossing her legs forced the satiny material to fall and reveal a smooth chocolaty expanse of bare leg to mid-thigh, tormenting his imagination. He locked eyes with her, and she cocked her head at him and smiled in invitation.

His already ragged breathing ceased as he watched her slide her dress past the mid-thigh point. One inch, two inches. She kept up the movement, crossed and uncrossed her legs again, and drew his attention to the darkened valley between her legs. Is she wearing underwear? Did she wax?

"Shit." The ragged word rushed through his teeth as he launched out of his seat to join her.

"Little girls who tease get punished."

Her eyes searched his face, a light of mischief danced through her expression. "I'm counting on it."

His response was swift and consumed him. He couldn't hear any of the soft music that played in the back of the limo for the blood rushing in his head. His hands fisted in her hair. He dipped his head and hovered above her lips for several beats. Her mouth parted in open invitation, pink tongue moistening her lower lip.

He tried to be gentle, but one taste of Champagne and chocolate and Izzy, and he forgot all about gentle. He cupped her head and held her in position while he explored every nook and cranny of her mouth with his tongue. Blood rushed and roared, and drove him to brand her, make her his, he didn't know if he could stop even if the limo were on fire.

She clamored to get closer to him, and straddled him to get better access. Her kisses were curious and sensual as she nipped at his lips, and he could have spent the rest of his life kissing her.

Gasping, he fought for control. He broke the kiss and locked eyes with her. Brushing fly-away strands of her hair out of her face, he tucked them behind her ear. "You are so unbelievably beautiful." She dipped her head shyly, but he held her head in place.

"You make me feel beautiful." Breaking eye contact, she looked around. "I think we've stopped."

Reluctant to let her go, he took a deep breath. She was right. The limo had crawled to a stop. "I guess we'll have to wait until we can get inside. Do you think you can wait that long?"

She groaned like a plaintive child forced to wait till Christmas to open her presents. Bending her head, she nipped, then licked his neck. "But I don't want to wait." She moved against the ridge in his trousers, forcing a groan out of his throat.

Shit. Neither did he, but the chauffeur would open the door in a minute so they needed to disengage. With pained reluctance, he shifted her away from him and led her out of the limo. Once inside the house, Jason could feel the tight rein of his control begin to slip and eventually fade away. "Izzy, come here."

****

Izzy had no choice but to obey. Every time Jason spoke her name, delicious tremors took over her nerves. She stepped toward him, her heart pounding in time with each step she took. Thud. Thud. Thud.

When she stood directly in front of him, she could smell a familiar musky scent mixed with cologne. Voice hoarse and thick, she said, "I'm here."

Mouth dry, she peeked her tongue out to moisten her lips. His eyes tracked the travel of her tongue. They clouded, darkened until she couldn't see his pupils. She couldn't help but sway into him, the energy of his body pulled her in.

"Put your arms around my neck." His voice lowered several octaves, and she shivered.

She obliged because it brought her closer to him and there was nothing she wanted more. When he dipped, she swore she'd feel the searing heat of his kiss, but he held back and only brought his lips close enough to tease and commingle their breaths.

In an instant, steel-gripped hands lifted her off her feet and forced her legs around his waist. She felt his hands on her ass and gasped in surprise. He kneaded her flesh bringing her core against his shaft.

"Jason."

"Remember what you did in the limo?"

"Yes, I—"

"Do it again."

Instinctively, she moved against him. Desperate to be closer. Desperate to feel all of him. He dipped his head to kiss her. His tongue teased her lips apart, eager to find its playmate.

She felt them move, and she assumed he directed them toward the back bedroom. However, when he sat and took her with him, she realized they were in the living room. The fire burned strong and high in the fireplace, warming her to the point of overheating. She gave him a quizzical look. "You don't want to go to the bedroom?"

He trailed scorching open-mouthed kisses from her ear down to her neck. "We'll get there." He took a nip out of her neck which sent shivers coursing down her spine. "I've dreamed about you on this couch since I saw you curled on it last weekend."

She felt the heat rise and flush her face. He'd thought about her. Dreamed about her. That thought filled her with feminine power. She rocked her core against him once, then twice, and he bit off a curse. "Damn, Izzy."

She did it again, unable to deny herself the pleasure of feeling the length of him press against her. "Mmm," she moaned, unable to stop touching him.

While she worked on the buttons of his tuxedo shirt, he grabbed fistfuls of hair with both hands, gently tugging her head back to give him better access to her neck. The combination of pleasure and pain sent another shiver through her body. "God, Jason."

He kissed his way back up her throat to her lips. "You like that?"

She muttered a yes, and he did it again with his left hand. His other hand traced a path of heat from her neck down the center of the dress. He alternated murmuring love words and taking nips of her neck, lips, shoulders.

His right hand found its way into the bodice of her dress, and he muttered another curse as he dragged his lips from hers. He took several sharp, ragged breaths. "You've been running around all night without a bra haven't you?"

She gave a slow nod, and he rewarded her with a brief flick of his thumb over her left nipple. Intense pleasure forced a cry from her throat. She wanted to tell him that a bra wasn't the only thing she'd gone without, but she figured he'd find that surprise on his own.

Jason dragged the top of her dress down, and she wiggled to get her arms out of the sleeves. His eyes transfixed on her breasts with such intensity, she wondered if something was wrong. She looked down to see his bronzed hands splayed over her dark skin. His hips rocked, and she smiled. She wondered if she could die from pleasure.

She dragged his shirttails out of his pants and went to work on the rest of his clothes. She unhooked the clasp of his trousers and slid the zipper down. His hands constantly moved and touched, but they jerked to a stop when she slid a hand inside his boxers and released him from the confines.

He sat still for several heart beats as she stroked, jaw clenched. When she stroked him again, he growled out, "Izzy, stop. We should slow down." She could feel his sharp intake of breath when she pumped him again. He growled out another warning before he placed a hand over hers to stop her ministrations. "You're naughty, you know that?"

She almost laughed. If desire weren't pouring through her veins, and the ache at her core so strong she thought she might die from need, she would have. "I want you."

He released her and worked the piles of dress fabric to her legs. Strong, calloused hands grasped her thighs and trailed up her legs. When his fingers traced what would have been her underwear line, his half-lidded gaze widened, and he stared.

"Shit, if I'd have known—"

She rocked her hips against his seeking fingers, needing the penetration, needing the release only he could bring. "What would you have done if you'd have known?"

He smiled, locking his gaze with hers as he slid one finger into her fevered center. Izzy moaned at the penetration. "Jason, what are you doing to me?"

"Teasing," he replied and inserted another finger. He began a steady rhythm, refusing to allow her to take over.

"Please." She tried to drag in a breath. "I don't want to wait anymore."

He chuckled. "Impatient aren't you?"

"Yes." She pulled him to her so she could kiss him.

Grabbing the fabric of her dress, he bunched it together and pulled it up over her head. Completely bare, Izzy felt the prickling unease of exposure, and she wanted him just as naked. She tugged at his shirt until he dragged his arms free, a task made more difficult by his fascination with her breasts and the silken folds between her legs.

His trousers demanded more creativity. He pulled a condom from his pocket, scooted to the end of the couch, and shimmied his legs free. The tremble in his hands as he sheathed himself sent a little thrill all the way down to her toes. Before she could fully recover, he shifted her into position and moaned her name. She was everything he'd ever dreamed of.

Gripping her tight, he slowly levered them down back onto the couch and sheathed himself inch by inch. Izzy gasped his name as he filled her, and seared her tender flesh. The fit was snug, but her body accommodated and stretched to fit around his large size.

"Jason," she breathed.

"Baby..."

"Too big."

"God, you feel so—" He gripped her tightly to him caressing her back, hands moving to grip her cheeks, he moaned. "Baby, move for me."'

She didn't need any invitation. As her body adjusted around him, she gripped his shoulders for support and used her legs for leverage.

When she leaned back for a better angle, he dipped his head, taking her left nipple between his lips. As he laved and suckled, she felt the deep ache at her core. He grazed her nipple with his teeth, and she could feel her impending orgasm.

He felt it as well because he stopped and mumbled against her breast. "That's it. Let go. Come for me, baby."

Jason kept up the same slow and steady rhythm as if he were in no hurry at all. But, his clenched jaw, and his insistent stroking of her flesh, said he was as far gone as she. He kept up their rhythm and locked his lips with hers. His thumb circled her clit, massaging it into fevered attention.

"Jason, I..."

"Yes, Baby..."

"I, I…."

"Come on, Baby, come on…" Spoken on a guttural growl as he pumped and increased his movements. He never removed his lips from hers.

The tingling spasms began at the base of her spine and spread until she barreled toward the edge of the cliff. On a scream, she came apart in his hands.

She clutched him to her as he bucked his hips and increased the speed and force of his thrusts. Roaring, he joined her in a freefall off the cliff.
****

A deep chill woke Izzy out of her slumber. She peeked an eye open and looked around trying to see through the pitch black that surrounded her. She reached for her blanket, but snatched her hand back when she came in contact with hard searing heat. Jason. Memories flooded over her as she recalled the limousine — the couch — the floor.

She bit back the moan as her body responded to the memories. She'd been his to do what he wanted with, and she'd loved every minute of it. It wasn't like she'd never had sex before. Just never sex like that. Raw and dirty and so satisfying. With Jason she could do anything with no fear.

She sighed when Jason pulled her close to him and turned her over on the rug so they could spoon. As she nestled against him, the hard length of him nudged against her ass.

He couldn't possibly.

"Hmmm, baby. You cold?" he whispered into her neck.

She nodded and murmured something noncommittal. She didn't feel nearly as cold now resting against his heat, but they couldn't stay on the floor forever. She wiggled to get closer, and he growled.

"Damn woman, I'm not a machine." But that didn't stop him from lifting her leg and shifting behind her to align his eriction with her warm femininity.

She felt him searching for something with his free hand.

"What's the matter?"

"Damn honey, I think we're out of condoms. I left a couple down here, in the hopes you might, erm, come to Malibu. I didn't think we'd go through them all."

She felt a flush warm her body from the inside. "Oh. I uhm. I've been tested in the last year, and I'm on the pill."

He hissed in a breath. "I had a clean bill of health at my last check-up. But we can just go upstairs. I'm pretty sure I have some more around here somewhere."

"I don't want to wait."

"Are you sure, Izzy? I—"

"Shut up and make love to me."

He chuckled and drew her back up against him. "Somebody sure is bossy. I could get used to this."

As he entered her with slow precision, she gasped. She hadn't thought her body could handle any more, but her flesh parted and stretched to accommodate him.

"You sore?" He stilled, waiting for an answer.

"A little, but don't stop."

"I don't want to hurt you." The twitch of his dick inside her tight channel wasn't voluntary, but the movement made her push against him.

"You're not…hurting me. Don't…you…dare stop," she breathed out.

He chuckled, but inched forward again. "What the lady wants, the lady gets." And he wasn't kidding. She felt every ridge and vein of him as he moved within her and wished she could have felt this every time. The contrast of his soft satiny skin against the hard column of his dick was enough to make her quiver.

They didn't have the same urgency as their previous lovemaking sessions. He took his time, as if in no hurry to ever leave. With aching tenderness, he kissed her neck and shoulder whispering words of love into her ear. He told her how beautiful she was, how much he loved being inside her. How much he needed to touch her. How good she felt bare.

All words any woman would love to hear. She felt the telltale clamping of her inner walls and moaned as the pleasure and spasms increased. "Oh, God, Jason." He wasn't far behind her, as he gripped her hips hard enough to leave bruises and thrust into her. She felt the warm flush of his seed as he tumbled over the edge in release.

"Jesus. Izzy." After he shuddered, he held her for several minutes before he shifted away.

She stretched languorously and watched his tight butt walk into the bathroom nearest the kitchen. He turned on the bathroom light and for a moment, the light backlit him. He looked back at her and smiled that smile that always made her ache. "You're beautiful, Izzy Connors. I'm so lucky."

And, because she knew he meant it, she swiped at the tear that rolled down her cheek. She loved him, and he would break her heart.

Chapter Twenty-Nine

Jason woke alone. Bright orange rays didn't illuminate his bedroom, so the sun couldn't be up yet. However, when he reached out to touch Izzy's warm pliant curves, all he felt were the rapidly cooling sheets. Only the barest hint of her scent remained.

He rolled out of bed and trolled the house looking for her. She couldn't have gone anywhere, she didn't have a car. Although she could have a called a cab, but she wouldn't have left without so much as goodbye. Would she?

After a thorough search of the upstairs, he found her in the downstairs bathroom adjusting her dress with haste, as she tried to finger comb her hair.

She was leaving? After the night they'd spent together, she'd leave him and try to sneak out in the middle of the night? Hurt and anger tightened the vise on his vocal chords as he spoke. "Going somewhere?"

With a stunned yelp, she whipped around to face him. "Geez, Jason, you scared the shit out of me." Her fingers fidgeted with her earrings, and she turned back to the mirror. "It's getting really late, or rather early. I need to get home."

Her lack of eye contact infuriated him. "So, you were going to leave without so much as thanks for the fuck?"

She turned back to face him. Her eyes flashed daggers of hurt, her lips flattened before she spoke. "It's nothing less than I'm sure you've done."

He staggered back a step, the sting to his emotions hurt as much as a jaw-numbing slap. "I didn't sneak out of bed with you, Izzy. You're the one who's running. Not me."

Her shoulders sagged, and she hung her head. "Shit, I'm sorry. I—I don't know how to do this, okay?" She scraped her wildly curling hair behind her ears, she folded her arms across her chest in a gesture of protection. "I've never had a one night stand. I've never slept with a man whose modus operandi is to have sex with several women a week." She held up a hand. "Not that I'm complaining, because obviously, practice makes freaking amazing, but I'm not the girl who can look at you in the morning and be happy you chose me for a night."

"Where do you get this shit from?" He forced his anger back into its cage as he took a step toward her. "Yes, I've slept with a lot of women. I can't change any of that. And, maybe I've been less than pleased to find some of them in my bed come morning, but, Izzy, you're different. Everything about you, me, us is different. Do you really think I'd wake up, take one look at you after last night and say, 'Gee, thanks, but I've had enough?' Shit, I'm still hard with need for you."

Her gaze leveled with his. But for an instant, her eyes flickered to his boxers. Eyes wide, they flicked back to his gaze. The need reflected in her eyes sent sparks of craving to his belly. "You're not a one night stand for me."

He could see her softening and let out the constricted air he held in his diaphragm.

"This isn't a one night stand?"

He shook his head. "No."

"So I guess I didn't need to sneak out of bed?" She wrinkled her brow in a sheepish half smile.

"No. You don't need to run away, Iz. I—" He couldn't tell her he loved her. She'd run for the hills. "I care about you." That was better. Still left him a way out of a stinging rejection.

"You have to promise me one thing."

He pulled her into his arms and relief washed over him once she circled arms around his waist. This was where she belonged. "For you, anything."

She peeked up at him from under full lashes. "When you're bored and you've had your fill, you'll tell me like a grown up. Don't leave me to guess. I couldn't take that."

"Izzy, don't be — "

"Promise me."

His eyes searched hers. She was serious. She needed him to make that promise. "If the time comes when this isn't working, not that it ever will come to that, but if it comes, I'll show you enough respect and tell you like a grown up."

Like hell. Now that she was back in his life, he wouldn't let her go. "Now that we've got that all sorted out, can we go back to bed? I'd like to see what other types of debauchery we can engage in before I take you back to your respectable life."

****

"How does it feel to be a rock star?"

Izzy's head snapped up from her proofs as Jessica threw the Arts and Culture section down onto the proof littered light table. Displaced air whisked strands of hair into her face.

"One good review is hardly rock star status, Jess." Izzy swiped her wayward strands behind her ears. "Besides, all I care about are sales."

Jessica rolled her eyes and hopped her ample bottom onto a corner of the light table, further displacing Izzy's proofs. "Oh, c'mon, you can't tell me you don't care about reviews."

"I don't," Izzy said as she resisted the itch in her fingers that urged her to pick up the newspaper.

Jessica narrowed her eyes. "You can't lie to me, Home Skillet." Jessica waved the well-worn paper under her nose. "You know you want to read the reviews. Better yet, I'll read the reviews to you."

Izzy's hands cramped from clenching her fists too tight. What's the worst that could happen? Even if there was a bad review, at least there was one good one. She could live with one good review.

"Okay, read them, but only the good ones. I mean I don't want to know if anyone thinks my photos are pedestrian or they use ridiculously large words that I can't pronounce and don't really want to know what they mean."

"Got it, I will give you only the pros, and I will use little words as if speaking to a five-year-old or my eighty-two-year-old grandmother."

Unable to quell the queasy roll of her belly, Izzy took a seat. Reviews could be brutal. She'd seen a review of her last Homelands book. On an ugly scale, it had come amazingly close to a ballet dancer's mangled feet. And those were the not-so-mean bits.

"Go on. I suppose I'm going to hear the worst of it from Simon anyway."

Jessica blinked at her. Once, twice. "That's just it babes, there isn't a bad one in the lot. All good reviews."

Beads of sweat scored delicate paths down Izzy's back. "What do you mean they're all good?"

Jessica rolled glitter-laden eyelashes. "You look confused. I really do need to use little words, don't I?"

"Jessica!"

"All right. All right!" Crinkling sounds of newspaper echoed in the studio, accompanied by the low whir of the air conditioner. "Photographer Z Con brings a delightful blend of whimsy and solitude in…" Jessica used her fingers to track her place on the paper as she read. "A brilliant showing of newcomer Z Con to the world of professional art work. The artist uses her…" "Brilliant…" "Wonderful…" "The artist juxtaposes… Wait, I was supposed to use small words, wasn't I?"

Izzy felt the fist around her neck loosen its deliberate death grip, allowing air to flow freely into her lungs. They liked her? They'd actually liked her work?

She made a grab for the paper, but Jessica held it out of her reach. "No, no, no. You didn't want to read the reviews remember? Too busy working yourself to death, remember?"

Izzy sighed and feigned surrender. The instant Jessica let her guard down, Izzy snatched the wrinkled papers from her friend's hand. Grinning, she said, "You should know better than to buy my fake out."

Jessica shook her head. "Oh, I'm not buying anything. It was a diversionary tactic."

Dubious, Izzy lowered the paper, brows furrowed. "Let my guard down for what?"

Jessica snatched the paper back. "You think you can waltz in here after a night like the one you had and not share the deets with me? We're supposed to be buds, pals, comrades."

Izzy dodged the rolled up paper aimed for her head. "What the hell are you talking about?"

"Jason Cartwright, you little minx. Spill your innards, or there'll be hell to pay," she threatened with a wave of the paper.

A hot flush started at the balls of Izzy's feet, meandered its way over her calves and weakened her knees. Not fair, she wasn't the only one with some explaining to do. "How about you tell me about you and Simon first."

Fierce crimson blotches stained Jessica's cheeks. "What? I—"

Izzy folded her arms and cocked her head to the side. "The coat check? Seriously?"

"Shit, Izzy, I'm so sorry. I had too much to drink and he…Well…God, I can't believe I'm such a fuck up." Her shoulders rose to her neck as she inhaled enough breath for another verbal torrent. "I never meant to hurt you. I didn't plan it. I swear. It just sort of happened. And I'm not even really sure how. We were fighting, and the next thing I knew—"

Izzy rolled her lips inward to contain a giggle. "You two were going at it like a couple of rabbits on speed."

"Shit, well, yes. And—wait." Jessica paused her stream of consciousness to study Izzy's face. "You're not upset?"

Izzy rolled her eyes. "Gosh no. A, we already broke up. And B, I think we can both agree that he's absolutely the wrong fit for me."

"Yeah, I know. But I still should never have even gone there. And I swear to God, if I hadn't had so much bloody champagne, none of it would have ever happened. I mean, I broke the ultimate girl code. It's never going to happen again, and I mean never. Gosh, I can't even stand the guy. And—"

"Jess."

Jessica snapped her mouth closed, and Izzy laughed at the wide-eyed contrition in her expression. "It's really okay. Don't beat yourself up. I've noticed the chemistry between you two on more than one occasion. Something like this was bound to happen. Well, either this, or I'd get a call in the middle of the night to help you move a body."

"What, you knew this was going to happen?" Izzy nodded.

Jessica blew her bangs out of her eyes. "Well, you could have told me before I started freaking out about the horror my life had become. I had no idea what to say or do. I kind of hoped I could forget the whole thing."

"Why?"

"Because it's Simon. Because I can't stand the guy. Because I didn't want to hurt you."

"We've established I'm not hurt. We've established he's Simon. We haven't established if you really can't stand him, or if you're in denial." Then, looking from side to side as if looking for eavesdroppers, Izzy lowered her voice. "Was he any good?"

Between her blue-green hair and crimson face, Jessica looked like Christmas. "Hell yes. But I'll never do that again. Just because you have unbelievable sex with someone doesn't mean they're a candidate. Besides—" Her eyes wide, she placed her hands on her hips. "Enough about my idiotic mistakes, give up the goods, girl. I want to hear all about your night of debauchery."

Surprised at the sudden turn in conversation, Izzy hedged. "What makes you think I slept with him?"

"You mean besides the fact you have the all over sex sheen going? Besides the fact you look more relaxed than I've ever seen you since I've known you? Besides the fact every time your phone vibrates, you hop up like a rabbit?" She shook her head. "Nothing."

Izzy felt her lips form a small "O." It wasn't supposed to be obvious. Jessica was supposed to think she'd come home on her own and crashed in bed from the high of the successful opening.

"Don't even think about lying. You were also in here before I got in at seven, which means you made a special effort to get here before me and not look suspicious. Thereby, making you even more suspicious."

Izzy willed the floor to open and swallow her whole, but nothing happened. When willing didn't work, she tried prayer to God, the earth mother, and the patron saint of humiliation. None answered her plea. She cleared her throat. "I get in early sometimes."

Jessica hopped down off the light table. "Yes, my dear, but you're a creature of habit. You come in, make a beeline for the Red Bulls, which will kill you by the way. You turn the computer on and have your read through TMZ.com. You make an attempt at a healthy breakfast with some instant oatmeal, then you get to work."

Izzy jutted out her chin. "What's your point?"

"My point is, where's the Red Bull can? Where's the bowl of instant oatmeal? And why are you hovering over your phone like a hooker guarding her street corner?"

Defeated, Izzy didn't bother to hide the giggle as her shoulders slumped forward. "Okay, fine, you're right."

Jessica's high-pitched squeal sliced through the calm and sent reverberations of energy all around. "I knew it, I knew it! Okay, so tell me, was it totally worth it?"

The corners of Izzy's mouth moved jerkily into a full on grin as if pulled by two kittens hell bent on reaching the butterfly stud earrings in her ears. "Completely well worth it."

"So he tastes as good as he looks?"

Izzy dropped her head in her hands, unable to contain the giggle fit. "Better."

"You lucky bitch. If only I could have a one night stand with someone like Jason Cartwright. I can't believe it. He looks like…"

"I think it's time I got back to work, Jess."

Jessica shook her head and dislodged several strands of green streaks onto her rosy cheeks. "O. M. G. Stop the blogs! Honey, you're not—you didn't fall for this guy again… Did you?"

Izzy shook her head and busied herself with the now disarrayed proofs on the table. "No, of course not. It was nice, fun. But that's the end of it."

Jessica's eyes narrowed. "You're doing that eye aversion thing you always do when you try and lie. Oh, Iz, honey, no."

"Relax, okay, I'm not falling for him. It's a fun fling thing. He's that guy, you know. Easy to get caught up with, but I'm fine. I'll keep my wits about me."

Jessica gnawed on her bottom lip. "Babes, when I suggested you ride that pony, I thought you needed to get over that thing you've carried around for him all this time. I never thought you'd—"

Izzy grasped Jessica's hand across the table. "And I haven't. He beds a new woman every other night, and they all fall all over him. I'm not one of those girls. I'm grown. I wanted him, I had him. No biggie."

Jessica shrugged but her eyes remained narrowed. "If you're sure. Guys like Jason Cartwright, they're good to look at, but no good for relationships. Not a few weeks ago, he was photographed with Sabrina."

Izzy told herself she didn't feel like her heart had been tied to an iron anchor and dropped into the center of the ocean. She told herself she was in no way falling for Jason again. When her phone buzzed insistently on the table, sounding like an angry swarm of bees, she told herself it wasn't disappointment to see the name Simon flash on the LCD.

☐

Chapter Thirty

Don't stare. Don't stare. Don't stare.

No matter how many times Izzy told her eyes to stay on their task and keep all of her fingers intact as she sliced onions, they insisted, needed, pleaded to follow Jason around her brightly lit kitchen.

She drank in every move he made. Bronzed hands contrasted sand-colored countertops as they sifted through proofs. Muscled forearms bunched and released with every movement.

"Is the plan to concentrate on what you're doing or stare at me all afternoon?" He flashed her a grin that better women would have swooned at. Each casual glance, each oh-so-sexy smile, sent heated shivers zinging over her flesh.

Was this what it felt like to be infatuated? It had been so long she'd forgotten. One drawn out week since they'd "gone to Malibu", since she'd lost her heart again. They hadn't seen each other until today, and all she could do was think about doing something inappropriate on top of the countertops.

A slam of the front door slapped her back to the present. "Nick, is that you?"

The sizzle and pop of the heated oil on the stove told her it was time to add the onions. She looked over Jason's hand-written instructions on foolproof Pad-Thai. They seemed simple enough. As she added the onions, their pungent scent filled the air. She felt very chef like. No need to mention to Jason that she'd chopped the onions too small. Maybe he wouldn't notice.

No response sounded from the family room, but a shuffle from the doorway brought her around. A bloody-lipped Nick bore a sullen expression as he graced the doorway. He caught sight of Jason, and the scowl on his face deepened to a cartoonish snarl.

Izzy ignored the itch in her feet to run to him and cuddle him and planted her feet. "What happened to your lip?" She held up a hand. "And don't tell me you fell."

Nick didn't spare her a glance. He continued to glare at Jason, malice in his eyes. Her motherly alarm bells rang clear and loud, like a church organ in her head. Trouble.

Jason didn't seem at all perturbed by Nick's angry glare. He leaned back on the stool. Every bit the non-threatening male. "Didn't you hear your mom?"

Nick swung his head in her direction, but cast looks of disdain over in Jason's direction. "I fell… onto some guy's fist."

She knew it wasn't the cool thing to do, but Izzy let her mother's instinct take over, and she reached for him. He shook her off and turned his attention back on Jason.

"What happened?" Impatiently, Izzy tried to check his lip but he shrugged her off again. "Nick, just let me—"

Jason stood and moved over to the far counter, probably in an attempt to give Nick some room. "Did that happen at practice?" Jason's voice was low and calm.

"Yeah, genius. What do you think? 'Cause I'm her kid, I run with gang bangers or something?"

Dread curled its icy fist around Izzy's windpipe and made it impossible to breathe. "Nicholas Reems, I don't know what's gotten into you, but I have not raised you to be rude and disrespectful. Apologize."

Eyes wide, he stared at her, looking more like a wounded six-year-old than the man he pretended to be. "Can't you see, Mom? He's using you. It's just like the guys said. You're his flavor of the week." Before she could respond, he tore out of the back room into the yard.

Izzy staggered back from the force of shock hitting her in the chest. He'd never spoken like that to her before. Nauseous with anger and confusion, she eased herself onto a stool.

Jason placed an arm on her shoulder. His hand abated some of the chill that had seeped into her bones.

"I'll talk to him." Then indicating the stove, he added, "You might want to check on the stove."

Shit. Afraid to peer into the pan, she choked back the acrid smell of burnt onions.

****

Jason ambled over to the pool, careful to approach with caution. "You want to tell me what's really going on?"

Stubbornly, Nick shook his head. "Nope."

Jason shrugged. "Fair enough. But, I happen to know your mom's had a hell of a couple of months and doesn't deserve you taking verbal jabs at her." He paused. "Me? Maybe. But not her."

Nick considered, and puffed in a few shorts breaths before speaking. "Some reporter guy showed up at lunch asking a bunch of questions about you, and these guys at school cornered me after practice and said some stuff about how I think I'm all Hollywood and stuff."

Jason let the anger roll through him and then seep out. Nick needed to talk about it. He didn't need Jason to go on a rip about the reporters. He'd deal with the paparazzi issue later. He nodded. "Yeah, then what?"

"They talked shit about Mom."

Jason did his best to stay cool. He was sure Izzy would want him to throw in a bit about how violence didn't solve problems. "What did they say about your mother?"

"How I wasn't special just 'cause you'd taken my mom out once. And that she was just your flavor of the week skank. And some other stuff…" The words trailed off, and he snuffled, unable to continue.

"Other stuff?"

Nick clenched his jaw as blood infused his face. "One of them dropped the N-bomb and some other stuff, so I took a pop at him."

Jason could only guess at the other stuff. No wonder Nick had gotten in a scuffle. Bullying kids could be a pain in the ass. Ignorant, bullying kids could be dangerous. It was worse when they had muscle to back it up. Nick wasn't a small kid. "What does the other guy look like?"

Nick cracked a smile. "Worse."

Jason nodded his satisfaction. "Good, I hope you made 'em pay. But for future reference, violence doesn't solve anything."

"I'll make sure to tell her you told me that." Head hanging, he added, "I'm sorry about in there. I was rude."

Jason shrugged. "You had good cause to be a little miffed. Paparazzi showing up at school. It can be a lot to handle. I'm sorry you're in this position. That is my fault."

Seemingly off topic, Nick asked, "So, are you like dating my mom now?"

"I'm trying to, if she'll have me."

"Maybe it's not a good idea if she's a flavor of the week."

Jason got the message loud and clear. Nick was Izzy's protector, and he didn't want Izzy hurt. "She's not. I care about her. I'm trying to convince her to let me stick around a while."

"Okay."

Jason smiled to himself. As if it were that easy. Say okay, and all was right with the world. "Not so fast. You still owe your mom an apology."

A crimson sea washed over Nick's face as he winced. "I swore in front of her, and I was rude. That's going to be no phone for a month, at least."

"How about we start with dinner and a sincere apology. I hear it can take you far."

Chapter Thirty-One

Izzy needed a distraction. Screw a distraction, she needed sex. Because of Nick's mood the night before, Jason hadn't spent the night, and she was still humming with the tension. Every look, caress, stolen kiss, reminded her of her trip to Malibu. And all she'd been able to think about was another trip to Malibu, but their schedules weren't compatible, so she'd have to wait.

She scooted out of her office and went in the hunt of chocolate. If she couldn't have sex, Dove chocolate would make a fine substitute. "Hey Jessica do we—" She pulled up abruptly when she saw Jessica shove something in her desk.

Eyes wide, Jessica rolled her chair in front of the desk drawer as if to hide something. "What's up Izzy? What do you need?" She paused for a second then added rapidly, "I've got your appt book for the day. A couple of sittings, but nothing maj—"

Something wasn't right. Izzy scrutinized Jessica's ramrod-straight posture and tightly clenched hands. "What gives? What are you hiding?"

Jessica turned a shade of pink. "Uhm, so…." Her voice trailed off, and she looked away."

"Spill it, Jess. I haven't got all day. What's the matter with you?"

Jessica reached into the desk and pulled out what looked like a magazine from the desk drawer. "Iz, you have to promise me you're not gonna tweak about this?"

Izzy's brow furrowed. "Tweak?"

"Yeah, you know. Trip, bug out, push button panic, and shit a cold purple Twinkie?"

"Shit a wh—? Never mind. I know what to tweak means. Now show me what you're hiding."

Jessica pulled the glossy, weekly gossip rag from the desk. "I'm sure it's not what it looks like. You know how these people like to deal funk."

"Deal fu—"

"Hose, bag, make shit up…" Jessica's definitions trailed off.

"Give me the magazine."

Her hands trembled, but Jessica handed over the Us Weekly. Initially, Izzy didn't see any cause for alarm. But when her eyes trailed the bottom left corner of the cover, her heart seized, threatened to lock up and never beat again.

"The image is all fuzzy, and probably photoshopped to hell. It's probably not even him."

Izzy continued to stare at the image and the title above it. "Tennis' bad boy on the rebound from Cienna." The small print around the image added, "He never wastes any time."

Nausea overtook her stomach and churned her breakfast yogurt around and around in circles. How did these things happen? Needing to sit down, she stumbled to one of the reception chairs and eased herself into it. This could not happen to her. Could. Not. Happen. She told herself over and over.

Concerned, Jessica brought her a Dixie-cup of water. "I'm sorry, honey. I tried to warn you. Guys like Jason, you enjoy once and move on. They're not relationship types."

Izzy drew her head up. "What are you talking about?"

Jessica's dark brows drew in. "Ain't we talking about the same thing, honey? Your wannabe man. Two-timing like a Mo' Fo'?"

Izzy was confused. "Huh?"

Jessica's eyes rolled. "Mother Fu—"

"I know what Mo' Fo' means Jess. I'm confused about him two-timing."

Jessica's mouth thinned, and her eyes widened. "I didn't know you were so down with the open relationship thing—"

Izzy lost the tenuous tether on her emotions. "For fuck's sake, Jess. He's not two-timing. That's me in the photo."

Jessica did a perfect impression of a frog's bugged eyes. "You're shitting me."

Izzy shook her head. "I shit you not."

Jessica grabbed the magazine and thumbed through to the feature page for a bigger image. Izzy wanted to curl up and vanish. Things like this were not supposed to happen to her.

Sure enough, there was a bigger image. Clear as crystal, she could make out Jason's face. Thankfully, God heard her prayers, and her face was obscured. However, her head was thrown back in obvious ecstasy. Her skirt bunched up around her upper thighs. There was no question what they were doing.

Jessica's voice broke through her haze of despair. "I don't get it. When did this happen? I thought you didn't do the do until last week?"

"We didn't. This is from when Nick and I stayed in Malibu. If you look closely enough, you should recognize the skirt. It's yours."

Jessica narrowed her eyes and scanned the image again. A grin spread across her face. "Hey, what do you know? My skirt is famous."

"I'd taken your advice, like the moron I am, and tried to seduce him. We were having some serious extracurricular activities until he saw a photographer on the beach with his creepy telephoto and serious flash."

"Holy cow."

"I know. Needless to say, that put a stop to any fun we were having. He called security, but I don't think they ever got the guy."

"My, my, Izzy Connors. You are an adventurous one. On the balcony? I never thought you had it in you."

Heat flushed Izzy's body. "It was your idea for me to go and get what I wanted."

Jessica conceded. "Yeah I guess you're right." She indicated the magazine and asked, "What are you gonna do about this?"

Izzy stood up. "The only thing I can do. I need to talk to Jason." She checked her watch. "He has physical therapy downtown at twelve. I can probably catch him before he starts."

"I mean what can you really say? It's not his fault someone got a picture of you guys."

"It might not be his fault, but when people start splashing pictures of me on a magazine, something about it isn't right. He lives a high profile life, and we don't."

"Hmmm."

Izzy's eyes narrowed. "What's the hmmm for?"

"Izzy, you chose to try a relationship with this guy, even against my better warnings. You chose to jump right in. You can't pick and choose the parts you want. You gotta take it all, the good the bad and the ugly."

She wasn't picking and choosing. She was trying to protect her family. Maybe she'd gotten too carried away with Jason. Maybe they needed to slow things down. Maybe she just needed to talk to Jason.

"I know. I'll talk to him. There has to be a way to keep us out of the glaring paparazzi bulbs. Like normal people."

****

Jason knew she'd be in the lobby before he even got into the building. He'd seen her car as he pulled into the parking lot. He'd also seen the US Weekly that morning. He was such an idiot. Should have just gone after that photographer himself as opposed to letting security try to find him.

Then those pictures wouldn't have come out. In truth, though, nobody would recognize her in the photo. They'd all recognize him, though. He didn't want to think about the hell Nick would catch at school if any of the kids found out the woman in the picture was Izzy.

He walked into the lobby but didn't pause when he saw her. He lowered his voice, mumbled, "Follow me," and motioned her in the direction of the locker rooms.

She looked askance but followed him anyway. When they were in the private changing room, he dropped his bags before he turned to face her. "Paparazzi followed me to the gym. They're not allowed on the property, but they would have loved a shot of you in the lobby."

Eyes wide, her full lips parted. "Are you serious?"

"Since last night, they've been on me like flies on shit. The only reason they haven't found you yet is every time I'm coming to see you, I switch cars and drive around aimlessly for an hour before actually coming to you." He shrugged. "Either that, or they haven't put two and two together that you are my photographer and date to the opening last week. It won't take long though."

She turned to stare at the door they'd come through. "Is that how you live your life every day?"

He nodded. "Pretty much. Sometimes it's my own fault. I'm out at a club and do or say something stupid. Mostly, I'm going about my life and they're not there, but if they smell a story, they'll hang around until I'm less interesting."

"I—I didn't really realize what it must be like. I mean you're coming to physical therapy. What's so interesting about that?"

He shrugged. "They're hoping I'll injure myself even more, and they'll get a photo of it. Or they hope I use PT as a ruse to meet a beautiful woman."

She ducked her head in embarrassment. "You're not supposed to say stuff like that. I'm here to read you the riot act."

He cringed. "Us Weekly?"

"So you've seen it?" He splayed his arms. "What the hell, Jason? Is this what it's going to be like? People following us around everywhere?"

Desperate to calm her down, he reached for her. "You have every right to be pissed."

She shrugged out of his hold. "Damn right I do. You can imagine my shock when Jessica showed me the stupid picture worried you were going to hurt me. You can imagine her shock when I told her I was the one in the picture."

He couldn't help the shit-eating grin tugging at the sides of his lips. "Was she jealous?"

"Jason!"

He laughed. "I'm sorry, baby. But this is part of it. If you want to do this, we can continue to try to exist in the little cocoon of your house or my house, but I don't want to. I want to live our lives. Go see a match of Nick's. Maybe take one of those photo vacations you always talk about. I don't want to hide."

"I don't suggest we hide, but—"

"Then what do you suggest? If your suggestion is you walk away and pretend we never met, I'm not interested. We'll find another solution."

Deflated, her shoulders sagged. "Well that just takes the sport out of being pissed."

He pulled her in close. "Baby, I know it's not what you signed up for. But remember, you're giving me a chance. Giving us a chance. I promise I'll do what I can to keep you and Nick out of it. Right now, they just think you were a date to an event. They don't know that you're—" He abruptly stopped himself before he revealed too much. It was too early to tell her he loved her. She'd bolt. He amended his statement. "That we're involved. They'll find out soon enough, though. And, when they do, the best way to get rid of them is to live our lives. They'll get bored eventually."

She folded her arms across her chest, but her spine and shoulders softened. "I don't want to be the subject of tabloid magazines. It was a real shock to see myself on the cover of Us Weekly."

He grinned at her and hoped for forgiveness, hoped she'd adjust like he'd learned to. "I gotta say, you look like you were having a blast though."

Annoyed, she smacked him on the arm. "That's not funny."

He dodged another swat and drew her closer so she couldn't take any more swipes at him. "C'mon, tell me the truth, you came all the way down here because you missed me didn't you?"

She wiggled and tried to free herself, but he held her tight, breathing in her unique scent of jasmine, vanilla and spice. His memory flashed to their night in Malibu. The way her hair felt between his fingers. The petal soft texture of her skin. The way her legs tightened around him when she was ready to come. He needed her. But, like last night, making love would have to wait.

Once he and Nick had come back inside, and Nick had apologized to Izzy, they'd had a fun night. Nick salvaged the Pad-Thai. They'd laughed. Played a spirited game of Gin Rummy. Like normal people. First time he'd felt normal in years.

Jason hadn't touched Izzy aside from the casual touches of two people in close proximity. After his chat with Nick, he figured it was a good idea to give Nick a chance to adjust to the idea of him before he started groping his mother in public.

But he missed her. Missed the smooth glide of her skin on his. Missed the way her eyes darkened when she was about to—

She giggled. "Jason, I think the racket in your pants wants to go a couple of games."

He groaned, but didn't let her go. Planting kisses on the baby-soft hair at her temples, he murmured, "Forget games, he'd like to go several matches."

"Several huh?"

He nodded as he tried to temper the insistent urging from his body to be as close to her as humanly possible. "A whole tournament."

She rose on tiptoe, and he bent his head to meet her half way. She brushed her lips to his before breathing out, "We should do something about that and give him a proper workout."

His erection jerked inside his shorts. Izzy would be the death of him. "You shouldn't tease a starving man like that."

"Who's teasing?"

"Iz—"

She wrapped her arms around his neck pulling him in for another kiss. Her lips tasted of coffee and strawberries, the flavor of her drifted over his tongue and drew him in. He smiled into the kiss and wished he could stay like that forever.

Her hand traced a path from his shoulder and only stopped to explore his chest, before it moved down to the waistband of his shorts. When her hand reached beneath the thick elastic waistband, every nerve call in his body screamed Danger Will Robinson, Danger.

Delicate fingers eased around his already engorged erection. When she pumped the length of him slowly easing her hand from the base to the tip, he bit off a stream of curses. "Damn it, Izzy, what are you doing? We—"

"You want to argue with me? Or do you want sit back and enjoy this?"

He knew when to shut up.

Backing up against the training bed all the while tugging at his shorts, she released him from the confines of his shorts. When the hard length of him sprang free, her eyes widened with mischievous glee. He had no time to register the look before warm breath encircled his dick.

He squeezed his eyes shut and willed his body to relax. He was not a fourteen-year-old about to embark on his first sexual encounter. He had some control. Didn't he? It had been a while though. He'd missed her.

He lifted his head and peeled his eyes open to look at her. Nothing was more erotic than watching her full lips engulfing every inch of his penis, then slide back and release him.

Too tempted, he wove his hands into her hair, the thick texture enough to drive him climbing toward the peak. "Izzy." Her name came on a breath he didn't know he had left in him.

When she traced her hand up his thigh, he knew we wouldn't last long. Using every non-verbal cue he could think of, he tried to warn her. "Izzy, wait. I'm—"

She didn't listen.

One hand continued to work the length of him in alternating turns with her lush mouth. The other hand traced a path up his thigh until it reached his balls. The instant her fingers grazed the sensitive skin, he knew he was lost.

She knew it as well. He could swear he saw her smile through his haze of ecstasy. As he soared over the cliff of dizzying pleasure, her mouth milked every last drop of his essence from him.

She released him and grinned. "So exactly how does one evade the paparazzi?"

Chapter Thirty-Two

Brash ringing permeated Izzy's cocoon of lustful relaxation. She reached for the phone, ready to pitch it across the room when she realized she wasn't in her bed, and it wasn't her phone. She lifted her head and took in the sleek contemporary furniture.

Jason's.

With Nick at a sleepover, they'd snuck in under the cover of night. That, and she'd ducked down in the car once they'd hit the coast.

The phone shrilled again. She stretched and released the protesting groans of muscles unaccustomed to such — vigorous use.

"Jason, phone."

The running water of the shower was all she heard. Groaning, Izzy wrapped a sheet around herself for modesty, not that she had any left. Giving semi-public blowjobs could do that for a girl.

Without knocking, she entered the bathroom, smiling at his rendition of Living on a Prayer. "Hey, Bon Jovi."

The sexy smile she'd grown so accustomed to spread across his face with a lazy ease.

"No free shows, Princess. The toll is you have to join me."

Her laughter bubbled up in her chest. "Oh no you don't. I'm not getting my hair wet this time. It takes forever to dry." When she slid the glass door aside, she scooted out of his reach. "Not to mention you'll be really late for your meeting."

"But I have to drop you off anyway, and you need a shower too." He waggled his eyebrows.

"You're incorrigible."

Playfully, he flicked water at her.

"Jason!" She held the phone over the toilet. "Try that again, and the phone gets it."

He held his hands up in surrender. "Okay, okay. But you'll have to make up the toll charge."

"Looking forward to it. Your phone's blowing up."

He ducked his head under the showerhead. "Hmm, called more than once? Probably Aaron to remind me not to be late."

"I thought it might be important."

He grabbed a towel off the shelf. "Could you pick it up if it rings again and tell him to chill. I'll be there on time."

Izzy smiled as she meandered out of the bathroom. This was all a dream. Things like this, men like Jason, didn't happen to her.

Through half of her adult life she'd gone through the motions of dating. Of relationships. Of sex. If this was what all the fuss was about, she could shoot herself for missing out.

Thanks to Nick's sleepover, she and Jason had some uninterrupted alone time. Perfect alone time. She shoved the cloud of doubt that threatened to rain on her bliss to the far reaches of her brain. He wasn't permanent, but she deserved to be happy for a while, no matter how long it lasted.

Another persistent ring brought her back to present. "Hello, Jason Cartwright's phone."

A long pause of silence followed.

"Aaron, is that you?"

"I must say, Izzy, I applaud you for going after what you want."

Sabrina. What the hell was she calling Jason for? "You've got nerve. We haven't seen you since you humiliated your son at his exhibition match a couple of weeks ago. So much for turning over a new leaf."

"Look who finally got a backbone. Must say, I'm impressed." Her chuckle said anything but. "Now, be a dear, and put Jason on the phone."

"You can't have anything to say to him. He already turned you down for money. It's sad you keep trying to insert yourself his life. He's not dumb you know, he'll figure it out."

"Isn't it enough that you stole my son, now you want my cast offs? Sad, sad, Izzy. When will you get a life of your own and stop trying to live mine?"

Izzy felt the anger rise, ebb and hum on her skin. "You should take better care of what's yours in that case. Otherwise, they will find somebody better geared for the job."

A stream of shrill epithets flowed over the phone line. For once, Izzy wished she could see Sabrina as she pitched one of her infamous tantrums.

"Sabrina, as much as I'd love to listen to you, I need to get dressed. I'm afraid we stayed in bed too long. Did you want me to give Jason a message?"

For a full minute, silence ruled the airwaves. When Sabrina spoke, she kept her voice controlled and level. "Maybe you should ask your new boyfriend about the last time we slept together. I'll bet the money he paid me to keep quiet, he doesn't tell you the truth."

"You're lying."

"I have no reason to lie. He's already paid me."

Despair treaded heavy footsteps on Izzy's former happiness. "No, he said he didn't give you any money. He said—"

"We both know he can't be trusted, the faithless prick."

Sudden awareness sprinkled with fear tingled at Izzy's brain. "Is he Nick's father?"

"Oh, this again? You really are a one-trick pony. We've been through this already."

"And I want the damn truth out of you, for once."

"Truth is, I haven't the foggiest. But once you ask your boy toy about our past, I think your numbers might add up. I was never as smart as St. Izzy. But I'm sure you'll figure it out. Do tell Jason to call me. We have a few more things to discuss."

Cold filled Izzy's marrow at the silence on the line. Slimy, icy, fear crawled over her skin. Jason could be Nick's father. She'd suspected, but suspecting, and suspecting with cause, were two different things. She clutched her hand to her belly and prayed she could quell the rolls of nausea. Jason had lied to her.

Jason came up behind her, hair damp from the shower and placed feather light kisses on the nape of her neck. "Was that Aaron calling to tell me to get my ass in gear before—" He stopped talking when she turned to face him.

"It wasn't Aaron."

She watched as the tension ebbed onto his shoulders. "Who was it then?"

"Is it true, Jason? You paid Sabrina?"

His normally tanned face blanched by varying degrees. Both of his hands raked though his wet hair. "It's not like she made it out to be."

"Then what is it like, exactly?"

"Izzy—"

"Because right now it sounds like you lied to me."

A long breath escaped his lungs. "Sabrina's been blackmailing me."

****

Some things you couldn't take back. Jason knew by the shock on Izzy's face, this was one of them. Part of his brain screamed for a recall button as he watched Izzy's lithe, naked form gather her clothes and retreat into the bathroom. He couldn't lie. Couldn't evade. Couldn't pretend.

No more hiding.

"I didn't lie to you at first."

"Just in the end." She shook her head. "She said you went back to campus to see her. Is it true?"

"I didn't go back to see her, I went back for you."

"Bullshit. You never came back for me."

He reached for her hands, but she pulled away from him. "I did. I'd heard from Coach about how you'd had a hard time, and—"

"So you came back to see me after I cracked up on the court. But then you accidentally fell into Sabrina's bed?"

"It wasn't like that."

"Right. And how do you account for the fact I never saw you?"

Hot, fierce shame washed over him. "I went by your place and ran into her before I ran into you. She told me you were dating some guy, Bryce or something. Pre law guy."

"Bryce? He's gay."

His back stiffened. "Yeah, I guess it wouldn't be the first time she lied."

"So you couldn't find me, so you jumped in the sack with Sabrina just for shits and giggles. For old time's sake?"

"I know. It's the dumbest thing in the world I can say. I was so rotten drunk. I was happy you were happy, but I wanted to punish myself because I'd let you go."

She shrugged. "I don't give a shit how it happened, it still happened. And even if that's old history, the fact is, you've had a million opportunities to tell me the truth, and you haven't."

"I was young and stupid. I tied one on that night at some stupid house party. I got so drunk I couldn't see my own feet. Sabrina was there and—"

"So what? Sabrina asked you for money to keep it quiet, and you forked it over instead of telling me the truth?"

Shit. "No. At first I told her no. But after what happened at your place, she said things would get worse for Nick if I didn't give her the money. I just wanted to protect you."

"Protect me? You were being Jason Cartwright, selfish prick. You talk about not wanting to be that selfish asshole who only thinks about himself, but that's who you are. Sleep with Sabrina, lie to me, pay Sabrina off, it's all about protecting yourself. You always take the path of least resistance."

"That's not who I am, Izzy."

"Then who the hell are you? Because I don't know."

Why hadn't he told her? Why had he lied? Why hadn't he told her earlier? Had he sensed her growing attachment and, in typical fashion, needed to shake her off before it got too sticky? Too messy? Or worse, had he feared he'd fallen so irreversibly in love with her, he wouldn't be able to escape with his heart intact if she left him and not the other way around?

He cleared his throat, choosing to interpret her question. "Izzy, I'm sorry, I can do better, be better. What can I do to make this up to you?"

"That's just it, Jason, you can't go and wave your magic wand and make it all better. Simple fact—I can't trust you. Another simple fact, Sabrina has some hold on you, you can't seem to shake free. If you'd just told me when we first started, this wouldn't have been that big a deal. Just a blip. I would have forgotten it."

Shame gave way to defensive anger. "Are you so sure? You wear your pride like a fucking badge. You've been looking for an excuse to run, and I just gave you one so you're out the door."

"You can pull that reverse psychology shit on me all you like. It doesn't change the fact you're a coward."

She went into the bathroom, presumably to get ready. The soft click of the bathroom lock signaled the irreversible closing of the door on their relationship.

Chapter Thirty-Three

"So when do you plan on coming out of this funk? The whole broody, depressed, jilted lover thing is so last year."

Izzy's head snapped up from her task to glare at Jessica in her newly blonded form. "This coming from the woman who changes boyfriends as often as she changes hair color."

The biting words escaped her lips before she could wrestle them back into their prison cell at the back of her throat. The stabbing pain in her chest, fear clutching at her belly, constant state of nausea, and pure as spring water rage—none of those were Jessica's fault. If she needed to blame anyone, she'd blame herself. Then she thought better and added Jason on the list.

Jessica deflected the jibe with aplomb. "I'll let that one slide, Muff. I know you're pining." Jessica plunked herself into the overstuffed beanbag chair in Izzy's office. "I told you not to fall in love with the guy."

Izzy shoved the proofs in front of her aside. She didn't need to review them anymore, she had the perfect ones for the SI shoot and for her editor. She was too distracted to focus on getting the gallery pieces out to their new owners, so she tried for busy work. "Jess, I'm sorry. I didn't mean it. I've just been…" Unable to find the right words, she spread her arms. "I'm sorry."

Jessica gave a brusque nod of her head. "Forgotten. I get it. He's a bastard. But I'm worried about you. You look a hot mess."

Izzy cringed as she sat back to take in her outfit and wondered where she'd gone wrong this time. "I'm a little wrinkled maybe, but hardly a hot mess."

"No, not your clothes, though they could use a little color. I'm talking about you. You've been walking around like a zombie for the past week. You've dropped a few pounds…" She paused and frowned. "Though, I'd love to know your secret for that. And don't think I haven't noticed you've made yourself sick with worry. You're drinking tea and eating saltines like it's your job to stave off nausea. Frankly, if I'd known what kind of effect he'd have on you, I never would have suggested you get together."

Izzy shook her head. "I'm fine." When she realized Jessica wouldn't accept that answer, Izzy added, "I'm upset, sure, but I'm not heart broken or anything." She tasted the lie on her tongue and decided to swallow the bitter flavor.

Jessica worked her lower lip. "Okay, Slim. If you say it's not a heart problem, then what gives? The distracted, snippy, forlorn-looking Izzy isn't much fun at all. I'd like the other one back, please. She may have also been distracted, but at least she was also fun and witty."

Izzy considered. She didn't want to have to relive the exhausting disappointment or the heart-shattering pain, but maybe if she shared, she'd stop feeling so miserable and be able to let some of it go.

"Jason slept with Sabrina."

Jessica's movement to her feet was so fast it caused a draft to wisp hairs into Izzy's face. She picked up a paperweight. "I'm gonna kill that mutha trucka." Jessica tossed the paperweight between her hands. "Then I'm gonna go after that skinny, coked out bitch, and show her what it really means to hurt. Withdrawal's got nothing on me."

Izzy couldn't help the laughter that skipped out of her mouth. "Damn, remind me not to piss you off, okay?"

Jessica's lips curled in a baring of teeth, but her tone lightened. "You like? I've been practicing my sassy black woman routine." She tossed the paperweight again. "That doesn't mean I can't do murder. That fucking prick. I figured he'd get bored, or stop calling, but to sink lower than a pile of ant shit and sleep with that, that…" She gesticulated wildly while she searched for the right word. Jessica's eyes widened when she found it. "That Cu—"

Before she could complete the phrase, Izzy jumped in. "Easy does it. What would the Mormon rocker say?" The intricate pain of resentment, nausea and jealousy coursed through her as she spoke the next words. "It wasn't recent. After he left for the pros. He came back to school. They got together."

Understanding there was no longer a need for the imminent bashing in of Jason's head, Jessica put down the weight. "Okay, maybe we need to back up. I'm confused."

"Yeah all right. You already know he left that night fifteen years ago."

Jessica plopped back down in the beanbag chair and grabbed a handful of jellybeans from the candy dish on Izzy's desk. "God, I heart a good soap opera. Go on."

"Well, apparently he came back about six months later. To see me." She sighed. "Or so he claims."

"Hmm. Guy comes back to see girl. Guy doesn't see girl, but somehow finds he accidentally-on-purpose got naked with girl's best friend?" She blew out a breath. "So Mr. hot-enough-to-melt-in-your-mouth thinks you're moron enough to drink this brand of Kool-Aid?"

Izzy shook her head in exasperation. "I don't know. Sabrina never told me he'd come to see me. He never made the effort to see me. But I wouldn't put it past her to deliberately not have told me."

"So you know what I'm gonna ask you next right?"

Already on the same page, Izzy nodded. "Is Jason Nick's father?" Izzy massaged the bridge of her nose. "I honestly don't know. I've considered before, but the timing was all wrong. And, even now, with what I know, the timing is still iffy. Nick was born a month early according to Sabrina. Only she would know for sure."

"Honey, I'm sorry. I can only imagine what you're dealing with."

Izzy's lips trembled into a semblance of a smile. "I appreciate it. I wish I knew what to do now. I don't even think Jason's considered Nick in the equation. If he's Nick's father…" She grabbed a tissue from the dispenser on her desk. "I don't know what I'll do if he wants custody."

Jessica frowned and appeared not to hear her. "Wait, so how did you find this out? He just blurted this all out?"

Izzy blew her nose and recounted Sabrina's call. When she was done, she slouched in her seat, exhausted from the effort.

For several moments, Jessica sat and said nothing, merely blinking. Every few seconds or so, Izzy could see the brilliant blue of Jessica's eyes disappear behind the purple plumage of plum shadow, only to reappear again, scarcely a moment later.

Finally, she spoke. "No wonder you're full of piss and vinegar, Sweetie. I would have killed that bitch by now."

Izzy blinked back. "I'm too tired to kill anyone. Trust me, I thought about it. Besides, I'm too cute to go to jail."

Jessica considered. "Good point." She gave Izzy a pointed look, she added, "So are you going to tell Jason he might be Nick's father?"

Chapter Thirty-Four

How had her life gone from zero to shit so quickly? One day Izzy had hum drummed along in an uneventful life. Now she had hot tennis players, paparazzi, and a drug-addicted crazy woman in her life. Though, to be fair, the drug addicted crazy woman was more of a staple.

All she needed was some good old fashioned Bravo to take her mind off of everything. As her brain left the world of reality for the world of reality TV, she heard the scrape of a key in the lock. Had Nick forgotten his new set of keys again? "You gotta learn to remember your keys, Nick."

Swinging the door open, Sabrina, not Nick met her on the other side. On reflex, Izzy swung the door closed, but Sabrina used her foot to block it from shutting.

"Izzy, wait. I need your help."

She didn't feel like she had the strength to not kill Sabrina, so Izzy just stared in wonder at Sabrina's audacity. "You want my help. After everything you've done to me, to this family, why should I help you?"

"Look, I'm a mess. I've made some horrendous mistakes, and I have no way to get out. You're all I have left."

"I thought you had Jason."

Sabrina tried for her best expression of contrition, but Izzy could see through it. "Would it help if I said how sorry I was? I never should have gone to Jason. Never should have blackmailed him. I had nowhere else to turn. Tony would have hurt Nick if I didn't pay."

Izzy shook her head. "We had a deal, Sabrina. You could stay here as long as you were clean. I thought it was healthy for Nick to see you, but I was wrong. You bring destruction and lies everywhere you go. You're permeated with it. You honestly can't help yourself."

Sabrina sniffed and clasped her hands together. "I know. I know. I screwed up. I thought I could get the money and pay Tony, and he'd leave me and Nick and you alone. I thought of everything I could. I should have just stayed away. I'm a user, but I'm not all bad, Izzy. I'm not. I wanted custody of Nick for the wrong reason. B-b-but I only wanted to put things right. I need help, okay?" She used the back of her hand to swipe at the trail of liquid that pooled on her upper lip.

Izzy shook her head, vehemence written on her face. "No, not okay. You try to exploit him for his trust. You blackmail Jason. You vanish for days on end. You show up at his tennis match high. You. Hit. My. Son." She put up her hands. "Not this time. You can't wipe those things off with a simple apology. Get off my property."

Sabrina lifted her face, tilting it to a bruise on her cheek. "He's going to kill me. He said he'd kill Nick too." She sniffed and clamped her hands together.

Izzy stood in front of her, arms folded, not budging. She saw the signs. The twitching. The pinpoint pupils. Sabrina was high. "Sabrina, I'm sorry, I've had enough. You can't do this to yourself or to Nick. I'm not going to do it to him."

"Look, I know." She bit her lip. She took a deep breath before she shoved past Izzy. "But I'm serious about needing your help. I can't do this by myself. I've got to pay, or we're all in trouble."

Izzy shifted her position, but it was too late, Sabrina was already in the house. She clenched her jaw. "I'm not giving you money. I haven't got it. From the looks of it, you need to get back into rehab."

"Shit, Izzy. I need money. Bad things will happen if I don't pay."

"Then you need to find a way to pay on your own. I won't to enable you anymore."

"Izzy, c'mon—"

"And while we're at it, you've got some things to come clean about. We're calling Jason."
****

Jason's stomach flipped over with nerves. She'd called. It meant she wanted to see him right? Missed him. If he could just see her and explain. Maybe she could forgive him. Or at least not hate him entirely. Shit. Who was he kidding? He missed her like crazy, and he would do anything to see her. Even have her shoot him off her front steps. The doorbell rang, and he knew this was the moment of truth.

Unprepared for the need that clawed at him when she answered the door, he reached for her in an automatic gesture. As if touching her, holding her would put it all right again. "Izzy, I'm so sorry. I—"

She shifted away from him. He thinned his lips and shrugged, making his way inside the doorway. It was too soon. Through his mind, a thousand different apologies ran. He searched for the best one, but none of them were good enough. He settled on, "I've really missed you."

"This isn't why I called you over."

"I—oh."

"You might as well bring him in. What you're asking about concerns him as well."

The cool, nervous sweat in his palms turned hot in his fury. He knew that voice. He walked around Izzy and stalked through the living room in the direction of the voice. When he found Sabrina sitting at the dining room table, she sneered up at him.

"You always did have impeccable timing, Jason. Were you already on your way here?"

"What the hell are you doing here? Haven't you done enough damage?"

Her resounding laughter was devoid of any real humor. "Don't blame me because you got caught in a lie."

Izzy's voice came low and flat from behind him. "Will both of you just shut up? Jason, have a seat."

He braced himself against the bookcase. "I'd rather stand." He looked from Sabrina's half smug, half jittery expression to Izzy's tight lipped strained one, knowing he wasn't going to like what he heard.

"Okay, suit yourself." Izzy levered herself into a chair, and he tried not to remember the last time he'd seen her. The censure and the disgust in her voice kept him awake nights.

"I hate to repeat myself, but what's she doing here?"

"Truth and consequence time, Sabrina. I want the truth. Is Jason Nick's father?"

Jason felt the furrow in his forehead before his brain fully computed Izzy's question. "Now, wait a minute I—"

Izzy didn't let him finish. "Sabrina, for once in your life, take responsibility for the mess you've created. I want the truth."

Sabrina eyes widened before visibly forcing a swallow. "Jason."

Jason waited for the revelation to come, but Sabrina looked frozen on the spot.

"God damn it, Sabrina, spit it out." Izzy's shout echoed into the kitchen. Sabrina opened her mouth, then closed it again, and her lips trembled. She parted them again, licking her lips before speaking. "Nick is our son, Jason." She sniffed and used the back of her hand to scratch her nose.

Jason stood to his full height and cocked his head in an attempt to hear her better. Sabrina took a step back like any prey would with a predator in their midst. He fixed his gaze on Izzy. "Are you serious?"

Izzy looked at him, confusion etched in her eyebrows. "What the hell do you mean? Did you hear her?"

A brittle smile cracked his lips. "Oh, I heard her. Only problem is I've heard it before."

The tears tracked freely down Sabrina's makeup smeared face. "It's the truth, Jason. It's not a lie this time."

"That's the problem when you cry wolf Sabrina." Izzy shook from the anger. Looking at Jason, she asked, "Will you take a paternity test?"

He turned his gaze to Izzy, incredulous. "You're serious?"

She nodded, somber eyed and tight lipped. She looked like hell.

"What makes you so sure I'm the father?"

"Listen, you son of a bitch." Sabrina pushed herself out of her seat. "I'm not a liar. I don't have to explain myself—"

Izzy interrupted before Sabrina could finish. Walking over to the bookcase he leaned against, she pulled a folder out of the drawer and handed it to him. "I took these at your house. The resemblance is striking enough. I knew I needed confirmation from Sabrina that it was even possible." She searched for the right words. "It didn't hit me until you told me you'd come back, that you could..." She cleared her throat, not looking him in the eye. "That you might be his father."

He stared at the photos, awareness dawning in his eyes. He didn't look at her when he asked his question. "When were you going to tell me?"

Her eyes snapped to meet his, and she folded her arms across her chest. "After you dropped the bomb on me last week, I suspected. I needed Sabrina to confirm it was possible."

"You've suspected for over a week. When were you going to give me the heads up? Or were you just waiting to leak it to the press first?"

"Don't. You. Dare." She shoved a finger in his chest to make her point. "Don't you dare. You were the one who lied to me. Without a confirmation, I couldn't very well—"

"Yes, you could have very well. You're always on and on at me about trust." He waved the photos at her. "You kept your mouth shut."

"You're the liar, Jason. For weeks, you looked at me and lied."

"We've been seeing each other for weeks and not once did it occur to you to mention, hey, you know, the kid, I might be his father."

"You act as if I kept him away from you all these years. I didn't know for sure until Sabrina confirmed it."

"But you suspected, and you kept it from me."

"I'm not the only one with my suspicions. You must have suspected. You can do the math, or did you take too many tennis balls to the head?" She put her hands on her hips, eyes flashing with contempt. "What, Jason, did you think I'd hit you up for money? Did you think I'd tarnish your oh-so-stellar rep?" She ran a hand through her hair. "Shit. I knew I should have tried harder not to trust you. But I wanted to believe in you. As always, I guess I was naïve."

He worked the muscle in his jaw. "You've been looking for a reason not to trust me since I met you." He straightened. "Well, I guess you found one." He took the photos with him as he strode to the door. "Set up a paternity test and a time to sit down with Nick."

"I don't think it's best to tell him before—"

He pierced her with a stare. "You really think I'd let you determine what's best? You're not even his mother."

Chapter Thirty-Five

Jason drove for hours trying to get the image of Sabrina telling him he had a son out of his head. A son. She hadn't been lying. The look on Izzy's face had told him that. And Izzy. She'd lied too. How could she have known and not told him?

You lied too. But he wasn't in the mood for his own truths.

He drove the 101 until he came to the nondescript beach bungalow. He didn't bother to knock and walked straight in.

"Y'know, I could have been butt naked getting it on with some hot model." Aaron came from the kitchen wielding a beer for each of them.

"When was the last time you had a hot model?" Jason looked at him askance.

"That's not the point. The point is I could have been... in theory anyway." He gave Jason a long look. "You look like shit."

Jason took a pull of his beer. "Feel like it. I got a kid."

Aaron choked on his beer. "Come again."

"You heard me. One stupid mistake, and I got a kid. You want me to tell you where babies come from?"

Aaron frowned. "You mean the stork doesn't bring them?"

Jason glowered at him under hooded lids.

"Who's the kid? And who's the mother?"

Jason, relieved that Aaron's first questions weren't if the press had wind of it all yet, relayed the story. Aaron listened for the most part, standing next to Jason on the deck not saying anything.

After he finished, Aaron put his beer down. "Does the press know yet? We'll need to figure out a way to contain the whole abandoned kid angle."

Good ol' Aaron. He had a job to do after all. "No. And we'd better keep it that way. I don't know how Nick will react, and he doesn't need that. And I didn't fucking abandon him. I didn't know about him."

"Hey, bro, don't be so touchy. It's just a question." He took a swig of his beer, then he added, "I told you dating that chick would be complicated. Though I had no idea how complicated it could get. Only you could get in this much shit."

"I need to figure out what to do."

Aaron cast him a look. "None of my business and all, but you should talk to the lady. Sort it out. Amicable like."

Jason stared at him and frowned. "You have got to be kidding me."

Aaron shrugged. "I'm just saying. She loves the kid is all. From what I can see anyway." He shrugged. "Look man, you dropped a bombshell on her a week ago. You were always better at telling chicks what they wanted to hear, not what they needed to hear. It's better for the kid if you guys work this shit out away from the limelight."

"I can't believe you, of all people, are saying keep it out of the press." Jason wasn't sure what he was going to do. But the last thing on earth he wanted to do was deal with this.

"Yeah, never let it be said I don't have a heart. Even if it is made out of a gin and tonic cocktail."

Aaron had a point, though. It was in Nick's best interest that he work something out with Izzy. But what arrangement did he want to work out with her? It wasn't like he wanted a kid.

Did he?

No matter what, he'd meant what he told her. Nick would find out from the both of them. No matter what.

****

"Mom? Is something wrong?"

Izzy looked from Nick's concerned expression to Jason's stoic one and wished there was an easier way to have this conversation. "Yeah, I—" She shook her head before she started again, this time trying for a united front. "We wanted to talk to you about something. Both of us together since this involves all of us."

"You know your mom will always love you no matter what. Nothing will ever change that." Jason tried to help, but only made it worse if Nick's expression was any indication.

Izzy's stomach rolled as Nick's expression turned from giddy excitement, to mild worry, back to excitement again. Shit. They needed to just spit it out already. "So you know how I've been looking for your birth father?"

He nodded encouragingly as if to urge her on. "Yeah, so you can adopt me."

"After talking to Sabrina, we need to discuss a few things with you."

He stood abruptly. "Damn, Mom, just tell me. Whatever it is. Do I have to go live with her? Are they taking me away from you? Does my birth father want custody? What? Just freaking tell me."

From the corner of her eyes, she saw the muscle in Jason's jaw tick as he gnashed his teeth.

His voice was low and controlled. "Nick, have a seat, what your mother has to tell you is hard enough without you getting upset."

Both she and Nick snapped him looks that said shut up. She sent a small prayer to whoever might listen and gave Nick the truth. "According to Sabrina, there's a chance Jason might be your birth father."

Nick stared at her with his head cocked for several moments before he turned his attention to Jason. "Is it true?"

For the first time she could recall, she heard poignant grief in Jason's voice. Unable to turn to face him, she wondered what he'd look like through her lens.

"She never told me, Nick. I had no idea it was even possible."

Regardless of Jason's words, Nick wasn't interested in reason. "Is that why you've been so nice to me? To get close to me?"

Anguish in his eyes, Jason looked at his son. "No. I promise I didn't know. If I had, I would never have abandoned you like that. I would have been there."

Mutinous, Nick stood and stared at Jason. "Yeah well, I didn't need you. I had my mom."

Jason stood to face him. "I know Izzy did the best she could, but that doesn't substitute you having your father around. I'm sorry I haven't been there. But I hope to be there for you now."

"Bullshit. I don't need you." Then as if realization dawned, wide eyes stared at Izzy. "I won't live with him."

Her heart broke at the pleading look he gave her. "No of course not."

She spoke just as Jason said, "Well, nothing's been discussed yet."

Nick crossed his arms. "Well, I won't. If you try and make me, I'll run away."

Izzy stepped between the two of them. "Nick, you will do no such thing. Nothing has been decided yet, mostly because we need to have a paternity test done. If it comes back positive, we need to have some conversations about where to go next. Until then, there's no need to get upset."

Jason shrugged. "No one's upset. Nick and I are having a conversation."

Nick's eyes didn't waver from Jason's. "I'm not leaving you, Mom. I don't care what those stupid tests say."

Jason folded his arms around his broad expanse of chest. "We'll see what the Judge says."

She stood between the two of them, as they geared for battle. So much for a united front.

☐

Chapter Thirty-Six

Jason hadn't paid attention when the taxi passed the security gate. After his chat with Nick, he didn't have the energy. When he saw Sabrina's compact form exit the taxi, he ground his teeth. "What the hell are you doing here?" Jason stood with his arms crossed, legs braced apart. His lips thinned as she drew nearer.

"I have a few things to say. You can hate me all you want, but you'll hear me out."

"I think I've heard you out enough."

"I know. I wish I could say I'm sorry and mean it, but I'm not, so I won't. I just needed to see you before I left town."

He turned his back on her and stalked into the house. "Why does that not surprise me? So what's the deal? She's sending you to rehab in exchange for what?"

"I, ah, I get to go to rehab if I promise to leave Nick alone until he's ready to see me." She fiddled with the clutch purse in her hand. "I know as far as you're concerned, I'm an evil bitch."

He leaned up against the dining room table, light streamed in through the sliding glass doors behind him and lit her face in shadow. "You're right about that. You're an evil bitch, but then not much has changed since we were kids."

"I never should have kept you from Izzy when you came back. I never should have kept Nick a secret from you. I never should have blackmailed you. Just about the only good thing I've done in my life is leave Nick with Izzy. I couldn't take care of him, and let's face it, Jason, you would have been a useless father."

"I never got the chance to make that choice for myself. You stole that from me." Jason could have sworn he saw remorse flit across her pretty features.

"You can moan about it all you want. The truth is we all made mistakes. Maybe I should have told you about Nick, maybe not. But you tried to keep our past secret from her, and that's on you. Not me, not her, but you." She swiped at her nose. "I needed the money, so I got it from the logical source."

"You're a piece of work."

"Don't I know it."

"You used Nick's safety, and my feelings for Izzy against me."

She shrugged. "I don't deny it."

His voice chilled by degrees. "Then what the fuck do you want from me, 'cause I get the impression you're not feeling all that sorry."

"You don't have to listen to me, but I'm here to ask you to go easy on Izzy and the kid. They need each other. If you want custody of him, fine you have a right to him, but you've got to share it with Izzy."

"Why would you give that to her? From what I can see you've never even liked her."

"I don't, but she's done right by me when she didn't have to. She's the best parent for Nick. Always has been. None of this was her fault. Not like she knew he was yours." The muscles in her lips trembled into a semblance of a smile. "If she'd known, she would have fought all the more to adopt him sooner. She's always loved you."

Chapter Thirty-Seven

Izzy retched into the studio's corner wastebasket. All she'd been able to think about was Nick's paternity test. The lab had called that morning. Nick was for sure Jason's son.

She'd asked the doctor if he was sure, and he'd assured her without a doubt that the results were accurate. Damn them with their 99.86% probabilities.

Her entire world was falling apart, and her body knew it. Spitting out the bile, she straightened. Maybe it was a bug. Between the gallery opening, and Nick, and the whole Sabrina-Jason thing, her schedule was erratic and hectic.

"When were you going to tell me?"

She whipped around to face Jessica. "Tell you what? That I'm sick?" She shrugged and added, "It's no big deal. I hope it passes soon though, I can't afford to be run down now, between paternity tests and press people, and my editor and additional clie—"

Jessica shook her head, interrupting. "Honey, even you can't be that distracted." Moving forward, she handed Izzy a cup of water. "How late are you?"

"Late?"

Jessica rolled her eyes. "You know preggers?"

Izzy's stomach rolled. Too nauseous to process the question, she hugged the wastebasket to her chest.

Jessica continued. "With child, lack of Aunt Flo, about to be Shamu the whale?"

Izzy swallowed around the nausea. "I'm not pregnant, Jessica." She waved a hand. "It's got to be the flu. Simon had it last week. I'm not pregnant," she stated more adamantly.

Jessica kneeled in front of her. "Is it at least possible?"

"No, of course it's not po—" Izzy halted, suddenly remembering making love on the rug in Jason's living room. She remembered the smooth moist tip of his erec—Shit. She'd forgotten her pills when she and Nick stayed at Jason's. She'd made up the pack, so she hadn't given it much thought. She cleared her throat, cast a guilty look at Jessica and nodded. "Yeah, it's possible."

There was a time for lectures and a time for support. Jess knew her well enough to know now wasn't a lecture time. "Right. So first things first. You need to pee on a stick."

In a flurry of activity, she made notes, grabbed calendars and rushed into the reception area. "I'll call your doctor for a confirmation sometime in the next couple of days, but you'll probably feel better after you know for sure," she shouted from the reception desk.

She strode into the studio, oversized hobo bag in hand, and rummaged through it. When she procured a pregnancy home kit from the bag, Izzy stared, agog.

"You carry around pregnancy tests in your bag?"

"You never know when they're going to come in handy." She shrugged.

Izzy grabbed her hand. Voice shaking, she whispered the one fear she'd been unable to admit to herself until now. "Jess, what am I going to do? You see how Jason is about Nick? I don't know if I can do this."

Jess squeezed back. "Right now, you don't have to do anything except pee on that stick. You're a strong woman. You can do this. And anything you can't do, I'll do. And your mom and Nick. So what if Prince Charming is full of warts?"

Izzy felt the weak smile tug at her lips. "He's a particularly resistant species of toad. No amount of kissing turned him into a prince."

Jessica smiled back. "Maybe you didn't kiss him hard enough?"

Izzy's smile widened hand pointing at her belly. "Well, I did more than kiss him—several times. If that didn't aid the transformation, I don't know what will."

Jessica choked on a laugh. "That's the Izzy I know. You're Izzy Connors, and you've got people who love you. You can move mountains." Jessica paused. "Including deal with the horde of paparazzi on the lawn outside."

Izzy felt the blast of a migraine coming on. "You're shitting me."

"I shit you not. Looks like the story leaked about the paternity test."

"Shit." She took a deep breath. "Shit, shit, and more shit."

"Look, I'm already on it. I called the cops to remove them. You'll probably want to talk to the toad before anything else leaks to the press. You don't want that."

No, Izzy didn't want to talk to the toad, but she was fresh out of options. She didn't know if she was strong enough for two custody battles with Jason.

Chapter Thirty-Eight

Was she really too cute for jail? Would the DA prosecute if she shot a member of the paparazzi and buried him in the desert? Wiping her hands down her jeans after she placed a casserole in the oven, Izzy went to pull the drapes in the family room. Thanks to the security Jason had sent over, the paps stayed on the street, not her lawn. But when the sun went down, they'd have a clear view into the house. Her neighbors had already complained as had she, but there was little the police could do.

She walked down the hallway to her room with every intention of lying down for a few minutes. She'd had a headache going on a week solid now, and it showed no signs of going away.

"Nick? Have you finished your homework. Jessica can take it in the morning if you have."

He didn't answer her. She sighed. He'd been impossible since she and Jason had sat him down. Rude, staying up late, talking back — all uncharacteristic. He was going through a lot, but she'd only put up with so much before she started slapping on the consequences.

She stood outside his door and knocked. "Nick, did you hear me about your homework?"

Tempted to open the door, something she would have done before the age of twelve with no qualms, she knew better than to open unannounced now. "Nicholas, if you don't open the door in three, I'm coming in."

When he didn't open the door, she went in with the full expectation to see him brooding on his bed, the sounds of Snoop Dogg blaring from his earphones. But she didn't find anything, he wasn't there.

Quickly she backtracked to the living room, not there either. She did a quick sweep of the rest of the house, calling Jessica at the studio in the process. "Jessica, is Nick there?"

Izzy heard the snap of a popping bubble in her ear. "No, ma'am. But you just left here yourself. He didn't pass you?"

"Oh, God. Jessica, he's gone."

****

Jason walked his body through the series of stretches Brian insisted on for dexterity. His muscles weren't used to so much torture, but since his life was such a mess at the moment, working out was one thing he knew would relieve the tension. Make that the only thing.

Izzy wasn't on the menu, and he didn't want anyone else. He heard the doorbell mid-stretch. God damn it. They didn't give up. The reporters had never been so bold as to come straight up to the door.

He yanked open the door and stepped back in shock. "Nick? Are you by yourself?" His eyes scanned the front lawn for Izzy.

Nick's eyes were stormy as he walked into the house. "What's the matter, Dad, aren't you happy to see me? Am I going to ruin your set up or something?"

He stepped aside to let Nick through. "I'm happy you're here, Nick. I'm just wondering how you got here. Did your mom drop you off?"

Nick scowled. "Don't you mean my glorified babysitter?"

Damn. He'd seen the papers. "Nick, I'm sorry. I never meant for any of this to happen." Jason led Nick into the kitchen and handed him a soda. He almost thought better of it after he remembered Izzy didn't want Nick to have too much sugar. What the hell? She wasn't there.

"Nick, the press sucks. I take the good with the bad. But they had no right to go after you or Izzy, and for that, I'm sorry." He took a deep breath. "I'm just trying to make it right."

Nick didn't look like he believed him. "Do you know what the kids at school are asking me? They keep asking what it's like to have my own mammie. And if that now you're my dad if I'll move to the big house."

Jason sucked in his breath. He figured it would be bad, but he hadn't taken into account the kinds of things that people would say. "Shit, Nick. I'm so sorry. I screwed all this up." He shook his head. "I only wanted the chance to get to know you better."

Nick sniffed and swiped at his face. "Is all this why you pretended to like me? 'Cause you were trying to figure it out?" He sniffed again. "Or were you trying to get close to my mom?"

"Nick, I—"

"'Cause that's what she is. I don't want to come live with you." Nick glowered and lifted his chin as he glared.

Jason felt like an ass. He knew he was an ass. "Nick, I never intended to take you away from your mother."

Nick scowled, and his chin went up a fraction. "But the court, they might make me come and stay here. I'm not coming."

Was he that bad? "You don't have to come, Nick. But I will come to you." Jason added, "I know better than anyone that just because a guy makes a donation doesn't mean he's a father. I didn't know about you, so I missed out on getting to be a dad. But now that I do, I'm going be there for you if it kills the both of us."

"What if I don't want you around?"

Jason smiled. "I figure you'll get used to me."

Nick squinted. "Are you sure you're not going to come make me live here?"

"I'm not going to make you do anything you don't want to. Like your mom, I want what's best for you." To Jason's surprise, he meant it. At first he'd been angry because he hadn't known about Nick, but he knew Izzy had taken good care of him.

Nick nodded, and the tension ebbed out of his shoulders. Shyly, he peered at Jason over the rim of his Coke can. "I, uh, when you came over that day…" He paused before continuing. "I thought you and Mom were gonna say you were getting married or something."

Well, hell. That, he hadn't expected. "If your mom didn't hate me, I'd say it might have been a possibility."

Nick shrugged. "She doesn't hate anyone. Not even people she should."

Jason had a suspicion Nick meant Sabrina, so he didn't say anything to encourage the line of thought. "How did you get all the way over here?"

Nick gave his classic teenager shrug. "Cab. I snuck out the side door of the studio so the shutterbugs wouldn't see me."

Snuck out? "Good thing you were able to avoid them, but does your mom know you're here?"

Nick cringed and had the grace to look remorseful. "I might have forgotten to tell her."

Jason clenched his jaw. "Nick, that doesn't work. You have to call her." Jason strode to the cordless and dialed the number he'd committed to memory.

When she answered, he didn't bother to mince words. "Izzy, it's Jason. About Nick."

She didn't let him get out another word before she started sobbing into the phone. "Jason, he's gone. I've called every friend he has and sent Jessica on a hunt all over the neighborhood. I almost asked the damn cameramen if they'd seen him."

"Izzy, relax. He's here."

"What?"

"He's here. He's safe. I can drive him home after—"

"No, I'm on my way." She hung up before giving him the chance to respond.

When she appeared forty-five minutes later, he wondered what traffic laws she'd broken to get from Pasadena to Malibu in such record time.

She stormed in searching around for Nick. When she saw him, she grabbed him in a hug so fierce, Jason worried about Nick's air supply.

She pulled back examining him. "You know you're grounded, right? No phone, no friends, no practice."

Sheepish, Nick nodded as she squeezed him again. Jason watched from the foyer, a little jealous of the bond they shared. He hoped they'd be able to let him in at some point.

"Nick, can you give us a minute? I need to talk to Jason."

Nick nodded and made himself scarce, knowing where to find the media room.

When Nick was out of earshot, she rounded on Jason. "Did you ask him to come here? Do you have any idea how worried I've been?"

Jason stalked over to her. "No. I didn't ask him to come. His arrival was as much a surprise to me as it was to you. And the moment I found out he didn't have permission to be here, I called you."

She nodded and looked around as if she wasn't sure about which way to look. "He's okay. He wasn't hurt or anything when he got here?"

He reached out to pull her into his arms. "You saw him. He's fine."

She trembled in his embrace. "I was so worried. Then I was mad. Then I thought some crazy paparazzo had gotten him. Then I started to freak out that some crazed fan of yours got him."

She spoke so fast, Jason had to strain to hear every sentence. "He's okay. He's safe. So are you. Everything will be okay."

He pulled her into him, needing her close. This was the first time she hadn't fought him since Sabrina had told him about Nick. He hushed her and stroked her hair.

He held on as long as he could, telling himself he only needed to hold her a little longer and everything would be okay.

She pulled back to look at him. "Jason?"

"Yes, sweetheart?"

She furrowed her brow, then wiggled out of his grasp and ran to the bathroom off the hallway.

"Izzy? Are you okay?" He knocked on the door. "Baby?"

She flushed, and he could hear the sink running. When she opened the door, her skin was clammy, and she averted her gaze. "I didn't expect you to follow me."

"I wanted to make sure you were okay."

"I'm fine. Nothing wrong with me that hasn't been wrong with women for millennia."

He frowned. "I don't get it. What's wrong with you?"

She buried her face in her hands and mumbled something unintelligible.

"Try again."

"I'm pregnant."

Chapter Thirty-Nine

"You're what?" Jason breathed, eyes wide.

Suddenly the hallway felt too small, as if Jason was using all the air she preciously needed. Izzy shoved past him and walked into the living room. She didn't make it far before he took her arm and turned her around.

"Izzy, tell me again."

Exasperated, Izzy blew her bangs out of her face. "I'm pregnant, okay?" And because she was so raw and scared, and more tired than she'd ever been in her life, she continued in anger. "And yes, it's yours. And yes, I'm the idiot who missed a pill. And no, I'm not trying to trap you, and no, I don't want anything from you. And no, we won't be working out custody."

He put up his hands in surrender. "Izzy, easy. Calm down. I wasn't—I mean I didn't—" He took a deep breath and raked his hands through his hair. "You have to give me a second to process this. I went from having no kids, to one kid and now two. It's all a bit much."

"A bit much." She kept her voice low. "How do you think I feel, Jason? I'm finally going to have a baby, and the father is none other than the man fighting me for custody of my other child. You don't even want children."

"Now, wait a minute." He couldn't let her continue. "I've never said I don't children. I've never given much thought to family. Mostly because mine was so shitty." He took a breath. "It's just a bit more than I ever thought I'd have to handle."

Izzy shook her head. "Again, this is all about you. Poor Jason. You can't spin this."

"Is that what the hell you think I've been doing?"

"Damn it. You're going to do what you always do, put on a show."

"What the fuck? I—"

She put up a hand. "You'll play the part, Jason. You always do. To the tennis world, you're this perfect god. To your friends, you're this consummate party boy. To Nick, you're the perfect mentor, to me the perfect lover. And now..." She spread her arms. "And now? You want what? You want to be the perfect father? Provider? Which is the real you? You're such the consummate actor, Jason. I never know what to believe from you."

"That's not fair, Izzy. I've been exactly the same since you met me."

"No, Jason, you haven't. You've got this shiny, glossy layer you use to mask who you are." She stalked into the living room.

Rage contorted his face. "Your damned pride keeps getting in your way, and you'll never see the truth."

"And what truth is that?" She stared at him, praying, hoping wishing.

Several beats passed, their breath mingling. "I'm in your life forever now, Izzy. You're going to have to get used to that."

Chapter Forty

"Mr. Cartwright, I must say this is most unusual."

Jason folded his hands to keep from fidgeting. "Judge Robertson, I appreciate you taking the time to meet with me."

The judge's usual stern expression softened. "Are you sure you don't want Miss Connors present as this affects her?"

"No. No. That's the last thing I want." He ran his hands through his hair. "Look, last time we met, you asked me to work on visitation and custody and give thought to the best arrangement for Nick." Jason swallowed around the lump in his throat. He knew what he had to do. What was really best for Nick. Doing the right thing wasn't easy though.

"As a professional athlete, I can't provide him the kind of stable environment he needs."

"You seemed certain about your place in Nicholas's life. What's happened to change that?"

He tried to avoid the judge's shrewd gaze, but eventually gave up the fight and leveled his gaze with the older man's. "Nothing has changed. I am certain about my position in Nick's life." He drew a deep breath. "I'm even more certain about Izzy as a mother. She's brought him up to be a smart, vibrant, talented kid."

He sniffed and looked around the judge's office at the photos of different families on his wall. "I had nothing to do with that. I won't punish him because I want to be part of his life. He's old enough to know if he wants to spend time with me."

Judge Robertson looked down at his papers again. "Would you at least like to think about it? Take another day or two to make this kind of decision." His worn hands traced over the papers. "This can't be undone."

"I know it can't be undone. And I need no more time. It's the right thing to do. I'm sure of it."

Judge Robertson wielded a heavy sigh. "Fair enough, Mr. Cartwright. I'll process the necessary paperwork for you to sign away custody of your son."

****

Izzy blew down the highway like the devil was on her trail. Since leaving Judge Robertson's office, all she could think of was getting to Jason. Elation, confusion, anger, nausea, all warred for top billing in her body.

She swore as she swerved to avoid a collision with the slow moving truck in front of her, Izzy took the Malibu exit. As she approached Jason's, uncaring about the voyeuristic paparazzi, she sped past the front gate security with barely a pause.

Jason was on the front steps before she'd even thrown the car in park. "Izzy? What the hell's the matter?"

Izzy panted as she climbed out of the car. "Jason, I know what you did." She took a deep breath. "I have no words."

He gave her a tight smile that resembled more grimace than expression of happiness. "All I want, is for you and Nick to be happy." Then with a wistful tone, he added, "The little one too." He gestured them inside, away from nosy eyes.

"Jason, I know how hard it must have been to give up your parental rights." Her hands itched to touch him, convey her thanks, her relief.

"It was. But it was harder to think about how unhappy Nick would be with me." He ran his hands through his hair. "I'll make sure you get back child support for Nick and take care of all the medical bills and child support for the baby."

"Jason, you don't need to do that for Nick. I've taken care of his education. His college fund is flush."

He reached for her. He wrapped his arms around her and squeezed tight. "Izzy, I want to. I know it can't have been easy doing it all yourself with no help all these years. At least let me do this."

She pulled back from him and nodded. "We'll work out visitation. I want you to have as much access to the kids as you want. It's important."

"Thanks." He smiled. "You'll take good care of them." Gone was his usual brash confidence, leaving a shell of vulnerability.

All the love she had for him squeezed at her tear centers and threatened to brim them over. "Thank you. I — I don't know what to say."

"Don't thank me, Izzy. We've already done enough damage to each other. I don't think I can take any — "

In a rush, she said, "I love you." Knowing Jason, she knew she had to qualify it. "I don't want anything from you. I just needed to tell you. I know you don't really do the long term relationship thing and it's fine. But after what you've done today, I can't let you walk away without knowing how I — "

She didn't get to finish her monologue before hot firm lips pressed to hers, demanding a response. As with every time he touched her, her blood sizzled and popped.

"Izzy, I love you too. I loved you the first time I saw you play. I loved you the moment I walked into your studio the first time. I love you."

Her blood tap-danced in her veins, and Izzy almost didn't hear everything he said. "You love me?" *He loves me.* "I know you don't really do relationships. I — "

He pulled her against him. "I want to be with you. I want to be part of our children's lives. See every part of them grow up. Support you. Make love to you every night and every morning. I want it all. What do you think I've been trying to tell you for weeks?"

"My stupid pride always gets me in trouble."

He dipped his head and grazed her lips with his. "Don't I know it, but I'm willing to hang in there, if you are."

"You love getting your way, huh, Ace?"

"Always."

Epilogue

"So, I think I want to go see Sabrina next weekend."

Izzy turned her attention from the cooing baby in her arms to give Nick a long look. "Are you sure? Do you want me to go with you?"

He shook his head as he tickled his little sister's feet. Chubby, mocha hands slapped at Izzy's chest as a gummy smile displayed deep dimples. Nick grinned back. "Nah, it's okay. I just want to fly up for the day. Get a chance to talk to her."

Izzy handed Nick the baby as she rifled through one of the bags to hunt for a bottle. The stands at the match didn't provide much legroom, so she needed both her hands to get what she needed. "If it makes you happy, then that's all I want." She blinked away sentimental tears as she watched her oldest child hold her youngest. How in the world had she gotten so lucky?

"You're not upset?" Worry laced Nick's words and his brow.

She gave him her most reassuring smile. "You have every right to want to see her and have your questions answered. So, no, I'm not upset."

"Cool."

The announcer's voice reverberated through the stands as the officials on the court prepared for the awards ceremony. "Ladies and gentlemen, allow us to present to you, this year's Men's Grand Slam Champion, Jason Cartwright."

Izzy and Nick stood immediately and clapped like maniacs on speed, determined for their cheering to stand out in the roaring crowds. Baby Kara also clapped chubby hands together beaming a dimpled smile at daddy. As soon as Jason finished shaking hands, he sprinted for the stands and scaled the wall to greet them.

Laughter bubbled in Izzy's chest as he wrapped her in a drugging kiss. "You're a loon. You could have hurt yourself scaling the wall like that. I'm going to need my husband in top condition later."

Teeth nibbling at her lips, he chuckled. "Yes, ma'am. Understood."

"Do you two have to maul each other like that in public? It's kind of gross." Nick's voice dripped with teenage sarcasm, but his face beamed with pride.

Jason turned his attention to his children, enveloping them in a sweaty bear hug. Planting a slobbering kiss on Nick's forehead, he laughed as Nick grumbled with embarrassment. "I didn't want you two to miss out."

Kara reached her arms out from her brother's hold, exclaiming, "Da!"

Scooping her up, he whirled to face Izzy. "Did you hear that? She called me Da. Her first word was Da."

Izzy laughed. She didn't have the heart to tell him Kara had already started calling Nick, "Ik" over a week ago. "Yeah, I heard her."

As Izzy surveyed her family, she couldn't help but think, even though she no longer played tennis, she'd won everything she'd ever wanted, Game, Set and Match.

A word from the author...

Nana's love of all things romance and adventure started with a tattered romantic suspense she borrowed from her cousin on a sultry summer afternoon in Ghana at a precocious thirteen. She's been in love with kick-butt heroines ever since. With her overactive imagination, and channeling her inner Buffy, it was only a matter a time before she started creating her own characters.

Waiting for her chance at a job as a ninja assassin, Nana meantime works out her drama, passion and sass with fictional characters every bit as sassy and kick-butt as she thinks she is. Though, until that ninja job comes through, you'll find her acting out scenes for hubby and puppy while catching up on her favorite reality television shows in sunny San Diego.

Visit Nana at http://www.nanamalone.com

Other Books by Nana Malone

Sexy in Stilettos
©2012 Nana Malone

~ 4 out of 5 stars - Picked by Poison ~ "I liked
Nana's writing style and how she made her
characters quirky and fun, and not the usual
romantic type."

Blurb:

What's worse than having to watch your sister
marry your ex fiancé? How about when that fiancé
fires you from the family business?

Hyper-organized, event planner Jaya Trudeaux is
used to doing things by the book and never making
waves. It's a strategy that's served her well until
she finds herself in failure alley with no fiancé, no
job and her thirtieth birthday looming. Maybe it's
time to change her methods. Starting with an
unlikely date to the wedding from hell.

The only thing that can tie carefree playboy, Alec Danthers down is his formidable step mother. When she calls him home to help find his wayward brother, he never imagines an uptight, list making, sass- talking woman would make him think about putting down roots.

Can Jaya put the lists down long enough to enjoy the ride that is Alec? Will Alec stop running long enough to recognize true love?

Warning: Sexy, sass talking women will make you laugh, cry and want a pair of killer footwear.

Reluctant Protector
©2011 Nana Malone

~4 - A Pack Howl from Kayla - Bitten by Paranormal Romance~ "This book kept me thoroughly entertained from the first page to the last. I went into it expecting a decent paranormal romance and came out of it with so much more. I can't wait for the next parts of the series to be released so I can enjoy them just as much as the first book. "

~4 - Four Black Hearts from Paranormal Romance Party~ "The first thing that I have to say is that this book is Very HOT!!! I didn't have any expectations but I was very happy to have received this book to review! It's more Romantic Suspense with some PNR elements but I enjoyed it very much...I was hooked on The Reluctant Protector!"

http://theparanormalromanceparty.blogspot.com/2012/03/review-reluctant-protector-by-nana.html

Blurb:

For five years, Cassie Reeser has been her brother's personal lab rat. Peter's experiments have made her a stronger, faster, better human. And she's not the only one – he's been experimenting on others as well. For five years, escape has eluded her. Until now. When she finds out he plans to sell her as a human weapon she knows it's now or never. To make her escape she'll sacrifice family bonds and leave behind the one person who's ever helped her. Cassie's learned to shrink from kindness and to never trust anyone. She knows the day Peter finally captures her will be the day she dies. To elude her brother and save the others, she'll have to risk her body and her heart. What she doesn't expect is a chance at a normal life.

Seth Adams is used to sifting through lies to find the truth. As a former war correspondent he knows what evils lurk in the world. When he finds Cassie hiding out in his car trunk, her story sounds like a fantastical dream. But, before long, he witnesses firsthand what she's talking about when they're attacked by a group of Peter's soldiers. As a result, he goes through his own transformation into a super human and realizes the extent of what Cassie is running from. Cassie might not think she needs his protection, but he'll die before he lets her brother have her back.

Available for purchase on www.nanamalone.com

Coming Soon From Nana Malone

- Sultry in Stilettos Coming November 2012

- MisMatch – The much anticipated sequel to Game, Set, Match

- Wounded Protector – The latest in the Protectors Series